ALSO BY ANTHONY HYDE

The Red Fox

CHINA LAKE

CHINA LAKE

ANTHONY HYDE

ALFRED A. KNOPF   NEW YORK
1992

For

Sylvie & Richard

Brooke

Kathy

Trapper (P. M. Stevens)

Rita

—and good times at Lac Bernard

Sidewinder, AIM-9

One of the most influential missiles in history, this slim AAM was almost un-American in development for it was created out of nothing by a very small team at NOTS China Lake, operating on the proverbial shoestring budget. Led by Doctor McLean, this team was the first in the world to attack the problem of passive IR [infrared] homing guidance, in 1949, and the often intractable difficulties were compounded by the choice of an airframe of only 5in (127mm) diameter, which in the days of vacuum-tube electronics was a major challenge. . . . The first XAAM-N-7 guided round was successfully fired on 11 September 1953. The first production missiles, called N-7 by the Navy, GAR-8 by the USAF and SW-1 by the development team, reached IOC in May 1956.

AA-2 Atoll

Unlike most Russian weapons this AAM is beyond doubt a copy of a Western original, the early AIM-9B Sidewinder. When first seen on 9 June 1961, carried by various fighters in an air display, it was almost identical to the US weapon. Since then it has followed its own path of development, and like Sidewinder has diversified into IR and SARH [semiactive radar homing] versions. . . . Like AIM-9 versions, IR missiles have hemispherical noses transparent to heat, and radar versions slightly tapered noses that appear opaque. Current carriers include all later fighter MiG-21s, with four missile shoes instead of two, and the MiG-23S swing-wing fighter which also carries later AAMs.

—BILL GUNSTON,
Modern Airborne Missiles

I want to thank Cyril Levitt for his help and company in Germany; HJ for hints from her psychedelic past; and people in California, who told me the secrets of China Lake.

PART I

Black Bodies

black body (Phys.). A body which completely absorbs any heat or light radiation falling upon it. A *black body* maintained at a steady temperature is a full radiator at that temperature, since any black body remains in equilibrium with the radiation reaching and leaving it.

black-body radiation (Phys.). Radiation that would be radiated from an ideal *black body*. The energy distribution is dependent only on the temperature and is described by *Planck's radiation law*. See *Stefan-Boltzmann law, Wien's laws.*

—*Chambers Science and Technology Dictionary*

CHAPTER 1

Later, Tannis often wondered if there'd been a warning, some clue he'd missed. Presumably someone had been watching him, so there must have been a change, which he should have picked up, in the routines around him. He didn't like it. He didn't like the idea that anyone could get the better of him. He hadn't been "operational" for years, but he was a professional all the same. . . .

As best he could, he went over the preceding days—the cars behind him driving to L.A., his phone calls, a man he hadn't known outside his bank. He wondered: had some detail, among all those details he kept track of, been out of place? had there been some crucial, subtle difference? But he couldn't say for sure. . . .

In truth, he suspected nothing. Everything seemed as usual, and that Friday night appeared no different from a hundred others. Since his retirement the days had all run together anyway and he was never exactly certain where he was—April? November? '58? '85? It made no difference to him. He was as timeless as the desert, and never "looked back" in the usual sense, his past fading like the contrail of a jet in a high, white sky. His life was like that; apparently it had never quite materialized, or had long since dissipated and dispersed. He'd caught the tail end of a war that had become a myth and had waited for the next one, a myth in a different way, for it hadn't come at all and now seemed as strange as movies on the

Late Show, part of a world that might mysteriously stand still or be attacked from Outer Space. But it hadn't happened. They'd unleashed the mighty atom and broken through the sound barrier and nothing had happened after all. Now no one mentioned those days, and only old men like himself, he noticed, still wore 100 percent nylon shirts—the "miracle fabric"—or remembered how exciting transistors were. Perhaps he was part of a generation that had bided its time too long, and their time had never come. Now they were trapped in a peculiar past, heroes of a history that didn't lead to the present they were in. As a consequence they were not quite visible to those around them. Once they'd been familiar, even famous, but now they were forgotten, like old songs that had sung out of every radio. With Tannis this was especially true. Out of his navy uniform he was somehow unrecognizable, and when people did recall him, they were usually shocked: wasn't he dead? hadn't he moved away twenty years ago? Not that this troubled him. On the contrary. He preferred his anonymity. Perhaps he was anachronistic, but his life and times were very much his own. He did not buy Jap; he did not know what disco was, or had been. Besides, he still knew the words to those old songs. As likely as not, waiting for the light to change, he'd beat them out against the steering wheel: *When the moon hits your eye like a big pizza pie that's . . .*

Still, even if he wasn't up to date, Tannis knew he was somewhere in "the Reagan Years," and there was that Friday-night feel to the glass in his hand, and it had to be late spring or summer, because there was no fire of mesquite branches flickering on the hearth behind him. But it could have been any other Mojave night. Sipping tequila, smoking a Lucky Strike, he stood before the big picture window in the living room and watched the evening sun go down, thinking idly of some gold stocks he'd invested in, Hemlo, Franco-Nevada, Breakwater. Tequila and the sunset—for Tannis this was close to ritual, and for about twenty minutes he just stood there quietly, his weight canted a little to one side, sipping at the liquor and staring across the desert toward the low, black hills that hid Los Angeles from view; and at a certain point (somewhere beyond the dunes, the salt flats, the smooth, stretching shadows of the great red rocks) his eyes lost focus, or their focus shifted, so there was that characteristic internal *flexion*, a shift in his persona, his self losing itself out there, like a spirit, so that his vision took on an extraordinary clarity, like someone looking through the wrong end of a telescope, or indeed someone with second sight, and if there'd been a premonition in that wilderness, he would have felt it. But he didn't. His mind just drifted, thinking of gold, and the men who'd looked for it here in the Mojave, in Randsburg and the Panamint: and then, more generally, to other men who'd stared across the desert in just this way—Rommel, Cochise, St. Anthony, Lawrence of Arabia. He began to make a list, wondering what quality had joined them, deciding, in the end, that they were all men of vision, looking for hope and glory and finding—But this was hardly a foreshadowing of anything that happened, though it was exactly at this point, 7:42 p.m., that the phone began to ring.

He turned from the darkened window, listening. And then he walked across the hall, where he kept his little office, and answered as he usually did—the way security people always do—without giving out his name.

"Yes."

"Tannis?"

"Who is it?"

"Tannis . . . ? It is you, isn't it? I recognize your voice."

And for one fleeting instant, a crucial instant, Tannis almost recognized the other, the past offering itself like a forgotten dream . . . but no, it couldn't be, he was dead, no, he was long gone. Hadn't they all, like himself, died twenty years ago? And then it slipped away. It was the voice of . . . but it was gone. And he replied, "That's fine, but I don't know yours."

"I don't suppose you would. It was a long time ago, Commander."

In fact, this was not his rank; but even if it had been, Tannis sensed immediately that the caller was not a navy man because . . . because commander was merely a term of address, not a rank superior, or subordinate, to the caller's own. No, the caller had no rank. But there was something about the voice he did remember, although even as the memory formed he realized that this voice had deliberately hidden itself, swallowed itself back, muffled itself with time and distance, all the miles of the desert night and all the years. And then, even as Tannis was drawing closer, the voice switched away again, took another turning down the tunnel.

"*Nos conocimos muchos años atrás, mi almirante. Yo soy un amigo. Un viejo amigo . . .*"

Tannis checked himself, and for a last few seconds the momentum of the day, so ordinary, carried on. He'd been to the bank, he'd fixed a rake, he'd watched the sun go down. . . . Now the phone had rung. This man had answered, "An old friend, from many years ago . . ." It was possible, of course; "Commander," the man had called him, though he'd been promoted years earlier to captain. Or perhaps it was a joke, and he should play along. But this wasn't the kind of joke he liked, and he rarely played along. "Who the hell are you?" he said. "*¿Cómo se llama, amigo?*"

And the man replied, "*Mi apellido . . . no tiene importancia.*"

"My name is not important . . ." But now, suddenly, Tannis knew it was. And he felt irritation, simply because he couldn't remember who this joker was, though it had been right there, at the tip of his tongue. "Listen," he said, "listen, amigo, I don't talk to people unless I know who in hell I'm talking to. So what's your name?"

A peculiar sound came down the line, a kind of cluck; a rather prim and proper sound of disappointment and disapproval that, when he thought about it later, created the impression that the man might be European, German or Dutch, or even French—though he definitely wasn't Mexican. Tannis had spent his life in the desert, and knew every variety of Mex—from the flat tones of the border towns to the plummy eloquence of the *distrito federale*—and he knew this wasn't native. The man *clucked* again. "No, Jack. You should understand. Not my name. Not on the telephone."

"Suit yourself. I'm hanging up."

"No. Listen—"

"Five seconds. I'll give you five seconds. That's the first one. Two, three, four—"

"Just hang on, Jack. If you want a name, I'll give you a name. Harper. There's a name for you. David Harper. If you really don't know who I am, you must still remember *him*."

Harper. In fact, Tannis hadn't heard the name in at least twenty years and hadn't thought of it since . . . but he couldn't remember when. And oddly, though he recognized the name instantly, it was not actually Harper he thought of, or not directly: quite another memory filled his mind, really a memory of a memory. Years before, he'd been driving down to San Diego and at a certain point he'd looked away from the highway—an instant like the scissoring of a camera's shutter—and glimpsed a little ranch, squeezed between two huge tract developments, a sight so anachronistic it was itself an opening on the past: a paddock, its rails painted a gleaming white, with a woman riding around it on a coal black horse, a cowboy hat dangling from her neck and bouncing on her back. Then, the hat had turned the key: all at once a flushed, excited face was looking up at him and a lilting English voice exclaimed, *Heavens! I must look just like Dale Evans!* Harper's wife . . . Now he even recalled her name. Diana. He remembered her because . . . but with Harper, the woman, and everything that had happened it wasn't a question of having to remember at all; again, he simply knew. Except there was a peculiar oddity, for when he tried to summon Harper's face, there was nothing, a total blank. What had Harper looked like? Tannis had no idea. But already his mystery man was prompting, "Tannis? Are you there?"

"You're not Harper."

"No. Of course not. Harper could be dead for all I know. But you remember—"

"I remember Harper."

"Good, my friend. Because that's what we have to talk about. The old days, if you like. The good old days."

"So talk."

"I told you. Not on the telephone."

"Maybe it's not so important then."

"No games, please. We don't have the time, believe me. Just listen: in Ridgecrest there's that restaurant where everybody used to go, the Hideaway. It's still there, I see. Go there—"

"I don't think so."

"You will. Let's say it's a chance I'll take. Be there by nine o'clock. Go in—"

"Like hell."

"Just keep quiet and listen to me. Go in. Order something, if you like. I'll be later. You understand? I must make sure that you're all alone."

"Fuck off. I won't be there at all."

"That's enough . . ."

And then the line was dead.

Harper . . .

For a moment Tannis didn't move. Outwardly he seemed completely calm. And when he did move, he only lit up another Lucky with his old brass Zippo and ambled back to the living room, precisely retracing his steps, ending up exactly where he'd stood a few moments earlier. And everything was just the same; nothing at all had changed. The window, the desert, the setting sun . . . It seemed that nothing had happened after all. The tequila was exactly where he'd set it down, and he raised the glass, as if offering a toast, toward the last few rays of sun that slanted across the sand: mescal, the desert sun distilled. The taste of the liquor trickled through him (that taste of charred wood against the teeth), and as his arm came back he saw the image of his face flicker for a moment, ghostlike, in the darkened window, but he stared right through it: *why couldn't he remember what Harper looked like?* beyond the wash and alkali flats, into the boundless emptiness. A moment ago . . . What had he been thinking? It would be best to go back to that, pick up where he'd left off. Something about . . . He'd been thinking . . . *There was nothing out there.* No, that's what he thought now; and then he remembered that he'd been thinking of other men who'd looked across the desert as he had done so often, wondering what *they'd* been looking for, men like Rommel, Cochise, St. Anthony. They were all men of vision *and once upon a time he too . . .*

But at once he broke off this series, for it led, inevitably, forward; and he still wanted to work backward, as if hoping to find a place to detour: some path that would carry him *around.* So, turning away, his eyes lit on the book he'd been reading earlier, *Doctor Faustus* by Thomas Mann. This was typical of Tannis. For he read only the greatest books, the books that everybody claimed to read but rarely did, like *Don Quixote* or *Moby Dick.* This one was a paperback, and he'd bent it over, to mark his place, and now he opened it again and scanned down the page, seeing where his thumb had marked a word, theonomy, for he'd stopped to look it up—if he didn't know a word, he always did: "the state of being subject to God's authority and rule." Subject to God! It made him laugh, and then he thought, No wonder the bastards did it, meaning Mann, the Germans, and the war.

But then his mind began to work back farther, along the path the book had made, for he'd bought it on the way back from L.A. the previous week. He remembered this: he'd driven down as usual, and he was fairly sure that nobody had followed him, but he'd taken the long way home, driving up the Coast Highway to Point Mugu (the site of the Pacific Missile Test Center) and then doubling back through Pacific Palisades. And it was then, as he wound along the narrow road through Rustic Canyon, with its million-dollar log cabins nestled in the woods, that Tannis had been reminded that Mann had spent the war here; and it had occurred to him that even though he spoke absolutely fluent German (this was, in fact, one of the foundations of his career as an intelligence officer) he'd never read a word of Mann's; so he continued his detour all the way to Bakersfield and bought the book. He'd been reading it this afternoon, before . . . But he still wasn't ready for "before" and "after" and already was leaping back again, this time along the lines of the war and Germany. *April 1945*. Bavaria. Yes—he'd been walking back to his jeep (it was not a question of remembering; he was there, smelling the woods, feeling the firm-packed pine needles beneath his feet, then stopping as he saw the German through the trees: the shock of it, stifling his breath, as if he'd come upon a wild animal) and as he came up to it, he saw a German soldier scrounging in the back. The man was probably looking for food: he was half starved. They all were. The German had no weapon; his uniform was in rags. Looking at him, *looking at him when the man didn't know he was standing there*, something happened. He felt absolutely calm. He knew he was going to kill him. He *could*. He lit a Lucky. The German only noticed him when he cocked his Colt, putting up his hands; smiling; perhaps not believing; attempting to summon an expression of friendliness, entreating—and then, looking him straight in the eye, Tannis had shot him right between the eyes: seeing in the man's eyes, in the instant before he pulled the trigger, a reflection of his own. On the German's body he found a few identity papers, which he burned, but also a brass Zippo lighter, which the German must have taken from a dead GI . . . And as the memory faded, he thought how odd it was, that he could remember exactly what that German looked like, but he couldn't remember Harper. *Harper*. He thought of Harper. Somehow, it seemed, he'd made the detour. He was back in the here and now. Yes, what *did* he look like? There had to be a picture of him, in his office. Harper. It was difficult to characterize what he represented to him. The buried body? The skeleton in his closet? His almost-Waterloo? Harper had been British, so such associations came to mind. *A blot on your copybook, old boy*. In general, *a near catastrophe*. But not quite. And what had happened in the past made no difference now, he told himself. Harper was a door that was now swinging mysteriously open, but he already knew there was nothing down that passage.

Tannis took a breath—he seemed to have been holding his breath—then turned his old brass Zippo in his hand. He was in his office now and remembered that he'd come in here to look for a picture of Harper, and his eyes moved over the wall behind the desk, a wall covered with photographs. They were mostly of himself at various times and places—his life, in black and white: standing beside the Little Giant, the machine the CalTech scientists had used to extrude propellant; in his fine new uniform, ready to leave for Germany to uncover the scientific secrets of the Reich . . . March 1945: crossing the Rhine in a rubber boat, nineteen hours behind Montgomery . . . April: sitting in his jeep, down some forgotten Bavarian road, a Lucky pasted across his mug . . . A few weeks later: looking every inch the spy in a khaki trenchcoat, chatting quietly beneath the pines of the Hermann Göring Institute with Adolf Busemann, inventor of the swept-back wing—they'd cabled his calculations direct to Boeing in time to redesign the B-47. . . . Finally, bending over, Tannis found what he'd been looking for, a group shot of some visiting scientists at NOTS, mostly Brits from Aberporth, the British base in Wales, presumably in 1959 or 1960. Harper was standing at the back, but he must have moved, for his face was blurred, and Tannis turned away again. No, he couldn't even remember what Harper looked like. Where was he now? *Harper could be dead for all I know.* Yes, but coming back to haunt him, brought back by this mystery man, the *viejo amigo.* Who'd known him a long time ago. Or so he claimed. But when, precisely? Presumably around the time that photograph of Harper had been taken. But he wasn't Harper. Standing there, Tannis played the call back in his mind, and he was fairly sure of it. But who the hell could he be? Names went through his mind again, half a dozen, he tried to match them to the voice, and if one seemed most logical—a scientist who'd certainly known Harper—it also seemed impossible, if only because the man was dead. Dead. Yes, they were all dead, or at least they ought to be.

He lit another Lucky. Did it make a difference? It had all been so long ago. The man he'd been was long gone too, and the events, the facts, even in his own mind, were a blur. The Tushino Air Display, June 9, 1961, and the photographs of the MiG-15s with the copied missile clearly visible underneath their wings. The photographs had been the final confirmation—they'd known a good deal earlier—but now the investigation, all the interrogation teams, had rolled into action. Harper, the poor bastard, had just been in the wrong place at the wrong time; it was no wonder, he decided, that he couldn't remember what he looked like: he really had nothing to do with it at all; he was just a convenient fall guy, from everyone's point of view. *Jack, why in hell are you putting yourself on the line for the little jerk? The kid did it, let's wrap it up, let's end it. Do you really want this investigation to go on?* Not that there'd been any danger of *that*. Had he spent a lifetime in the navy not to understand bureaucracy? *They* knew a sucker better than anyone on God's earth; they would have hushed up Adolf Hitler if they hadn't seen something in it, like promotions, for themselves. And British security, he remembered, *your opposite number, old chap*, had gone along quite happily after one brief spasm of loyalty—but then they'd almost managed to hush up Philby. In the end Harper had probably been grateful. Because they didn't even charge him . . . though he was actually doing them a favor, because if they had laid charges there would have been a trial and headlines, BRIT TRAITOR HANDS RUSSKIES OUR BEST MISSILE. No, it was simpler and much more discreet to take away his clearances, blackball him in every lab that ever hoped to make a nickel out of Uncle Sam. Tannis wondered what had become of him. Certainly, he'd been finished as a scientist, and he was just in his twenties. There'd been a child, he knew, right in the middle of the whole business, but the woman had left him anyway. Supposedly Harper had become a drunk, but he wasn't sure of that. He remembered the woman again, Diana, with that high-toned Brit voice that makes any woman sound like a virgin, even when she's panting for it.

He ground out the Lucky. Contempt, that's what he felt; for all of them. But why should he care at all? There wasn't the slightest danger to him, he was fairly sure of that. As a threat Harper meant nothing, not now. There was, really, only one difficulty. Harper was innocent. Harper had been framed, as Tannis had certainly said at the time—a suggestion that had threatened people *then*, but couldn't now. Still. It meant that Harper was a loose thread, and someone—this amigo joker—might be trying to unravel it. You never knew what might happen when things became unraveled; and Tannis again remembered that German on the road in Bavaria and the look in his eyes before he squeezed the trigger. Yes. He could do this one just the same, if that's what it came down to. But why take the trouble? Let this character go to the Hideaway if he wanted. They served a great prime rib. And then, if he was still looking for trouble, he could come on here . . . and he'd be waiting for him.

But though these thoughts and questions went through his mind, they were essentially formal and academic. For a few moments Tannis hesitated, because he'd been caught off guard, whether he liked to admit it or not, because his complacency had been disturbed after all these years. But there was never any doubt about what he'd do. In that part of the desert everyone knew Tannis had a mystery. Some thought it was personal, others professional; a few sensed some peculiar twist in his career. Certainly, many people assumed he still had a connection to "intelligence," sophisticates guessing the DIA or the NIS, while the less knowledgeable bet on the CIA or the FBI. And a few people, who actually knew him, pointed out that he'd begun as a scientist, at CalTech, and speculated that some failure had deflected him. A failure . . . only a very few people might have connected Harper to it, for only a few people, even inside the United States military (so great was the navy's discretion about the blunder), knew the true story of how Sidewinder, the first heat-seeking missile in the world, had fallen into Russian hands. And failure, in any case, was not necessarily the way Tannis thought about it. But there was no way, even after all this time, that he could let it go, and even as these thoughts were slipping through his mind, Tannis was kneeling down to open the locked drawer of his desk. Inside was a padlocked cashbox, and inside this was his big old Colt, the same gun with which he'd killed that German. He took it out, pushed in a clip, and worked the action. Then he thumbed on the safety and stuck it in his pocket, as heavy as a hammer. . . . Of course he was going to go. He was going to go because curiosity killed the cat. Because he wanted one more time around the track. Because all he could do with his secrets now was carry them to the grave. The reasons didn't make much difference. Tannis was who he was and did what he did; that's all.

There was, in fact, only one more detail. For as he left the house, Tannis felt the wind against his face and stopped, turning; moving ceaselessly across the face of the earth, the wind had now chosen to touch *his* face, and he lifted his eyes. The Mojave night was sprinkled with bright stars, and now, for an instant, they gave him the light to see. He could see it, feel it: that day, more than twenty years ago, the soft, hot sand beneath their boots as they trudged up the wash at Darwin Springs, the FBI man panting along beside them, the rutted jeep tracks. And finally David Harper's face, but still not clear enough to recognize, just so young, so frightened, and so innocent.

CHAPTER 2

The base at China Lake lies 150 miles northeast of Los Angeles, just off U.S. 395.

Founded in 1943, it was originally known as the Naval Ordnance Test Station, or NOTS; in 1967 this was changed to Naval Weapons Center (NWC). Under either name, however, almost no one has ever heard of it—in contrast, for example, to nearby Edwards Air Force Base, where Chuck Yeager broke the sound barrier and the space shuttle lands, or the Miramar Naval Air Station, in San Diego, with its "Top Gun" school. Even in the navy itself, China Lake is virtually unknown. And those who are familiar with it often speak of it suspiciously as being "outside the loop"—a maverick reputation that serves to underline the fact that NOTS (to use the older term, as Tannis normally did) is different from every other base the United States Navy runs. It operates under navy command, but its history connects it to outside, civilian institutions, especially the California Institute of Technology, in Pasadena, and although some naval personnel are stationed there—in particular, the test pilots of the VAX squadron—most of the population is civilian. Moreover, these people are all scientists, engineers, and technicians, "damned professors," as they were called in the beginning. But their achievements are undeniable and silence all the critics, for China Lake has produced some of the most effective military ordnance in the world, from the barrage rockets used in the 1943 invasion of North Africa to the explosive lens charges in the first atomic bombs and a vast array of guided missiles and bombs, Zuni, ASROC, Shrike; above all, Sidewinder (AIM-9, as it's known officially).

Most of these weapons are launched from aircraft, and this has dictated a good deal about the base, especially its remoteness and its size. China Lake is huge—more than a million acres, 1,800 square miles, an area greater than Rhode Island's. This immense territory is divided into two great tracts, separated from one another by a narrow civilian corridor running up the Panamint Valley through the town of Trona. In recent years the range to the south of this line has been used to develop "stealth" technology and electronic warfare countermeasures (ECM), but it's the northwest section of the base that's the more important, for the airfield, the laboratories, and the community itself are all located here. Forming a rough rectangle, this area is considerable in itself, for it stretches about 45 miles from east to west and 25 from north to south. The upper, northern half is tableland, rugged hills, and valleys where wild horses and burros still roam, and high up on the faces of the cliffs, which have names like Renegade Canyon and Cactus Peak, one can still see the strange etched drawings, called petroglyphs, made by a long-vanished race of Indians. (The drawings are an official historic site and are scrupulously protected by the navy.) To the south the hills give way; the land becomes flatter, merging with the desert; and finally, in an abrupt slope, it runs down to the depression that is China Lake itself. Of course, there has been no lake here for ten thousand years, although once this part of the Mojave was covered by a chain of them, hundreds of feet deep, which ran from the Sierra Nevada in the west all the way across to Death Valley. Now only the dried-up beds of these lakes remain, this particular one resembling an enormous scar, hard and hot, and gleaming white with the deposits of borax, calcium, and silica that Chinese laborers mined during the 1880s, thereby contributing the name. Forming a clear, level expanse, almost like a natural concrete, this is perfect for the base's test ranges, and they are laid out in a great arc across it, extending back for about ten miles; Baker, Charlie, and "G" ranges (never George, because it stands for Ground). South of the ranges, along the old lake's shore, is the base itself. Originally the buildings were all Quonset huts, and they are not much more elaborate today: simple, functional buildings, mostly of one story. In fact, the working side of the base has changed little over the years; on the other hand, the residential district is now much smaller. Originally it housed ten or fifteen thousand people, but today the population is less than half that number; the decline, however, is more apparent than real and derives purely from a technicality. In the beginning China Lake was officially a "temporary" wartime facility that, in theory, the navy could have shut down at any time, so no bank would extend mortgages to people from the base who wanted to build in the area. But this was changed in 1962—with the help of President Kennedy, no less, the base was declared "permanent"—and most of the civilians immediately fled the rigors of base housing, though only as far as Ridgecrest, the civilian town that has grown up around the base perimeter. Today it has a population of some twenty thousand, with schools, a hospital, and a community college (the great local pride), and its neat streets stretch back almost to the highway. Most of the houses are pleasant ranch-style bungalows, and there is no outward sign that many of the inhabitants are top engineers and chemists. In fact, the only odd thing about the town is its name, since there isn't a ridge or a crest for miles. But that's a part of local lore. In 1940, before the navy came, the area's ninety-six inhabitants had petitioned for a post office, asking to be called Sierra View—a suggestion that was not unreasonable since you can see the Sierra Nevada from here—but the government rejected the request on the grounds that California had enough sierras as it was. Accordingly, alternatives were called for and posted on the bulletin board of Bentham's General Store. Rattlesnake Gulch gained some adherents, as did Gilmore, the brand of gas that Bentham sold; but in the end it was a stranger passing through who supplied the winning nomination—years before, he'd enjoyed good times in a place called Ridgecrest, in Missouri. All the same, the choice has worked out well: with its bungalows and carports, its porch lights abuzz with moths, the town clearly takes its inspiration from the suburbs; if not Ridgecrest, it could have been a perfect Buena Vista, Maple Heights, or Greenwood Glen.

For Tannis this was the landscape of his personal history: he'd lived most of his life in the desert and knew it like the back of his hand. He usually said he'd been born in Sparks, Nevada, although his military records listed the other candidate, Los Angeles. In fact, Tannis couldn't be sure—he was a bastard. He'd no idea who his natural father was, and his mother, having attached herself to the man who'd given Tannis his name, decamped six months later and was never heard of afterward.

Tannis had probably been five at that time, although he wasn't even certain of his birth date. If his father—as Tannis thought of him—had ever known it, he'd forgotten, for those kinds of details never much concerned him. He was the sort of man who was always on the move, looking forward, not back. He loved plans, projects, dreams, traveling: though his voyages never took him beyond Oregon to the north and Panama to the south. He worked in construction and on the railways, sold tract houses and Mack trucks but always thought of himself as a prospector. Over the years he even made his share of strikes. The biggest of these, near Riddle, Oregon, allowed him to take Tannis to L.A.; usually they only staked him to a few months gambling.

For Tannis, as a boy, this life was not as colorful as it sounds; he seemed to spend most of his time waiting around, ignored, half forgotten: *Just stay here a few minutes, son.* . . . But never entirely forgotten: his father always stuck with him. And he had another saving grace, his intelligence, which was acute enough to see the intelligence in his son. After the age of five Tannis never lost to him at checkers; and after his third game of chess, Tannis never lost at that. So, whenever possible, his father put Tannis in school; ultimately, when Tannis was fourteen or so, he took him to Los Angeles and got him into high school. Since Tannis didn't have any academic records, he was given a series of tests to determine which grade he'd enter. Most of these were mathematical, for it was assumed that this would be his weakness; in fact, the opposite was true: in any secondhand bookstore trigonometry texts are usually cheap, and Tannis was already reading them for pleasure. So even though he'd scarcely heard of Shakespeare and would have had difficulty locating India on a map, he was started in the junior year and promoted halfway through. He graduated third in his class, then wrote a scholarship examination that got him into CalTech. And it was CalTech that led him to China Lake.

In fact, to be precisely accurate, CalTech led him *back* to China Lake, for, as he liked to tell people, he'd been there before anyone else knew the place existed, working across it with his father, who'd made a halfhearted search for the Lost Gunsight Mine, which some people claimed lay in the Coso Hills. He even found a little mercury and actually staked a claim, which the navy eventually bought from Tannis, his father having died. But that was years later. At CalTech, certainly, it would never have occurred to him that his personal history and the larger history of the world would intersect. His goals were purely personal, though even that formulation was probably too precise: his conception of success was entirely abstract; his grade scores, as far as that went, would have been a good approximation. As the youngest student on the campus (he must have been close to that) he had to run fast to keep up and didn't have much time for the war in Europe. Certainly he was barely aware of the Council on Defense Cooperation, CalTech's way of planning how the institute could make its contribution to the war effort. On the other hand, Tannis knew Charles Lauritsen, its leading member, by sight, for Lauritsen was something of a hero, the man who'd developed the world's first million-volt X ray. But he knew nothing of Lauritsen's trip to England in the spring of 1941, where he was shown a new British explosive, cordite; nor did he have any idea that one of the peculiar properties of this substance—you could shape it, extrude it—made it ideal as the propellant in small rocket engines.

Eventually everyone knew about the rocket program itself. Lauritsen's initial efforts were discreet—a rocket that towed targets for naval gunnery practice; a "retro-fired" antisubmarine rocket—but his first great success was very much public knowledge. This was a 4.5-inch barrage rocket that CalTech designed, developed, tested, and manufactured in only seventy days so that it could be used by the thousands in support of American troops going ashore at Casablanca on November 8, 1942. It was an effort so massive that it almost monopolized the school; CalTech secretaries actually did much of the final assembly work in the gym, and the rocket casings were piled up in the halls.

By that point Tannis was thoroughly involved in the project anyway. He was perfect for it. His research interests involved the behavior of gases under pressure, and his academic adviser was Bruce Sage, who was in charge of propellant extrusion at Eaton Canyon (and would eventually become head of the Explosives Department at China Lake). More than this, he had practical experience; how many other students had first handled nitroglycerin at the age of nine? For it was now he earned the nickname Cracker Jack. And besides this, Tannis could run lathes, mix solvents, fix an engine; above everything else, he knew the desert. This last became important in the fall of 1942. By then it had become apparent that CalTech's rockets needed safe test facilities and a large proving ground. They were all air-launched, and there were obvious problems working with high explosives right in Pasadena. Two men had died already—on March 27, 1942, Raymond Robey had accidentally detonated several hundred pounds of propellant in the Kellogg Radiation Laboratory, and that same June, Carl Sanborn, a technician, killed himself while making a mixture of magnesium powder and potassium perchlorate in Eaton Canyon. To solve the problem Lauritsen turned to the navy, who'd already become involved around the barrage rockets. In June a directive from the commander in chief of the U.S. Fleet called for the expansion of rocket testing on the West Coast; and later in the summer, after flying for hours across the Mojave Desert in a single-engine Beechcraft, Lauritsen simply looked down and discovered China Lake. It was, in every way, exactly what he was looking for; there was even an old army dispersal airfield right beside it. But the next day, when Lauritsen took a party into the desert to inspect China Lake from the ground, the sand, the rock, and the creosote stopped them dead. But all that sand and creosote put Tannis in his natural element, and a few days later, when they decided to try again, it was Bruce Sage who suggested they ask Tannis to come along. "Didn't you say you'd driven a Mack truck across Death Valley?"

"Yessir. A Bulldog. They'll go anywhere."

"Well, come on then. It's either you or some anthropologist from USC. We'll probably run into Paiutes."

Tannis was familiar with the desert in a way that no one else was; he knew how to keep the sand out of his nose, and out of a carburetor. He could use a gun. He always made sure, if you were going out there, that you took enough water—which invariably seemed too much to begin with but barely enough at the end. He was handy and he was willing. So he was always around and actually saw the first tests, the first flights off the airstrip, the beginnings of construction. Yet in his own eyes his position was anomalous. He sometimes felt . . . like a mascot? like the last boy picked to play? It was unfair; he certainly never suffered a slight. Yet he felt a constant frustration that he couldn't quite pin down. He was close but wanted to be closer; he wanted to jump some barrier, leap across. He wasn't sure what he wanted. He wanted to . . . fly. That's what he finally decided. He loved to fly. The first plane he flew in was an NE-1 (the navy's version of the L-18 Grasshopper) that had been assigned to NOTS, and he made friends with the head test pilot, Tom Pollock; in fact, he still had a picture of himself and Pollock, poised above the NO STEP on a TBF Avenger's wing, inscribed "Someday you'll be up here with me."

But of course that didn't happen. In 1944 there were very few young, single men with chemistry degrees who spoke fluent scientific

German; Tannis was snapped up by the navy, commissioned inside seventy-two hours, and sent to Europe as a member of a technical intelligence mission. Working as a spy (well, more or less) he remained in Germany until 1947: long enough—though this must have been happening before he left—to extinguish the scientist in him. When he came back, still in the navy, still in security, it was almost inevitable that he be assigned to a research installation, like White Sands, Dahlgren, or China Lake.

In all the years since, he'd never left, though he'd had opportunities. In the sixties, when the service intelligence operations were gutted to staff the DIA (Defense Intelligence Agency)—a revenge for the failure at the Bay of Pigs—he could have gone there, off to Washington. But he stayed where he was (Tannis had no taste for bureaucratic wars) even though, in his own words, he was reduced to being a glorified security guard. And when naval intelligence finally did come back, he was offered a job in the NIS (Naval Investigative Service) but turned it down; he'd just finished the house, south of Edwards Air Force Base, where he intended to retire, and didn't want to give it up. Or so he said. But people who knew him sensed the truth was different. It was a strange thing to say, since this was the desert, but he would have been a fish out of water anywhere else. This was his world, his universe. He couldn't breathe city air, sea air, jungle air. He needed the desert. "I'm like an old lizard," he'd sometimes say—it was a conceit he cultivated. Tannis, he was so familiar you didn't notice him. Tannis, just another Joshua tree signaling from a hill. Tannis, just one more sign on the nighttime highway: WIND GUSTS NEXT TEN MILES. He relished such anonymity, such familiarity, and it was entirely appropriate, that Friday night, that he was heading for the Hideaway. It was another fixture, one more part of the unchanging landscape. Like any other "company town," China Lake has always had a particular place to go; the sort of place, people would say, where you could drink but also take your wife. Tannis could remember the first of them, a bar called Poppa Ludo's (which some people claimed was actually built with materials filched from the construction of the base itself), and after that came the Village or Towne's. The Hideaway was almost indistinguishable in this series, typical of a certain kind of restaurant in California: the local establishment that is known to everyone but that also maintains a peculiar discretion, a reminder, perhaps, that its antecedent is the roadhouse. Low, dark, recessive, betrayed by only a single strand of neon, it stood well back from the highway, behind a large, unlit parking lot. Clinging to the desert night, it seemed to encourage clandestine intentions: a woman's laughter hinted at couples going off together in the dark, and the obscure entrance, around the side, implied that you might have to knock to gain admittance. But of course you don't, and Tannis didn't. He knew, as everybody did, that the Hideaway's prime rib is always excellent and its welcome warm and friendly.

Tannis had arrived late. But he didn't care. His mystery caller would wait, he would have no choice; and perhaps, in any case, Tannis already guessed that the Hideaway was only the beginning of the trail. So he'd taken his time coming across the desert, sticking to back roads, side roads, or no roads at all—at one point he'd run right off the highway, driving half a mile across the hardpan, and then stood nonchalantly, with his hands in his pockets, on top of the cab of his old Dodge pickup, checking back along his route. At the Hideaway, when he'd arrived, he was just as careful, noting cars and license plates, for this was a public place. He didn't want surprises. Perhaps in the back of his mind was the caller's fear, however improbable, that his phone was tapped, so that even if no one was watching him now, his every move might have to be accounted for, could become a potential item for interrogation. *On the tape your caller told you to be at the Hideaway by nine o'clock, but according to the hostess* . . . She was a tall woman with a limp and a bouffant hairdo (still keeping faith with Jackie, with her girlhood) and there was no way she wasn't going to recognize him, so he didn't try, lighting up a Lucky with his Zippo, giving her his biggest smile.

"Captain Tannis . . . Nice to see you. It's been a time."

"That's what I was thinking."

All the same, from every point of view, he wanted to be discreet: he wouldn't try to hide, but he didn't want to stand out either. If the caller was here, he didn't want to scare him away; and if it all came to nothing, he wanted to be able to shrug it off—I came, I saw, I ate a steak . . . what else do you expect me to say? So he ordered what he always did, prime rib (rare), baked potato (with sour cream), tossed salad (and ranch dressing), Schlitz, and tried to hang back, particularly hoping that no one else would recognize him, come up and say hello. And then, instinctively, he was almost certain that the man wasn't there, that this was some sort of test, or preparation. Or perhaps he was even being mocked. I know something you don't. Can't you guess? Harper. Sidewinder. The early 1960s. He was being taken back to that time, almost taunted by it. For the same people, as he looked about, could have been sitting here twenty years ago. The restaurant hadn't changed much either, its decor low key, the ambience vaguely Western—heavily varnished tables and a mural along one wall that featured a Mexican figure and a motto. Harper, Tannis thought, must have been here and read it. "It is morning. The warm sun absorbs the chill and dampness. My eyes open slowly. Today I shall take a glass of wine and heap my tortilla full. Today I shall be easy with myself and those who touch my life." When the waitress came, she brought a min-iature loaf of bread on a wooden serving paddle, ranch-house style; and as he bit into a slice—he had certainly read Proust—he wondered if the taste might recall the caller's name, or at least Harper's face. But there were no revelations, and he realized that either Harper, or this mystery man, could have been sitting at any of these tables and he might not have known. He didn't recognize a face—and on a Friday night there were a lot to choose from. He guessed: a teacher at Cerro Coso College. An engineer at McDonnell Douglas. A highway inspector. A real estate man thinking of buying a strip development. A lot of couples. But also one large navy party that was undoubtedly from the base, aircrew in their caps, a naval aviator in a windbreaker, and a couple of civilians in suits and ties. The noise level in the room dropped suddenly, and everyone could hear the flier say, "Of course, you can always tell a navy wife—she's the one that's overdressed." The whole room laughed, which was typical—the Hideaway had always possessed the easy, confidential atmosphere of a place whose clientele is largely composed of regulars. But the caller, Tannis concluded, wouldn't be one, otherwise I'd know him; and a stranger would stand out. So whatever way you looked at it the odds were against his being here at all, and the interrogation he kept running through his mind would draw a blank, at best the kind of lead that's only busywork:

So he wasn't there when you arrived?

I'd say not.

Still, you didn't go into the bar, or the side room. Why was that?

I was trying to make it work. I didn't want to frighten him off. The arrangement was: he'd come to me.

In any case, you didn't see anyone you knew.

Not till later. Not in the dining room. Then Howard Angell came out of the bar—

When was this?

I was eating by then, say ten or quarter after. He was with someone else, someone I didn't know.

Who is Howard Angell?

He was a security director at Ford Aerospace. Maybe he still is. We worked together when they set up the line for Sidewinder at Newport Beach.

And he saw you?

No. He would have said hello. But he was there. Ask him.

Could Angell have been the caller?

Not a chance.

That's very definite.

His voice is wrong. The voice on the phone just couldn't be his, no matter what you did with it. Besides, I don't see how he could be connected to any of this. It wouldn't make any sense at all.

All right. But when you were looking around, did you think you saw anyone? Try to remember. What names began running through your mind, associations?

But there weren't any: he looked into a hundred faces but saw no fear, no threats, no hidden secrets—or anything else that might reach back *multas anas astra*. His coffee arrived. He drank it. Asked for more. Still nothing. Once, he went to the john, giving the man a chance to leave a note at his table. Another time, he bought some cigarettes. There could be absolutely no doubt: Tannis gave him every opportunity.

So by eleven o'clock—

Quarter past. I checked my watch. I knew you'd ask—

Anyway, you figured he wasn't going to show?

Or not there. I'd done exactly what he'd told me.

Not exactly. You were late.

What the hell. If he'd wanted to see me, I was there. That couldn't have been important. But I figured something else had frightened him off. Or possibly it was only a test. Anyway, there was no point hanging around, and so I didn't. The thing was over.

But Tannis didn't really think that it was over.

And he knew that this, implicitly, was an admission that the man, the caller, represented something really serious.

For an amateur might in fact have contacted him inside the Hideaway. But not a professional—a professional would have understood exactly the problems the Hideaway created for him; he would have sensed the invisible watchers, the inevitable questions. So if the caller appeared now it meant . . . but then it could mean anything . . . he had no idea what . . .

Behind him the low, dark building stretched back into the night, merging with it, and beyond the parking lot the lights and traffic on the road hissed distantly. From behind, a rush of sound and conversation erupted in the emptiness—a door must have opened; but then it closed, and silence folded around him once again. He waited a moment. He lit a cigarette—he let the light of the flame play across his face, almost like a signal. He could afford to, he knew. There were no witnesses here: there could be no contradiction of the account he would choose to give. He had passed out of view. The phrase "a window of opportunity" formed in his mind, and a small smile flickered on his lips. It was the sort of modern phrase he didn't like, "bottom line," "level playing field," "window of opportunity"; he preferred *zero hour, loaded dice, make your move.* But that's what it came down to, though in a reversed way, which pleased him; for this window of opportunity was his invisibility, an area of darkness. So they were on even terms, the caller and himself, for the first time. And he suddenly thought, You're just like me, and quickly, becoming more certain with each step about what he would find, he crossed the parking lot to his pickup. And of course there was an envelope underneath the windshield wiper. He carefully opened it. And unfolded a single sheet of paper, with a message spelled out in letters cut from the L.A. *Times*: MIDNIGHT TRONA AIRPORT SERVICE ROAD.

He looked around instinctively, but of course the man was long gone, the parking lot empty; there were just the cars, and the wind, and the desert behind, and the streetlamps along the road in front—the darkness and the light, the silence and the sound, lying in stripes across the night. He ground out his cigarette. Well, well. This was getting good, he thought. He checked his watch. 11:20. There was no time to hatch a plan, to do anything except what the caller wanted. How well the man knew him. He'd guessed, so precisely, the degree of his patience: how long he'd wait inside the Hideaway. Was that a clue? Perhaps this whole thing was a treasure hunt, the clues trailed in front of him—Harper, the Hideaway, now the Trona airport road. But he didn't have to follow them. He'd played everything by the book. Now he could just go home. Even if it later came out that the message had been left, he could just say he'd never got it. A kid took it, it blew away, that was a windy night. Or what the hell—discretion is the better part of valor; why should he go up the goddamned Trona road? The trouble was, he knew the caller would come back. No one went to this kind of trouble and then just let it lie. On the other hand, when he called again, he'd be ready for him. . . . But this was happening now, tonight—there was something in the air: with the wind or premonition, the back of his neck bristled and he smelled, yes he did, blood and saw the look in that German's eye. Tonight was the night for someone—he knew it. And so he got into the truck and backed it around, turning into the stream of traffic on China Lake Boulevard. There was a lot of it—cars, pickups, kids in jalopies and jacked-up vans celebrating a small-town Friday night: McDonald's and Carl Jr.'s went blinking by; somewhere, Johnny Cash was playing. He came up to the corner of Ridgecrest Boulevard (the same intersection where Bentham's store had stood) and then swung east and picked up speed. To his right was a zone of neon, motels and drive-ins; to his left, darkness, with a few lights twinkling in the distance: this was the southern perimeter of the base. But it was too dark to see. His headlights threw shadows from the fence and picked out the water pipeline, but in a second they were gone, and there was only the empty desert, and the night, black and polished; and after only a couple of minutes there wasn't a single light in his rearview mirror and he was sure no one could be behind him. The road unwound like a ribbon. It ran east for about fifteen miles and then turned him north, through Poison Canyon, lifting him up and through a spur of the Argus Range, a little pass that opened into one long plunging view across Searles Valley, the name for the southern extension of the Panamint. More than once, this view had made him think of Dante; like black smoke from a dreadful fire, the night sky rolled away for fifty miles, and on either side devastated peaks rose up, burned, jagged, iron black. The road switch-backed on a lip of rock, and he looked down and out. A few high stars revealed the valley floor, limitless, vaguely phosphorescent, like the tongue of a dying man: an excrescence of soda ash and salt cake, borax, lithium, and bromine. These were the salts of the ancient lake bed, mined at Trona. He descended toward its furtive lights—the glowing eyes of a dog by the road, anxious glimmers behind the curtains in the metal trailer homes, red warnings to mark the looming towers of the American Potash Company's mills. Then they too were gone, and once he was clear—though he literally had not passed a car—he switched his own lights off. Swallowed up, invisible, he drifted for a mile. But he knew exactly where he was and at a certain point began to slow; and seventy yards before the turn, though he couldn't actually see a turn, he killed the engine and geared into neutral. He floated through the black, silent night, his tires hissing softly, the wind rippling by.

He wound the window down. Cool air flushed his skin. He felt the truck slow very slightly; finally, instinctively, he turned the wheel, and the truck swayed easily around the turn. He coasted. A gentle grade carried him along. Vague shapes passed before his vision: a tilted derrick, with a swinging pulley; dark pits dug into the sand—and all at once, beside him, an enormous circling eye, crudely winking, like some totem . . . in fact it was the airport radar, with a whanging, pulsing hum coming from the electric box that served it. The radar, he remembered, was the excuse for the road. And as the radar disappeared behind him, the road petered out, ending in a circular asphalt patch so you could turn around. Gently he applied his brakes; the truck had already lost so much momentum that it stopped at once.

Tannis didn't move; for a good minute, as if on a dare, he didn't move. With his hands very visible on the steering wheel, but very conscious of the weight of the Colt in his pocket, he sat absolutely still.

Nothing happened.

The wind flickered shadows across the hood of the car, reflections floated across the glass in front of him, but the night was empty.

Relaxing slightly, he leaned out the window. To his left, at the edge of the asphalt circle, he could see an old wheelbarrow, missing a handle, tilted on its side, and a patch of gravel, lumpy with hardened cement; but there was no sign of another vehicle. And since he hadn't passed one coming down, or noticed anyone parked along the highway, he didn't see how anyone could be here, unless they'd dropped out of the sky. He ducked back inside the truck and checked his watch. It was three minutes after midnight. The caller, if he'd ever been here, couldn't have left. He felt a little uncertain. Slowly he opened the door of the truck and got down beside it, but carefully holding the door open so he had cover, at least on one side. The wind pressed his face; his nose, his eyes went dry. Tight to the truck, he edged along to the back of it and looked up the road. He squinted into the wind. The grade had been very slight, a little rise, but it was enough to hide the highway. Still, as far as he could see, there was nothing up there, only the great vague shapes of the mountains, guarding the base, that formed the horizon. More openly now, he strode around the front of the truck, then across to the edge of asphalt, and abruptly ducked down, getting himself below any horizon. Narrowing his eyes again, he peered all around, but he still didn't see anything. He was alone. His mouth tightened. He didn't actually think—there was simply a vacuum here, and he filled it. But the logic was clear. The man had blundered. Perhaps from an excess of caution, a fear of a trap closing in on him, he'd created exactly that possibility, set a trap that could be sprung on himself. And Tannis, springing up into a crouch, and running—and working the action of the gun as he ran—broke into the desert, his boots slipping in the sand. Twenty yards to the right of his truck was a thickish patch of creosote; the moment he ducked behind it, he was invisible.

Would he do it? Would he kill? That wasn't clear. But he might: that was very clear. His heart pounded. Catching his breath, he thumbed off the pistol's safety and stared back toward the road where the truck gleamed like a pearly shadow in the starlight: like a bait for a trap, where he lay in ambush. The peculiar silence of the desert settled around him, a silence that whispered constantly, as if the wind passed messages between the stars. And as he stared into the night he remembered the German, how he'd come upon him, by the jeep, just like the pickup, surprising him, a figure from *der Totentanz*, his uniform in rags, but standing erect at the end, when he'd seen the gun and finally understood. . . . Staring, Tannis felt the darkness dissolve under the very strength of his sight; and his hand, trailing down beside him, sifted through the crusty soil—caliche—and the present crumbled in his palm and he found himself repeating a lesson of his father's, naming each stone and plant and animal he could see: creosote, brittlebush, arrow-weed, and shad scale. And beneath the swell and fall of the wind he heard a little chirp and knew it was a Mormon cricket, and when his fingers dug out a lumpy cluster from the sand he brought it to his lips and tasted salt, knowing this was probably halite. Then above his head he sensed the movement of a bat, which meant there was a mine nearby. But there were a hundred, and of course he knew them all: to the east, the Ophit, Redhill, Virginia Ann, the Gold Bottom, Stockwell, Standard; and over on the base itself—the navy had supposedly filled them in, but no one quite believed this—the Mariposa, El Conejo, Mohawk, Ruth, the Sterling Queen . . . The names, the memories, flickered like bright lights as real before him in that instant as the twitch of a twig across his vision. In the silence, in that waiting, all of this existed, all at once, his father, the dead German, the revolving radar's hum. Then the wind came up again. A breeze caressed his neck, withdrew, brushed against his cheek; an eddy rose and twisted higher, disappeared; and then a great soft wave billowed down from the enormous sky and swept on by him, making the land bow down before it, this wind feeling like ice against his heated skin. For those moments, with the gun's weight pressing against his flesh, he was part of this, and each breath of that wind seemed individual and alive, separate spirits moving around him, breathing on him, calling to him—calling what? And how much time went by? He scarcely knew. Five minutes certainly. Or ten. But suddenly his mouth was dry. He sniffed—so imperative was some scent. Blood was rushing in his ears. His eyes strained out. . . . He knew something was about to happen; his finger tightened. . . . And then it came—an explosion so near he almost felt the fire of it, so violent it seemed some ultimate compression of the universe or his very heart. Or at least, poised on the lip of violence himself, that was what it sounded like, though his mind knew instantly that what he'd heard was nothing more (but then also nothing less) than the discharge of a high-powered rifle.

The shock was extraordinary: like that moment, on the very edge of sleep, when you jerk awake. And for one instant he actually thought his own finger had pulled the trigger; and in the next, that he'd been hit. But even as his blood raced, he knew that the bloody halo in the corner of his eye was the afterimage of the muzzle blast. Which meant that the shot had come from the area behind him and to his right. He twisted around that way. The darkness shimmered. He might have heard a cry. Yet he wasn't sure: and almost instantly, silence descended, as if two hands had closed against his ears. Then the breeze came up, and he could hear sand sliding across the hardpan and the low buzz of the transformer for the radar. He didn't move—or only his eyes moved. But there was nothing to see, or nothing definite, only shapes that swelled against the darkness and shadows that opened into other shadows.

For five minutes he was frozen there. He was absolutely still. Finally, sensing a void in front of him, his tension eased. Yet he was very cautious. He stared up the road, back toward the truck. Nothing. He shifted left, then right. Nothing. Only then did he allow himself to lose the concentrated focus of his eyes and check his watch. It was twenty-seven minutes after midnight, so he'd been here for almost half an hour. . . . What had happened? He waited—for five minutes, timed. When there was still no sound, he rose to a crouch and began moving to his right, dodging from one patch of shadow to another in a broad circle around the area of desert where the shot had come from.

Ten minutes later he found the first sure sign, grotesque and ludicrous: a hat, caught in the creosote bush ahead of him.

A Western hat, but woven from straw—a farmer's hat, a hat to keep the sun off. Yellow straw. Silhouetted against the sky, it had a clownish look—it would have been the hat worn by the hero's portly sidekick, with a name like Andy or Gaby or Slick, flattened in every pratfall but always resurrected and dusted off. He watched it for a second, bobbling in the wind, then ran across and snatched it down . . . an ordinary cheap straw hat, but with a bloodsoaked brim. He pushed it into the sand. Looking about he could see no evidence of its owner. But the wind was blowing from the left—it would have been pushing the hat before it—and he began moving cautiously in that direction. And perhaps five minutes later he almost stumbled on it, literally, his foot stepping into a pool of shadow, then pulling back as he realized what it was.

He froze, and stared.

The dead man lay in a hollow, a hollow thrashed out in the sand. Now he was curled there in a constricted fetal posture, his hands thrust between his legs, his shoulders hunched, as if he had attempted to compress himself, to squeeze down some last dark tunnel. He'd been shot in the chest, and probably through the lungs; there was a lot of blood. It glistened in the dark like oil, and the man's face, drawn in to his chest, was covered in it. After a moment, to see him better, Tannis kneeled, pushed the barrel of his pistol against his cheek, and eased the head back.

At once Tannis knew he'd never seen this man before—and that he had nothing to do with David Harper.

Professionally, Tannis took him in. The man was short, five feet six or seven. One hundred and forty pounds. Thin white hair. He was clearly an older man, at least as old as Tannis himself, with hard, bony features: thin cheeks, a sharp nose, eyes set deep in bony sockets. The eyes were open and still gave the face expression, narrowed in pain or concentration; and again Tannis thought of a tunnel and a man trying to find the light at the end of it. A miner? But no one, today, worked the mines in these parts. Yet he was a workingman, or gave that impression. He had thick, rough hands. And he was wearing a navy jacket of heavy cloth, and heavy trousers, some sort of serge, and on his feet were thick, black, lace-up shoes. A workingman . . . but perhaps a workingman dressed up to pay a visit since, beneath the blood, there was a shirt and tie. In any case, probably not a local man. When he crawled here in his final agony, one of his trouser legs had rucked up above his shin, revealing cheap nylon socks and a patch of pallid ankle. Winter skin, city skin. To match the hat: a man from the city, afraid of the desert sun. Or at least that was a tentative conclusion. To confirm it, Tannis used his gun again to roll the body on its side, the man's limbs shifting loosely inside his garments, already incoherent. Kneeling beside him, he patted the man's hip pocket, felt a wallet, tugged it out, and then reached stickily inside the jacket, pulling out a clutch of paper. Stepping away, with his back to the wind, he spread out these findings on a Kleenex, then worked the Zippo. In the dark the orange flame bent and flickered with a little cutting sound, and revealed the boarding pass for a Pan Am flight from Berlin to Frankfurt and a German passport issued in Bonn two weeks previously. He riffled through it. In life, in the black-and-white photograph, the man had looked little different than he did in death. But apparently his eyes were blue and he had gray hair. Height, 168.3 cm, weight 71 kg. His name was Buhler, Walter Joseph, born Leipzig, 1920. Flipping to the visa pages he found there was only a single stamp, made in New York, nine days before. A German . . . an old German workingman . . . Which was certainly a surprise, but nothing in comparison to the one he discovered when he opened the wallet. It was made of brown leather, old and polished smooth, and held a fair amount of money, U.S. twenties and some deutsche marks, as well as a passbook from the Berliner Bank, a receipt from a motel in Lone Pine . . . and an identity card issued to Walter Joseph Buhler by the *Volkspolizei* in Karl-Marx-Stadt, the Deutsche Demokratische Republik, the DDR. The passport was from the West, that is, but Walter Buhler was from the East.

A dead East German, here.

An East German, shot dead within ten miles of the United States Naval Weapons Center, China Lake. Tannis stood very still and heard the questions begin again.

What did you think right there, looking down at Buhler's body? Let's play psychiatrist. What was the very first thing that came into your mind?

We had an informer about Harper. We got a tip. That was the connection. That's what came into my mind. It was the same man who'd given us the tip on Harper.

I don't understand. You're not saying that Buhler was an informer?

No, it was the other way around. I was thinking of the man who'd called me. That was the connection, you see. I suddenly realized that there was no real tie-in with Harper at all—this had nothing to do with the original case—except that the man who'd called me had given us the tip back then. Do you see? Now, somehow, he'd found out about Buhler, this East German, and he still had my name—that's why he'd come to me—and he was going to tip me off again. Harper really didn't have anything to do with it.

You received the original tip on Harper?

Yes.

What was it?

It's in the file. Once a week, Harper went into the desert, a particular road. Supposedly, he left something there. An hour later, a car came along and picked it up.

A drop?

Yes.

But you weren't sure about it?

It sounded a little too good to be true.

And what did you think this time, with Buhler?

I'm not sure I didn't think the same. Except . . .

Except what?

Maybe this time I was the guy being set up.

In fact, that was what he thought; that was the first thing that came into his mind. But as he looked down at Buhler's body, he wasn't sure he believed it. It was hard to imagine that this old man, in a funny straw hat, could be a Communist agent. And yet, he knew, that's what he had to assume, because everybody else would. But who the hell was he, really? And what did Buhler have to do with him? Lying there like that, with ants in columns already marching toward his blood, the body seemed curled in a question mark, which summed up the situation perfectly. The wind sighed, and he let his mind swing free, listening to the scratching of the creosote, the sifting sand. He wanted to get away; just leave. And who would know? If a bell is rung in the desert, does anybody hear? But he knew he couldn't . . . not just walk away. He knew at once that he had to tell them; and he imagined, quickly, what was going to happen. The sheriff's squad cars on the road, with their flashing lights . . . the barrier of tapes delimiting Buhler's resting place . . . the deputies linked arm in arm as they made their "pattern search" around the body . . . The FBI, the security people from China Lake—they'd all be there. . . . He saw it all, looking down at the dark, huddled body; then he lifted his head and looked into the dark distance. He could see nothing: the darkness was as deep as an abyss, and the bushes seemed to drift between the shadows, the sands to rise and fall in waves. But then, he knew, in such darkness no one could see him. He was alone, all alone in the dark, and now he felt a peculiar, precise resolution of himself—the coming to sharp focus of the elements in a lens—and slowly his breath escaped, then easily filled his lungs. He was on the edge of some deduction, a revelation. But not quite yet. It was still a distance away, the distance, precisely, between himself and the dead German, and just then, almost inadvertently it seemed, he caught sight of Buhler's body once again. Well, well, what have we here? He moved over to it. He sauntered around it. He stood above it, looking down. It was like looking down a deep black hole. Repulsion filled him, for the ants were now crawling in a small black line up the dead man's cheek, and down, across his lips, hesitating there, and then feeling inside his mouth. This dead German . . . *Those fucking German bastards* . . . The phrase, spat out of so many muddy faces, drifted through his mind, like the memory of a scent, familiar and yet exotic. Falaise. Ardennes. Remagen. Might these not be the names of perfumes in some half-forgotten language? Which, nonetheless, he recollected. The war. The beginning. Which had now come back. All those poor dead fucking Germans. Just men to kill . . . and he remembered then the dead German, by the jeep, the ants had eaten him up a lifetime ago. Just like this. The soldiers of great ancient armies. He watched them now. They tickled at poor Buhler's ear. They traced the line of his slackened jaw. They got right into, they worked down between his teeth. . . . This German, that first dead German. Why did I do it? Why had he done any of it. . . . But it was another question that now found an answer: the distance closed, his mind made something new, the little deduction now came to him, withdrawn before—his nostrils quivered with it. Yes. He was, after all, the only witness. He was the only man who'd experienced this night, who'd hidden in this darkness, felt the rise and fall of the desert wind. And so he might be the only man to ask the question *How had the killer come and gone?* Yes, he would be the only one to ask it because the answer would seem so obvious—he'd used a car or truck that Tannis simply hadn't seen. But there hadn't been one; about certain matters Tannis knew himself to be infallible. So how, indeed, had the killer done it? The question was so curious that he lit a Lucky and thought it through—stood there, straddling Buhler's body, and worked it out. Then, moving quickly, he went back to his truck. He found a flashlight in the glove compartment and looked back toward the body, fixing its position, but then walked across the little circle of asphalt in the opposite direction. After three steps he began to run, the gun in his right hand, swinging at his side, the flashlight in his left, but switched off, so that he was running in the darkness. He ran faster. Then faster still. He ran like some spirit escaped from Ballarat, the ghost town up the road, or a madman, or a *loco*, or an Indian, like some mad Paiute—for it is mad to run across the desert in the darkness; that's just the time your foot will find a snake—but he kept on anyway, a steady lope, his breathing strangely easy, as if the wind were blowing through him, turning finally, making an enormous loop back toward Buhler, so that no one would ever find his footprints or know what he had done. And then he almost stumbled into what he knew he had to find.

A wash.

A dry gulch.

Or what passed for one in this dreadful place. The rains of a hundred years (falling a pitiful few inches every other year) had carved a groove into the desert plain. Slipping down its bank, he reached the bottom. It was surprisingly deep, for the walls reached his shoulders. Now he turned on the flashlight. He followed the spreading beam: as though walking down a tunnel or a mine shaft (had Buhler been at home here?), his light like the lamp on a miner's helmet. And he seemed to be descending. He felt a hot, dry draft. The wind rose higher; a gust drove sand like smoke against his face. He squinted, ducked his head. A bird flew by, with soft, slow-beating owl's wings. A piece of creosote skittered across his path. Back and forth, he swung the light. Deep in burrows in the bank, white eyes were staring out, and for one fleeting instant, trapped inside the beam, a milk snake went twisting on its way. For twenty minutes he pushed along, then advanced more slowly: and at last he saw them, set concrete hard in the gray caliche . . . and no more difficult to follow than the white line down the center of a road. The tracks of a horse. It was that simple. Fresh as spit, he thought, and smiled, catching his breath; but then he began to run again, a steady trot, the light marking the tracks' twisting path. After a quarter mile he reached a place where the tracks made a little compounding of themselves. The horse had been tethered here, he knew, and he could see the marks where its rider had scrambled up the bank. He scrambled up himself, shining the light, and could see, even from here, the spot where Buhler's body lay.

A horse . . . that was how he'd done it. Had Buhler ridden too? Or had he come a different way? With the wind blowing stronger in his face, Tannis slid down the bank and raised his light, flashing it along the wash, looking for the answer. But the darkness swirled, the beam flickered like a candle, and there was nothing more to see.

But he'd seen enough. Kneeling down he pressed his palm into the horse's hoofprint and smiled. He'd go back and call them now. But here was something they wouldn't have to know. A secret. Of the most precious kind, for Tannis knew it was bound to lead him somewhere.

CHAPTER 3

During the next six days—from the Friday, that is, to the following Thursday—Tannis watched the official investigation into Buhler's death unfold.

His vantage point was privileged, but not necessarily close, for the dynamic of most security investigations is centrifugal and he was quickly swirled to the periphery. But it wasn't hard to guess what was going on: he'd done it often enough himself. There'd be a lot of chaos and confusion as offices and communications were established, and then the drudgery of routine—interviews, reports, and meetings. And everything, he knew, would be compounded by the very size of the effort, which in this case was considerable. There were a lot of strangers in Ridgecrest that week, and everybody in town knew that the FBI had taken over all the rooms in the Miracle City, the old motel right across from the base where the navy always puts people up.

By Monday afternoon, however, things had settled down a little. Tannis learned that the sheriff was out of it, and he drove up to Independence, the county seat, and found him in a coffee shop. Tannis had known him for years. He was a big, shrewd, even-tempered man, not the kind who looked for trouble, and Tannis suspected that he was just as happy not to be involved; but, on principle, he put on a mild show of resentment—the local man displaced by outsiders—and allowed the details of the autopsy to be pried out of him. However, there were no great revelations; Buhler had been shot at close range with a .30-30 rifle, dying more or less instantly. The sheriff confirmed as well, though Tannis had noted the receipt in Buhler's pocket, that he'd been staying at a motel in Lone Pine, and on his way back Tannis turned in to look at it. Sierra Peaks, it was called; split logs, a cedar-shake roof, the parking spots marked with hitching posts. Sitting across the road Tannis thought of Buhler with his straw hat and heavy blue suit; everything about him was incongruous, though in fact he could imagine him here. The motel had just the rustic quality that might appeal to a German; perhaps a man who'd never taken a holiday and had put on that funny hat to get himself in the mood. But it hardly smacked of espionage.

The next day he managed to learn a little more. In Trona there's a weekly newspaper called the *Argus*, and it had received a number of calls about what had happened on Friday night—people reporting "strange lights in the desert"—and the FBI was worried that the wrong sort of story might come out; so the Special-Agent-in-Charge asked Tannis, who knew the editor, to have a chat with him. Of course, this was a way of including Tannis as well, of keeping him on side, and by way of reward, he was then given an informal briefing on events-so-far during which he was told that the FBI's legal attaché in Bonn—known in their jargon as a *Legat*—had established that Buhler's identity was apparently genuine and that he'd legally crossed into West Berlin about six months previously. He'd come alone, he had no money, he'd made no attempt to hide himself; apparently he had no clandestine intention whatsoever.

Then, on Wednesday, Tannis picked up another tidbit—though he wouldn't understand its importance for several days—this time by taking advantage of the kind of bureaucratic anomaly only someone like him would have known about. Ninety miles southeast of China Lake lies Barstow, a small town of no particular importance except that it happens to straddle a number of major interstate highways and several smaller ones (including the old Route 66). As a consequence, virtually every fugitive fleeing Southern California is bound to pass through it, and so the FBI has long had a three-man unit there, a Resident Agency, or RA. These are the smallest organs within their bureaucracy, but as it happens the Barstow Agency is the closest office to China Lake and its senior agent, a man named Iverson, had been the first federal officer to reach the scene the previous Saturday. He'd actually done very little, for it was obvious that the case would ultimately be handled from Los Angeles, but he had "federalized" it (under Section 533, Title 28, of the U.S. Code). Because of this, the Barstow Agency automatically became the Office of Origin, the OO, for the investigation, which meant that under standard FBI procedures it received a copy of all reports connected to the case. Tannis knew Iverson, looked in at his office on Wednesday, and they had lunch together. Without pushing too hard he discovered that Barstow had received a huge transmission direct from Bonn, apparently a massive security file the Germans had already compiled on Buhler. It was the size of a book, but Iverson showed Tannis only a single page. "This was what got them all excited. You read German; maybe you can tell me why." Tannis read through it. It was a standard medical report, stating that Buhler had suffered from a heart condition called cardiomyopathy. Iverson nodded as Tannis finished his translation. "That explains it. There was a big panic. They took the body to L.A. and did another autopsy." Tannis checked, discovering that cardiomyopathy is a serious heart disease, often the result of alcoholism.

What all this meant he simply didn't know; on Wednesday night he was as confused as anyone. But he'd taken part in enough investigations to know that they always came full circle, which meant coming back to him. So he just bided his time, poking and prodding a little. He called Howard Angell in Newport Beach to see if the FBI had called him, which they hadn't, and one afternoon drove back to Lone Pine, where he knew a man who rented horses. He took one out—he hadn't ridden in years—and then chatted about vets and where you might buy feed, and if there were any riders up the Panamint: not so far as he knew. . . . There couldn't be anything very directed about this; something would happen, or it wouldn't.

And then it did. Bill Matheson, the security director at China Lake—that is, the man who now held the position Tannis had filled for so many years—called and asked him to come in the next morning. "They've decided they have to know about Harper. Of course, you're the obvious one to ask."

"Is it official?"

"Let's say we'd appreciate your cooperation. But we do it here, on the base. The NIS has sent in a team from Washington. They want to keep it all in-house."

A request, not a command; made through Matheson, not the FBI directly; to take place on the base rather than in a Bureau office. Tannis drew the obvious conclusion: the investigation was in trouble, they needed favors, and he was being rallied to the colors. What he probably underestimated, however, was the effect of his reputation: they were being delicate with his sensibilities. Over the years, he'd put the fear of the Lord into more than a few people and at the very least had a reputation as a difficult loner. Besides, he went back so far; he could pull rank on any of them. In all that followed, this gave him leverage, and more subtly, in ways he didn't realize, it gave him another advantage as well: only an anachronism could have understood what was going on, and Tannis, uniquely, lived both *then* and *now*.

Thursday morning, when he got up and shaved and dressed, it was as if he'd got his old job back. And his mind slipped back. As he drove across the desert, with the high sky as white as well-washed denim, it might have been twenty years ago. There was a subtle shift in his perception, as though in a reversal of technology a color film had been washed to black and white. He was in a time machine that took him back to a world of cast-iron engines, vacuum tubes, Bakelite, cork-tipped cigarettes.

Oddly, at China Lake, scientifically so up to date, this wasn't difficult to maintain. So little had changed over the years, for the very layout of the place, planned as carefully as a suburb, locked it in the patterns of the past, a past dated by the very "modernity" of its low, flat-roofed buildings. There were differences, of course. In the old days there'd been a checkpoint guarded by marines, M-1s at the ready; but that morning he lined up behind salesmen from Raytheon and Martin Marietta—three-piece suits and fancy briefcases—and received his pass from a smiling secretary who worked quite unprotected in the air-conditioned reception room. And the main road in, Lauritsen Drive, was not dirt anymore but the most immaculate asphalt, as smooth as satin ribbon—again, a brand-new subdivision came to mind. Yet these small touches were only the gentlest impositions of the present; otherwise, the past persisted. For example: the interview took place in "the White House," as the base headquarters was called, one of the original wooden buildings, full of sunlight and bright varnish, like a yacht club or a hotel on a tropic isle. Offices opened elegantly off a mezzanine, and in the conference room, with sunshine falling through the slats in the venetian blinds, there was a sense of time suspended, as though, peeking out through those blinds, you might see a gentle scene of palms and glittering water, with a Mitsubishi Zeke circling to make its run. In fact, like most other American military institutions, China Lake owed a good deal to Pearl Harbor, and in that room those days didn't seem so far away, President Reagan's smiling countenance neatly symbolizing the ambiguity, a subtle confusion between then and now.

In any case, even if they didn't quite understand the cause, this dislocation of time affected everyone. The two FBI agents, and even the officers from the Naval Investigative Service, were huddled together at the back of the room, looking uncomfortable and out of place, as Tannis came in. With the toe of his shoe one of the FBI agents was fiddling with the shiny brass plate that covered an electric outlet set into the floor: an anachronism, he had just decided, that was probably designed to serve another, perhaps a 16mm movie projector. In the same way, looking at Tannis, both the navy men saw something that was not quite right, though neither of them ever put his finger on what it was: Tannis, in fact, was dressed in an old uniform, the light khaki that used to be the navy "fatigue" before summer whites came in; but then neither of them had ever seen such a costume, except in photographs. Taken together, all of this gave Tannis the upper hand; the *subject*, as the FBI labeled him, was actually in control—the interrogated found answers to all his questions. The Special-Agent-in-Charge, a man named Olin Nickel—he was from Los Angeles, where he was head of a large counterintelligence team— found no way to break through this. Later he claimed to his assistant (the younger man, an Assistant Special Agent called Colarco, who'd been fiddling with the outlet cover) that this kind of result was inevitable when you had a divided authority, though both of them understood that this didn't really explain it. As for the naval officers, they ended a little happier. Their posture (as they termed it) was in part defensive, protecting both their own bureaucratic position and the navy's reputation against a civilian agency, and so the fact that very little happened was, if not a victory, no worse than a draw. Their team was led by a full commander, a man named Benson, a young, tough veteran of the bureaucratic wars in Washington and Norfolk, but he also had a deputy, a big glossy black getting heavy around the belly who was called Lieutenant Commander Rawson, and he was the final discordant note. In that room, in that subdued, golden light, his crisp white uniform really demanded a napkin folded across his forearm and an expression rather different from his easy, confident nonchalance. Languidly he smoked a Kool; from time to time he checked his big gold Rolex. When "the White House" had been built, the U.S. Navy accepted no blacks at all. Matheson, the base security director—their host and chairman, nominally in charge—was aware of Rawson more than of the others. He didn't really mind blacks, but there'd never been many at China Lake and, despite himself, he was still from Arkansas. So he was self-conscious, a tic developing in the corner of his eye; otherwise, he was small and quick and already, at fifty, well on his way to becoming a little old man—correct, upright, a deacon in his church.

Tannis didn't become aware of these various currents immediately. Feeling at home himself (how many meetings had he attended in this very room?) he was actually a little puzzled at their unease and at first kept quiet, as he worked out the play of tension. Typically this revealed itself through an argument around procedure. After making introductions and getting them to the table (the navy and the Bureau took up positions opposite each other, while Tannis, the elder statesman, assumed place of honor at the head) Matheson made some introductory remarks. And these were clearly guarded. He thanked Tannis for coming in. It was noted, for the record, that he had done so voluntarily. Everyone expected to make great use of his vast experience. And of course he could speak freely, for everyone was cleared, right to the very top. Then he referred to a "general agreement" that they were less interested in rehashing the events of Friday night than in obtaining some general background. "What it comes down to, Jack, is that we want to pick your brains. We want to broaden things out. As I was telling Agent Nickel, when it comes to this place you're a walking archive. You can tell us about Harper, give us a history lesson, whatever you think we need."

But this consensus broke down immediately; clearly, some previous argument had not been settled. Nickel leaned forward; he was a man who would literally press home his points. There were a number of questions, he said, that it might be useful to go over; some details needed clearing up; he was certain Captain Tannis wouldn't mind. Yes, Nickel wanted more than general background—there were certain specific questions about the captain's story, points that didn't exactly tally. . . .

But Rawson, the black, took a drag on his Kool and made a face. "Olin, we agreed we wouldn't *plod*."

They argued doggedly, and watching them Tannis began to sense, for the first time, how much they clashed: not simply with each other, but with this place, himself, and whatever might be happening. This was especially true with Nickel. That room had set Tannis up for the old days, when FBI agents had shared certain qualities with the clergy: they had faith, or at least accountancy, they had a determined, incremental rationality; whereas Nickel was pure bureaucrat. In a small way, at least for public consumption, Tannis had cultivated a contempt for such men; the day before he'd smiled knowingly when the sheriff had said, "Nickel's the kind of cop who'll never get flat feet, but I bet he has a hell of a case of hemorrhoids." It was the reaction of a field man to a desk man—and Tannis had spent his life in the field—but in fact men like Nickel interested him, if only because they proved how much the field had changed. Intelligence operations were now run by bureaucrats to achieve bureaucratic ends, so it was inevitable that men like Nickel should understand them best. And there was nothing soft about Nickel, even physically. His suitcoat rucked up around his shoulders as he leaned across the notes that were spread over the table; his face was gray with tension. His expressions—a quick look up, a tiny smile—ticked off the facts, matched them to some invisible form. He knew where he was going. He had his eye on two issues. The first was obvious, the caller, but the second was more subtle: What, exactly, did "Harper" mean? But he came at it from an unexpected direction and made everything dependent on the offhand remark that Tannis had made about an informer in the original Harper case, a crucial tip that had tied Harper to the Russians. Nickel, who eventually overcame Rawson, worked up to it. "On the basis of your statement, Captain, you believed that the man who called you actually wanted to talk about Harper?"

"Yes."

"That was your first impression?"

"That's right."

"But isn't it true that you backed off from that?"

"No. Not exactly. But when I thought about it, I realized he could have meant it a different way. He could have been saying, 'I want to talk about Harper.' But he might have just been using the name to get my attention. Remember, if you go through my statement you'll see that he only brought Harper's name into it when I threatened not to meet him."

"So you agree it's possible he might only have mentioned Harper's name to get your attention. And going on from there—this isn't in your statement—I understand you speculated that he might have been the individual who gave you a tip about Harper at the time of the original case."

"Yes."

"You confirm that?"

"As speculation, sure."

"We've all read the file, but let's keep things straight. This was an individual who telephoned you on April five, nineteen sixty . . ."

"Yes."

"And back then, he disguised his voice?"

"Yes."

"In the same way that the man who called you on Friday did?"

"No, the original informer . . . he just covered the mouthpiece with a handkerchief, as I remember. Nothing fancy. Whereas the man who called me on Friday . . . actually, he really disguised his voice by dropping into Mex."

"Still, back then, he gave you a tip that Harper was going to make a drop—"

"Not exactly. He said that Harper was going to drive down a particular road at a particular time, near Darwin Springs; supposedly he did this regularly. Harper did show up, and a while later a car with four Russians in it went down the same road, but nothing was *dropped*. Harper was under observation the whole time and nothing happened."

"And Harper explained all this"—Nickel looked down at his notes—"he said he'd been told, someone had told him—"

"It was his wife. He claimed he'd received an anonymous letter, that his wife was having an affair. She was supposed to be meeting someone out there. She used to go riding a lot. She did too. I remember—"

"But did you believe that story? Harper never produced the letter."

"No. I didn't believe that end of it. He made it up on the spur of the moment and then stuck with it. I've no idea what the hell he was doing out there."

"Well, forget that a moment. You had a tip he'd be out there, and he was. What I'm worried about now is this informer. I just want you to remember: this informant, back then, spoke to you, and only you?"

"Yes."

"So, bearing in mind that he disguised his voice, it might have been the same man in both cases?"

"Yes."

"And in both cases, he probably knew you?"

Tannis shook his head. "Probably, but not necessarily. Then or now. We did a lot of work on who that man might be, how did he know Harper was going up there, but all we ever concluded was that he had to be a local man."

"So he *could* have known you?"

"Could. Yes."

"As this man could have known you?"

"Yes."

"In fact, on Friday, he assumed that you would recognize him. Or at least he thought you might. It was only when you didn't that he brought Harper into it, as you just pointed out."

"Right."

"And so you thought—"

"Agent Nickel, let's not make too much of this. It occurred to me, I *speculated*, that this character wasn't interested in Harper *now*, but that Harper could have been the basis of our previous connection, a previous connection which this man kept saying we had. So I thought of that informant. Back then, he'd obviously known something about Harper, and he knew enough to call me. And maybe I was right. After all, on Friday, if he'd wanted to talk about Harper, why didn't he?"

Rawson, leaning on his elbow, sprawled a little on the table, murmured, "An old legal principle, Olin. We intend the natural consequences of our acts."

"Something like that," said Tannis. "If you concentrate on what actually happened, Harper's name lured me to the Hideaway, and then the note took me up the Panamint, so getting me to Trona was probably the point of the whole exercise. For whatever reason. Maybe Harper had nothing to do with it all. At the same time, I'd say you don't want to miss the woods for the trees. Whatever he meant, he did *know* about Harper, and he knew that I knew."

"Oh, don't worry, Captain . . . Commander . . . That fact defines our universe of suspects. What I'd like to do now. . ."

Rawson began to argue again. Tannis listened less carefully; he wasn't sure what it was all about, but he was coming to one conclusion from Nickel's line of questioning: although they were interested in Harper, they really wanted to avoid him. In fact, that was his first impression altogether: they were avoiding something, falling back. Some

obsessive point was bothering them, so much so that they missed the
great clue, even as they gave it to him. And in fact Tannis himself was so
intent on working out what was going on that he almost missed it too. But
he did just catch it, and no doubt this could be put down to his peculiar
advantage: the strangely flattering light that fell upon him in that room,
the echoes of voices he could pick out of the corners, his sense of déjà vu
as a ring of water sparkled on the long, varnished conference table. There
were no statistics, or probabilities, or parameters; it was a pure deduction.

By this point they'd circled away from Harper back to the caller
himself, and Nickel had won another point with Rawson, who finally
crossed his arms over his chest and looked sideways down the table with
an expression that was part boredom, part contempt. Matheson was fidg-
eting; whatever he'd planned here, it clearly wasn't working out. Benson,
the nominal leader of the navy team, had still barely said a word. Colarco,
Nickel's assistant, glanced around with bright, sharp, curious eyes; he was
learning from all this, like the sharpest child in the class. But finally
Nickel began to read out a list of names to Tannis: the idea was to jog his
memory. As a last shot Rawson muttered, "Is this what they call *free
association*, Olin?"

Nickel ignored him. "You should know all these names, Captain.
What I want to know is whether they might have been the caller."

"Uh-huh. If they ring a bell . . ."

"Robert Chapman."

Tannis shook his head.

"That's a negative?"

"Negative."

"Jonathan Frank."

"Negative."

"Carver Davis . . ." It was an interesting list. Tannis wondered how
they'd put it together. His old phone bills. His personnel file. Some had
been classmates at CalTech whom he barely remembered. And then there
were the security files he must have handled more than twenty years ago.
And random shots.

"Denovan Hill."

"Negative. He's dead."

"For Christ's sake, Olin . . ."

But he remembered Hill. Hill had been part of the team that had
gone to Formosa in 1958. There'd been three scientists from China Lake,

plus the navy, plus the CIA. Secretly they'd equipped a squadron of Nationalist Sabres with Sidewinder, and the next week they had shot down fourteen Chicom MiGs, the first planes in history to fall victim to a guided missile. The Formosa Crisis had ended promptly. . . . Nickel droned on. Scientists, support staff, navy types. They seemed to be in no special order, but then, at a certain point, Nickel stopped reading and nodded to Colarco, who pulled a microcassette recorder from his pocket and pushed a button.

"The same idea, Captain. But these are voices."

In fact, many of these voices (dim memories came back to him) belonged to the names on the previous list, which meant they had to come from wiretaps that were twenty-five years old. Most had been edited. He was hearing only one side of a conversation. Several voices had foreign accents, and Colarco smoothly rewound the tape and ran those through twice. A couple were clearly Englishmen. And at one his ears pricked up. "It's the power takeoff. . . . That's right. But I'll have to go in to Oxford anyway. Evidently they don't. . . . No. No, if those checks arrive, just pay them in as usual. . . . Right . . ."

"That's Harper," he said at once, really blurting it. He had recognized the voice instantly, though he also knew instinctively that this was how Harper sounded *now*. The voice was older, stronger . . . though, despite this instant recognition, there was still no image of his face, he still had no idea what the man looked like. But they'd have a photograph of him. The tape kept on. More voices. A good ten minutes of them, snippets, snatches. Even a few women, which summoned a groan from Rawson. Then one voice speaking German; it took his mind an instant to adjust. "I already told you many times, I came because of my heart, because I need special medical attention, and because I no longer have any ties there. My family is dead and most of my friends . . . Yes, it's true, my sister is still alive, and I suppose, yes, I will be preparing for her. But even that's not certain. She's younger than me. She won't be able to retire for several years, and by then . . ."

"Negative," Tannis said. "But I'd guess that's Buhler."

At which point, for the first time, Benson intervened. "You're right, Captain. But if you don't mind, Agent Nickel, I think this is taking things a little far. The captain's statement was very clear. The speaker might have had a German accent, but he did speak English—I am right about that, Captain?"

"Uh-huh."

And then Rawson, still leaning on the table, exhaled some smoke and murmured, "Understand, Captain. We don't know much about Walter Buhler, but we do know this: he couldn't speak a word of English. Not a word. There's no way he could have been your mystery caller."

He couldn't speak a word of English. There it was. Tannis sensed its importance at once, though he didn't quite know why. But it didn't get past him. It stuck. And he sat back and expected them to follow up, but they moved right on. Nickel said, "All right, Captain. I won't go on. I assume if you do come up with a name, you'll let us know."

"Of course."

"Regardless of the consequences."

Matheson said, "I don't think any qualification is required."

"I'll withdraw it then. But I think it is on the record, Captain, that you never believed Harper was really guilty?"

"That's in the file."

"And in fact, Captain, this was the major case of your career."

"No."

"No?"

"I had bigger cases than this in Germany. Harper, you might say, was the major *unresolved* case of my career."

"Captain, this case was officially closed twenty-five years ago. There's nothing unresolved about it."

"Don't be so sure. No one ever went to jail."

"We both know what that means: absolutely nothing."

Tannis could now see where Nickel was going, but Benson cut him off, whether in deliberate obstruction or subtle collusion, he wasn't sure. "Let's not take it too far, Captain, but if Harper didn't do it, who did? Who do you think gave the Russians Sidewinder?"

"If the case is resolved, surely my theories about it are irrelevant."

Benson smiled. "Well . . . maybe. But you have to understand, Captain, I have *no* theories about it. And as Commander Matheson says, you're the archivist, the historian."

Tannis shrugged. "All right. Why not? You have to go back, though. Conceivably the Russians had Sidewinder as early as '58, but you have to go back earlier, to '56. October twenty-nine—that was the start of the Suez War—"

Rawson said, "You might have to explain about that to our civilian colleagues."

"The Israelis, the British, and the French invaded Egypt. The Israelis destroyed the Egyptian Air Force on the ground and without air cover their army was destroyed. The Suez Canal was put out of commission."

"Actually," put in Nickel, "we know all that. Our guys won."

"Except there were difficulties. For Eisenhower. If he sided with the Israelis and the British, that just made him an imperialist and pushed Nasser and the Arabs closer to the Russians. But the Israelis were our boys really; everybody knew that. So in the end Eisenhower stopped them—that was the very end of the British, that one week—but in the years right after that war we tried to put on a balancing act, trying not to favor either side. Or *look* like we were favoring either side. This was especially the case when it came to weapons, particularly planes and missiles. To the Israelis, planes and missiles were most important of all. Outnumbered the way they were, they had to have air superiority. That meant they had to have Sidewinder, and they had to have an assured supply, a supply that couldn't be held up by Congress and that wouldn't embarrass us. The solution was obvious. In 1958, 1959, 1960, this place was crawling with Israeli scientists—the mess out here was keeping kosher—and in 1961 the Rafael Armament Development Authority began producing a version of Sidewinder under the name Shafrir. . . . You understand, I'm not saying the Israelis gave it to them, but it was during that process it happened."

Benson, ever so slightly, cocked his head and looked thoughtful. "None of this is in the file."

"That surprises you?"

Rawson grunted. "What you're saying, then, is that Harper was real convenient. That's what it adds up to. Even the fact that there wasn't quite enough evidence to charge him was okay. It just let everyone off the hook." He leaned back in his chair; it creaked under his bulk. "But let me ask you this. Do you have any evidence to suggest that Buhler's death, anything that's happened since Friday night, would support your notion?"

"No."

Rawson nodded, and cast an eye toward Benson; this was what they'd wanted. But at once Nickel leaned forward. "But isn't it true that you would be happy to see the Harper case reopened?"

"Not particularly." Tannis held up his hand. "This is ridiculous. What you're trying to suggest—"

"I'm not suggesting—"

"But I think you are, and I don't like it. You're insinuating that I've used Buhler's death to dredge up the Harper case. But just remember, I'm a retired officer of the U.S. Navy. I was once security director of this place. And you're conducting an investigation into a security threat against this nation. So I'm not about to give you, or any other federal official, false evidence about anything, no matter what my private feelings."

Matheson's lips made a thin, prim line. "Good for you, Jack. That needed saying."

"And anyway," Tannis kept on going, "if there is a connection, Buhler tends to confirm—what should I call it?—the standard version, that Harper did it."

Tannis watched Nickel's face go quizzical, anxious. Then he realized why. He'd worked out their line, and it was instructive. The only evidence connecting Buhler's death to Harper was his report of the phone call, and they were trying to say that he'd made that up, that the caller hadn't mentioned Harper at all, or at least that he'd meant something else by bringing in his name. Which meant that for some reason he didn't understand they wanted to disentangle Buhler's death from security considerations altogether. Which was all right by him, God knows. He'd play it any way they wanted and still win.

Nickel finally said, "I don't understand what you're driving at."

Benson eased in. "I'd say that all you mean, Captain, is that Buhler is from the East, he *might* be KGB, and so that creates an unfavorable context, from Harper's point of view, in which to bring the whole thing up."

"Something like that. You read the file. The big piece of evidence against Harper was his trip to Czechoslovakia."

Benson, in fact, had read the file. "He claimed he was visiting an old friend, Miroslav . . . the Unpronounceable. Some old friend of his father's who'd paid for his education or something."

Tannis nodded. "Harper's father was a technician, an armorer, at RAF Benson during the war. That's where British Photo Reconnaissance was based. Miroslav Rechcigl was a pilot, first in Spitfires then in Mosquitoes. They got to know each other. He was Harper's godfather. In 1948, when the Communists took over Czechoslovakia, he went back to try and stop them. Of course he didn't. And he was trapped there. But he had a lot of money in a British bank account, mostly his accumulated flight pay from the war. He managed to transfer it to Harper and that's how he got to Cambridge. He was grateful. He wanted to thank Rechcigl and went to see him."

"And didn't tell anyone," said Benson.

"But that wasn't the crucial point," said Nickel. "What you're leaving out, Captain, is the fact that Rechcigl continued to fly for the British after the war—they were flying Mosquitoes on photo-intelligence missions over Russia until 1950. We have to assume that the Czechs knew that. They must have been on to Rechcigl—and from there, the step to Harper is pretty short."

Tannis said, "You can assume it if you want, but there was never any proof. Just the opposite. Harper's visit was impromptu; Rechcigl had no idea he was coming. And the way Harper told it, Rechcigl was worried the whole time, because it singled him out as having connections in the West."

Nickel broke in here and said, "But I'm not arguing with you, Captain. It's beside the point. Because I don't see what connection all that could have to Buhler. Buhler was East German, not Czech. So far as we can establish, he had no connections with any intelligence organization, either in Harper's time or now. Let me put it on the record: at this point in time we haven't been able to establish any link whatsoever between Buhler's death and the Harper case."

"Except," Rawson put in, "you say the caller brought up Harper's name."

"But," Benson added, "that could be accounted for in several ways. That's why the point is so crucial. And I'll admit I'm intrigued by the captain's speculation—about the original tip on Harper, I mean. It could make sense. The informer is a local man. Years ago he learned something about Harper and passed it on. Now he discovers that an East German is staying in a motel in Lone Pine. He calls Captain Tannis, wanting to tell him about it. When it seems that the captain might not listen, he drags in Harper, so the captain will take him seriously."

Tannis said, "Of course, the trouble with that is that he didn't tell me about it. And Buhler wasn't simply staying in a motel; he ended up in the desert with a bullet in him."

"So," said Rawson, "you don't believe your own theory. . . . No, no, I understand. You didn't advance it as a theory. What I'm wondering is this: going back to that theory of yours, and this *is* your theory—about the Israelis, I mean—supposing you were right. It almost turns that original tip into part of a frame-up."

"Maybe. Or just a screwup."

"But no one believed you at the time. In fact, some people said you were so convinced that your friend Harper was innocent—"

"He wasn't my friend, Commander. Mostly I don't like the British. And he was a stuck-up, tight-assed British kid—"

"—that you almost suppressed that tip, didn't act on it, that there'd been several others."

Tannis smiled. "You're lucky, Commander. I never hit people who wear glasses."

"Glasses?"

"That's right. 'Some people said'—those are your glasses. Of course, if you were to take them off—tell us what *you* say. . . ."

Tannis actually began getting up from the table, a gesture that was almost certainly theatrical, although Rawson looked immediately panic-stricken, and Benson, pushing his chair back, only a little less so. Nickel smiled. In front of him he had an old file, from the original Harper case. Someone had written in the margin, "*Tannis*"—the name had been underscored so heavily that the pen had cut through the page—"what a son of a bitch, the kind who'll put a rattlesnake in your pocket and then ask you for a match."

In the end Benson played diplomat, things settled down, and Tannis agreed to be pacified, though at a price. They broke for coffee, but immediately afterward he took the initiative completely. "So let me in on it," he said. "How come you're all so certain Buhler was no spy?"

In saying this, Tannis had no idea what to expect by way of an answer; he was only making explicit the fundamental problem. And despite the tensions between Nickel's group and Benson's, it was a problem both of them faced; that's why they kept swinging back and forth between infighting and collusion. They'd found themselves in no-man's-land. What they were facing clearly went far beyond their usual experience—police methods, the techniques of perimeter security, the rules for keeping diplomats in line. But Tannis wasn't disturbed at all. He lit up a Lucky. He'd killed a man in cold blood, after all—had any of these men?—he knew that definition of the cold war. He'd been in at the beginning, he knew what China Lake was all about. That's what he felt: a continuity between his own life and the air in that room and what he'd been hearing, a sense that he'd been here long before, a continuity that Nickel didn't feel. Nor Benson. Tannis watched him as he began to talk. Tannis could remember a time when navy officers had been the sons of navy officers, or the sons of somebody: the son of the owner of the First National Bank of some decent small town, or the son of the man who owned the local department store, or the son of the fellow who sold stocks and bonds. They were in the navy because that's who they were; and they lived up to it. And Tannis understood that. But Benson was the son of nobody. Benson had a Naval Career. He had degrees. He took courses. He could Communicate and Manage. He didn't smoke, and he took only a social drink. If he came under stress he took a Valium. Buhler, whoever he was, came from a different world, and so did Tannis, and so did that room. They were all part of a history from which Benson had been severed, and it was actually to Benson's credit that he was conscious of this sufficiently to feel uncomfortable. "Well . . . that's putting it bluntly, Captain, to say that Buhler wasn't a spy, and I wouldn't say we're *certain*. But in fact there's no substantial evidence that Buhler was a security threat at all. That's why the connection to Harper is so puzzling, that's why we've been so interested in nailing it down."

He glanced at a file in front of him; beside him Rawson swung around in his chair, stretching his arm over the back of it. Nickel rocked back, as if to indicate that his stint was over. Then Benson began. "We know a lot about Buhler—too much, you'd think, if he really was a spy. To begin with, those documents you found on him were all genuine. He was exactly who he claimed to be. He was born in Leipzig. He had an older brother and a younger sister. The whole family worked in the German railways, and—this got us excited for a while—they were all Communists. I mean by that they were all members of the Communist party of Germany, the KPD. The German police have the entire membership list, so we can be certain of it."

"The trouble is," said Tannis, "there's a lot of names on that list."

"Exactly. If all old German Communists were spies . . . And Buhler was very young, in any case, so he probably wasn't that involved. But both his father and the older brother were big in the trade unions, and when the Nazis got to power they were all thrown into a concentration camp. Buchenwald."

Tannis said, "That's where most of the KPD were sent."

"So they tell me. In any case, the father died there. But the two brothers were transferred to a satellite camp, near a town called Nordhausen. It's a railroad junction not far from Erfurt; again, that's what they tell me. Apparently this was a labor camp, not a death camp—we're still trying to find out more about it—but it was also dominated by Communists and there was some sort of internal Resistance. Buhler's brother was killed for being a member of it. Buhler survived, however. He was very sick, in the infirmary, but alive, when the camp was liberated. That was April 1945. Third Armored Division, First American Army—"

"So he must have had contacts with Americans, then?"

"Yes, and we're trying to run it down, though so far that hasn't come to anything. Probably it won't, because he didn't hang around for very long. By the end of the summer he was back in Leipzig. He claims he was looking for his sister and when he found her they set up house together. They got back on their feet. In fact, everything after the war becomes very normal. Neither of them ever married. Leipzig ended up in the East, but that didn't bother them since they were both Reds. Buhler went back to working for the railroad—he was a machinist—and did that for the rest of his working life. That can all be documented, by the way, because the State Railways publish an in-house magazine and every few years he'd win an award or commendation; there are even a couple of pictures. Anyway, time passed. Then, this past year he turned sixty-five, and retired." Rocking back in his chair, Benson now tapped a file with his pencil. "Here's an important point," he went on. "Apparently, under certain conditions, when an East German hits sixty-five, he's free to leave the country. Unless you've held a sensitive job, you can simply walk. You don't get your pension, and they only let you take what you can carry in a single suitcase, but you can go. It's a very neat way of passing on their geriatric problems to the West. That's what Buhler did. He simply strolled through Checkpoint Charlie this past January. January twelfth. Thousands of East Germans do the same thing every year, and the West Germans have programs to look after them. In a perfectly routine way Buhler was sent to a reception center in Giessen. They ran a security check on him there, which is where most of this comes from; that's where that tape we played comes from. It was a routine check, but of course the West Germans were interested. He *was* a Communist. He probably could have got out in '45 but he didn't try. Why was he coming now? The difficulty was, he had perfectly good answers to all their questions. He said he had a bad heart and wanted to be near Western drugs and hospitals. The Germans checked it all out, and it was true, and our doctors say the same; we had them do another autopsy in L.A. Also, according to the Germans, he was probably preparing the ground for his sister; she was younger, but would retire in a few years herself. It all checked out; so far as the West Germans were concerned, Buhler seemed harmless. They settled him in Berlin. He applied for a passport, the BND took their time, but approved it. Two days later he flew to New York. He stayed there overnight, then flew out here, to L.A. Clearly, he was doing *something*. He got out of the East at the first opportunity. He applied for a federal passport ASAP. But everything he did was aboveboard: he always used his own name, he made no attempt to cover his tracks. So far as we can tell, he didn't come onto this base or contact anyone who worked here. In fact, we're not absolutely sure he was ever in Ridgecrest. And on top of it all it seems he couldn't speak much English. He had someone in Germany—we think it was someone he met in Giessen—write out the English answers to the sort of questions you have to answer on a car-rental form, and at LAX he just handed this to a woman from Hertz. And the manager of the place where he stayed in Lone Pine says he could barely say hello." Benson turned a little in his chair, and shrugged. "So you see what you've got. An old man with a heart condition who couldn't speak English—he just isn't the sort of person you chose as an agent, not if you're the KGB."

"No. But what was he doing here, and why was he killed. You still have to answer that."

Rawson said, "This is an old Audie Murphy movie. You know, it was those GIs in nineteen forty-five. Buhler got into a poker game and won a map off one of them. It was supposed to show a gold mine. So as soon as he could, he came out here to look for it, but somebody beat him to it."

Tannis said, "Maybe that's not so farfetched as you think."

"We're looking at it," said Nickel. "That is, seriously, we're trying to find some private explanation for his movements."

"But if that's what it was," said Benson, "it's no business of ours. Which, you see, brings us back to Harper. That's why Harper is so important."

Tannis nodded. Now he did see. Of course, he took it with a grain of salt. They wouldn't be discounting Buhler quite as much as they pretended. He had been murdered, he was East German, and everything had happened so close to the base. But he was no agent—there could be no doubt of that. The only connection was Harper, and that connection was made through him. Which meant that he, Tannis, was the piano they'd have to move if they ever wanted to sweep this under the rug. So now it was his turn to backtrack. To plod. He didn't deny or contradict himself—he never once deviated from the simple truth—but, in a kind of self-inquisition, he raised doubts, entertained possibilities, explored alternatives. He tried to give some credence to the "original informant theory," since it had already gained a certain favor. "I wouldn't push it. It's only an idea. But I'll admit, when I think about it, they do have the same feel. . . ." He could see them relax as he talked, turn sympathetic. They broke for more coffee. The tone improved. He had a quiet, confidential word with Nickel. He wouldn't back down—he made that clear—but he wouldn't cause trouble either. They worked on, toward lunch. And as they grew happier together around the table, the time warp in that room came into play once more. But in quite a different fashion. The polarity was reversed. Tannis went back a long, long way, Tannis knew times they'd only read about, but all that meant, when you got right down to it, was that Tannis was an interesting old geezer. He was an old *old* man. His time was done. You didn't want to take him *too* seriously; God knows what he'd actually heard Friday night. Tannis saw it happening in their eyes, a glassy, indulgent look; and, as he kept on going, he swore they became positively bored. But they'd missed it. That's what he was finding out, as he went back and forth over the same ground, giving them one chance after another to see what was under their nose. And as Matheson summed up—"Jack, I think I can speak for everyone in saying what a help you've been"—he was finally certain that they'd literally overlooked it. Of course, eventually, they'd find it. When all was said and done, these men were professional policemen, but sometimes they let themselves be trapped by that. They'd work through every step of the routine (where Buhler had gone, everyone he'd talked to, where he'd spent his money) before they started on deductions, before they allowed themselves to *think*. But eventually they would think. So one way or the other he was probably ahead of them, but it couldn't be for long. So, when they invited him for lunch, he turned them down: "Gentlemen, at my age, if you have a drink at noon, you just piss the day away," because that's just what he didn't want to do. *An old man with a bad heart who couldn't speak any English*. Why, then, had he come to China Lake? Tannis didn't know the answer, or not all of it. But he did know this: if Buhler really had no English, it could only mean that the man he'd come so far to see, the man who'd probably killed him, *must speak fluent German*. And out there, in all that sand and rock, how many people could that be?

CHAPTER 4

Tannis didn't fool himself.

He'd got lucky.

The FBI and the navy had missed the obvious about Buhler because they didn't want to see it, but eventually they'd be forced to look. So his advantage was purely temporary; it might last an hour, or a day, but to count on its lasting very long at all was silly. He had to move quickly. But he also knew that this might be the only chance he'd have, so he had to get it right, which meant he had to take time to think. Still, he had the freedom to do that; for example, he was now sure that the original call hadn't been taped, which certainly gave him an advantage. So that afternoon, sitting in his office—in the dim light of his gooseneck lamp, with his photos on the wall—he relaxed and worked it out; worked it out as he drank his tequila and watched the sun go down; worked it out as the stars began to light the sky.

He began with his assumptions. Point one: Buhler and Harper were connected—that was the fundamental point. Nickel and Benson could play around with words, but there could be no other explanation for what had happened on Friday night. He, Buhler, and the mysterious caller had one thing in common, and that was David Harper. Point two: however odd Buhler's actions seemed, he'd been up to something; even Benson had conceded that much. At the very first opportunity, this very ordinary

East German machinist had made a beeline for China Lake, hardly a popular tourist destination; he must have had some plan in mind. And point three: since Buhler spoke no English, this purpose, whatever it was, must have involved a German-speaker; he literally couldn't have communicated with anybody else. Finally, it was this German-speaker who had then murdered him, either because of something unpredictable that had happened that night down the Trona road or as part of a deliberate plan, conceivably to frame Tannis himself. These assumptions seemed unimpeachable, and taken together they established three requirements that Buhler's murderer must possess: he had to be connected to the original Harper case; he had to speak decent German; and he must still be living in the Panamint.

On this basis Tannis began compiling a list of names, and of course the first one on it was his own. This was not quite pro forma. There was that slight element of doubt in his last assumption, namely, that the man Buhler had come to see had also killed him. So, Tannis considered, it was theoretically possible that Buhler had made his extraordinary trip to see *him*. But then why hadn't he done so? He'd been in Lone Pine for a week, according to the FBI, and all he had to do was look Tannis's name up in the phone book. Even setting that aside, there was another problem. If Buhler had wanted to see him, that meant that Buhler had most likely been killed to prevent them from meeting. But then why had the Friday-night caller, the obvious murderer, alerted him to Buhler's presence? There were answers to these questions, but they were all very hypothetical. At the same time Tannis had to admit that he met all the other qualifications. His German was excellent. He had first learned it in Mexico from an old German prospector, a friend of his father's, and later he'd taken it at CalTech; and of course his proficiency was one of the reasons he'd been recruited by navy intelligence in the first place. Finally, four years in Germany—much of it spent interrogating Germans—had made him truly fluent, so that even now he could shift his mind and hear his thoughts *auf Deutsch gesprochen*. So he could have talked to Buhler and of course he'd been connected to the Harper case and he'd never left the Panamint. Yet it was all so unlikely, he thought. He searched his memories, his files, he even went through old photographs, but he remained almost certain that he and Buhler had never known each other. He couldn't positively say that they'd never met—he'd met a lot of Germans—but it was hard to believe that a meeting he didn't recall could have been so important to Buhler that he'd sought him out forty years later.

Having eliminated himself, he went on to the next name, and that was Harper's. Also unlikely. But also not impossible. Was he in the Panamint? It was the third qualification that seemed to rule him out. Because the FBI would already have checked if he was here; he was prepared to bet that the tape they'd played with Harper on it had been made in the last seventy-two hours. It certainly wasn't an old tape, pulled out from Harper's interrogation, and no one would have a tap on his phone at this point, so the British must have done a quick, dirty, special job. But if Harper failed this test, he passed all the others. He *was* the Harper case. And he spoke good German. This was even part of the reason he'd been suspected. Tannis let his mind run back through the interrogation sessions, the one-way glass, the smudgy transcripts, the tapes that seemed to have been made at the bottom of a well, the endless briefings afterward. It was the Czech. The Czech flier had taught Harper a little German as a boy, on the grounds that he must hate the Nazis but not the German people. He'd learned it willingly: "There was a kind of subversive excitement about it ..." Tannis could remember Harper's saying this and wincing; it was not the sort of weakness you should confess to while being questioned about espionage. And then the last letter from the Czech, about the money, had been written in German. "*Ich werde es nie verwenden. Vielleicht wird es für Davids Ausbildung behilflich sein.*" But what could it mean? To imagine a connection between Harper and Buhler was to accept that Harper had been guilty, and Tannis was absolutely certain that he wasn't; it was one of the few things he could be certain of. And why would he have come back here otherwise? Revenge? Nostalgia? Some attempt to come to terms with his past? None of these answers worked, if only because he hated the place, hated the desert, he always had (though the wife had loved it), and so Tannis just couldn't see him out there now, in a motel, with a car parked outside, listening to the lifting wind. He'd been so uncomfortable. So tense. Withdrawn. Inhibited. No. It just wasn't Harper.

All this cleared the ground; eliminated, in his own mind, the possibility of some "trick" solution. Now he set to work in earnest. Letting his mind run free, drifting back more than twenty years, seeing in his mind's eye old files, old faces, remembering half-forgotten voices. He began jotting names at random on a memo pad; and if one name kept coming back to him more often, if one candidate certainly seemed more likely than all the others, he was still professional, methodical; he worked through each department at the base, Mike Lab especially—the Michelson Laboratory—where Harper had actually worked, and then he drew a rough organizational chart of the Sidewinder Program itself and carefully filled it in: Code 352, the Project Engineer; 3525, production and quality controls; 3527, aerodynamics, propulsion, launching; 3529, seeker head studies, fuses, warheads. Harper would have met people in most of those areas; by late afternoon, when Tannis took a break (a bottle of Corona, half a papaya, and lime), he had a fair stack of pages piled on his desk. Almost without exception the people involved were scientists or technicians. In age, today, they would run from dead to their forties, and by now most would be retired and could be living anywhere from Florida to Costa Rica. Stern, for example, had ended up in San Miguel d'Allende. Yes, he remembered that. In fact, he thought a lot about Stern. He was the instrument man; Stern made gadgets that measured microvolts at thirty thousand feet, then sent every quiver of the needle back. He was a genius of ingenuity, a fixer; his hobby—everybody knew it—was fixing watches, head bowed, loupe to his eye. Trying to recall his face, what came back was the image of his head bent down, all concentration, a stork going for a fish. Stern, because he'd measured everything, had known everything, at least theoretically he was a primary suspect, and he certainly spoke German. But it couldn't be Stern because Stern was dead, he'd died down there in Mexico, Tannis was fairly sure. Of course you can fix anything in Mexico, but he'd checked at the time, he remembered. Stern was definitely someone he'd kept track of, and it had seemed okay. Still, he had to be certain, he had to check again, and he knew just how to do it. Stern had been strange about money. Not greedy, but tight; careful. So Tannis took a nice, easy drive along Route 395 to Mojave and from a phone booth called the base, getting to an old acquaintance in Pay and Benefits. He wanted a favor, he said. He was trying to track down a few types from the good old days; he wanted their addresses. He gave in the names: Stern, Pritchard, Jackson, Kowalchuk—Pritchard was made up but Kowalchuk was actually on his list as well. An expert on reticle design, pulse triggers, target images, fields of view. Living in San Diego, as it turned out. Jackson, they had no record of. And they'd stopped Stern's pension more than ten years back. "He died in Mexico. No survivor benefits, so no wife. I had to look on the old tape files, they never changed it over." Well, Tannis knew his Stern: if he was alive, one way or another he would have got that pension.

So he struck Stern off his list, but then, over coffee, still in Mojave, he went carefully through the other names. All were American. All spoke German; besides the fact they knew Harper or could have known him, that was what they had in common. But in fact, he decided, the best way to sort them out was in terms of their linguistic abilities. They were all scientists and, like Tannis himself, were older than Harper, part of a generation in which German had still been the language of science and mathematics, so they could all speak it a little—they'd at least be able to finger their way through a newspaper. But he was looking for more than that, real fluency, and as he cast his mind back, that winnowed the pile. Then there was the other consideration: they had to be in the area—Buhler had traveled here, specifically. So he went back to the phone and dialed information for all the towns and counties in the area, from Los Angeles to Bakersfield to Bishop. This took more than an hour and exasperated several long-distance operators but left him with five names: five men who'd likely known Harper, spoke German, and still lived in this part of the desert.

The next step was easy. He simply called each man in turn, addressing the person who answered the phone in his own excellent German. Of the first four, only two managed a reply, and one of these was actually the son of the man he wanted, a former specialist in "rod" charges who was now bedridden. So he came to his final candidate—after Stern, the most likely of all, which is why he had saved him to last: Kenneth Helmsley, a distinguished chemist who had gone to some lengths to befriend Harper, a friendship, as Tannis recalled the details, that pointed out how brilliant Harper had been. For despite his youth and the fact that he wasn't American, Harper had been made a member of the Working Group on Infrared Backgrounds (WGIRB), an elite committee established by the U.S. services in 1954 to study the military applications and problems of the infrared. Two scientists from China Lake had been part of this group, one of whom was Helmsley. He spoke excellent German, because he'd studied there; he was a living connection to the first work on the infrared that had been done in Germany between the wars—which was interesting, Tannis realized, in another way. Helmsley had studied under a professor at the University of Frankfurt named Czerny, whose work had been funneled to the Zeiss Company in Jena in the forties; there, a team had developed an infrared device, known as the Kiel IV, that could be mounted in a fighter to detect enemy bombers at night. So there was a little line here. Had it touched Buhler? Certainly Jena was in the East—a good deal of the Zeiss complex had been dismantled and shipped to Russia. Moreover, as Tannis had discovered during his time on the Technical Mission, most of the other German research work into infrared radiation had ended up in the central and eastern parts of Germany that the Russians had taken over. In any case, whatever the links to Buhler, there was no doubt about the link between Helmsley and Harper: they had known each other *before* Harper had come to China Lake. Most intriguing of all, Helmsley still lived in Ridgecrest. So Tannis dialed his number with a degree of hope, but after five minutes of Helmsley's stammered (but passably accented) bafflement he was fairly certain that Buhler had never spoken with him.

It was now late in the day: late enough to conclude that his luck had run out, late enough to head on home. But he wasn't discouraged and remained convinced about the essential point: Buhler had come to China Lake to talk with someone who knew German; he would hang on to that.

The next morning, though not finally abandoning his initial list, he decided to come at the problem a different way; instead of working from Harper and the base toward the Panamint, he turned things around: he would go through all the names in the area and pick out the German-sounding ones. To narrow this a little, he made the assumption that the location of Buhler's death hadn't been accidental and that the killer lived somewhere in the Panamint Valley along the Trona road, that is, in the southeastern section of Inyo County. As a choice, Tannis knew, this was not necessarily so defensible. He was fairly sure that the access road had been chosen as a meeting place because the radar made any kind of electronic surveillance very difficult; and so the odds were that the killer, the mystery caller, actually lived elsewhere. But convenience, derived from the peculiar administrative complexity of the area, caused him to ignore this. As it happens, China Lake is almost exactly at the conjunction of three county boundaries. Ridgecrest and most of the residential sections of China Lake itself fall inside Kern County, which extends all the way to Bakersfield and has a population of around half a million, so it would be difficult for one man to search through the county records. But the situation is even worse in regard to Trona, the closest settlement to the murder scene, because it lies just inside San Bernardino County, which runs as far south as the perimeter of Los Angeles. So Inyo County was the easiest choice; though it covers an enormous area—across Death

Valley to the Nevada border, north to Yosemite National Park—its population is under twenty thousand. In any case, very early that Friday morning, he drove a hundred miles up Route 395 to Independence, the county seat, arriving around nine. Working back and forth among the tax rolls, voting lists, and telephone book, he began compiling a list of all German-sounding names in the Panamint section of the county, and around noon, when he came up with number nine, it rang a bell.

Vogel, Karl Rudolph.

He formed the words in his mind, pronounced them in English and in German . . . and there was something. Not a *viego amigo* exactly, not a certain explanation for that call, but something. And then it came to him, an association he could scarcely have expected: *horses*. Closing his eyes he had the same vision that had come to him as he'd held the phone a week ago: the road to San Diego and his glimpse of a straight-backed woman riding around and around a white corral, her hat flying out behind her. *Heavens! I must look just like Dale Evans!*

Yes. It all came back. Harper's wife, sufficiently British and middle class to know one end of a pony from another, had loved to ride, and during their time at China Lake she'd rented horses from a man named Vogel. Tannis had once gone riding with her himself, and he could remember her telling him about the place where she got her mounts, a "homestead" she called it, some poor ranch owned by a man whose wife had died. He was looking after a little girl; there was some sort of vaguely tragic domestic situation. But he couldn't remember whether Vogel actually spoke German, in fact, couldn't remember him at all, apart from the connection to Diana Harper. Had Harper done any riding himself? Thinking about it, Tannis wasn't sure, but he didn't think so; and there would have been no other way he might have met Vogel, for he was sure Vogel hadn't worked at the base and wouldn't have known any of the scientists—Stern, Helmsley, any of them. So the only connection was through the wife and the horses. And that wasn't absolutely certain. There was a difficulty, which he couldn't puzzle out. Vogel's ranch, and certainly the area where Diana Harper used to ride, was in the Indian Wells Valley, to the southwest of the base, but the Vogel in front of him now was paying taxes on land in the Panamint, twenty or thirty miles northeast, and a check with the land office showed that he'd bought his land only two years previously. So he'd moved; either that, or the two men weren't the same.

In fact, Tannis did not believe this. A lot of questions were unanswered—if he didn't know Vogel, how did Vogel know him?—but the coincidence was too pure: Harper, horses, Vogel, it all came together so very nicely. But if this was so, if the two Vogels *were* the same, he knew he had almost certainly discovered Buhler's killer, so even the smallest doubt could be disastrous. He had to check. Which again bought him up against the tangled local government in this part of the desert, for Indian Wells Valley is in Kern County, whose government offices are in Bakersfield, and Bakersfield was a hundred and fifty miles away. Yet he didn't hesitate. He filled his truck with gas, bought four KitKat bars, and headed off, arriving around three; and by that time he'd so precisely worked out the location of Vogel's ranch in his mind, that is, the ranch where Diana Harper had rented her horse, that he was able to find it in the second deed book they pulled down for him. And the two men were the same: Karl Rudolph Vogel. They had to be the same . . . yet there was a curiosity. According to the deed, Vogel had paid no taxes on the Kern County property since 1960, and there were now a variety of liens and attachments against the land. So it seemed that he'd abandoned it, even left this part of the country altogether, only to return many years later, when he'd bought the second piece of property. What had happened? Where had he gone and why had he come back? And why had he bought a new property, when simply paying the back taxes would have allowed him to reclaim the old one? But though these were interesting questions, their ultimate importance depended on the answer to a prior one: Did Vogel speak German? There was one way to find out. From a pay phone he dialed Vogel's number. A woman answered, in a voice that was strong, declarative, and entirely American in its accent. Tannis hesitated, almost hung up, almost spoke in English, but then tried anyway: *"Ja, ich möchte Karl Vogel sprechen."*

"Ah . . . I'm sorry . . . *Er ist in diesem Augenblicke nicht da* . . . I'm sorry, my German's not very good. But my father isn't here."

"I see. That's all right. You don't know when he'll be back?"

"Not really. He's in L.A. Could you leave your name?"

"That's okay, Miss Vogel, he wouldn't know it. But I'll call back later. Thank you."

He hung up and, with the phone still in his hand, took a deep breath. Perhaps the girl's German hadn't been perfect, but she'd shown no surprise when he'd asked for her father that way. Yes, he was almost sure.

He'd hit pay dirt. Vogel was the man Buhler had been looking for, the man he'd died to see.

By this time, it was four o'clock in the afternoon, a reasonable hour for a drink if you've just solved a murder case. And Tannis was tired. He'd gone hard all the previous day, and since seven that morning he'd driven 250 miles, perhaps more. But it never occurred to him to stop, any more, as he might have put it, than a crapshooter on a roll wants to pass the dice. From Bakersfield he drove to Ridgecrest, another eighty miles, where he paused for gas and a lot of Coke he bought in tins from the Qwik Korner Deli, but then was off again. One step following another, the logic of momentum carrying him on. Ridgecrest Boulevard. The Trona road. To his left China Lake flickered beyond the fence, flat, sere, dust-caked, a landscape of whitewashed brown, overlooked by Lone Butte, a purple humped scar with a chalk marker for the planes. The *logic* of momentum. Like a map with its legend. And he had found it out. Buhler—Harper—Vogel. He had traced the links. And as he leaned back and lit a Lucky, there was that characteristic shift within himself, so everything was magnified, sharper, and perspectives shifted, patterns emerged. Everything had meaning. First principles were clear. *If x, then* . . . Yes, the first principles worked their way through the data, sorting, sifting. It all meant something, from Buhler's crossing through Checkpoint Charlie to Diana Harper on a horse; from the Third Armored Division entering Nordhausen to the Tushino Air Display; and finally, *He couldn't speak a word of English*. Yes, out of this chaos, meaning had emerged. Like a winkle of gold in the sand in the pan. But he was the only one who saw it. It was his secret. Now, as he climbed through Salt Wells Valley and Poison Canyon, as he topped the crest that looked down on Trona, the whole world seemed to be his secret. He was himself a secret. Alone. The iron towers above the mills, the endless loops of the conveyors, the heaped-up ash and salt, the black pools of evaporating wastes—only he could see them. All across that valley there was no one else to see: only himself and God, if there was a God—and if there was no God, he truly was invisible. There was only himself in that vast place, no one else to know it, so that everywhere he looked he was looking in a mirror, a pool shimmering with a perfect reflection of his face. He knew everything there was to know; everything had become inevitable, fate. His eyes searched along beside the road, as if for horse tracks, as if tracing the links from Buhler's corpse to Vogel's name was merely a continuation of the tracking he'd started along that wash, a clear spoor lost on shale, picked up again, erased with a dragged bush, betrayed at last by the buried coals of last night's fire uncovered by the morning wind. And at precisely the right moment his eyes lifted up: in the desert, certain features are clearest at a distance, like the foundations of ancient buildings that reveal themselves only at altitude; Vogel's road was like that. Lifting his head, he could see it half a mile away: a too-regular, too-white line curving north and west across the flat surface of the sand. But once he was on top of it, this pattern was almost lost in detail. There was no sign, no mailbox, no real evidence of a road at all. But black skid marks betrayed where someone had turned, and he followed them.

At first the ambiguity of the track continued, the truck jolting violently as the land rose roughly, and he almost thought he'd been mistaken, that there was no road after all. But he knew, too, that he'd find it out. Of course he would. And just then he hit a flat stretch where you could see the ruts left by a grader as it backed around. With one eye on his odometer he pressed ahead. Four tenths . . . five . . . six . . . There seemed to be nothing around him but black rock, creosote, a haze of salt; a landscape that continuously fell back upon itself, one spot indistinguishable from another. But in such a place—monotonous, monochromatic, mesmerizing—even the slightest change in the lie of the land can conceal or reveal a great deal, and abruptly, coming up on the exact mile, the road climbed very slightly, curved around two large boulders, and below him, in the middle of a broad, shallow bowl he saw a trailer up on blocks. Burnished by the wind and sand, it glittered in the sun. Air conditioners protruded from windows at either end, a bent antenna stuck up from the roof, and three cast-concrete steps teetered before a narrow door. Scattered around it were a couple of oil drums, lengths of muffler pipe, a heap of bricks. It was like a piece of industrial wasteland, and the house might have been a boxcar abandoned on a siding. He slowed, then braked to a stop about forty yards away, waiting as the truck's rooster tail of dust eddied back against the sky and the hot ticking of the engine faded into silence. But no one emerged. After a minute he hit the horn. Still no one. But somebody had to be inside, for an old dusty car—it took him a moment to recognize a Peugeot—was parked beside the door. He got down from the cab, but moving very slowly, careful to keep his body behind it: Vogel, after all, knew how to use a gun. At the same time he deliberately left his own weapon behind the seat: the .30-30 Marlin he always carried there. To keep him guessing. Not to alarm him—yet. But then he wasn't sure himself, for as he narrowed his eyes against the glare and smelled the dry, hot wind, he began to feel very exposed, and was about to get back into the truck when he finally did see someone.

A little girl.

She was running around from the back of the house, running as fast as she could with her tongue stuck between her teeth and her arms outstretched on either side as she tried to keep her balance. She was angling away from him, away from the house, and in her determination she didn't see him for a moment, but when she did, she stopped dead. Stared. And then slowly turned her head away and called, "Mummy!" She stared back toward him, eyeing him; then again called, "Mummy!" But her voice was more commanding than alarmed, and when she looked back once more, she added, quite calmly, "We have to be careful. There is a rattlesnake underneath our house."

His surprise, oddly, came more from the child's presence than her statement: children, whenever he saw them, were a shock, an aspect of life he normally forgot, or overlooked. They weren't one of his assumptions. But for this very reason he always took them seriously, which, on those rare occasions when he encountered them, they usually sensed and appreciated. But now, though he believed her immediately, he hesitated, wondering how a little girl could fit in with Harper, Buhler, and Vogel, and the child apparently interpreted this as doubt. Coming forward and speaking rather sternly she repeated, "I *said*, we must be very careful, because there is a rattlesnake underneath our *house*." Then she added, "What is your name, please?"

"Cracker Jack." The girl smiled at this and Tannis asked, "The snake . . . which side of the house is he on?"

"In the middle, I think."

"It didn't bite you?"

"Of course not. If it had bitten me, I would be *crying*, silly."

There was no arguing with that, and Tannis turned toward the trailer, squinting at the black line of shade beneath it; in the heat of the day that was just where a snake would go. He couldn't see anything and was turning back to the girl when another figure appeared, also running, also from behind the house. This was a woman. She was out of breath and had a bloody scrape on her cheek. Like the little girl, she seemed to be circling away from the trailer, but as soon as she saw Tannis she stopped.

And he had his first impression of her then: a powerful impression of fear
and beauty. It was a dark beauty, short, dark hair, now a little wild, and
a long, tawny face, and huge, dark eyes. The fear was in the eyes—and in
that vast landscape, those eyes seemed all there was to see.

She was far enough away that he had to raise his voice, but he kept
it calm. "Where did it go?"

She leaned forward, resting her hands on her knees, and panted. She
looked up and finally gasped, "Underneath the house."

"What exactly did it look like?"

"A light color. Yellow . . ." Her voice began to tremble, but it was
a deep voice; it was the same woman who'd answered the phone, the
woman who'd said she was Vogel's daughter. "On the back there were
brown splotches and—"

"All right." It was almost certainly a rattlesnake. "Just wait there,"
he said. "You can show me. I've got a gun in my truck."

But she called out, desperately: "No, no, it's all right. It's all right.
When it's dark, it'll go away. By tonight . . . it will be all right . . ."

Tonight . . . all right. The rhyme hung in his mind as he looked back
to her. She was frightened, she'd seen a rattlesnake; under the circumstances, there was no reason to take anything she said too seriously. But
her words struck him as so odd that he stared and saw something falter
behind her eyes—as if those words had been an admission, an unintended
revelation. So that Tannis imagined *tonight* when everything would be *all
right*, with her lying awake in the dark while the snake moved beneath
her. How many other nights had she lain awake like that? Oh, a good few,
Tannis thought. He could just see her. And—here was the first connection between them—he knew that she knew what he'd seen, for she
turned when she reached the girl and gasped, "I'm sorry, I don't know . . .
Jesus . . . I don't know."

Tannis smiled. She was a woman. And unlike children, women were
not an aspect of life that he'd overlooked. He said, "Just get your breath,
take your time. They'll give anyone a scare. You don't usually see them
in the middle of the day."

Gulping air, she tried to smile. "That's what I thought too."

"Something probably frightened it, a hawk, or a king snake—believe
it or not, they hunt rattlesnakes." He smiled again. Without meaning to,
he'd come closer to her; all at once, he was standing there beside her.
Close enough to realize she was wearing perfume, a light scent of flowers;

an incongruous touch, but in fact she was carefully groomed, and was even "put together" in a simple way: a crisp white shirt with the cuffs turned back and faded blue jeans tucked into tan Frye boots. She stepped back a little from him, running her fingers through her hair and tipping her head back to reveal a flash of silver at her neck, something Navajo. For an instant it actually occurred to him that she might be Indian; she was dark enough. In any case, it was obvious that she was not from here, yet it was hard to say where she did come from. Mexico? That was not impossible; her darkness had something of that quality, and Vogel at least had spoken Mex, assuming he was the man who'd called, and yes, that's what he was assuming. On the other hand . . . His mind chased the question. Then resisted. What did this woman mean to him? Nothing. But that was the trouble: he was the one, after all, who'd found meaning in the chaos, and now everything had meaning. Everything—precisely— signified. Including this strange pair. But what connection could they have? The woman was half his age. When Harper had been in this desert, she would have been a child, a child the age of her own child or even younger. In his mind he followed the chain of this descent, the separate links, one fornication leading to another—but then she'd caught her breath, recovered herself, and smiled. "I'm sorry. I didn't catch your name."

"Jack," he said. And smiled as well. "Jack Tannis."

She nodded. "Marianne Vogel."

"I came out to see your father."

"You're the one who called, aren't you? This afternoon?"

He smiled again, and nodded, all agreeable. "I was in Ridgecrest anyway. I thought I'd just drive out. I haven't spoken to your father in quite a while, but he has this property in Kern County that I'm trying to buy."

"He doesn't own property in Kern County."

Tannis cocked his head. "No? Well, just barely, I guess you could say. The county's about to take it over." And he took a photocopy of the land register from his pocket and passed it to her. She looked at it with a frown, and he went on quickly, trying to give her no time to doubt or question. "Look, about that snake. You're probably right, as soon as it cools off, he'll go. But maybe not. That's the trouble. You just can't tell. And a bite from a snake like that, if it bit your daughter, it would likely . . ."

As he said this, they both looked over to the little girl. She'd wandered off and was squatting in the dirt, playing with two small plastic figures no bigger than party favors. In a quiet, rather confidential voice, she was talking to them. Debbie, one of the figures, was apparently going on a trip to Buffalo. She must be sure to write. When she came back, William would meet her at the bus. As she continued this dialogue, Tannis gathered that the little girl's name was Anna and that she was not in the least afraid. Which, he realized, was somehow part of it: the woman soaked up all the fear. "Just let me take a look," he said. "You stay with her, or maybe she can play in the back of the truck."

Marianne nodded, glanced at him . . . and then, as she turned away, there was a moment, not quite acknowledged, when the photocopy passed permanently to her, his little gift, her daddy's secret . . . and then he had his gun and was walking to the house.

He didn't fool. He walked all the way around it, twice. But if the snake was there, he'd worked his way well back into the crawl space. He peered carefully into this and saw a jumble of planks, broken tools, ends of chicken wire, old electric cord, but no sign of a snake. He went around the back again. Here there was more junk, in a randomness that defied all pattern: odd bricks and cement blocks, shingles, coils of wire, an oil drum filled with trash, even an old cement mixer, fossilized by its final project. But there were also five old tires and a two-kilowatt Yamaha generator—a line ran up to the kitchen window—with a half-full tank of gas beside it. Rolling a couple of the tires to the edge of the foundation, he spaced them out and then set them alight with gas from the generator's tank. At first this seemed to have almost no effect—only a throw of heat and a rippling of the air showed that they were burning—but then the flames took hold and they began to smolder. The wind was perfect, not too strong, but steady. In a moment, waves of dense black smoke were rolling underneath the house.

He went around to the front.

He could feel Marianne and the little girl watching from the truck, but he kept his own eyes on the shadows underneath the house. He could smell the burning rubber; in a moment a wisp of gray, gritty smoke appeared, followed, about five minutes later, by the snake itself. It emerged, in fact, right below the front door, winding across the second step, like a strange crack opening up in the cement. It was a yellowish sandy color, just as the woman had described, with a pattern of darker diamond blotches along its back. About four feet long, he guessed: it was a very large Mojave rattlesnake. It drew itself slowly across the steps, then down the other side; then it turned, hesitated—its black tongue was testing—and slid along.

He watched it.

He could feel the woman watching it.

And there was a temptation to turn, to watch her watching; but he'd been too long in the desert to take his eye off a snake, and he moved very carefully, circling it, so that a ricochet wouldn't carry toward the woman and the girl. The snake slid around a rock; slithered in the dust; winding along, moving a little faster. Leaning forward, he watched it, the sun hot on his neck, sweat tingling in the corner of his eye. He followed it. But he didn't want it to get away, to be out here, on the loose, and as it moved past the Peugeot—he was afraid it might go underneath the car—he took four quick strides, trying to cut if off; which was close enough. With astonishing speed, the snake turned about, and coiled. Tannis stopped. He was perhaps fifteen feet away. He raised his rifle, worked the lever action. Then, quite delicately, almost discreetly, the snake's head came up, and probed, and steadied; at which point Tannis had a flash of memory of Harper and his wife and a time, at dusk, when he'd been walking with them (one of the few times they'd all been out together) and they'd seen a snake, in fact a sidewinder, sidewinding toward them along the shadowed, wavy sand. And Diana had recoiled in horror, stepping back into Harper's arms (like a B-movie heroine, she'd later joked, and it was the only time he'd seen them in even this much of an embrace), and Harper had explained—yes, he could hear his voice but still couldn't make out that young, blank face—that this was the world's first infrared detector (thinking, naturally, of the missile): the snake, with its cold blood, as if not quite alive, while we glowed like coals, little constant suns, so that our heat, carried to the pits beneath its eyes and compared to its own cold self, told him where we were. One third of a degree was all it took; if you stood out from the background temperature by just that much, he had you. And now, up the Panamint, this one certainly had *him*, Tannis knew, staring at him with its lidless eyes, its tail up, though still not buzzing, its big wedged head fitting neatly between his sights, and, again, what did it mean? *Because this all meant something too.* And then he squeezed the trigger and the snake's head exploded in a spray of pink. It was over that quickly. He eased the rifle off his shoulder as the echo of the shot came back. He turned toward the woman. Her face was white. Her fist was jammed against her mouth. While the child simply stared as the snake's back end writhed and thrashed and died. Finally it grew still. He went over to it. His boots scuffed up the dust. He could feel the woman watching him. She'd been afraid of the snake. He had killed the snake. She was now afraid of him. He knew exactly how her mind worked. He could sense it on the back of his neck, the way she fitted him into the pattern of her fear. But he didn't look back again. Picking the snake up by the tail, he carried it behind the trailer, the thing thick and heavy, swinging from his hand, and tossed it in an oil drum that was full of trash. He pulled some rubbish over it so the birds wouldn't get it, then pulled the smoldering tires away from the house and kicked sand over them till they went out. This took a good ten minutes, and by the time he went around to the front again the woman and the child were gone.

The door was closed; he would have bet money it was locked.

He started up to it, but then stopped. Something held him; he felt a peculiar concentration of the atmosphere. He looked around; in the distance, jutting up against the horizon to the west, were the black, jagged hills of the Argus Range, but up close he couldn't see beyond the rim of this dusty, rocky bowl. The wind had died. Nothing moved. From the trailer there wasn't a sound, no sign that anyone was there. But of course she was watching him, and he thought, for a moment, that he'd simply felt her gaze; he was at a focus. But then he remembered something about Harper, remembered that he'd been an expert on "black bodies," perfect absorbers and emitters of the infrared: they drew it into them with absolute efficiency or let it radiate from them with no interference whatsoever . . . making a focus of a different sort. That's what he was feeling. It was the same phenomenon again; there was nothing else to see, no one else to watch. This was the only speck of life, and everything was drawn to it and radiated out from it. Vogel had been drawn here; so had Buhler; so had he. Why? The woman knew. The woman, the child, even the snake; for the moment, they were the heart of the mystery. He looked up at the door. She had the answer. But of course she'd lie, though he wondered why, because he'd know, he always did, he always knew when a woman said no but really meant yes or a man made a bet and didn't have the card. He was never wrong. So when he went to the door and she didn't come immediately, he thumped so hard the doorframe shook; and it was just barely possible, when she finally answered, for Marianne to offer, "I was running Anna's bath." And even then he came up the steps so quickly, and with such determination, that she wasn't quite able to get out of his way, and he brushed against her. He stood close to her, too close to be quite normal, but, just as he thought, it would have revealed too much for her to move away. He looked around him. After the bright light outside, the trailer seemed very dark, and he blinked, hearing more than he saw: the whir of a fan and a flicking ribbon streaming in its breeze; a running tap; a hum he couldn't place. His eyes adjusted. A low, dark living room; beyond, two doors. And a doorway with a curtain of beads. The kitchen was to his right.

"About the snake, I should thank you . . ."

But he didn't give her even that much: "Not if you don't want to."

She was leaning against the doorway to the kitchen. She tried to shrug but didn't bring it off. He could see she was afraid. He had the gun in his hand, after all, and he was a big man; in that small trailer he looked very big. He could beat her. He could beat the truth out of her; it was as simple as that. Beat her with his open hand. That was it, he thought; she'd be afraid of that, but she wouldn't want to admit it; so, for her, the trick would be to let him see the truth without actually telling him what it was, out of her own mouth, or forcing him to beat her. Which made it something like a game. *Playacting*. He smiled again. Near her, he could feel her heat—well, he was like that snake. He turned away, into the dark, cool living room. It was clear that he was going to look around, whether she liked it or not, but the pretense of normalcy—he sensed this—was so important to her that the thought would be forming in her mind, Why don't you come in and sit down? But of course she didn't say it; she couldn't trust her voice; by now it had all gone much too far. He went over to the doorway, the one with the beads. It was the little girl's room. A wooden bunk bed stood against the wall; there were dolls neatly tucked beneath the covers in the lower berth, while the little girl's dress was draped across the upper. On the wall was a faded poster, the colors badly registered, "Walt Disney's Living Desert." He stepped back. The beads rattled shut. At the side of the room was a little hall, and he could hear the child at the end of it, splashing in the bath. Besides this there was only one other door, and he opened it. Inside was another bedroom, with two single beds along opposite walls and a dresser between. It was very bare, a jail, a monastery, a boarding school. No rugs. No pictures. The only sign of habitation was a woman's hairbrush on the dresser and a mirror hanging above the dresser in which, behind him, he could see the woman watching him. And he smiled, looking at the beds, so she could see him smile. But I won't tell. He closed the door. Turned back. As she turned away, into the living room. Which had a little more character. On the floor, thrown down in every direction, were layers of rugs and blankets—Indian blankets, Navajo blankets, with more hanging from the walls. There was no real furniture, only cushions and more blankets, rolled up, to sit on. In fact, the room, with its darkness, did create the feeling of an Indian's tent, or a bedouin's. Could this be part of the truth? He wondered again if she might be part Indian, but then he stopped himself. The truth about her, about her and the little girl and Vogel, was much more obvious. Like the Purloined Letter. It was sitting right out in the open. In fact, he'd already seen it. From the back of the trailer, he could hear the little girl singing, "You deserve a break today . . ." He could see just a flicker in the woman's eyes as his attention touched her daughter, and this finally made her speak. "I'm sorry, my father isn't here."

"When did you see him last?"

"I haven't been here all week. I was in Laredo."

Indians . . . Laredo . . . the Rio Grande . . .

"But you think he's in L.A.?"

"He left a note."

"So how long do you think he'll be away?"

"Not long." And this was all sufficiently conversational for her to relax a little; but even as she did so, she caught herself. He watched her. Her face was beautiful, like a shape the eye picked out in rippling water or a patch of fern. She was hiding just below the water or in the ferns. She looked at him with her frightened eyes. Had he seen? That's what he saw in her eyes. "He's just buying a few things, he said," she said. "He's a rock hound. He looks for . . ." She shrugged.

"Buried treasure? The Gunsight Lode?"

She tried to smile. "Something like that." She leaned back, in the kitchen doorway. She took cigarettes from the breast pocket of her shirt, Virginia Slims, and lit one. "This property, you said . . ."

He watched her. Yes, it was like a game: animal, vegetable, or mineral. Twenty questions. Was he getting warm? He lit a Lucky. "You don't remember it?"

"I think I do now. But we left when I was even younger than Anna. We went to Arizona. Then down to Mexico."

"So you don't know much about it?"

"No."

"You wouldn't remember, say, if he kept horses there?"

"No. I don't think so."

"He doesn't have any now?"

"No. No horses."

But of course she was lying, and he smiled. In the oil drum, where he'd thrown the snake, he'd seen three or four vials clearly labeled sulfamethazine, horse medicine for strangles or pneumonia. He smoked the cigarette. They watched each other. Who'd blink first?—it was all like that. Everything still meant something. The woman, the little girl, the snake. All of it connected, to Buhler, Vogel, Harper. All of it was linked, and all of it was *coming back*. That, in a way, was the most extraordinary part of it, he thought. Buhler had gone from the concentration camp to East Germany—and forty years later had come straight here. Vogel had abandoned Kern County around 1960; now here he was, less than thirty miles away. And he couldn't forget himself, the observer who was an intrinsic part of the experiment. He had come back too. What did it mean that he was here, that he had killed the snake? The snake, like the emblem on a crest or a medallion, seemed to wind around, intertwined between the woman's beauty and her fear. Adam and Eve. The Purloined Letter. As he stood there, these set up associations that led him to a memory, in Munich, just after the war was finished, when he'd been sent to interview a Jew who'd been in Dachau, and he'd gone out to the hospital to see him every day for a week. The man was dying. They couldn't bring him back. But he was glad to talk, especially to an American, and asked him to bring some books, especially by Jack London; though he was not strong enough even to hold them in his hands, he asked Tannis to read out the titles to him, the titles of the stories and the chapter headings—"Bâtard," "Into the Primitive," "The Law of Club and Fang," "The Dominant Primordial Beast," "Who Has Won to Mastership," "The Trail of the Meat," "The Hunger Cry," "The Lair," "The Reign of Hate," "The Abysmal Brute"—these being the truths that had sustained him, or so he'd claimed. And Tannis, emerging from this parenthesis of memory, kept on, still thinking of the snake, twisting around the woman's beauty and her fear, thinking of Eve in Paradise, but that was exactly wrong, for the woman was no innocent; the child was proof. And he could feel it in her anyway. He could sense it. She was a woman who'd done it every which way. But then innocence was just another lie. We've always known, he knew. He knew it now. And she knew he knew. It was right there, lying in the open, yes, exactly like the Purloined Letter. She could feel it happening as well as he could, that thickening of himself, that slow, warm stirring. And there was nothing she could do about it. He could have her. He could put her over on her back. Fuck her. Right now. He could take her to the other room and fuck her with the child just behind the screen of beads: if he got up now and pressed his hand across her mouth, she wouldn't scream. No, she'd love it. He watched her eyes, that slow, dull, stricken look. . . . But then all at once, with a great rush and rustle, as the two of them were standing there, the little girl ran stark naked from the bathroom and thumped down on the floor. She was grinning and laughing, and this, oddly enough, restored everything to normal, as if he were just a neighbor who'd dropped by to chat.

"Anna! What do you think you're doing? Look at you."

She laughed. "I took off my clothes! You have big toes! Nobody knows! Have a long doze!" Then her face went very serious, as she realized Tannis was there, and Marianne scooped her up, giving her a little slap, and there was a piece of business: Tannis butting his cigarette, turning to one side as the woman brushed past him, a whoop from Anna; a moment that ended at the door of the trailer. But that was fine with him. Her initiative was pure illusion; he'd gotten what he'd come for. But he wanted to drive it home, make sure there was no doubt, keep the pressure on, because he knew he still had very little time. So, standing on the bottom step, looking back, he said, "You better tell your father when you see him, tell him that I came. And tell him—Friday night—that I spoke to Buhler. Buhler. He'll know who I mean."

And then he was away, without another word. Knowing she knew he knew. So now she'd run. She'd run, and she'd make tracks. And he'd come following after.

CHAPTER 5

Tannis was in his element.

The woman was afraid, terribly afraid, and Tannis knew about fear the way a compass knows about north: he was sensitive to it, as to a mysterious, primitive force. For Tannis, fear was the greatest magic, and Tannis had taught himself every magic trick and principle. Pick a card, any card . . . he always guessed which one.

He had that gift—talent or luck or genius; call it what you will. His mind could *leap*. He could think thoughts that no one had ever thought before. Once, sitting on the beach at Santa Monica (he was still at CalTech—this would have been around 1942, a year when the beach and philosophical contemplation were not yet mutually exclusive) he'd spent an afternoon contemplating the waves and tried to work it out. Listening to the rumble of the surf he'd tried to imagine the moment when Beethoven had thought of the theme for his Ninth Symphony, *alle Menschen werden Brüder*—surely one of the greatest thoughts anyone had ever had. It had changed the world; the world had been just a little different after that theme had been composed. But what had happened? Where had that thought come from? He wondered if the world itself had changed, cracked, or decomposed, thereby permitting Beethoven to think that particular run of notes. Or had he, truly, thought it up all on his own? Or was it chance? Perhaps his theme was already out there and he'd only stumbled on it, like Columbus discovering America. When you got right down to it, he considered, it was the question, Did God exist? If Beethoven had merely found his theme, God must have been its true composer; whereas, if Beethoven had created it himself, he *was* God, or so near it made no difference. Which people hated to admit, so they thought up words like luck and talent. For his own part, even then, Tannis had known where he stood. He'd already had thoughts no one else had ever thought, and he knew they had nothing to do with luck. But they had a lot to do with fear. Fear was the key. You always thought *against* fear, and all true thoughts had fear in them; you could certainly hear it in *alle Menschen werden Brüder*, you could feel that thrill, it made you tremble. Great thoughts frightened even the men who thought them. Sometimes the fear of their own thoughts drove them mad. Why? He thought he knew. Because all true thoughts, by definition, began as secrets; you were the only one who knew them. Yes, all great thoughts, in the instant that you thought them, as the tune went whistling through your mind, were secret. Which raised a question. Why reveal that secret? Why tell anyone about it? Why not keep that tune all for yourself? Well, he knew the answer; the fear was just too great. By telling, by confessing their secret, even great men tried to escape that dread. Their secret power, the power of their secret, was just too much. But not for Tannis. Long since, he'd known that he was stronger; he knew fear and was not afraid. And on that long-ago afternoon he'd watched the Pacific come rolling in and wondered about the other men, like himself, who'd refused, who'd resisted the fear, who'd sworn to keep the great secrets to themselves. They were not afraid and so kept the power of the fear, which eternally set them apart from other men. He'd smiled at that. Since this had all begun with *alle Menschen werden Brüder*.

That afternoon—and it was now late in the afternoon—Tannis wasn't actually thinking this, but as he left Marianne Vogel's trailer and walked back to his truck, all of it was working for him. The snake. The child. The woman and that stricken look. His mind had *leapt*, he was in that clear, bright space where he so loved to be; and as the sun declined behind dead volcanoes and a dry breeze stirred he enjoyed a whiff of ozone, the smell that collects around a thunderstorm, which also was the smell of fear. And perhaps it was compounded because he had the feeling that Marianne's mind had leapt as well, that the woman had come close to a secret even beyond the secrets that she knew. Immediately, it seemed, everything between them was reciprocal: they were working from the same assumptions; she too knew all the laws of fear.

The hunter and the hunted—that's how they worked it out. In the penumbra of the fear around her, they were indissolubly linked, like the antelope whose final flight provokes the lion's charge, or the rabbit that freezes as the stoat sneaks nearer. Panic and paralysis: the balance was so delicate. He wanted her to run, but not run blindly. She must run to Vogel; so she needed that much self-control; he had to give it to her. Accordingly, as Tannis felt it, they now made a pact along these lines: he would pretend and she would pretend, and so he wouldn't have to frighten her and she wouldn't have to be afraid. Though these thoughts were merely murmurings to confirm his instincts. For he knew exactly what to do. Two great boulders, like two buck teeth, projected from the lip of the crater where the trailer lay: he hid the truck and worked up the gap between them. From the top, he could see everything below. But was so discreet he scarcely looked. In fact, rolling on his back, he looked away, giving her every chance to escape because then she wouldn't. She would know that as her hand reached toward the door, his eyes would move and freeze her soul, like the peace of the stoat's dark gaze, the sweet promise of oblivion in the lion's. So she stayed quite still. And he stared down toward the house, the Peugeot, the slowly lengthening shadows, stared down across that distance. It was such an easy stare; and yet, in the sight of his eyes, he often thought, was the earliest form of magic, his first true secret. The oldest. At first a baby's eyes can't focus, and then they do, and everything resolves, in beauty, terror, magic. That very first look. *At first sight*. Second sight merely recaptured this, and he was a master of it. Space collapsed. Now, staring down, he was both here and there, he was a seer, he could see her perfectly; and then looked away to take her fear away. He could hear her thoughts. Like a woman walking down a lonely street who hears footsteps coming up behind her. She's so, so frightened, but she'll look back only when she's certain that they've stopped. And is then so afraid to run because as soon as she starts to run the steps will start again, oh so much faster. But that was their little pact. Turn around! Look back! See, there's nothing to be afraid of! So Tannis looked away, looked up, watched lights skid down the darkening sky: an F-18, heading back to Armitage Field because the tower closed at sunset; looked back, where the desert plants stretched out in luxuriant shadow (as if they grew only in the absence of the sun); and even looked inside, letting his thoughts wander through his body, his aching shoulder, his dry mouth—until he suddenly turned around, and there she was.

She'd moved, and too far to turn back.

The sun was down. It was the darkness, otherwise so frightening, that had finally given her the nerve. Because she would assume he couldn't see. But of course he could see. Still, he thought, she'd managed it very well. She'd turned out every light inside the trailer; the door, opening, was the faintest disturbance of the dark. But something had given her away, and as he caught her silhouette, Tannis realized she was carrying the child in her arms, wrapped in a blanket, as if bearing her away from a burning house or rushing her to a doctor—there was the panic that had drawn him. She moved toward the car, or the spot where the car must be, and disappeared within its deeper shadow. He listened. The door clicked open, a sound, so intense was the silence, like the crack of a shot, although, a moment later, as she closed it, this sound was oddly muffled, remote, removed, infinitely distant. Uncannily, it made him feel he was looking into the past, that this was already over and he'd lost her, he was too far behind. And for a second he did lose sight of her altogether. But in fact she was still there. She hadn't gotten into the car: she'd only bent over, putting the child into the back. And now she stood, and above the roof of the car, he could see her head and shoulders outlined against the light. She turned back to the house, shut the door. Came back; he could just follow her in the gloom. Finally, hurrying, she came around the car, opened the door on the driver's side, then apparently bent down, reaching inside, perhaps under the dash. For a moment he didn't understand. A gun? But almost immediately she slipped inside, and the engine drew a deep, coarse breath from the desert night. And a few seconds later Tannis was startled in at least two ways.

He had assumed that the woman would come right toward him, heading for the highway, and so he'd tucked his own machine neatly behind these rocks. But in fact she swung the car around and drove in precisely the opposite direction: away from him, past the house, into the deeper desert and the hills. And, the second surprise, she showed no lights whatsoever, a realization that struck him even as he understood that she was also getting away. With a curse he scrambled down the rock, then jumped, hitting the sand with a grunt and rolling hard onto his shoulder.

Lying there he listened, but already the sound of the car was lost, blocked by the upslope of the crater. Running to his truck, he decided that he could not risk lights himself, but leaned close to the windshield as he gunned it over the edge of the dip, the front end lifting just enough to give him one quick glimpse of the Peugeot in the distance. But then it was gone, and he was skidding down into the crater, where a pale cloud of dust eddied back out of the night, like fog. Instinctively, he steered out of this, but almost drove straight into the trailer. In fact, the dust was all he had to follow. Yanking the wheel, he turned back into it, skidded through a patch of soft sand, and picked it up—wisps of grit, then a layered, drifting mist, then a thicker, rolling cloud. He stuck his head out the window. Driving with one hand on the wheel, he narrowed his eyes, keeping the truck inside a kind of fluorescent gloom. Quickly, his nose filled with dust and his lips and gums were dry as paper. But he grimly kept his head out, the truck pitching and jolting, banging his skull against the window frame. At one point, the front end nosed down and with a great clang the oil pan smashed a rock and he cursed out loud, but then he began to get the hang of it. In the desert, after all, nothing could defeat him. And now he understood what the woman had been doing when she'd leaned in, under the dash. The Peugeot had no lights, but, as Harper could have told you, among the first applications of the infrared were the headlamps and image converters the Germans had fitted to move their tanks at night. Vogel, he supposed, must have fitted the Peugeot with a similar system, and she'd been turning it on, and now she could "see in the dark," but no one could see her. Yet her advantage wasn't total. It was remarkable that her car handled this terrain so well, but she would have to keep her speed down: even steel-belted tires had their limitations. Then the dust began to clear and he realized he was running on bare rock, a hard spine that probably bulged through a *bajada* that was spreading, like an enormous fan, from the mouth of a canyon that lay ahead. The black night rushed by. He drew his head in. They'd come a mile, he guessed, which meant the hills could only be a few miles on and she'd have to stop. So, for a last minute or so, he kept right up, but then he began to slow, hanging back, until he was barely creeping forward. And then he stopped dead, for he felt the ground slope abruptly under him. He stuck his head out again, but the dark spread all around. But she could only be a few hundred yards ahead. He made up his mind. He got out of the truck and ran around behind it and with the butt of the big Colt smashed both the taillights. Then he turned the truck around, until he was heading back the way he'd come, and flashed his lights. For an instant, they flushed the ground with a brilliant phosphorescence, but in the desert direction is everything, and since his taillights had not come on, he knew she wouldn't have seen anything. And, for his part, he'd seen exactly what he had to see. As expected, he'd been traveling along a broad whaleback of rock, boulders strewn on either side of it, with patches of lighter, softer ground between. When she came back—for that was what he was now thinking about—she'd stick to the rock, so he deliberately drove off it, down into one of the sandy hollows, well out of her way. Finally, he stopped the truck and turned off the engine. He listened for a second, but there was no sound except the wind.

The desert. The night. Pursuit. For Tannis, it was all second nature; he knew exactly what to do. For just an instant he stood beside the truck, getting his bearings, feeling the odd sense of claustrophobia that is part of the desert dark: that vast space, all closed in upon him, like a deep mine shaft, where one misstep could tumble you to eternity. But he was so accustomed to this feeling, this darkness was so much a part of him, that he could ignore it, and he moved quickly forward. He could see only about ten yards in front of him, but the wind was steady and he took his direction from it. He moved carefully—it would be easy enough to turn an ankle—and every few minutes he stopped and listened. But there was no sound except the press of the breeze across the sand and the rocks and through his hair. It was silent; he could almost hear his eyelids flutter. Then, after a time, he realized he was in a canyon: the wind swirled, and he sensed invisible walls rising up on either side. Of course, he was expecting this. Now he counted paces. After fifty, the ground began to slope higher under his feet; soon he had to lean against it, and very quickly the terrain changed completely, enormous boulders jutting up around him, massive, silent, implacable in the dark, great chunks of rock that had tumbled from high cliffs a thousand years ago. Instinctively he looked up and hesitated. And though he still couldn't see anything, he knew exactly what was out there. He had been walking up the mouth of a canyon, and now he was approaching its face, or possibly one of its sides. There was no obvious way to turn.

A canyon, at the foot of the Argus Range. It could be anything from forty yards wide to four hundred. In any case, he knew the woman had to be somewhere in it; even with a tracked vehicle she could have gone no farther. Finally, arbitrarily, he swung left, which was more or less south. Then, keeping the wind against his right cheek, he marched for about fifty yards until a line of boulders, like fragments of a gigantic backbone, stopped him. Now, even in the dark—there were still no stars—he could see a vast cliff rear up. This was the canyon wall. Slowly, with his left hand extended to his side, he turned and began moving around the base of it. This formed a rocky slope, like an abutment, and he moved slowly around it, knowing, theoretically, that if he just kept going he was bound to find her. But he actually didn't have to go far at all. Two minutes after he began, he saw a light flash. He stopped dead. The light flashed again. Held steady. A small white light. He didn't move. A light in the dark can be very deceptive, but he would have thought this was less than fifty yards away. He stared just a little to one side of it, to take advantage of his peripheral vision, and again the light flashed on. But then he realized that it hadn't really flashed at all. The light was steady, stationary: the woman, or someone, had simply walked in front of it. She did so again, her shadow swinging, and then he could see that the light was a beacon marking the mouth of a cave in the back of the canyon wall. A cavern. He stared. A huge shadow gaped. A hiding place within a hiding place, and she was waiting for Vogel to come to it.

Whatever his expectations might have been, to the extent that Tannis had formulated them at all, they certainly hadn't included this. Still, the very extent of the surprise was satisfactory; even if he didn't understand what all this meant, he thought, it must mean something. Yet it seemed to connect with nothing else. Sinking down behind a rock, he tried to work out where he was. They hadn't come that far; the Trona road would be only six or eight miles away. Beyond this, however, he wasn't exactly sure. There were still no stars, he could make out no landmarks, but he doubted that he would have recognized this spot even in the light of noon. A canyon, but there were dozens of them. The big ones all had names—the Revenue, the Homewood, the Shepherd, the Knight, the Thompson; but most were unnamed, unknown, rarely visited. All of them were rifts in the Argus Range, which rose up six thousand feet in front of him, and along their summit was the line of electronic sensors that marked the boundary of the base. What was Vogel doing here? As a hideout it was brilliant—right under their noses, the last place they'd look—but it was obviously more than that: everything he'd discovered today had been months and years in the planning, not days. So what was

Vogel up to? What had Buhler *interrupted*? That seemed to be the question, but, having come so far, he still had no idea of the answer; he could only wait there, hoping it would appear.

Over an hour passed. Then, very nearly at midnight, he heard a sound, a quick, skittering spill of rock. Somewhere metal struck on stone, and in his mind's eye he saw a spark. But he was not sure where. Turning slowly he looked behind him, but a moment later, from the opposite side of the canyon and higher up, he heard a harsh, heavy cough and a peculiar indrawn whining sound, which took him another moment to identify as the braying of a burro or a donkey. And then, a moment later, a horse blew softly; gradually these sounds drew closer, running together, and he understood that a small train of animals was making its way along a path that must wind down the canyon's face. He stared up, eyes searching; a small avalanche of stones sprinkled the dark with silver; and finally, like the details in the gloomy background of some old, dark painting, shapes modeled themselves from shadows. They were remarkably close. Four burros. And then a horse, led by a man. They rather jumped out of the gloom, as if right on top of him. Now the light flickered again in the cave. Then it burned up brighter and came forward, the woman holding up a lamp so its glow fell back upon her face. Her eyes gleamed. Her hair shone, full of golden highlights. Shadows swung like midnight torches in a great cathedral—almost literally so, for in this light he could see that the cave was sheltered by an enormous porch of overhanging rock. She held the lamp up higher ... he heard it hiss ... it was a gas lamp, with a mantle; and then she stepped ahead onto the canyon floor, the gas hissing harder against the wind, and when she stopped, the circle of its light fell not ten feet in front of him. Tannis held his breath. Around him boulders swelled like sentinels and shapes moved beyond the brilliance like creatures circling the fire's light—again, all this might have been drawn by an old master's hand, shadows swirling around some classical theme, *The Midnight Watch*, *The Flight*, *The Caravan Returns*. And for an instant a peculiar feeling passed over him, a kind of déjà vu: somewhere, he'd seen it all before. His mind, in characteristic fashion, almost made its leap, projected him across the gulf between here and there. But in fact he didn't move. And then, from way behind, the child called out, "Mummy! Mummy!" and then the woman herself was crying, "*Bist du? Bist du?*"

And the voice of a man came roughly back: "*Ja, ja, Marianne. Nach innen! Innen!*"

German.

They spoke German.

Of course they did. "Go inside." Yet she didn't immediately obey; instead she raised the lamp still higher, and Tannis could see the animals drawing closer, the burros with their big ears down and heavy boxes bulging on their backs—indeed, like an ancient caravan returning home— and then the horse and the man swayed inside the light, the man tall in the saddle but stooped and with a wide-brimmed hat drawn down tightly on his head by a leather chin strap. And before Tannis could actually see his face—who are you? why don't I know you?—the woman swung the lamp away and slowly, their hooves thumping softly in the sand, the animals moved off into the shadows of the cavern and then were gone.

Tannis didn't move. There was a sense of anticlimax. No, he hadn't recognized the man, but then he hadn't seen him. And his mind had *not* leapt, as he might have hoped, though somewhere inside he'd been tensed and ready. Half of him had gone ahead, so that, as the procession disappeared, he had the feeling of jumping back from a leap that had not quite been dared. He waited. The light momentarily left him dazzled, and the darkness, as it returned, was a kind of absence. He felt drained, empty. He could make no move. He'd missed—what? Time was frozen. And then, abruptly, the light was blotted out. A huge shadow came toward him. It was Vogel leaving again. It was too late, but Tannis suddenly realized that the woman had simply warned him off. And Vogel, on a small black mare that must have scented Tannis, for it blew and sidestepped away, was visible only for a moment before being swallowed by the night, the rattle of the horse's hooves disappearing up the canyon path, the way it had come down. Slowly Tannis turned back toward the cave. The light still burned; but after a time, it flickered and swung lower and then seemed to move away to the right. And then went out. He waited. Perhaps a minute passed. Then a much smaller light bobbed toward him, which he realized was simply the woman with a flashlight. She came just close enough for him to see her. The child, once more wrapped up in a blanket, was clinging to her neck. The light poked ahead and her car gleamed darkly for an instant in a patch of open ground beside some boulders. He heard the sounds of her getting into it, the engine starting. Again there were no lights. He listened. The sound drifted off; in a moment it too had disappeared.

They'd gone—the woman, back to the trailer; Vogel, into the hills. But still Tannis didn't move, powerless before the scene he'd witnessed. They were gone, and a certain pressure was released; but this was almost instantly transformed into a different tension, an overwhelming curiosity. What had happened? What was going on? He had to know. He had to *see*. He stepped ahead, feeling with outstretched hands through the darkness, and finally, out of breath—breath held—found himself before Vogel's cave.

He wasn't quite sure where he was, he'd so been *led*. The darkness, if anything, was deeper. But he could no longer feel the wind on his face, and some cooler undercurrent of the atmosphere had touched his nose. So he guessed he was inside the vaulted porch, the tumble of rocks that guarded the entrance to the cave. Taking his Zippo out of his pocket, he held it off to one side, out of the direct line of his sight, and worked it. Now, at last, he might see something. His heart was pounding as the little flame leapt up. But there was a moment of fumbling, cursing frustration: he was just outside the entrance, a steeply angled arch of rock about twice his height, and beyond this it was utterly dark, too dark; the flame of the lighter revealed nothing except itself. But the woman, he remembered, had moved the gas lamp before turning it off, and he edged sideways, following the curve of the arch as it swung down. At the point where it merged with the wall, he again flicked the lighter and metal gleamed. It was the lamp, set aside for the next time. With a grunt he picked it up, twisted at the valve; a second later the mantle threw a white fireball of light around him.

Ducking below the arch, he stepped inside.

But then, uncertain, he stopped. In front of him he had a dizzying, breathless sense of space—the cave was enormous; but as his eyes adjusted he realized he was not confronted with a fall, but a gentler slope, a ramp of very smooth rock, as broad as a highway, that angled down. Cautiously he stepped forward onto this, holding the lamp up. He went on about ten yards and stopped again. High above his head a rocky roof curved up and everywhere shadows stretched like banners. He might have been in the courtyard of a castle, or a tower, or, as he stepped ahead again, the runway of rock could have been the aisle of a great cathedral, for the lamp swayed before him like a censer, its reflection lighting tiny candles in the dark. As he went on, rocks glistened wetly; he could hear a little dripping water. His feet crunched gravel. Now he had the sense of a constriction, as if the space around him might be growing narrower; as if he was going through a pass, or a divide. It was difficult to tell, but he thought the color of the rock was changing, growing lighter, like sandstone. But in fact he didn't know; the darkness swallowed up the light, and all he saw was shadow. Instinctively, with each few steps, he hesitated; he kept fearing, in his ignorance, that he'd step into some vast, dark hole. But he kept on, and then he had a sense of the space swelling out again, and then the ground leveled and he seemed to be emerging onto the floor of a great valley, a huge rock canyon buried inside the mountain.

Halting again, he turned around and around with the light held over his head, as far out as he could reach. On his right hand broad shelves of stone rose up, like steps or the rows of an amphitheater, while to his left the ground was level, almost like a stage. Nervously, reluctant to leave his track, he moved toward it, like someone coming into a darkened hall to view a rehearsal. And it actually had that abandoned but expectant quality, as if in a moment someone would appear and he'd hear an echoing voice reading vaguely familiar lines. But such an actor, presumably, would have been a giant: the stage was so large. Which created a peculiar disproportion, for as his eyes penetrated a little farther in the gloom, he saw that the setting on this dramatic plain was domestic, peaceful, even pastoral; in fact, thinking of a cathedral again, it was something like a crèche. For at the back of the cave he could see burros moving contentedly around a long wooden manger and a metal water trough, which were set out in a strawed area illumined by a low pool of dim light. Calmly the animals lifted their eyes toward him and then, with little grunts, went on feeding. He waited, watching them, their appearance reviving the impression of antiquity that Vogel's arrival, in the light of the high-held lamp, had created in his mind; it really seemed that he'd been carried back in time. Yet the palpable reality of what he was looking at lent it a quality of parody; as he started toward the animals, holding the lamp up himself, he might have been some Victorian gentleman explorer whose white man's eyes were for the first time in ten thousand years looking upon a long-lost tomb, precisely the evidence of some great and ancient myth, a God who'd used a Virgin woman to carry the seed that would bring forth Himself.

But as he came closer to the animals he stopped again, swinging the lamp to one side to soften its glare. Because beyond the animals and off to the right was another tableau, even more startling than the first. It was less domestic, but also ancient in its associations: a grouping of three machines made of iron, obviously very old, and so strange in their configuration that they might have been instruments of torture in a medieval dungeon. *Engines*—they seemed to possess the older connotations of that word.

He moved slowly closer. From somewhere above there was a glow of light, and he could actually see them. All three were partly covered in a fine white dust but were also blackened in some parts and rusted in others. One involved a heavy iron wheel, like an immense spinning wheel or perhaps some kind of winch, although he knew that wasn't what it was, for an enormous jaw, like the jaw of a vise, was bolted to it. The second was apparently a derrick, like a pump for a deep well, perhaps an oil well. At the top, perhaps twenty feet above the cave floor, there was a wheel, run off a belt, presumably to lift a weight. And finally the third and simplest of these devices was clearly some sort of crucible or retort, blackened and pitted, with several pipes protruding from it.

Tannis stared at all this for a moment. The animals and these machines—together, the effect was bizarre. The animals, moving so contentedly around the manger, were as sentimental as a cheaply colored religious print, while the machines were like finely engraved illustrations in an old encyclopedia, their separate parts denoted *a* through *f*.

He went across and approached the machinery, realizing that this section of the cave made up a separate chamber; a rock wall, rising up toward the roof (though this was actually too high to see), sectioned it off. Against this wall was a large table, some metal shelves, and a litter of more commonplace tools, hammers, sledges, crowbars, a bucksaw. And also a generator. He could hear it running, and then he saw it, ingeniously enclosed by heavy padded baffles, like the sides and top of a box that didn't quite come together; presumably the gaps prevented overheating. He went over to it and looked inside. It was a gasoline-powered Yamaha generator, bigger than the one at the trailer, running very quietly. Beside it was a small electric panel with a series of switches. They weren't labeled in any way, but he moved one and heard a pump chug in some invisible recess of the cave; and then, as he twisted another, a string of lights came on around him: a line of bare bulbs along the back wall and two spotlights on a metal post about ten feet high just to the right of him.

Setting down his lamp and looking around, truly able to see for the first time, Tannis now recognized what this was: these strange devices were examples not of the Inquisition but of antiquated mining technology. More exactly, they were a "battery" of ore-dressing machines, the wheel-and-jaw device being a simple rock crusher, the tower a gravity stamp, and the crucible some sort of rendering retort. It could mean only one thing: somewhere, and fairly close, there was a mine.

Tannis stood there, staring.

For an instant he simply couldn't believe it—it was such a fantastic sight. But he reached out and touched the derrick and it was real enough, cold black iron. He almost laughed. He had to be mad, he thought; or somebody was. Suddenly the lines of the old song began going through his mind: *In a cavern in a canyon/Excavating for a mine/Dwelt a miner forty-niner/And his daughter Clementine*. Which, in an odd way, actually fitted the whole bizarre scene—the cave, the equipment, Vogel and Marianne—and also took him back to a boyish time when the fever of discovery might have been as intense as this, a time when you took dares and had heroes and laughed at girls, dug for buried treasure and cut up frogs to see inside. In fact, this discovery, so obviously the discovery of a closely held secret, infected him exactly that way, boyishly, cockily: Yes, by God, this was it, he'd done it. And he'd beaten them all, Benson and Rawson and those jerks from the FBI.

With this energy—in a fever, but determined to battle through it, and now finally, grimly certain that he would survive and triumph: that was the mood—he crossed over to the peculiar iron spinning wheel. He was right; in fact, it was a rock crusher. Proof: piled beside it were two boxes, like the boxes he'd seen on the burros' backs. He ripped them open. They were full of stones—quartz, quartz monzonite, rhyolites; he made quick identifications on the fly—chunks of rock about six or eight inches in diameter. He gave the machine a push; heavily, the wheel rotated, bringing the big iron jaw around and down through an iron hopper bolted to one side. He filled this up with the stones—it was not unlike the hopper for a meat grinder—then found a switch. He pressed it. The lights flickered darkly. A diesel engine fired. The whole device trembled. And then, slowly, the wheel began to turn, revolving with a crude laboriousness, a movement not quite modern—as if it should have been driven by steam—but perfectly in keeping with the nature of the place, like the Mills of the Gods. Just that implacably, the jaw swung around and ground down into the hopper, the wheel shuddering and almost stalling; and then it crunched through the rock and jerked around again. The noise grew deafening. Gray dust swirled up, and the sparks of iron striking stone flashed like lightning within a thundercloud. Tannis felt his throat go dry, the ground trembled beneath his feet. The rock, as it was crushed, fell through a screen into a collecting box below. Obediently, bending and lifting to the pounding rhythms of the machine, Tannis added more stone at the top, stone after stone until his hands were scratched and bleeding, but finally it was all reduced to gravel, pounds of it, stones ground down to the diameter of an inch.

He switched off the engine; his ears rang deafeningly in the silence, his body was soaked in sweat. But he scarcely paused. The collecting box had handles, like a wheelbarrow, and with a great grunt—it took all his strength—he trundled it across to the second big machine in the battery, the one that looked like a small oil derrick. In fact, this was a gravity stamp—unbelievably crude, but then it worked crudely. Fed through a gate at the bottom of the derrick, the gravel was heaped onto a number of heavy steel dies inside—in effect, a mortar; and when he turned on the engine, a wheel lifted an iron column, a pestle, weighing a thousand pounds or more up to the top and then let it drop. The earth shook as it smashed down against the dies. The shaft lifted high again. Tannis felt himself go dizzy; and as it slammed down once more, his breath escaped him. Staggering back he closed his eyes and choked against another cloud of dry, hard dust. But then a cool spray struck his face. Somewhere, automatically, a pump had come on, and a fine fountain spurted from the loose fitting around a hose—because the gravel, as it was pulverized, had to be continuously wetted by a stream of water, which washed it off the steel dies, through a fine screen and then down a narrow, sloped sluice box. The column rose and fell in a heavy, quick rhythm—it delivered perhaps seventy-five strokes a minute—with Tannis feeding in the gravel like a stoker feeding a fire, or like a revolutionary running a guillotine. The machine just didn't stop; and he, to keep up with it, couldn't stop either. An hour passed. Finally, just as he felt ready to drop, Tannis found that the collecting box of crushed stone was empty and he turned off the stamp and stood, gasping, in the silence.

Unhooking the pipe from the pump he splashed his face with water and took a long, cold drink. And rested, but only for five minutes; he timed it as carefully as a foreman. Then, summoning himself, he began prying up the dies at the base of the derrick with a crowbar; six of them, squeezed together in a metal box, rather like printer's type. They had been, he guessed, lightly coated with mercury; now they were thickly encrusted with a fine reddish grit. And from the upper section of the sluice box he withdrew a copper plate, rather like an old-fashioned film plate, which had also been coated with mercury and which was also encrusted with grit. He was astonished: there was so much of it. He looked about, knowing what he had to find, and found it at the back of the chamber, a rough worktable with shelves and tools. He took up a hammer and a chisel. This next task, he knew, really ought to have been done very carefully, so that the delicate coating of mercury on the dies and the plate would be scratched as little as possible; but that would be Vogel's problem, not his, and he hacked away roughly at the crust, chipping it off. Right to hand, for this was obviously where Vogel must have carried out these same operations, he next discovered a steel mortar and pestle and ground the little lumps and chips of the grit into a fine, bright dust. Now his eyes searched along the shelves, finding a tightly stoppered bottle. Mercury, of course, and like a sorcerer he poured out a thick silvery stream of it onto the ground-up grit. At once the dust began to separate, some of it sinking, but a good deal floating on the top as a scum. He dabbed this up, agitated the mixture, and repeated the process. Finally he poured off the last of the free mercury, leaving a sort of mud in the bottom of the mortar. With a wooden spoon he scooped this into a small canvas bag, which he then squeezed and twisted, wringing the mercury out of the mud and through the porous cloth, letting it drip back into the mortar. When all the mercury was squeezed out, he reversed the bag, and a blob of "amalgam"—the mercury, combined now with the metal that had been attracted to it—plopped onto the table. He formed this into a ball. Now only one step remained, and though he'd never done it before, he thought he knew how: after all, he had his degree in chemistry, however mundane such a qualification seemed in this strange place. So he carried his amalgam over to the retort, the last of Vogel's odd constructions. It was, in fact, the least outlandish, merely a small steel drum, slightly larger than a paint tin, which was suspended above an ordinary propane burner. In the bottom of it was a screw fitting with a metal gasket. He opened this, shoved the amalgam inside, then tightened it up again, taking the trouble to find a wrench, for he knew it had to be airtight. A pipe projected from the top of the drum, then bent at right angles to meet the ground. He found a bucket, filled it with water, then stuck the end of this pipe down into it.

After these preparations he then lit the burner, turning it up as high as he could, though actually the flame would not be very hot. It didn't have to be; that was the point. Mercury boils, and vaporizes, at an incredibly low temperature for a metal, less than 360 degrees Celsius; the equivalent value for silver being 2,212, copper 2,594, and for gold . . . for gold, it was almost 3,000 degrees. Thus the mercury in the amalgam would turn to gas, which would then flow through the bent pipe into the water, leaving solid metal behind.

Or that was the principle; in practice it took more than an hour to prove. Exhausted, almost oblivious to his peculiar surroundings—part dungeon, part workshop, part secret laboratory—Tannis waited. He dozed but couldn't sleep. He listened to the animals, the gas bubbling in the bucket. And tried to follow, into the shadows, the currents of air that dried his sweaty skin. How far did this cave go? When and how had Vogel found it? What had led him here? He let his mind drift along these questions, knowing he wouldn't find the answers, until he guessed that his alchemy was done; in any case, he could wait no longer. Rising, he turned off the burner, doused the retort with water, and, when it had cooled, unscrewed the fitting. He shook the drum. A lump fell out. It was somewhat larger than a marble, but smaller than a golf ball, and it was rather porous, like a clinker of ash or a piece of sponge toffee; and it had the dull, greasy color of dirty gold.

Gold.

As, of course, he'd guessed. "The ruling secret of all things." The secret behind all the others. Now he had it, in his hand, and he squeezed it in his hand; then, exhausted, closed his eyes and panted in the dark.

CHAPTER 6

With the gold in his hand Tannis fell into a swoon—that was the only word for it. It was as if he'd just finished with a woman. He fell forward in the same way, until his body was supported, wedged upright, against the iron frame of the gravity stamp. He blacked out, and his sleep was so deep that he couldn't have said whether it lasted for thirty seconds or an hour. He didn't dream. Gold is the stuff that dreams are made of, but this gold was real. This gold was as different from a dream as a boy's imagining of a woman is from the touch of flesh. In fact, when he opened his eyes, the dream was finally over: at last, the mesmerizing trance created by Vogel's strange arrival had lifted.

Or so Tannis felt as he blinked and looked about in the silence and the dust of this extraordinary chamber. He stretched behind him, stretching his aching back, and then lit one of his Luckies—as a way of telling himself that he'd returned to normalcy. Then, to underline this, as he quietly smoked and watched the animals around the manger—a manger, Christ!—he thought, I don't believe it, which seemed about as normal a statement as you could make.

Still, normal or not, everything had changed: everything had shifted. Tannis, recovering himself, had no doubt of this. Squeezing the little lump in his palm, he knew that it represented something truly fabulous. He imagined what his father would have thought of it. Gold ore is graded in grams per ton, and in the U.S. two grams is considered good, five or six would be extraordinary; whereas this was likely more than an ounce, thirty or forty grams at least: on a level with the original strike at Moodies in South Africa. If Vogel had actually discovered a commercial ore body of this richness, Tannis knew, it would be worth billions, literally, and even a small strike would be many millions.

Was it possible?

Yes, he supposed.

But not likely.

The great strikes in the Panamint had been silver lodes: the Cerro Gordo, Darwin, Greenwater, Skidoo. Still, there'd always been some gold, and there'd been a lot of it to the west of this place, near Randsburg. And everybody knew that somewhere between Tin Mountain and the Wingate Pass was a treasure cave, guarded by a balanced rock, that held the Paiutes' gold. Everybody, that is, except the anthropologists, who claimed the Paiutes had no use for gold at all. But what did they know? Old legends had proved out before, and in the end no one could deny what he was holding in his hand: for nothing in the world is more tangible than a nugget of gold. The fact that Vogel had discovered it was no doubt part of some crazy tale that only a fool would ever believe. Vogel the German; Buhler, a survivor of the camps; the last days of the war, the Reich in flames; a map folded across the heart of a dead GI. You could make up anything you wanted. Because the gold was real. And this fact, no matter how incredible, changed everything. It shifted everybody's motivation. Gold explained Buhler's trip from Germany, and gold explained why Vogel would have killed him. But what it didn't explain, what still eluded him, was the connection to himself and Harper. What had happened that Friday night? Buhler, Marianne, this cave, the gold. *Why tell him about it?*

The answer to this question seemed so remote, so unlikely ever to appear, that he could actually see an argument for going home and forgetting everything. He didn't see what he had to lose. Certainly, he had nothing to fear from the FBI. Their "scientific" method made one assumption: all history was written and foretold in the bible of their files. Everything was repetition. Being novel, Vogel's story became essentially inconceivable. So if he, Tannis, just walked away right now . . . But these thoughts in fact only flitted through his mind. He'd awoken from the dream, but it had carried him much too far. As he'd been thinking, he'd slipped down against the frame of the gravity stamp, so that he was leaning back against it, squatting on his heels. Now, in a quick, unconscious gesture, he rocked forward and reached behind him to touch the Colt, and what he thought revealed his true intention: no, there'd be no point in going back to his truck to get his rifle. Because . . .

In fact, he didn't have to be explicit about this conclusion: he knew that he'd try to find Vogel and that there was no point in shooting him, not from rifle range; he had to talk with him first, *find out what all this meant.* So the Colt would be all he'd need. Yes, he was going to find Vogel; he was going to take one of his donkeys or his horse and ride up into the hills and get him. Which meant he was going to go onto the base, because that's where Vogel was. It was the only place he could be: he'd come down this mountain and ridden back up it, and there was nothing else on the other side. But he'd have to move fast; a good general policy, but especially now, for when Tannis looked at his watch he saw it was already 3:00 a.m. And to delay, to delay meant waiting until tomorrow night, because he had to travel after dark. Apart from the obstacles posed by the terrain itself, though these were considerable, security in this wild part of the range would be light, at least on the ground. There were no fences, and the electronic sensors couldn't tell the difference between a horse and a deer, a man and a coyote. But once the sun came up, the air patrols would start. Which was why Vogel had turned himself right around: he would want to be under cover before daybreak. And that was why, Tannis concluded, he had to leave right now, if he was going to go at all.

But there was no doubt he was going to go. He knew, as few people could, the difficulties of such a trek, but at this point, having come so far, nothing could have kept him from making it. Besides, conditions could have been a good deal worse. Remarkably, he felt almost rested. And Vogel's magic cave provisioned him generously. There was water at the gravity stamp, and he found four tin canteens and a rubberized "Nauta" tank, to hold it. A tin box offered a selection of freeze-dried camping meals—Hardee's beans, Big Bill's Chili, "no-refrigerator" steak—as well as a Coleman camp stove; and he also came up with a blanket, a hat, an ax, and even an old pair of binoculars with a wanky lens; rather than going back to his truck to get his own, he'd take them. What he looked for but didn't find was a map; he would have to rely on his inner eye. As for transportation he had a choice: Vogel's stable consisted of eight donkeys, a horse, and a mule. Four of the donkeys were fresh, but he ignored them as being too small. The horse, the one Vogel had been riding when he'd arrived, was well settled in its straw, Vogel having taken a second, fresh animal for his return trip. This left the mule. He might have chosen it anyway. It would be slower than a horse but it had the surefootedness of a donkey, and that would be more valuable than speed going across the mountains. There was a saddle laid up near it, and he put this on; then the bridle, then tied on his load. Finally he got up himself. Now, perhaps inevitably, there was a small moment of comedy. With Tannis in the saddle the mule wouldn't budge. Tannis jerked the reins, prodded, kicked, but with no results. At length he got down. Immediately, without further prompting, moving neither in haste nor with reluctance, the animal stepped forward, leading him to the entrance of the cave: the mule was king, or at least prince, and would rule with an iron hand.

Which was more or less the way it worked. It was a trip that continued as it had begun: a little oddly, basing itself on luck and instinct, finding its direction along the path of least resistance. The mule was crucial; it knew where it was going, presumably because it had been there before with Vogel. In a sense there was really no difficulty tracking him; through these rocks, up these gaps, along these narrow ledges, there was only one path anyone could have taken; he gave the mule its head and let him find it. But this was easier on both of them because of some good luck. When they reached the entrance of the cave and the mule allowed Tannis to assume the saddle, he saw at once that the weather had changed. There was no wind and stars were out, glittering in a high, hard desert night. Looking up he made out a dozen constellations, Draco the Dragon, Lyra the Swan, Boötes the Ploughman, and Hercules the Kneeling Man. They lit his way, or at least the mule's; and since he didn't have a compass, they let him keep a rough check on their route. And almost as helpful as this light was the dropping of the wind. Otherwise, as they climbed steadily higher, he would have been very cold, for he had no jacket, just the blanket he'd found at the bottom of Vogel's food locker; as it was, the effort of keeping in the saddle was enough to warm him. In addition, the stillness helped the mule, for it allowed the scent of the horse ahead of him to linger on the trail: regularly, in any case, he stopped to enjoy a sniff.

But then the problem of following Vogel's track was never an issue. As Tannis well knew, you couldn't just ride over these hills, for they were at least four thousand feet high, so high that there was even green to tint their summits; if you were lucky enough to find a route, you kept to it. For Vogel this would have been especially true since, or so Tannis assumed, he normally traveled with his train of burdened donkeys. As they worked higher, Tannis even began to see how this route was put together, a winding ledge that carried to the tilt of a ravine, which was in turn a roundabout to work past a cliff. There were markers too, three boulders piled atop one another at every turn or ambiguity along the way, and at several points rocks had obviously been pushed in to fill a gap or levered out of the path. The mule took all this in his careful, picky stride. There was no sense in urging him to go faster; there was only one pace, and Tannis let the animal set it. Before a difficult passage, he'd stop dead and Tannis would get off, scrambling along behind until the going got easier. And at a certain point—a broad, flat ledge—the animal halted and looked about expectantly. Tannis, after a moment, got the point. From his hand he fed the mule (Prince, as he was calling him in his mind) a ration of Hardee's freeze-dried beans and then gave him water from his hat.

Taking a little water himself, he checked his watch. Already, at that first stop, it was twenty after four. They'd probably come less than a mile, but climbed fifteen hundred feet. Which left them that much more again. He got back in the saddle. The trail turned higher. In fact, in that pure, black air, with the heavens bright above him, his ascent seemed almost limitless, as if he were climbing some pop-song stairway to the stars: the distance from here to there was infinite, but the way was absolutely clear. And perhaps because he himself was up so high, because the darkness stretched out on either side, above him and beneath him, there was something magical about it, a levitation. But that was putting a good face on it. In fact, within half an hour every muscle and bone was aching with the jolting of the mule's cautious gait. His backside went numb. His legs were lead. His head began to throb. And yet, in the end, he made it: by half past five Tannis and Prince the Mule had reached the summit.

Summit was probably not quite the right word. Tannis wasn't exactly certain where he was, but he knew he'd been climbing through a pass, not over the hills directly, and finally they'd mounted a gentle crest. From the ridge at the top of it he could see that the land sloped sharply lower below. Reining in the mule he twisted around in the saddle. They were very high, high enough for scrub grass, piñon oaks, and pines, heavy, swaying shadows in the dark. This was not the desert but *sierra*, high ground. An eddying breeze, a complex movement of the air, washed across his face—a sensation you never felt lower down. There was even the smell of water, or the smell of something besides the odorless desiccated air itself, and the sweat smell of the mule. You never smelled sweat in the desert. But indeed he was very high above it. Five thousand feet, he knew; maybe six. And this pass was a low point, a V between the hills: to his left and right they rose up steeply, and beyond them other hills rose higher still, shadows against the sky. He wasn't sure, but it was possible that the slope looming immediately to the north of him was the Maturango Peak, the highest in the Argus Range—almost nine thousand feet above sea level—which meant that the hill on his left was Parkinson Peak, only a thousand feet lower. But in fact he wasn't sure: there were four major peaks in this area, like the knuckles on a fist, and he could have been one pass too high or low. Though this made no difference in terms of the decision facing him, because all of the hills sloped down toward an open rocky wasteland of flats, gulches, and canyons called the Etcheron Valley, the sort of terrain in which a man on horseback, viewed from a helicopter, would stand out like a beacon. For the moment, he admitted, Vogel had beaten him. It was possible, of course, that he was only a hundred yards ahead, holing up. But if he was heading toward the other side of the valley, he'd already be halfway across it and riding hard. There was no way to catch him, not before the sun came up. Already, behind him, the sky was lightening, and he could sense his own shape forming among the shadows. It would soon be dawn. In the old days of the Test Station, when all the planes were propeller driven, they'd actually kept tropical hours, flying their sorties before the desert heat could build, while there was still enough atmosphere for an airscrew to get a grip; and, following this tradition, China Lake still liked to get its planes up early. So Tannis knew he had to get under cover. Twitching the reins, he turned the mule along the ridge, which rose gently and then more steeply as it merged with the shoulder of the hill where it formed a rocky point: boulders, jammed together into a massive overhang, to which one old black oak was clinging. Looking out from this promontory, to his right, through a screen of ponderosa pines, he could see the trail again, a deep groove of shadow winding lower in the pass; looking straight out, there was nothing at all, merely the clear, hanging blackness of the void. The point jutted out so far from the hill, he guessed, that once the sun came up he'd be able to see right along the valley. As a vantage point he wouldn't do much better. He could wait here and see what happened at daybreak, then decide if he could take the risk of going on, while also keeping one eye on the trail in case Vogel doubled back.

So he dismounted. The mule, having suffered a change of routine, seemed a little confused but found some grass and began working his way back into the trees. Tannis let him go. Now that he was down, he felt exhausted, trembly. He drank some water, then made himself keep going, building a fire, piling up rocks to hide it, setting it going with grass and pinecones. Its flame tore a little hole in the night. He warmed himself and then mixed up some of Big Bill's Chili in an enamel cup, dutifully adding a packet of spices as it heated. A few minutes later, eaten with the tip of his Buck knife, it was edible, or at least he ate it. Finally, wrapping himself in the blanket, he leaned back against a rock and smoked a Lucky. Slowly he felt his fatigue spread through him, his body at last demanding nothing of itself. The soft night moved around him, the shadows and the wind. He closed his eyes.

But he didn't sleep. Instead he fell into an exhausted restlessness in which his mind wouldn't stop working. Images filled his brain: Vogel and the donkeys, illumined by the lamplight; the cave and its iron machines; Marianne's child playing in the dirt with her little dolls, her legs spread open; and gold in bars and nuggets, gold washing from the sand, gold spilled from iron ladles. But these images never quite ran together in a dream. Then a thought began going around and around in his mind, the idea that he wasn't following Vogel but was being *led* by Vogel. He was like a dog, chasing its own tail. Vogel was important only because he'd mentioned Harper's name; but the only proof that Harper was involved was that Vogel said he was. And could he even be certain of that? Was he absolutely sure that Vogel was his mystery caller? Round and round it went, an endless loop: and nonsensically he remembered what they always said about China Lake, that it was "outside the loop." Everywhere he looked, no matter where he faced, he saw the same thing, and no matter how far he walked, he ended up at his starting point. What was he doing here? It wasn't because of Vogel. Vogel was nothing to him. Vogel, as far as he could tell, was an old man who'd once lived near the base, moved away, and then come back—and perhaps had struck it rich. But that had nothing to do with him. Last Friday night he would have hung up if Vogel hadn't mentioned Harper's name. So Harper was the key, Harper, whose face he still couldn't recall. Everything followed from that. But

Harper, given what he'd discovered in the past few days, had nothing to do with this either. Harper had never been a spy, he had no connection to East Germany or to Buhler; and he had no connection to a cave in the desert. So why had Vogel mentioned him? How could Vogel have known that Harper even existed? It made sense only one way, or so he began to think, and perhaps, in his mind, he was feeling again the strange attraction that had drawn him into the picture of Vogel's arrival. For he now concluded that the only logical explanation was that he himself was Vogel, or that Vogel was a part of himself, split off. On Friday night he'd called himself. He'd pretended to be Vogel. Or he'd dreamed that the call had come. Which was absurd, but in some strange way, this solution satisfied him for a moment; and perhaps he actually did sleep, and dream, for all at once he jerked awake. His eyes opened. He was staring—out, out, into the blackness beyond the hill, where the night wind drifted. And now a single thought overwhelmed him: Get out. He should get up and go, forget it, walk away; and in his mind's eye he saw the particular brick in his patio where he had long ago buried a heavy iron cashbox filled (and periodically replenished) with first-class tickets to Rio, Hong Kong, Singapore, Bombay; tickets to Paris, Frankfurt, Rome; tickets on a dozen different airlines, Pan Am, Qantas, JAL, Air France, Lufthansa. They were as good as cash, and they could take him anywhere. He should fly away. And as his eyes came into focus and he looked out into the valley, where the last of the black, shining night hung in a great sheet toward the west, he wanted to lean out, rest himself upon the desert sky and glide away. Yet he knew he wouldn't, he couldn't. Something nameless held him back, and all he could do was lift his eyes to the stars, still shining, swinging high above Wild Horse Mesa, Louisiana Butte, the Darwin Wash. And he was still staring at them as he finally fell back and slept.

But Tannis could not have slept for very long. With the first smoky light of dawn he was awake again: chilled, stiff, tired. The restlessness of the night came back to him as a vague sense of unease that left him feeling cautious, though, no matter how he'd passed the night, that would have been the case: from this point on, he knew he'd have to move very carefully. He would either find Vogel today or he wouldn't at all, so he was close to the end, whatever that might be.

But at least caution was possible. For the first time he could really see where he was and where he was going. Drinking some water he looked around, discovering that he'd made his camp on a rocky ledge that nosed out from the hill, but then curved back on itself ever so slightly. He was actually very well hidden. Directly beneath this ledge the hill fell away sharply, merging into a long, rocky slope—ridges, ravines, one long drop for a cliff—that finally descended to the great valley below him. To his right, much more gently, the hillside led down through the pines and oaks to a broad, rocky ravine. This ravine formed the pass that had led Vogel across the mountain, and as he looked down Tannis could follow its course as it angled lower, doubled back on itself, petered out for a time among rocks, but finally emerged on the valley floor. His ledge, in fact, was a perfect vantage point. If he had had the time, he realized, his best plan would be to await Vogel's return, assuming he would return, and ambush him here. But he didn't have the time, or the food or the water, so somehow or other he was going to have to cross that valley, for Vogel certainly had to be on the other side.

Theoretically there was no reason this should have been very difficult. With Vogel's binoculars he looked across the valley to the gray line of hills and bluffs opposite. The prism or the lens on one side of the glasses was askew, so he had an oddly canted view, but it was clear enough to judge the distance and estimate the terrain. He guessed eight miles, even less; and the ground, though rough—rock, hardpan, gravel, pavement—was certainly passable. In fact it would take only a few hours to get to the far side. But it was more complicated than that. Vogel had gone to earth—since he'd found some kind of mine that was, in all likelihood, literally true. So he'd have to be tracked and then ferreted out. That could take a lot of time. And of course it compounded the second problem, the possibility of a patrol; out there, he thought, setting down the glasses, he'd be very easy to spot.

Should he take a chance? The temptation was to make a run. Vogel had to be close: in the desert, even if you're devious, you don't take the long way around. Looking down from his ledge he could see that the trail ran into the valley only half a mile to the north of him; almost certainly Vogel would have gone directly across the valley at that point, or only worked right or left a few degrees. Say ten degrees, Tannis thought, and panned with the glasses over the arc of territory on the other side. What he saw was mostly bluff, mesa, rugged *bajada*—tough going for a horse. But there were several ravines; they would either run through the hills or dead-end in a canyon. In any case, Vogel must have gone up one of them; it was just a question of tracking him. And if worse came to worst Tannis could simply work his way across the mouth of each ravine in turn till he hit his trail. He would be exposing himself, of course, especially from the air, but once he was across the flats of the valley he'd find some cover. Anyway, the security patrols tended to concentrate on the perimeter.

These were all arguments to leave at once, but in fact Tannis put down the glasses and didn't move. Because, though tempting, he knew he mustn't. Because there'd be not only the regular patrols, there'd be special patrols. Buhler's murder and the investigation would ensure that. *After consultation with law enforcement agencies and NIS, helicopter perimeter patrols were flown on an accelerated basis.* Yes, he thought, they'd step up the patrols because it was the simplest way to cover themselves, show that they were doing something. So he went back into the trees, gave Prince some water, and tethered him under the biggest of the pin oaks; then he found a niche for himself farther out on the ledge.

He waited.

Forty-three minutes later he heard the helicopter.

It was behind him, back up over the higher hills, the beat of its rotor reverberating down the slope, fading away as it dropped down into a ravine, then thumping closer. But actually it was not very close at all, for sound played tricks in the hills. When he finally saw the flash of it, it was a good mile off, tilting in a turn that carried it over the valley. As it climbed he saw its white navy markings—it was an SH-2 Seasprite, the standard navy helicopter. Dipping down, it headed up a ravine, back into the hills, and quickly disappeared. But Tannis got right down, tucking himself in behind a rock, for they would certainly have cameras on board and probably infrared sensors; the hot surface of the rock would mask him. Three or four minutes passed, but in the end it wasn't even close, for they passed behind him, higher up the slope, and all he heard was the whine of the turbines and the heavy thumping of the rotors. Then that was gone, suddenly; again, it must have dropped right down below some height of land. Cautiously Tannis stuck his head up. But there was nothing to see, and though, after a moment, the sound of its engines came drifting back to him as the helicopter leapfrogged among the hills and ravines, this gradually dwindled as its search pattern carried it away, higher into the hills, to the east. He knew just what they were doing: flying along the perimeter, keeping the boundary hard to starboard. And they weren't looking for anything in particular, he thought; they were merely filling in a form, writing a memo. Above all, since they were keeping so close to the perimeter, they didn't suspect that anyone was *inside* the base at all.

Or at least that was his deduction, and now he knew he had to run the chance of being wrong. There was a chance the helicopter could double back on its course, but he might have to wait hours before he could be absolutely sure it had gone, and he couldn't afford that. He could delay no longer. Running back to the mule he threw on its saddle, and before the animal knew what was happening it was being led down the hill, back through the pines, to Vogel's trail. And then he headed straight down it, not pausing at all; first riding the mule; then, when it grew too steep, getting off and leading him, tugging him on, picking his way over the rocks and through the small stands of stiff, barbed pines. In some ways going downhill was more difficult than the climb had been; but now he could see, and that made all the difference. The trail followed the run of the land, and at every ambiguity—should he turn this way or that?—he looked for one of Vogel's discreet markers, and always found it. Hawing and hollering, Prince protested, setting his ears back and digging in his heels, but on this downslope Tannis had all the advantage and just jerked him ahead. To begin, they were under cover, the oaks and pines hiding them in a camouflage pattern, the steep banks of the ravine pitching dark angles of shadow he moved between. But increasingly, as they moved lower, they came into the open. The trees gave way to scrub and brush, and the course of the ravine was lost in a broad spill of boulders and rock. And soon the hot, dusty air of the desert, moving up to them, hardened the light of the early morning sun. Finally, blinking in its brilliance, he found himself on the level, at the desert's edge.

He reined in. A little ahead, like a lighthouse marking this arid shore, was a great boulder, fissured, as if by lightning, and he urged the mule forward into its shadow. It was the last cover for miles. Immediately ahead of him, eking out the last shade of the hills, was a hummocky stretch of sagebrush and creosote; but then the flats began, cracked, crushed, silent, still—a single gray image filling the eye, then endlessly repeating itself. It was almost hypnotic, exhausting even to look at; it seemed to take an effort of his will to lift his eyes to the dark line along the horizon where the land lifted again, forming the hills and buttes where Vogel had lost himself. Narrowing his eyes he contemplated this vista and reviewed his earlier calculations. The distance was actually not that great. The mule was fresh. If he rode him hard, he could be across that stretch in an hour. But of course he couldn't ride him hard. Where had Vogel gone? From this point that question would be harder to answer. The mule might know the way, but that meant keeping to *his* pace, which would be leisurely. He doubted if there would be any markers; even if Vogel usually came through here at night, there would be enough light to see his way, and he could use a compass. So, Tannis considered, he would have to track him. That wouldn't be impossible or even difficult if he had a little luck, but it would be slow. Two hours. Three. During which time he and the mule were going to stand out like a splash of paint.

It was this thought, consciously, that made him hesitate; but in truth it was the anxiety of the night returning. As his eyes searched the sky—the perfect, immaculate blue of some surrealist painter: dotted with three white clouds, as puffy as a child's—he again had the feeling he'd missed something crucial, right under his nose. It was all so obvious. But he couldn't see what it was. He'd forgotten something; in a moment, he was going to remember and say *of course*. And again a voice told him to go back, to get out while he could. Vogel, like an alchemist, was leading him on, as he'd lured him down the Trona airport road, but how could he turn back now? Shading his eyes he stared into the distance, but if he was searching for a sign that would give him permission to flee, what he saw was exactly the opposite. For a bright eye now winked in the ether—a quick flash, many miles to his left, low on the western horizon. He knew at once it was a jet; it disappeared, but his eyes moved instinctively along its trajectory and picked it up a moment later. It must have just rotated off Armitage Field, and now it was circling, gaining height. He felt behind him for Vogel's glasses. But even before he got them up, the plane was banking, and he caught the profile of its high, swept-back wings, and then, as it came toward him, the nose-intake of its engine grinned like a shark. So he knew it was an F-8, a Crusader. It was an old plane; it went back almost as far as he did. "The Last of the Gunfighters," it was called, and in 1957 John Glenn used one to make the first supersonic flight across North America. These planes were no longer operational, but a few still survived here, for the weapons center used them as test-bed aircraft. Which was the point. For there was no way the range safety officer would let it fly a test with a helicopter drifting around in the airspace. So there was absolutely nothing to stop him, and as the rumbling backwash of the big Pratt & Whitney turbojets reached him, Tannis was already geeing the mule onto the desert.

So Tannis felt disquiet, but in no way did it mar his efficiency. He'd tracked everything from jeeps to coyotes across this desert and he knew what he was doing. He let Prince do the work, Prince and his own sharp eyes: picking out the flash of a hoof against the hard clay, following the flight of a crow a mile ahead till it lighted on a spill of manure. And once he got down, and crouched, and scanned the horizon, picking out the half-buried body of a Firebee drone: one of the old Sidewinder targets, there were hundreds scattered through this desert, this one nosed in almost gently, its red paint scoured away by thirty years of wind so that now, catching the sun, it flashed like a beacon. Which was just what it was, a way point, for when they rode up to it the scuffing of Vogel's tracks was all through the sand. He'd turned here. Prince, it seemed, even remembered the spot, for he put his nose down like a hound and trotted ahead. So it wasn't that hard, and on the far side it became even easier, for they struck a mile of good clear prints across badlands where the salt lay like a crust on the earth. By that point he was getting close. He used the glasses. Ahead was the line of bluffs, hills like lumps of gray clay that had puddled there and dried rock hard, cracking along their margin. These fissures were ravines, or canyons. Three lay more or less opposite him, the bluffs crumbling down into three stubby points like the fingers of a truncated hand. Vogel, he assumed, was up one of them, though that was not quite certain. It was just possible that one of the ravines led through these bluffs to the valley and hills on the other side: these formed the Coso Range, and the Coso Diggings had been a famous silver lode. There were hundreds of mines back there, and when the navy had come here they'd had to buy out over a thousand claims, including that claim of his father's. Yet, Tannis considered, if Vogel was heading that way he'd taken the long way around; it would have been far simpler to work his way down from the northern perimeter of the base, from Darwin, and he would have been in the hills all the way, instead of this dangerous open area. No, he was sure of it: Vogel was near, dead ahead, up one of those ravines.

Tannis moved forward. The sun was now higher in the sky; he and the mule carved a black shadow on the smooth gray ground—they made that much of an impression—and as he drew closer to the bluffs he became more clearly a figure in the landscape, dwarfed by their size, but moving more clearly now before their stillness and immobility. It was a trick of his mind; but Prince's steps seemed louder and the muscles of his shoulders more defined, working in all their intricate connection beneath his glistening coat. Yet the sky was that same smooth blue and the three clouds hadn't moved, nor, it seemed, in relation to them, had he advanced an inch. But step by step he drew nearer to the hills ahead, Vogel's tracks swinging slightly to one side, then turning more abruptly, and almost certainly eliminating the most eastern of the three ravines. That left only two. These formed a natural divide, and perhaps a quarter mile before them the ground changed, rising in a slope of rock and gravel, the mound of silt left by the rivers that had once flowed down from their channels. Here Vogel's tracks were lost—the ground was stony and strewn with boulders—but Tannis merely loosened the reins and let the mule find its own way. He moved left, again decisively rejecting the opening to the east. The slope steepened, enough that he began to reach and dig with his forefeet. Almost imperceptibly the mouth of the ravine now began to swallow them up, although, to begin, it was not very impressive, forming a broad, indistinct opening with rather gentle banks that rose no more than thirty feet. It seemed to go nowhere, there seemed nowhere it could go to. Up ahead, apparently, the side slopes did rise much higher but curved around, dead-ending in a U-shaped canyon. But when he reached that point, Tannis saw that the ravine actually turned sharply here, constricting through a pass, beyond which it opened up again. He hesitated, then went ahead. And as soon as he was through the pass, he saw that the ravine went on, much narrower, with steeper, higher banks on both sides, banks sixty or eighty feet high, so high and steep that the sun hit only the upper part of the slope, the floor of the ravine lying in cool, brown shade. He rode into this for fifty yards and then realized he was trapped.

He drew up the mule. He didn't move. He looked around, and there was no doubt that he was in a trap, a trap, he realized, that was at least two thousand years old. Taking out Vogel's glasses he scanned the cliffs on either side of him, and everywhere he could see the petroglyphs, hundreds of them, thousands, pecked into the surface of every rock: stylized figures of men, sheep, and dogs; and abstractions, shields blazoned with arms, and stick men like dream men, three-toed, phallic, horned, and many-eyed. And as his glasses moved up toward the rimrock he saw three dummy hunters, big stones balanced one atop the other to make a man, like a snowman or a scarecrow. He knew exactly what they represented, for he'd personally discovered many of these sites. There were hundreds of them scattered all through the hills and canyons of the base. They had been made by an unknown race of Indians, Indians who had disappeared long before historical Indians arrived in this part of the desert. They were the "ancients"; they had hunted with spear throwers, called *atlatls*, even before the bow and arrow, and their quarry had been the bighorn sheep whose images were the chief features of the petroglyphs, drawn with big curved horns and leaping legs. Modern Indians had assumed these representations were religious, depictions of gods or spirits, but some of the scientists at NOTS, taking up the puzzle of their meaning as a hobby, had recognized them for what they were: equations, calculations, descriptions; they'd been designed to draw the sheep up into the canyons and gorges where they were then killed from ambush, the hunters hiding in stone blinds along the canyon walls. As science it had been superb, perfectly predictive, capable of replication down the generations; in fact, to the point where the sheep had been hunted to extinction, and the hunters had disappeared themselves. These strange markings were their only surviving trace, though from them Tannis drew his own particular deductions. Most important: he was not in a ravine, a traverse through these hills, but a canyon, a dead end, with no way out except the way he'd come. So Vogel was almost certainly up ahead. Tannis could even guess that he'd be in a cave, one of the ancients' occupation sites, and might well have him under observation now. He did not quite feel this. He didn't exactly have that sense of someone watching. But he still didn't like it.

Above all, he didn't like his exposed position up on the mule, so he slipped quickly down from the saddle and stepped back, keeping Prince between him and what lay ahead. With a prod Tannis got him walking. After twenty yards the rocky ground suddenly ended in a stretch of sand, a "sand tank" it was called. The wild burros and horses that still roamed this section of the desert would come here and paw down into the soft ground, for there'd be water there for much of the year; and running up its length, he saw the tracks of Vogel's horse, walking, apparently in no hurry. He looked up and around. At this point the walls of the canyon were very high, and only the western rim still caught the sun. Beyond it everything was backlit, and he knew that someone could be hiding there and he wouldn't see him—but then how would Vogel get up there? In any case, he had to go on or turn around; there was simply no other choice. So he gave the mule another dig. Ahead, the canyon grew even narrower; it was possible to imagine the sheep milling here in panic, and on both the right and left he could see the old hunting blinds. They were built higher up on the slopes, so the hunters would be shooting down, rings of rocks piled on top of one another, like fossilized nests or children's snow forts. They were only a few feet high, just high enough to hide a crouching man, and he stood a moment, surveying each in turn, which was the reason he now saw that one of the blinds was different; it had fallen in. This could have had no importance—especially, it would have been impossible for anyone to hide there—but just because it stuck out and caught his attention he walked up to Prince's head, took the reins, and suddenly urged him, hard, up the slope toward it.

So that was chance, in other words an accident; he had no intention, merely an instinct to disrupt the regularity of the pattern he was making as he worked up the canyon. But when he got up there, he was glad he'd done it; now *he* was looking down, and it was an advantage. With the glasses he could actually see Vogel's tracks winding up the canyon and could see, as well, that another fifty yards along they made a second sharp turn. And he decided he would not go beyond that point, not on the mule, but would make a reconnaissance on foot.

Coming to that decision he went over to Prince and fetched his canteen, taking a drink from it as he rested one foot up on the stones of the hunting blind, and now noticed it again. The blind, made up of chunks of basalt, had collapsed in on itself, though, he realized, in a rather orderly way, the walls having fallen into a conical heap. So it was not just a pile of rocks, and as it occurred to him how curious this was—for what could have disturbed these stones at all, let alone have rearranged them in such a regular way?—he saw a flash in the sand beside him. Bending down he picked up a dime, a shiny, thin American dime with Roosevelt on one side, the Torch of Liberty on the other. *In God We Trust*, 1959. He held it up between his fingers, twisting it to catch the light. 1959. That was so close to the crucial year. Harper's year . . . though of course it could have been dropped at any time since that date. But as he stepped back and looked down at the rocks he realized that it hadn't been dropped at all. He pulled at the stones, pushing them aside, and almost instantly, for there were really not that many, realized what he was going to find. The hunting blind had been transformed into a cairn; beneath the rocks were bones, and then more bones, a pile of old bones: old bones burned black. A human skeleton, in fact. The skull was smashed, but the long bones of the legs, and the flutes of the pelvis, were unmistakable. The ribs had separated from the chest and from each other, but lay neatly nested, a progression of curves, and at the very bottom, lying on the sand, he saw a hand. Palm down. Black and desiccated. But delicate. Perfect. Like an old black lady's hand.

He stepped back. For one moment he didn't move. That seemed very necessary. But then it was impossible not to look around, at the dead signs pecked into the rocks, at the dead stone hunters perched high up the slope, at the still, quiet course of the canyon leading to that turn ahead. His breath seemed poised inside his chest: everything hung in balance. For now Tannis certainly knew that he had been trapped, led on, seduced, not discovering but revealing: brilliantly deducing nothing more than himself. He had been led up here as surely as those long-ago sheep had been. Yet now, at the last minute, there was nothing to do but brazen it out. He understood nothing. Why, a quarter century before Buhler, had another man been killed, here, in this desert, fifty yards from Vogel's track? And who was it? And once again, what did it have to do with Harper? He had no answers to any of these questions; all he had left was his will, the peculiar power of its inertia: bluff, *I dare you*. And so, though it was insane, he stepped over to Prince and swung up in the saddle, exposed, and doubly exposed, and then rode him quite calmly down the slope and turned toward that second turn. He stared that way, toward it. His eyes fixed on it. And something in his vision . . . So often, it was a question of his vision, not simply what he saw, but how he saw it, that summoned Tannis more intensely to himself: the bright, small image through the wrong end of the telescope; a shaft of sunlight bent through still, clear water; or nothing more than a polished windowpane. But now Tannis could see just that clearly as he stared toward the turn of the ravine. Yet he must have had eyes in the back of his head as well. This was the sequence: he ducked, down and to his right; a bullet passed behind his neck; and then the mule reared as the roar of the shot exploded down that canyon.

From behind him.

And he jerked the mule around.

He stared, and saw forty yards back—he must have walked right by him—a man with a rifle in his hands. He was tall and thin, a thin old man in a wide straw hat. Standing in one of the hunting blinds.

"Jack . . ."

It was all he said. But there was something about the voice. But then he was bringing the rifle up. He aimed. Now Tannis had to die. There was simply no other choice, for any man who takes the trouble to buy a gun will learn to use it well enough to make that simple shot—a man-size target at under fifty yards. And yet it never occurred to Tannis that he was going to die; now that this moment had arrived, he feared it, feared the next two seconds, no more, say, than he would have feared taking a sip of coffee. But it was clear that he had no salvation. Except for God. And it was God, in fact, who did save him, God from a machine, deus ex machina, literally, as if Tannis had summoned him. For at that moment the F-8 he'd seen earlier came flying up the canyon. Probably it had no business being there. It was too old a plane, and too heavy, to go stunting in, but perhaps the pilot, hiding below the level of the radars, was playing hooky, enjoying himself for once, making this low-level pass at 400 miles an hour just for the hell of it, a proof of his own fine skill. And he flew it so cleanly, came over Vogel so directly from behind, that Vogel never heard it coming, the sound of the engine roaring a hundred yards behind. All at once it was simply there, a great brutish presence, the unpainted hull polished bright. Then it was on top of him, that pure sound of power, that sound unto itself. It knocked Vogel flat. He fired but had no idea where the bullet went. And then the plane was over the mule and Tannis, and the mule went mad, bolting, charging down the canyon the way he'd come, up to Vogel and then past him. And by that time, Tannis had his big Colt out and was firing back behind him with no chance of hitting anything but keeping Vogel's head down. Which he must have done. And then it was too late. Jack was gone. Jack was long gone, Jack was once upon a time. And at long last, he truly did know everything.

PART II

Target and Background

The sources of infrared radiation may be natural or man made, but a more useful classification to the worker in infrared technology is that of target and background. A target is an object which is to be detected, located or identified by means of infrared techniques. A background is any distribution or pattern of radiant flux external to the observing equipment which is capable of interfering with this process. An object may thus at one time be a target and at another be part of the background, depending on the intent of the observer. . . . Summing up, it may be said that "One man's target is another man's background."

—HOLTER, NUDLEMAN, SUITS, WOLFE & ZISSIS,
Fundamentals of Infrared Technology

CHAPTER 7

David Harper looked across the room, where Anne Brahe was knitting a sweater for Derek, her ten-year-old son. She worked quickly, head down, unaware that he was looking at her.

They were in her cottage, which lay on the outskirts of Kirkcudbright, in the southwest of Scotland, and were sitting on either side of a small stone fireplace. A low mahogany table lay between them. On David's side the table had been cleared away so he could repair an Aaton 16mm cine camera, while on Anne's there was a straw basket holding two balls of navy wool; beside this a pattern booklet was held open to her page with an empty coffee mug.

They'd been working busily for about an hour, occasionally talking, though not about anything of great importance.

Both had lights drawn near them and sat in the brightness of them, but the rest of the low, crouched room was darkly shadowed; shadows that lay across the roughly plastered walls and were highlighted, above the mantelpiece, by the reflection from a row of framed photographs. The images were lost in the dark, but each knew what they were: a polar bear, a hummingbird, a leopard leaping. It was after midnight. The mood was subdued and peaceful. Anne's needles clicked. From time to time there was the creak of springs as they shifted in their places—Anne was sitting on an ancient chesterfield, David in an enormous, sagging armchair—and sometimes a gust, blown here all the way from the Solway Firth, pressed against the window glass.

David watched her a moment longer and then took up the last piece of the camera housing and screwed it into place. When he was finished he hefted the camera in his hand, then set it down. And then he fitted his screwdriver back together—he'd been using one of those five-in-one screwdrivers, each tool sliding into the handle of the next larger. Tightening the cap over the last, he laid it on the table. This made a little sound and Anne glanced up. "Finished?"

"As much as I can do."

"Will it work, do you think?"

"Probably. But I have another camera, anyway."

She'd knitted on, as she'd spoken; now her hands rested in her lap and she did look at him, seeing him quickly, in all his familiarity, only noticing, as she always did, his strong mouth, beautiful but very masculine. Now the bright light and shadow sculpted it. "Didn't your father fix cameras?" she asked.

David nodded. But he felt awkward talking—he was suddenly aware of this. "That's right," he said. "In the RAF. Reconnaissance cameras—great big things. If he'd been doing this, he'd have been finished half an hour ago."

"So photography comes naturally to you. When you think about it."

"In a way. But I was never very interested as a boy. It was the planes—I wanted to be a pilot, and then I thought I might be an aircraft mechanic. If I hadn't gone to university, I suppose I might have done that."

"Except you *did* go."

"Right. So now I'm an amateur mechanic."

She smiled, and then looked down to her work again. She'd been determined to finish the first sleeve, at least down to the cuff, before going to bed. Working on, she was silent a moment, but then she laid her hands in her lap and looked up again. "I don't suppose many children get to be what they want to be when they grow up. Not nowadays. Derek wanted to be an explorer, like Scott. Then it was a sea captain. But of course he'll be steered away from all that and end up pushing paper."

"Except there are ship's captains. And ballerinas all start out as little girls. So I suppose some do."

"Maybe that's one of the great divisions, then. Those who do, and those who don't."

He didn't reply, and she went on knitting. He'd been withdrawing, unnoticed, into himself as they talked; and now, leaning back, he moved farther into the shadows, away from the lamp. When he moved—because he moved—a current passed through the room, flowing through the darkness from the front of the room, the dark windows, and spilling in a bright cataract where she sat; and then it pooled, darkly, all around him. He watched her quietly from within this. His gaze, under his dark, fine eyebrows, was very steady and direct—all he wanted was to look at her. He could see her very clearly; she could have been sitting in the sun, perhaps just having come out of the water; she had that kind of brightness. She was wearing a white terry cloth dressing gown over a blue cotton nightdress that covered her from throat to ankle, down to the straw sandals on her feet. Earlier she'd washed her hair; almost dry, it lay in broad, smooth strands, combed back flat across her head, golden, but full of coppery highlights. In the same way, her very white skin seemed dusted with copper and gold, and her full, dark lips were perfectly outlined by a paler, silver line. He'd once seen a Viking artifact, an iron buckle, outlined with a silver filigree; and he thought of that. She had a windswept, northern, Viking beauty. There was nothing luxurious or exotic about it. It was a plain beauty; at thirty-six she still had the beauty of a schoolgirl. And the pleasure in looking at her, simply looking at her, was rather like the pleasure of a boy looking across a schoolroom at a girl who has no idea he is watching. All absorbed, she worked the intricate movements of the needles. He watched her hands. They weren't elegant, in the usual way; she had blunt, bony fingers, with slightly prominent knuckles; at once a memory came to him, trailing its particular history and context, its whys and wherefores, but he didn't trouble to hold this in his mind. All he wanted was the image of her. She'd waded out into a shallow, slow-moving stream and was kneeling on a rock, washing out a sweater. Her blue jeans were wet and dark to the knees where she'd waded, and the white shirt she was wearing pulled up, as she bent forward, revealing her brown back, the knuckles of her spine. Her hair had fallen forward and he couldn't see her face; but her hands, closed in childish fists, worked the fabric of the sweater back and forth, back and forth . . .

His cock thickened, uncurling and pressing against his belly. But he didn't move. For a moment he felt a wonderful, deep, full satisfaction; but then dread swept across him—all his limbs were light, his blood raced, anxiety raced through him—he was afraid; not of her, exactly, but more obscurely, as if he was afraid of himself, as if he really was a schoolboy again, as if the original innocence of his desire had been condemned by some perverse trial or process, as a different, darker impulse. What was he going to do? Would he do it? In the darkness he couldn't see himself; and what would she see? That was unclear, but in her eyes, rising out of the darkness, he would certainly be transformed, monstrous or angelic. In a way, because of this, he really was thrown back to the very first time; his circumstances now were not so different. He felt his throat dry and constrict, choking on the words he couldn't say. This was precisely the difficulty; he was virtually compelled to be as tongue-tied as a schoolboy. The whole history of their relationship and his particular status in that house—they'd been friends for so long; he'd been friends with her dead husband; he was a kind of uncle to her son—made words impossible. Anything he might have said and that she might have answered would have tried to hedge the risk and preserve what, he knew, could only be a memory. If he did it. There could be no going back. He suddenly ached, in mourning for those memories, thinking of that same afternoon when she'd turned in the doorway and called back to him, asking if he wanted anything in town. The easy familiarity of her voice was something he would never hear again, or not in that way. They'd been so close, but their very closeness defined an unbridgeable gap; it could only be leapt over. So he waited, still in the dark. And at length his anxiety passed off. In its wake came weakness, trembling. And he was soft. Almost he reproached himself, felt a childish fury, a bloody frustration. But like an old, bad habit he knew that this was also a reflection of the past, to be ignored. So he just sat there and kept looking at her, seeing her so absorbed, watching her face, her lovely hands, her breasts, all in the light, and then he was hard again and he rose and went across the dark space between them and sat by her.

He sat close enough to her that she looked up, startled, her dark lips parting with surprise. He kissed her at once; he gave her no chance to conquer her confusion. Her lips spread softly under his as his mouth pressed down. It was a long, slow kiss, and it said everything; from that moment, there could be no doubt. But the moment he let her go, he was kissing her again, very gently, searching delicately, until he caught the swell of her upper lip in his and softly closed around it, gently tugging, until it slipped away, slid slowly back. And then he let her go again, and this time he leaned away.

Releasing her, he felt released himself. Relief passed through him, a soft, airy rush, like a breeze passing across his skin. He was all gone. He could have slept. He was like a gambler in the instant before the dice turn up, eyes closed before his fate. Now it was up to her. But not quite. She looked away, she turned away. It was the moment when she would say no, or at least consider it. He could see the doubt in her eyes, and fear. And as he watched, he watched the light die in her eyes and her skin go slack; now the light did not glow off her skin. He could see her slipping away from him, but quite calmly, whether to ease her passing or bring her back was, for an instant, not quite clear, his hand lifted to her face, to her cheek, and his thumb stroked up until it nestled in the soft hollow beneath her ear; and with this slight purchase, he worked against the tension of her body until it broke. She murmured, a small assenting sound deep within her breast, as if speaking to herself, and then she came the other way, passed over to him and was in his arms, her mouth turned up, his breath breathing life back into her.

How long had she been waiting? Only later would he wonder when she'd last had a man. Her mouth was so tender, awkward, a child's. This was something she no longer knew, or had forgotten; her lips turned on his, caught some past moment of her life and brought it back, gladness, a happy morning, her husband, kisses for her child, a kiss good night. In the same way, when he opened her dressing gown, her breasts seemed to surprise her with immodesty, swollen even before his hand closed on them; and when his fingers found her nipples, she gasped, again as if surprised, then groaned, remembering, finding what she felt again. Drawing the long nightdress over her head, she seemed to offer the whole history of her beauty; she was a child, she was a little girl; and when she emerged and shook out her hair—a movement so unconscious, quick, and intimate that he might not have been there—he lost his breath, she was so beautiful. She was a beautiful woman. Her hair shone about her face, her freckled skin sparkled in the light. Leaning back, her breasts pressed up, she gave him a prideful look, flushing with pleasure, like a girl who's secretly proud that her breasts are bigger than the other girls'. That was her secret. She loved her tits. Well, he showed her how lovely they really were. He kissed them, and she sighed with every kiss. Playing with her nipples, he sucked them out and pressed them back, while down there his fingers slipped into her and made her happy another way. She was groaning now. Yet she caught herself. She pressed him off her—her fingers clawed against his chest and held him back; and for a moment, almost still, their heads nodded together, cheek to cheek. Then she pushed him back a little farther until he was half standing, half kneeling on the chesterfield. His cock rode up between his thighs and she looked down. She wanted to look at it. So she did. Then she reached down and took it in her hand, gripping it firmly, but rather clumsily, as if wishing to reassure herself that it was real, and truly there. She held him like this for a moment, then eased him back a little more. And when she looked up at him now with her fine blue eyes, she was all herself, grown up, caught up, right up to date; with him, accepting the consequences of what had happened. She knew who she was, and he. Like a proof of this, she now spoke for the first time, whispering his name, David, David, and then, almost casually, like an animal drinking, she slipped her mouth down over him. He scarcely felt this, she was so very gentle, touching but not touching, licking but as lightly as the air, soft, considerate, coaxing, assuring and reassuring, and only slowly squeezing down, first with her lips and then reaching down more deeply, tightening, catching him up but almost as quickly letting him go, before she finally sank down on him. Then he pressed into her, he sank into the back of her throat, he gave himself over to her. He groaned. And this was what she wanted. She whimpered in response, a little sound of her own desire; a small, fearful cry that lost itself in a murmur of delight, as if again something was lost but had now been found. She licked it. She sucked it. And then her mouth went wild. He almost lost control, but a sweet, light coolness was spreading over him; her mouth was like a spring, welling up from some dark secret source, a refreshment for both of them: bathing him even as he burned, cooling her so she could hold his heat. Finally, as she let him go, her lips were glistening: as simply as a child, she wiped her hand across them. Then she pushed her hair back—with a hand on each side of her face she pushed her hair and tossed her head back—and then she rolled away, on her back, on the chesterfield, her face turning to one side upon a cushion. He was still half dressed. Calmly he removed his clothes and then stood there, his swollen cock jutting out toward her. She spread her legs, as he kneeled in front of her, one foot still resting on the floor. He went up in her with a single stroke. She smiled, and he might have laughed, it was so easy. Pulling him down, she pressed his face against her cheek. He began to move, all of him, all the way, each time: that was what she wanted, this was where she wanted him, and with a mischievous little tightening, she held him there. He groaned and she let him go, but at once took him back again. He was hers. She'd waited so long, she certainly wasn't going to let him get away. Back and forth they went, playing a game of tag, of hide-and-seek, and in the end she wiggled her ass for him and reached up and gave him a friendly kiss, so sweet a kiss that he went right up her, all the way, sighing as he got there. Then, all stretched out inside her, he rested, with his head upon her breasts.

She was folded around him, enclosed around him, she cuddled him up there. He waited in a deep, still darkness. And then he rose up. Slowly, he took it out. Then he put it in again. And then he fucked her, each stroke as smooth and clean as silky brushstrokes through her hair, and she was lost, she was waiting for him, everything was waiting for him, and all he had to do was take it, go ahead. He reached out, then reached out farther. And then he had her. But precisely then he could feel himself begin to come, the start of it, a deep, heavy thickening behind his balls: the pressure of it. In an instant, a flash, something passed over him. For an instant he could see himself; he could see his face. He knew what he was doing. He was making love to Anne Brahe, in her small, dark Scottish cottage. He thought of Axel, her dead husband and his old friend. And he knew his own name was David Harper. Once upon a time . . . once upon a time: his whole story hung there in that instant, who he was, his skills, tastes, habits, knowledge. He was himself, he was in control, and he clamped down then, he stopped himself, and a fierce, determined, deadened potency spread up his cock. He took a sly turn inside himself. He could go for hours. He was as hard as iron. Steel. Coming out of her, he was as bright as a knife about to sheath itself. Yet this all happened in an instant. And she felt it, she understood. But didn't panic. "Please, David," she said, in a voice that was absolutely calm, quite normal. "Oh, please," she called, in a voice that simply asked for what she wanted. Which, miraculously, was only what he wished to give. A feeling passed through him, at once grave and light; like forgiveness. And he flung caution to the winds, let something go, and she did too, rocking back, taking him all down in her, shaking him to his very root and crying out within his arms, and with a last deep, tender stroke he lost himself inside her.

Later, in her bed, they made love again, quietly, lying side by side, for she was thinking of her son, sleeping in the loft above. And then they slept. And then awoke. They lay together. He told her how, and when; he told her why, as far as he understood. She told him that she hadn't known, but must have. With the cool night around their skins they talked until the sun came up, the present hardly long enough to hold what they had to say. As for the past, it certainly seemed dead and gone, as far as Harper was concerned; there was no way it could rise up again. He had survived, he had come so far, he was still alive, and never thought that coincidence, the arbitrary power of the world *out there*, could touch him; so he didn't think, or speak at all, of the labyrinth of history that led back, through him, to China Lake.

CHAPTER 8

But half the coincidence, even if David didn't know it, had already arrived. What had happened between himself and Anne was now irrevocable, and its loss, implicitly, would be catastrophic. This was the point that would prove so crucial. In that sense, the next two days only deepened the inevitability of what would follow. Because they were in love. In those first tests that new lovers face they carried what they felt into the outside world, from whispers in the dark to ordinary voices in the light, and nothing spoiled it. They loved when they did not make love. They loved silently. They were in love when they were still. At a certain point, out in the country, looking for golden eagles to film—this was why he'd come to Scotland—David grew so absorbed that he didn't think of Anne for an entire hour, which, when he realized it, brought a moment's panic, as if he were awaking from a nightmare. But there was no reason to be afraid; everything he felt was right there, waiting. At another time he found that a tune was running through his head that he couldn't get rid of. He didn't know what it was, but when he hummed it Anne remembered it at once—there was that line, *Do you believe in magic?* Of course that was laughable, and they did laugh; they laughed a lot at themselves over those two days, but there was a kind of sense to it, David thought. It was as if he was sliding back through those gates of childhood, the other way, when you ceased to believe, when heroes and dreams were lost. Now he'd recovered that time again, and if the magic he commanded was rather modest, it was as much power as he wanted. With his lips against her breast he felt his whole life in him. The sun did not shine more brightly for them, but they saw all the light it had to give. He'd found the power, with her, that changed himself, and so, to the extent that he desired, the world was changed.

In all this only two problems might have truly troubled them, but these proved to be no problem at all. The first was Axel, Anne's husband, who as an added complication had been a crucial friend for David. In fact, David had actually known him before Anne. He was a wildlife photographer who'd died in Kenya in a plane crash and had given David his start, or rather his second: David had designed some special infrared equipment for him when he'd been making a film about nocturnal animals, and it was Axel's encouragement that had led him to take up photography himself. That had been the beginning of a good deal—his "new life," as he'd once considered it—and after Axel had died, his attention to Anne was a kind of repayment for this. It might have been considered that he had now overpaid the debt, but Axel had been sufficiently the melancholy Dane to have an anxious, pressing way of trying to arrange the happiness of those around him. When they came to talk about him, sitting in the little cottage parlor with his photographs above the mantel, it was easy enough to invoke his blessing. On the other hand, the second problem, Derek, might have been more complicated. Even that first night, in her bed, David had been aware of how conscious Anne was of him, sleeping above them. Derek had established himself in the old sleeping loft at the back of the cottage, even removing the stairs and replacing them with a rope ladder that he could pull up after him; and David could feel a restraint in her, felt her listening for him as he slept above them. David wondered what he should take from this. Was she reminding him that she was encumbered, that she and Derek were bound up together, inextricable? But then, he thought, the message might have been quite different, a reminder to herself that the boy could not be the whole of her life, that already they were moving apart. But in the end, if Derek was a problem, he solved it himself. For he knew at once that something had happened. He knew that very first morning. He took one look at them, sitting in the kitchen—neither Anne nor David actually daring to speak, Anne buttering a piece of toast into tatters—and his eyes went wide. But then he smiled, accepting the obvious as precisely that, *of course*—even, *it's about time*. And David could feel their relations shift, like the tumblers in a lock. But they were closer. There was even a sense, in his acceptance, of relief. Absorbed for a moment, he sat quietly, and then, with his breakfast in front of him, just seemed to get on with life. "Will you be filming the eagles today?" he asked.

"Yes. If I'm lucky. But I'm fairly sure there's only one of them. I couldn't find a nest."

"Why would there be only one?"

"I'm not sure. I don't think it's a young bird, so—"

"How can you tell?"

"They have white on their wings, underneath."

"So perhaps it's looking for another one."

"Or it might just be hunting."

"Right." Derek glanced down at his milk. Then, without the least hint of embarrassment, he asked, "You have a son, don't you?"

Anne went rather still.

David nodded. "Yes. He's called Tim. But he's rather older than you. In university."

"I thought you weren't married, though?"

"Now, Derek—"

"I was divorced a long time ago, when he was still a baby."

"So—"

"Really, Derek. Please. You're being rude."

Equably, with an entirely deadpan expression on his face, Derek turned a little. "Don't you remember, Mother, what Mr. Robinson said was the best thing about being Scottish?"

"No, I don't."

"You don't have to be English."

"Well, I am English. And I suspect you're only an honorary Scot. So behave yourself."

"All right already," he replied, holding up one palm—a gesture, in fact, that was absolutely American—and then dashed off to get ready for school. But apparently everything, or at least something, had been settled to his satisfaction, and David, only slightly bewildered, had felt a shift in his own status: by the end of that first day Derek was treating them with a discretion that implied they were already a couple in his eyes. And David could see that Anne was pleased and relieved by this. For her part, looking to David's past and present situation, she had no particular anxieties, and her curiosity, over those first two days, was all for the present. She knew about David's estrangement from his son, that they saw each other only for rather painful, ritual dinners—she'd once been with David on the evening he set off for one. But although she understood that this must be a factor in *his* life, she had no reason to believe that it would affect *theirs*. As for his divorce, she thought nothing of it. He never mentioned his wife, and she had to work to remember her name—Diana; but since David had left her before Anne had even met him, it never crossed her mind that trouble might come from that direction. At the most she was conscious of an obscurity in his past, a break, something not quite explained. But this was not equivalent (which would have been important to her) to any sense that he was keeping something from her or was less than open; it would never have occurred to her that she couldn't ask him anything.

And she was right. David had never told her about what had happened to him because there'd never been any reason to; the consequences, in his own life, had long since been assimilated, and he didn't think about it now. If he had he would have assumed that the story would just come out, in its own good time, and certainly, on that third morning, he had no idea that his peculiar past would return to haunt him now. The only foreshadowing of what would happen was of the faintest kind. Alone in the cottage—Derek had left for school, Anne was in Kirkcudbright shopping—he took his second cup of coffee into the sun-room, which was now Anne's office. After Axel's death, partly at his own urging, she'd started technical and scientific translating, and idly, wandering about, he picked up the paper she was currently working on. It was German—she had German, Dutch, French, Danish, and some of the other Scandinavian languages—and he tried to read it, slowly working through the first pages. The language he could cope with and even, in a general way, the subject—it concerned "anomalous dispersion," the behavior of wavelengths in certain materials, and this might have served to remind him how far in the past that part of his life now was. Yet he didn't think about that directly. Instead, a different sort of memory came to him, an image of the hedgerows at the end of RAF Benson where he'd played as a child. He had a sudden flash of it, could feel the wind in his hair, could smell the tangle of privet and barberry, chervil and stitchwort, all atremble with birds and butterflies. In his mind's eye he could see himself, a little boy in shorts and a rough wool sweater, standing stock-still, holding his breath, frozen, waiting, watching. And when a butterfly flew out, he'd gasp at the beauty of it, fluttering up, like a speck of light, an emperor or an admiral or a peacock or a blue—he'd learned all their names, borrowing books from the library, and collected them in bottles and trays. Sometimes, too, looking up into the washed blue sky, he'd catch the bright glint of a plane drifting down to the runway, the memory so clear now that he squinted his eyes, as if he could actually see it. Then he could: it was a Canberra bomber, the jet they'd used to reequip the Photo Reconnaissance Units that flew out of the base. The planes had fascinated him. He'd learned their names as well, all their designations; they were still as clear in his mind as they'd ever been. PR.3s were the Canberras, PR.10s were Gloster Meteors; and he remembered his father showing him one of the old Mosquitoes, a PR.34 back from Malaya, for it was this strange wooden plane that his father had worked on during the war and the plane that Miroslav, his godfather, had flown. They'd used something called the F.52 camera, and he could hear his father's voice, the pride in it: *That was the great thing, you know, those cameras, they made all the difference.* All this passed through his mind, and he tried to remember how old he must have been. Certainly he was at that age when he was discovering science and hating girls, a boy: taking the first steps to all he would eventually gain and subsequently lose. Though he didn't actually think this. He was long past thinking of it, an elision in his thoughts slid over it, his mind moving instead to Derek, who was something like the same age now, who in fact built model airplanes, as his own son had once done. And then he was thinking quite differently altogether, remembering his conversation with Anne, when she'd confessed to a little fear. Derek was on the edge of puberty; for all she knew, he was so private now, he could be into it. But what if he didn't change? What if he stayed a boy forever? David had laughed at this, and smiled again now, and had told her not to worry, that Peter Pan always did grow up.

But these memories and thoughts, which at least theoretically might have been connected in his mind to China Lake, were gone in a flash, and then he was on his way, hurrying, telling himself he had work to do. And he did. He was shooting the last footage for a film about golden eagles, and this area of southern Scotland had once been part of their range; he was hoping that there were still a few left. So he headed off, driving down to Kirkcudbright. A small fishing and tourist town built on the basin of

the river Dee, it had long been a favorite of painters, mainly watercol-
orists, but today the sun made it bright as a Kodachrome: the fresh-
painted shop fronts gleamed, the glare flashed messages between the first
tourists as they ran about in their cars. Crossing the river he looked back
to the turn of the harbor: a man in red rubber boots trudged across the
glistening mud toward a sailboat, varnished as bright as a child's first
penny, and the fishing fleet leaned against the jetty in a gay tangle of lines
and masts. Then it was all gone behind the trees and he sped up and
passed into the countryside. Here, too, the sun was brilliant, the highland
cattle blinking against it on the hillsides, and the white daisies and yellow
buttercups sparkling in the valleys where they marked the banks of the
streams. He was no longer thinking of anything. He simply let the bright
day flow all over him and around him. He was happy, light, like the light
that flickered down through the oaks, and calm, like the still shadows in
the dark, walled turns where the road switched back. Swinging north he
ran down into Gatehouse of Fleet, a village with a long, narrow high
street and a couple of pubs where it was claimed, not too improbably, that
Burns had written some of his poems. The tourists here were fishermen,
the talk all of "the water." Two leaned heads together on the bridge,
giving him a slow countryman's look as he went by. He turned off just
beyond, and then the road narrowed, with walled fields to his left and a
deep valley to his right; through a screen of ancient, moss-covered oaks he
could see the Big Water of Fleet at the bottom of it. A crow flapped lazily
through the sunshine, sheep trotted away from him in prissy, ludicrous
panic; and then, after a mile or so, the road turned sharply to the left.
Coming up to this bend he slowed right down. Ahead of him the land had
changed, the woods rising up over a hard, brown range of hills. A narrow
road ran parallel to these woods, blocked by a gate and a discreet sign,
NATIONAL NATURE RESERVE—CAIRNSMORE OF FLEET. He turned in. Immediately there was little to see, only the woods on his left and then an old
farm to the right whose broad, grassy fields stretched down to the river;
but then the woods petered out and he could see behind them, where the
land rose into a rocky moor edged by a high, steep cliff. This was the
Clints of Dromore, a precipice that formed a sheer drop of a hundred
feet. An abandoned railway line, which had also been hidden by the
woods, curved around the base of it, ran past the farm, and then crossed
over the fleet on an immense brick viaduct. Passing through the farm
itself—the farmer gave his usual friendly wave—David followed the road

down to the river, then beneath one of the great arches, so immense that the Rover seemed like a Dinky Toy miniature. On the other side the road doubled back on itself and climbed the steep hill on which the viaduct was built. He geared down and went up this. Now he was very high and looking back the way he had come. The Clints of Dromore, even higher than he was, lay to his right; behind him, stretching back from Dromore, was the moor, and directly below him lay the valley and the farm, its smooth green fields enclosed by the river. The eagle was hunting here, drifting over the moor, catching the updraft from the cliff, diving into the valley to kill.

He got his equipment together—the Aaton 16mm camera, a belt battery pack, two film magazines, light meters, his Leica, binoculars—and set off. The ground was lumpy with hummocks of grass and hidden boulders; he had to clamber over the rubble of some old stone fences, but since he'd already been up here four times that week, he knew the easiest route. It was not that difficult. Dromore was like a giant, lying on his side, contemplating the valley below. The drop from his shoulder down his rough, craggy breast formed the great cliff, which was unscalable from directly beneath, but the top of the viaduct, where David had parked, was somewhere around his ankles, so that he was now making the relatively easy ascent along the slope of his leg and thigh, then, more steeply, up his torso. It took about forty minutes to reach the top. Now he was very high. The farm buildings were tiny. The river curved around in a smooth, dark loop. He could see all across the green fields of the valley to the brown hills on the far side and even beyond them, and over everything stretched the high, bright sky. The wind pressed his face, making him squint; and he felt, as he always did, the pleasure of this, to be alone in the great space of the world, under this light: a pleasure that had been the salvation of his life and so, again, could have made him think of the past. But he didn't think at all; he just felt it: standing upright, with the pack eased off his back, his damp, flushed face cooled by the wind. Then he got busy; like all wildlife photographers, he'd often been caught out, his quarry appearing before he was ready. So he hurried. He'd left a lot of equipment here before, in an aluminum case lashed down under a tarpaulin, and now he opened it up. It contained rock climbing gear, ropes, tackles, picks. He'd already set out his pitons so there was little to do, and he was set to go in a moment. He walked over to the edge of the cliff. In a standard maneuver he intended to lower himself partway down the face of it, thereby getting himself off the horizon, outside the bounds of the bird's usual perception of danger. As usual he had three separate lines. On the first he sent down his camera and lenses, lowering them to a large rock that protruded from the cliff face; he would be able to stand on it. The second was a safety line, which he clipped to his chest harness. And the last, led through a three-part tackle, was connected to a bosun's chair in which he now strapped himself. He looked down. And it was a long way down—a first long drop to the old railbed, then a second to the valley floor. But he had no fear of heights and turned around and leaned back—you always go down a cliff backward—and stepped over the edge.

For an instant he was weightless: all his weight was taken by the rope. But then, reaching down, the toe of his heavy boot found a crevice a couple of feet below and his weight shifted onto it. He paused just an instant, testing, then brought his left foot lower. The rope was taut; in his mind's eye he could see it tightening against the staggered line of pitons on the top of the cliff, and he payed out a little, easing the tension. He took another step. This looked very dangerous, even spectacular, but there was a simple trick to the whole procedure: all you needed was nerve. With his weight leaning backward and enough tension on the rope, his body maintained a constant angle to the cliff, and he worked against this purchase. In a few minutes he'd reached the only difficult part: about eight feet down, the cliff face jutted out slightly in a sort of horn. To get beyond this he had to push off, swing out, let go the rope—and fall, and then brake the fall, grabbing hard on the rope, taking the strain on his forearm, so that he swung back against the cliff. Feet first, he thudded against it. He steadied himself. After that, it was simple. He rather bounded down, in a rhythm, and quickly reached his rock. Tying off the rope, he drove three pitons into the cliff with his rock hammer and ran a separate line through them to his safety harness. So now he had the main rope, his safety line, and this extra insurance. Secured in this way he tested his rock; it was firm, level enough, but not quite large enough to let him turn around on. Still, behind him, the cliff curved inward a little, so he could easily lean back and rest against it. Altogether it would be a good place to work, and he got himself ready, drawing the pack with his camera toward him. The battery pack went around his waist, the camera hooking into it. He screwed on a 50-150mm zoom lens and then took a series of readings with his light meter—against the sky, to his right and left, and then the darker valley. He set the camera accordingly, opening up as much as possible, his usual practice when filming birds in flight, sacrificing depth of field to get as much color as he could. Not, of course, that there was anything to film. After all this trouble the sky was empty; he couldn't see even a crow. Which meant there was nothing to do but wait.

Boredom. People found it hard to believe, but this was the chief hazard of his occupation. Clinging like this to the edge of a cliff, dangling beneath a waterfall, wedged into the top of a tree—even peril, he'd discovered, can be tedious. And it was invariably uncomfortable. The wind was cold. The straps of the bosun's chair dug into his thigh. His muscles developed a straining, rhythmic ache. And his eyes, ceaselessly moving, could not relax their vigilance, though he was certain, after just five minutes, that it would be unrewarded. Only his mind was free. His thoughts roamed around, haphazardly connected. The great arc of the sky made him think of the ancients' universe, with its interlocking spheres. His gaze ran over the horizon, the brown hills in front of him, and he thought of Conrad, writing novels of the South Seas in a London house, dressed in a suit and tie. Which made him think of Axel Brahe—because of the accent he had never lost? the melancholy line of those distant hills?—and his obliging nature, his tolerance, his rationality, which had nonetheless represented some resistance in him, a stubbornness, limits beyond which he wouldn't go, a denial. Had this not held Anne away from something vital?

Anne. Of course he thought of Anne. He remembered a time, in London, when they'd had lunch, the three of them, though even as this came back to him, he recalled that Axel had gone away from the table when Anne had smiled and said to David, "Are you going to tell me who she is?" Yes, he smiled now; he could remember that all quite clearly. He'd blushed. He hadn't told her, but it was interesting, he thought, that she'd wanted him to know that she'd guessed. She'd seen what had happened, and of course it couldn't have been more ordinary. He was just back from his first holiday in years, his first *since* (but he didn't think *since what*), two weeks on one of the Caribbean islands. There, in all that sun, that blinding light, he'd rediscovered the beauty of the world, his wonder at it. He'd spent all his time on the beach, by the sea, or walking in the hills. He'd climbed a mountain. He'd seen monkeys, egrets, pelicans. He'd watched the sun go down each night, caught the green flash twice. Though he'd had no snorkel, he'd rented a boat and dived, gliding over the bright bottom until his lungs were bursting. Birds, butterflies, the ceaseless wind—he'd felt it all. For two days he'd been on the verge of tears, and the right priest, he'd later suspected, could have converted him to anything. But there'd been a woman; for it was here that he'd put an end to the celibacy, almost unnoticed in his life, that had persisted for years. A holiday romance. He refused, even in memory, to be embarrassed by it: he was even now too grateful. It was banal to other people but still extraordinary for him. And Anne had noticed. Surely there was some significance in this, although, as he began to track it down, his mind shied away, trusting to it—*Zen and the Art of Archery*, a book he'd read twenty years after everybody else—and his thoughts moved on, fluttering like a butterfly across a meadow, the butterflies he'd seen in the Caribbean alighting in the hedgerows at the end of Benson's runways that he'd recalled that very morning. He thought of that again: how he'd caught them and killed them with a drop of chloroform dripped on cotton batting. To know nature, you had to kill it. Nature, Tooth and Claw. And then he tried to decide whether the camera he held in his hand was really so different from his collecting bottle. A year ago he'd been in the Caribbean again, working this time, and he'd heard a child jeering at a tourist, "You wanna take my picture, gotta pay ten thousand dollar." So they were tired of being specimens, collected by a lens; and would his eagle, supposing it could speak, not say the same? The trouble was, he thought, there was no such thing as Nature; every bird and animal on the face of the planet existed only on man's sufferance. Nature had been entirely humanized; there was only human nature, and what was that? A big question, and he steadied his mind on it for the next hour; in fact, until the eagle came.

It caught him by surprise. It shouldn't have, but it did, drifting over the moor behind him and then suddenly appearing, a black shadow, almost stationary, against the bright blue sky. Forty feet above him. Fifty yards to his right. At once he had the camera up, the motor running. He focused. The huge bird twisted slightly, and now he had it in all its glory, the light glinting on its plumage, its gold and copper head, wingtip feathers feeling for the air like fingers. A young bird: he could see a pale patch beneath its tail. But still immense, close to three feet high, the wingspan six. For a moment it just hung there. Then it caught an eddy backing off the cliff and rode it up—they never worked against such updrafts—and he followed it higher, until it was just a silhouette. He held on it all the same and a moment later was rewarded, for it sank back down, closer to him, though he had to twist right around in his harness, since it had also drawn closer to the face of the cliff, and then it sideslipped closer still, and he had a perfect shot in profile, with its fierce flat head and huge hooked beak, aquiline, *Aquila chrysaetos*, that's where the word came from. And then it banked, and even condescended to work its wings two lazy beats, and drifted out over the fields in front of him. He followed it out and would have hoped that it might hunt, but actually, at this point, he had all he needed. He'd been working on this project for over a year, filming the birds in Lewis and Skye and Rum and Tiree, and all he needed was a few shots here so the narrator could intone, *Driven out of much of its range, a few pairs still hang on, even as far south as Galloway*. But ten minutes later he got a bonus. The bird came back. He'd lost it, out over the river, but then it appeared again, to his left, drifting along the margin of the cliff above the old railbed. Just in case, he'd changed his magazine, and he began to film again, focused tight. The bird just drifted on, closer and closer to him, so tight, in fact, that he wasn't able to see the ground and had no idea that anything was there. Until the eagle dived. Like a bomb or a missile, propelled by three great wing beats, a disturbance of the air he could almost feel against his cheek; driving down so hard and fast, he knew the shot would be a blur (but that would work) until he had the focus back again and could see the rabbit, dashing, panic-stricken, all stretched out, along the gravel road where the rails had run. But in the open nothing can run fast enough. The bird struck—an explosion of dust and back-beating wings. One orange talon reached and clenched—did he hear a scream?—and the rabbit kicked, kicked, kicked, and died. It was over that fast. But then, as so often, the tables were turned. The awkward movements of the grounded bird perfectly expressed its fear, all advantage lost. Anxiously it grabbed up its prey, hopped, staggered, lumbered up— and then was all grace again, lifting and rising, climbing above the cliff and then vanishing from view. *Ironically, an abandoned railway cutting—a monument of the civilization which destroyed its habitat—here provides Britain's most noble bird with a perfect hunting ground.*

David relaxed, leaning back against the cliff, wedged there. He had exposed less than seven minutes of film but was exhausted, soaked in sweat, the camera a lead weight at the end of his arm. But he could not have done much better. And it was not even noon. He took a breath. He rested a moment. He was sufficiently cautious that he didn't want to move until he had his strength back. But then he did, and there was certainly no reason to stay. He had everything he'd come for. So, cautiously, he reached out and hooked his equipment bag over to him. He packed up. It took a certain discipline not to rush. But he had long ago developed exactly that discipline, checking and double-checking; not with anxiety but a practiced thoroughness. He checked the safety line, a real hard tug, both at the attachment to his harness and the length running to the cliff top. And he still kept the shorter line, attached to the pitons that he'd driven into the cliff just above where he stood. Finally he tested the line that would pull him up. The free end of this ran up to the top of the cliff and then through the tackle, which gave him the leverage of a large winch, and then came back down to a double attachment, one to the bosun's chair and a second to his safety harness. He now gave the free end a good, whipping pull. It seemed all right. But as soon as he pulled the other end something did not feel right. There was too much give. With a frown he pulled it again. And again. And the rope literally came away in his hand. It had simply parted; it drifted down, snaking against the rock of the cliff, and dropped, dangling, thirty feet below him.

He was utterly astonished.

Never before had such a thing happened to him.

He didn't even think: if he had not tested the rope, he would have fallen, to be caught by the safety line, hopefully, but a terrible fall just the same. Initially, in fact, he was more angry than afraid. He pulled the fallen end of the rope up to him and looked at it. But he couldn't tell what had happened. The rope was almost new, but it had somehow parted or unraveled. Or something had severed it. A rock? The edge of a block in his tackle? But the rope was Kevlar, a material whose other uses included tire cord and bulletproof vests. It was inconceivable that it could have come apart like that. But it had. What was he going to do?

He looked up. The top of the cliff now seemed a long way off, a rough black line mocking him against the brightness of the sky. And the rocky outcrop above him was suddenly a major inconvenience. Well. He swore to himself, at himself, but he knew what he was going to do, all right. Here was just the reason you had a safety line. He would have to climb the cliff. And he'd done enough rock climbing to know that he could, to know it was not even that difficult. He had his pick. Pitons. He even had a good length of rope, however suspect. He'd go up at an angle, around the outcrop, working along, as he faced the cliff, to his right, and then coming back to his left a little: there was a channel in the rock that way where he'd have a foothold. It was only twenty feet. But of course it seemed a mile. He was daunted. He was afraid. And perhaps he was even more afraid because of what had happened these past few days, because his life now meant so much more to him. But he didn't think this. He was in a trap, and he would have to work his way out of it. That was all. He looked down.

And then he looked down again.

Something had caught his eye. Somebody was down there, on the old railbed, watching him. A man. His face upturned. He had binoculars. Because of the binoculars, and because he was a hundred feet below him, David couldn't see his face, and he had only the vaguest impression of him: a big man in a blue nylon jacket bloused away from his body in the wind, an older man. But it was clear that he must have seen what had happened, for he lifted his arm and waved. But then an instant later he turned away and strode off, big strides, down the road, and a moment after that, because of the way the cliff curved, he was out of sight. A bird-watcher, probably; he, too, would have been looking at the eagle. David waited. What would the man do? If he went for help, he'd likely go to the farm, and the farmer would fetch the ranger. David strained his eyes; the wind had come up, cold now under the brightness of the sun. But there was nothing to see, at least for the moment, and he realized that the man's disappearance, rather irrationally, had left him irritated. He was embarrassed. He didn't want to be rescued. He had a sudden flash of what might appear on the evening news: they'd get a helicopter, winch him off. Ludicrous. On the other hand . . . He swore again at the bloody rope. What could have happened to it? He tried to think what he should do. He had to admit, he was in a predicament. But even setting aside the more ridiculous scenarios, there were reasons that any help might actually prove a hindrance. Would anybody know what to do? The ranger *might*. Still, was he going to trust a rope anyone else put down? He looked away, along the cliff. He still couldn't see the man. There was only one way he could go: along the graveled roadbed to the viaduct, then down to the road that curved back through the farm. He kept watching, undecided; but then he kept watching out of curiosity, because the man did not appear again. After ten minutes there was still not a soul in sight. He looked away, telling himself it was like watching a kettle boil, and busied himself, checking his safety line—it would now become the main line, if he climbed up from here—and then going over the end of the rope that had parted; could he make use of it? could he trust it? Finally, he looked back once more. But he still couldn't see anyone, and now felt irritation of a different kind. Had the fool not seen what had happened to him? Where was he? He looked at his watch. Another five minutes passed. The hell with it, he thought. There was no sense waiting. He would just have to make the climb, which was what he should have done in the first place.

But ten minutes later, as he was about to start, he realized there was somebody on top of the cliff.

He heard a grunt, a few pebbles came slipping down, and then the free end of the line that had parted suddenly jerked upward. He looked up quickly, but he couldn't see anything except the end of the rope as it disappeared over the edge of the cliff. And then, a moment later, a fresh length of rope came sailing down toward him, past him, falling way below him. He reached out and grabbed it. But almost immediately it began running back up. He let it slide through his fingers, looking up, and he did see someone then, one glance of a face, high-domed, reddish, ob-scured by aviator sunglasses. Then it was gone, and more rope was paying down toward him; he could hear it running through the tackle. This was the other end of the line, and it had a loop; the man had tied a bowline in it. It came down toward him, catching on the jut above him, backing up for a second, but then spilling off. It kept on coming; the man payed it out too far, and it ran well past him. Then stopped. David looked up, expecting to see the man, who clearly had not gone for help but was simply doing it himself. No one appeared, however, and after a moment he caught the free end of the line and gave it a pull. He could feel the resistance of the tackle, but it ran smoothly, and the looped end of the line rose up to him. Now he was undecided. The man, clearly knowledgeable, had simply replaced the bad line. But did David want to trust him? He seemed to know what he was doing. The bowline, though David didn't really need it, was correctly tied. And the free climb he'd been contem-plating was hazardous. In the end he attached the looped end of the line to his bosun's chair and began hitching himself up. In a few moments he was scrambling over the edge of the cliff, back where he'd begun.

Now, for a moment, the anxiety he'd been feeling caught up to him, and he just sprawled where he was, not really thinking of anything. So it was a minute or so before he realized something: the man, whoever he was, had gone. There was no one around. The barren, rocky cliff top was deserted. He got to his feet and called out, "Hello there!" But there was no response. He walked along the cliff where it rose a little. From here he could see a long way, back down the slope of the giant's leg, and finally he did see a figure, just for an instant, hurrying along, near the viaduct. But then the man, assuming this was the man, disappeared again as the ground dropped away. It was bizarre. He kept staring. And a little while later he saw a small car driving along the farm road. His rescuer? But he had not stayed long enough even to receive his thanks.

For a moment David stood where he was, on the edge of the cliff, looking into the distance. He felt puzzled. Why had the man left so hurriedly? Perhaps, he thought, he would have felt embarrassed to be thanked. It seemed a weak explanation, but then he wasn't obliged to provide any explanation at all. So he tried to shrug it off. But now, for the first time, he sensed that something was wrong. Something had happened. He had no idea, still, what it might mean, but already he knew it was important. And he wanted to get away.

Of course, even as he was feeling this, he was dismissing it; but he couldn't, quite. It dogged his steps. He felt annoyed. He could not get away fast enough. He hurried. But he had to make two trips, one with the camera pack, then a second with the aluminum equipment box that held his ropes and gear. He worked back and forth, walking with his head down, his eyes looking right in front of him, working as fast as he could to get away. But he wasn't fast enough. Circumstances, like a shooter, had led him perfectly. As he came back the second time he looked back across the valley and saw Anne's car, a battered old Polo, coming past the farm, and by the time he reached the viaduct she was waiting, her face all anxious, by his Rover. She came up to him. She was about to put her arms around him, but then she hesitated. Her face was stricken.

"David, I'm sorry. But I've got bad news. It's your wife. Apparently . . . I don't know how to say it. Your son called, just as I got back. He got my number—"

"What is it?"

"She's dead. She killed herself. Oh, David. In Wales, some place called Aberporth."

And he was stunned. Whatever premonition he might have had, it would never have been of this. And for a moment his surprise itself kept the impact from him. He set down the box. "I don't believe it," he said. "It's not possible."

"I know, but—"

"What did he say?"

"He didn't really say anything. Just that it had happened. And it was important that you come. Whatever you felt, he said, you had to come."

"My God . . ." Diana. What did he feel? What should he feel? Should he feel anything at all? "Did he sound all right?"

"Yes, I think so. He seemed calm. I didn't—you know I've never met him. I didn't feel, really, that I could question him. He was only worried, I think, that you wouldn't come."

"My God. Yes. Of course I will."

She eased herself against him and put her arms around him. "Do you want me to come as well?" she asked.

He held her. He shook his head. "No. I don't think so. It would only bother him. He was very close to her. My God. Christ."

She held him tighter. "This is awful."

"Yes."

"Are you all right?"

He nodded against her shoulder. "I just can't believe it."

"I know. But David, it doesn't . . ."

Her voice trailed away, her objection hanging in the air; but he knew what she meant, and hugged her tight, pressed her so he would always feel her. No, it didn't have anything to do with them. It would make no difference to them. That was what his arms around her said, but already he was wondering. Already this felt like times before. Why did he feel discovered? Caught? As if someone had been watching, waiting until he came into the open. And why, as he drove back to the cottage, following behind her car, did he see that face above him on the cliff, and think of Tannis, Tannis, Tannis, that American navy man, walking toward him across the empty desert?

CHAPTER 9

All David could do was go.

Anne drove him to Glasgow; he flew to Cardiff. By seven o'clock he was on the road—the A48, Swansea to Carmarthen, then north to Cardigan. He drove too fast, probably deliberately; it kept his mind on the road and off what had happened. He made good time. Turning north along the coast, he picked up the first signs for Aberporth and it was still not ten.

Like so many places in Wales, the village was described by its name. *Aber* means a river that flows into the sea; *porth*, a landing place, which at this point took the form of a scallop of shingle and sand at the end of a bay. It wasn't very much of a beach, but on this coastline of high, rocky cliffs it had formerly provided enough of a refuge for a fishing village and now was the excuse for a small resort. But it was too early for holiday makers; coming in from the highway he didn't pass a soul, and when he reached the village it seemed almost deserted: the shops were shuttered, the Chinese take-away was dark. Many of the houses bore neat, swinging signs—Cam Calch, Gwyn Hafod, Pen Llys—and rented out rooms to the tourists, but only a few cars were parked in front of them. Unnoticed, gliding along in the dark, he turned down a steep incline that ran toward the sea. At the bottom of this road was a little patch of park; below it lay the beach, gleaming darkly, for it was washed now by the phosphorescent waves of the ebbing tide.

Switching off the engine David got out of the car, wanting to stretch his legs. From Cardiff he'd phoned ahead to a bed and breakfast, and they'd agreed to wait up until eleven, so he still had plenty of time. He walked over to a stone wall that looked down on the beach and leaned against it; and now all the thoughts and feelings of the day pressed in, as dark as the sea and the night. He was, he realized, completely confused. He wasn't sure what he should feel. Whatever he felt, felt wrong; however much he felt, it didn't seem enough. As he squinted down at the water, a lick of spray struck his face and a memory came back to him, a memory from the days when he and Diana had first started seeing each other. It was in Cambridge, in the early summer. They'd been walking together behind King's College, across the Great Lawn toward the river. The sky had been full of sun except for a single dark cloud, whose shadow had moved slowly toward them across the green grass. Without speaking they'd stopped to watch it, and then they'd held hands and run beneath the edge of it, a soft shower falling against their faces, trickling over their cheeks as Diana laughed and laughed. He could almost hear her laughing now, and he thought how amazing it was, that day was now so far gone; and it seemed amazing, too, that he and Diana had ever had that kind of moment together. But was this truly sorrow he was feeling? He knew that some part of himself was waiting to cry, but he knew, too, that he wasn't going to cry. For even as he was feeling all this, he'd been wondering if his emotion was excessive, almost a presumption. That was, no doubt, part of the problem; he didn't know what to feel because he wasn't sure what he had a right to feel. After so much had happened, what sort of claim did they have on each other?

But the consequences of that question were inevitable: he felt the guilt, as black as the sea out in front of him, that underlay everything else. No one could rationally claim that he was responsible for Diana's killing herself, but it didn't make any difference. If it hadn't been for him . . . He glanced quickly, almost surreptitiously, off to his left, seeing now what he had carefully avoided looking at before, the low, dark headland with the red and white lights twinkling above it: the radars, the radio masts, the telemetry arrays that marked the Royal Aeronautical Establishment, RAE Aberporth. It didn't seem to have changed since the day he'd first seen it more than twenty years ago. He felt a little flutter of anxiety in his chest; and then, as he'd known he would, as he'd known he would have to, he began walking toward it along the short, dark street that ran across the little harbor, past the entrance to the beach, with its gloomy public convenience, and then, on the Pennar Road, up the hill on the other side of the village.

The road, darkly lined with trees, thick and dark and Welsh, curved up and then leveled off; and then, after a time, he could see, spilling around a bend, a slick of yellow light that shimmered on the asphalt. He kept on. Around the bend was the floodlit fence, topped with three strands of electrified barbed wire, and the signs that warned about guard dogs in English and Welsh—RHYBUDD: CWN GWARCHOD AR WAITH—then the main gate. Everything about it was so discreet. The crash barrier was a neat brick wall; the guardhouse was little bigger than a call box; the signs, obscurely posted by "The Procurement Executive, Ministry of Defence," merely pointed out that those who sought entry must have the correct permit issued by the MoD Police. In fact, considering that it was one of the most secret defense establishments in the United Kingdom, it looked perfectly ordinary and had a kind of universal institutional air, like a mental hospital or a training school, at worst a prison. In relation to the town, that's how it had always been: discreet; the other side of the local economy, assumed, or only vaguely defined—"the base," "up there," "the Establishment," "up the hill." He slowed down as he drew nearer. The spotlights around the entrance spilled shadows back among the buildings, although a few of the more important were separately lit themselves: the Admin Wing, the Main Laboratory, the Small Explosives Building. All the structures were much the same, no more than two or three stories high, built of red brick, the mortar immaculately pointed, the window frames glistening white with freshly renewed paint, while the grounds around them showed all the attention of the MoD, with the lawns neatly trimmed, the gravel paths laid out in perfect curves, and the shrubbery precisely clipped. No, he decided, nothing had changed, or at least nothing that he recognized, and as he stopped and looked, he thought he recognized almost everything. But this recognition, he realized, contained nothing specific, no precise memories or images or feelings. Only an odd sense of distance. Then, bizarrely, he was offered a precise definition of that distance, for he saw that a man was hurrying toward him along the side of the road, a short, rotund individual stepping smartly along with his hands thrust into his raincoat pockets. He was clearly taking his evening constitutional; a small Scottie was trotting energetically along behind him. By the time David noticed the pair, he realized it was too late to move away without being obvious, so he stayed where he was, waiting as the man's face tightened into a smile and a little nod, and he offered a clipped "Good evening." David returned his greeting, and then realized that he actually knew who the man was. Of course. His name was Eric Williamson. He was a chemist. Warheads . . . rod explosives—a little train of associations came back to him as he swiveled around, catching a last glimpse of the dog and his master as they disappeared in the darkness. But there was no doubt about it, the man was Williamson: for some reason his stiff-legged, hurrying gait had been indelibly imprinted in memory. They'd started to work about the same time; there'd been a reception to welcome them both, and he'd actually shared a toast with this man—in the bad South African sherry with which every British military institution had been supplied in those days. It was an extraordinary coincidence, he thought. Or maybe it wasn't. Williamson had stayed here—why not?—enjoying the sort of career he would have had himself. Presumably, he'd worked up the ladder, all the ladders: first marriage, second; children; school; second assistant, first; director; lab head; director, division. In fact, Williamson had lived the life he could have led himself, which only underlined how different, how irrevocably different, his own life had been. It was astonishing that this place had once been part of it, that he'd passed through those gates every morning, ready to play his role as the Young Genius in Residence. No wonder, he thought, that he didn't know what to feel about Diana. He'd become so different from the man who'd known her: the person he'd been more than twenty years ago was a ghost trying to grieve for a stranger. It was inevitable that all his feelings seemed undermined and suspect.

But now, as he stared toward the entrance gate—lit like a flare against the darkness—a different kind of alienation swept across him, a feeling of remoteness that was also menacing. The yellow lights gleamed on the wet road. The iron trefoil fence marched around the curve. The ghostly illumination of the buildings hung against the night. A dog barked; a patrol was coming. He had the feeling he was being watched. He turned away. He had to stop himself from running. He wanted to escape. This place, Aberporth, Diana—even his son?—represented a catastrophe he'd barely managed to survive. And he knew that here was another reason he couldn't feel too much, he couldn't cry, for the tears, inevitably, would be partly for himself. And he knew he couldn't risk self-pity. He'd conquered it once before; he couldn't take the chance again. And he didn't quite feel safe from it. Not here, where the past was so palpable, where it still lived and breathed. That was the frightening part: the past had just kept on, persisting regardless of him or his wishes, so that all sorts of questions he'd assumed were settled reared up again.

Anxiety began to eat away at him. In his bed and breakfast, despite the hour, he was welcomed with a cup of tea, and the cup trembled in his hand. Trying to relax he ran a bath in the cold, fluorescent bathroom down the hall, but each time he eased inside himself tension snapped him back. What was happening, what had started in these last few days? Did it have anything to do with him? What did he really feel about Diana? In his dressing gown, with the lights turned off, he lay down on top of the bed. But he wouldn't sleep. He thought about Anne, in an attempt to calm himself. But that only brought more questions. How did she think of him? What image came into her mind, along with his name? His whole body, naked? His face? His voice? What did his voice sound like to her? Did she think he was good? kind? gentle? There was no phone in his room. But if there was a phone, he thought, and he called her and asked, what would she say? She had a dear friend, an American named Jessie, who lived in Cornwall. They wrote to each other almost every week. He wondered if he would be in her latest letter, and what she'd say. Had she mentioned him before? *I think I must have mentioned an old friend of mine named David Harper. An old friend of Axel's too. A photographer. He sometimes stays with me and he's been here all week.* She'd say a little something about him, but she wouldn't beat about the bush or play coy. Yes, she'd come right out with it. *I love him.* She wouldn't say, *I think.* But whom, he wondered, was she in love with—and could he have told her? Perhaps that was the trouble with this place, he thought. The existence of his old self raised doubts about the new; made him provisional, suspect, a question mark. That's what had happened. That's what this all meant, coming back here. And then he slipped back into a memory, from a very bad time, about as bad as it had gotten, years ago, after he'd left Diana, after he'd given up. He'd been drinking heavily, had just been fired from another teaching job—even his Cambridge degrees hadn't saved him. And his car had packed it in. The estimate from the garage had been impossible, for he had no money. He was desperate. It was the last thing he was holding onto, that car, though it was just a Vauxhall, a good sensible middle-class car—why had he ever bought it? But he was desperate, and decided to repair it himself. So he borrowed some tools, got hold of a manual, and for three days, with the car jacked up in a vacant lot, he worked away. And what he was doing, he had realized afterward, was a kind of rewrite of his personal history. He was detouring around Cambridge, his "brilliance," all those teachers who'd discovered him, pushed him, and he'd gone back to the time when he was just the sort of kid his friends had been: they could fix anything, with their own two hands. They didn't talk, or write things down; they simply saw the arrangement of the parts and took hold of them. It had been a revelation to him. You wanted something, you took it. You just did it. Simple. He had forgotten how easy it was. And this, in a way, had been a turning point, though he hadn't realized it at the time. But six months later, setting out to buy his usual bottle of Bell's (and perhaps a second), he simply hadn't, but instead had wandered into a cinema that was running a film called *Morgan*, a comedy about a mad artist (who might just as well have been a scientist) who kept dressing up as a gorilla. But he'd laughed, how he'd laughed, sitting there the whole afternoon and into the evening. Ever since, the Vauxhall and the movie had been linked in his mind; rebuilding that car he'd begun to rebuild himself. But what had he built up? Was it he? Or something false?

But he actually did fall asleep, thinking of the film. It distracted him just long enough—it was as if he'd caught himself looking the other way, and hid. He ducked down behind a great black wall and disappeared. He was gone. Only his mind kept working; whatever was troubling him had one last anxious run. He wasn't quite asleep, but he seemed to dream. He had forgotten something. He was in some school. His college. Apparently, going into an examination, he had tried to summon the entire course into his mind, and something was missing. He could see a room, filled with row upon row of desks, and he had forgotten something. He couldn't remember what it was. Wien's formula, Rayleigh's and Jeans's, Planck's, Stefan's law, Boltzmann's constant . . . *radiant excitance, M, for a given wavelength, lambda, equals the first constant times the reciprocal of lambda to the fifth times* . . . Names, formulas, equations—all rushed through his mind. He was trying to remember everything at once, and couldn't; something was lost. His mind raced, around and around, looking for it. Finally, with a start, he awoke, or became conscious. Staring up into the darkness, he suddenly whispered, like a prayer, or the element of a catechism, "5.6697 times 10 to the minus 8 W m to the minus 2 K to the minus 4," and then repeated this twice, mindlessly, for a moment not aware of what the expression meant. But then he realized that it was the actual value of Stefan's constant, sigma, which allowed one to find the radiant flux per unit area emitted by a black body for a given temperature.

Black body.

The phrase dragged him fully into wakefulness.

For a minute, heart pounding, he lay perfectly still on the bed, as if he'd had a nightmare. He was startled and amazed in just that way. But then, as he got his breath and looked around and found a patch of lightness in the window, he wondered what the nightmare was, exactly: that he remembered so much? or that there was something, after all, that he'd forgotten? But then his long day caught up with him, and his head fell back, and his eyes closed, and he slept.

The next morning, as he awoke, the previous night and day seemed like a door closing behind him: trapping him in a peculiar labyrinth where the past lay around every corner. His future was lost, he was going around in circles, retracing his steps, returning to his starting point, which he'd been so certain he'd left behind, and the remembered taste of whiskey filled his mouth, so foul a taste, and with such terrible associations for him, that he ran to a side window and spat it out. But then, looking up, all he could see was Aberporth—wet rooftops, the gray sea running up reluctantly to the land—with all its memories. Resolution, as he summoned it, seemed only a grim, hopeless resistance before the inevitable. The ground had shifted beneath his feet and now he was sliding downward.

Everything reinforced this.

When he phoned his son, the conversation was brief, but the hostility was palpable, like a rope burning across his hands. He phoned Anne—if there was hope, it lay *there*—but of course she didn't answer; he hardly expected her to (she must have been driving Derek to school; rationally, he knew this), for he had that old feeling that his luck had turned. His old fate had caught up to him. As he set out for Diana's house everything undermined him. In the area where most of the scientists had always lived, between the highway and the base, around the single runway of the airstrip, the hilly streets and lanes were as complex as a contour map, but he found his way unerringly, as if it was twenty years ago and he was coming home from work; and in somebody's drive, as a kind of proof, he even spotted a turquoise Morris Minor, the first car he and Diana had bought together. And though he hadn't seen it in years, he recognized the house at once. Similar to its neighbors, it was two stories high, vaguely Tudor in style, with the beams, shutters, and trim painted the same dark green they'd always been. He'd installed the porch light himself, and it was still there, a faux antique of iron and stained glass, the fitting at the top now a little crooked, so that it hung at an angle. Yes, everything was familiar in just this way, and yet every memory and association was tugged out of him against his will.

Sitting in his car for a moment with the motor running, as if he had not quite decided to stop, he was amazed that he had ever lived here or could have contemplated doing so. He felt a sudden swell of self-contempt. No wonder, he thought. Looking at the light he imagined Williamson clambering up a stepladder, screwdriver in hand, to repair it. It was a house, he thought, that was Williamson's dream come true. And he hated himself for having taken that dream as his own, even for a minute, even if he'd resisted. For he had resisted, however weakly; he could give himself that much. Diana's father had bought it for them as a wedding present, which they'd hardly been able to turn down; but even at the time it had left him feeling vaguely resentful. And years later, after their divorce, he'd sometimes thought that Diana had married him as a way of escaping from her home, but her father simply hadn't let her go. It was all so banal, he thought. Resentful daughters, clinging parents, grammar school boys full of insecurity—what a soap opera their life here would have been. It seemed so unreal. Looking at the house, sheltered by the obligatory oaks, he imagined an old film, an American film, but set in Britain because it would star Cary Grant, driving a roadster along back-projected lanes and then turning in here, where his girl would come running down the steps, tennis racket in hand. Suburbia-in-a-village. And all illusion. And the illusion, he thought, was belief itself; everyone here was dedicated to seeing the Emperor's clothes. Of course, he'd believed as well, and Diana . . . but he was not sure, as he considered this, about Diana. Had she actually believed the script, or simply acted her part? She seemed, now, so much more mysterious than before. In the time they'd lived here, he remembered, she'd always assumed an air of superiority, as if she was putting something over on them all or knew a secret they weren't in on. There'd always been that hint of contempt. Had it extended to him? Certainly, he'd often felt that she'd respected him more *after* their divorce than during their marriage. She'd been far more sophisticated than he had been, more complex and subtle in the expression of her feelings, so something devious would not have been beyond her. But then, if she had not believed what these people believed, what *had* she believed? Because she must have believed something, or felt something. Her suicide proved it: something had been worth dying for. Money? Some man, a lover? Her health—she'd always worried about her eyes, for her greatest passion was painting. Before that it had been photography, and if anything had happened to her vision, perhaps she might have become desperate enough to take her own life.

But as soon as he thought this, it seemed incredible. The trouble was, he thought, desperate was a word that didn't fit her. He had been the desperate one. Looking back, he could see that very clearly. The feeling of alienation he felt right now—everything beyond the clear glass of the windscreen was so utterly remote—seemed only an echo of his knowledge, all those years ago, that he didn't belong in this place, as if, from the very start, he'd known that some calamity was going to strike, as he knew now that it was going to strike again, with this soft, silent explosion of anxiety in his chest. He'd wanted to run then. He wanted to run at this very moment. Get away, get clear away—he could feel all his instincts telling him to go.

But, of course, he didn't run. Instead he leaned forward and switched off the ignition. He knew, even if he did run, that he would have to see Tim first. And perhaps this sort of resolution, a determination to press ahead, despite his foreknowledge of what would happen, was characteristic of all his dealings with his son, the awkward by-blow of the whole catastrophe, China Lake, Aberporth, his life with Diana, in this dreadful house. He was a pure locus of the pain, all the more so because of his innocence. How would he be taking it? What would he be like? David didn't know, couldn't know, never knew: they had known each other so strangely, so irregularly, that their relations were always out of sync. Tim, Timothy, Timmy . . . he was always outgrowing a name just as David was becoming used to it. Now he braced himself, drawing in the smell of the air and the trees, letting it revive him. He went up to the house. On the porch there was a smell of musty leaves and damp brick. A memory suddenly filled him, the smell of glass as his nose pressed against a window, the precise window and the circumstances absolutely lost, but the peculiar dusty smell preserved as an emblem of loneliness. But he was never quite sure about that: which of them, Tim or himself, had lost more from the break of their relationship, which was the lonelier because of it. Tim, in any case, acknowledged only a certain resentment or righteousness, which never quite became anger and was usually hidden behind his reserve. Typically, he now kept David waiting, and when he finally opened the door he hesitated, blocking the way, as if there was some real question as to whether he'd let his father in. He was tall, as tall as David, and filled up the doorway. Except for their height, however, there was no special resemblance between them. David, with his dark hair and easier, looser body, might actually have had something Welsh about him, while Tim was fair, with freckled skin, and looked vaguely Irish.

David, as usual, had to speak first. "Tim, how are you? Are you all right?"

"Yes. Of course I'm all right."

David could feel himself shrink back inside. Of course he'd said the wrong thing; but then he always said the wrong thing, and what is the right thing to say to a son whose mother has killed herself?

He waited. And then with a relenting gesture Tim stepped back, an abrupt, awkward movement, like a boy, a little embarrassed, who has suddenly remembered his manners. This had always been his paradoxical quality: that his exterior was boyish, immature, but it wrapped around a person who always seemed older than his age. And it was not unappealing, David had often felt, if only he could touch that inner watchfulness. But that was Tim's inviolable, hidden core. He wore Adidas, he was passionately concerned about South Africa, he wore all the badges of his troop, and yet he didn't seem to belong, not anywhere.

David followed him into the hallway. "I phoned from Cardiff last night, to let you know I was coming. But there wasn't an answer."

Tim gave him a glance that was almost challenging, as if to imply that he didn't have the right to even hint at this sort of concern. But the basis of their relationship had always been David's insistence that he had precisely that right. I am here; I am part of your life; I have the right to care for you; despite everything, David had never backed down from this. He had been prepared to endure every injury to his feelings to keep up that claim. At the same time he had never pushed it too far. For an instant now he wanted to embrace his son, but such a gesture, he knew, lay across a line it would have been disastrous to cross. "I'm sorry," he finally added. "I know how terrible you must feel."

Tim ignored this. "I went out and drove around. I just couldn't stay here. I had to get out. I didn't get back until late." He hesitated. "I'm just getting up now. I've made coffee, if you want some."

"All right."

"You don't have to have it."

"No. I'd like—"

Turning on his heel, Tim walked away, leaving David standing in the hall. He turned to follow, but then didn't move. Alone, he suddenly felt a peculiar sense of trespass. This was Diana's house and she wasn't in it, and she never would be again. His very presence was a kind of violation. His being here was wrong. She was dead, and yet he was the ghost. On the other hand, everything was so very normal; Tim was in the kitchen, and when David stepped through an arch into the lounge he found himself in a perfectly ordinary room of a certain type: the Williamsons' lounge in the Williamsons' house, he thought. The pale blue Wilton carpet was precisely centered on the polished oak floor, while the sofa and two armchairs, immaculately upholstered in a glazed fabric of a darker blue, were neatly arranged around a fireplace tiled in blue and cream. The walls and ceiling were done in a soft cream, and the sunlight, falling through sheer curtains, was subdued. A discreet scent lingered in the air—the clean carpet, lemon oil, the bowl of irises on the mahogany table before the window. All this was perfectly peaceful and pleasant, but the peculiar nauseating feeling he'd had outside passed over him again, for he seemed to be stepping back into a middle-class home from his childhood, the sort of place where he would always have been on his best behavior. The people who lived here would have had condescending smiles and perfect accents, they would have read *Punch* and driven an A40 or even something grander, like a Wolsley or a Jag. He glanced up at the ceiling; in its center was a plaster rosette, picked out in the same blue as the carpet; before fashions had changed, a small crystal chandelier would have testified to greater pretensions. He felt disgusted that he'd ever wanted to live in such a house. Had he, though? And even though it was the sort of room Diana had grown up in, it was almost equally shocking to think of her sitting here, on that sofa. Of course, she would have known exactly how to sit, with her legs crossed, with her teacup perfectly balanced on her lap, with her left hand idly twiddling at the single strand of pearls around her neck as she listened to her host; because, definitely, she would have been a visitor in this room, and half of her would have been laughing at it. She had *left* this sort of room; this was the lounge in her parents' home and represented all that she had fled. He had a sudden fantasy. Diana hadn't killed herself at all but had staged her death so she could disappear and then surface somewhere else with a new identity. She was starting over. He had stepped into the past, she had stepped out of it—in some peculiar way, they'd traded places. For an instant he could actually imagine this being true, and he was so struck by it that Tim, coming into the room, gave him a look. "Is anything wrong?"

David let out his breath. "I don't know. It's this room. There's something about it . . ."

"What?"

"It's just not like her. I can't imagine her here, somehow."

Tim was going to argue, but then he stopped himself. He shrugged. "I suppose this was the room for other people, as far as she was concerned. She spent most of her time upstairs. She'd had a wall taken out of her bedroom, so there was enough space for a couch and an armchair. And she used one corner for her painting. I think, when she was by herself, she often ate her meals there. She could live up there."

In a tower.

Rapunzel, Mrs. Rochester, Mary Stuart. He thought of women in towers, trapped by wicked witches or madness or rival queens. What had trapped Diana? And even as he thought, Don't be silly, he knew he wasn't being silly: she had killed herself. If he had to imagine *that*, he had the right to imagine anything. There was nothing silly about this at all. But Tim went on. "I don't spend a lot of time here either. I've poured out the coffee in the kitchen, if you want it."

They walked through to the back of the house. The kitchen, too, was rather old-fashioned, everything dating from the fifties; it was as modern as "the jet age." Fitted cabinets with aluminum handles. An old Electrolux fridge. And a set of chairs, with a table, made from steel tubing and covered with some early "easy wipe" fabric, but not cheap: once this sort of thing really had been top of the line, and a little horsehair stuffing was leaking from one of the chairs; plastic foam had yet to be invented. He realized that this room must be almost unchanged from the day they'd moved into it, and on the counter, he noticed a set of tea/flour/sugar canisters, in clear Perspex, that his aunt had given them as a wedding present. So Mrs. Haversham could be added to his list of trapped women, he thought, jilted, shamed, living perpetually with the evidence of her catastrophe—but why? Nothing had compelled her. The question that had harassed him last night again pressed forward. Why had she stayed in Aberporth? But then he sat down and Tim poured out the coffee. David tried to look at him, but Tim looked away.

"Tim, listen—especially now—we have to find some way of talking to each other."

"I suppose so. I suppose you'll want to know what happened."

"That's not what I meant."

"But maybe you already do know. You probably know better than me."

"I doubt that."

"I'm serious. I was thinking this morning—" He stopped himself. Then he said, quite levelly, "You know, I have to keep thinking, She's dead. I have to think that about every ten—"

"Tim, if you want—"

"No, no. I was just going to say, the day I got here . . . In the garden—you can just see it from here, right out that window—it's nothing, really, just that she was having trouble with the irises, they hadn't come up properly. She didn't really like gardening very much, but she wanted me to help her. I think we were dividing them or something. So out there, right now, there's a hole she dug and a spot where we scattered the dirt around, and I thought, this morning, that I'd go out and fill it in, but I couldn't, you see—you can see why—but it made me think about the garden, and when you phoned this morning I remembered how much I liked it down there when I was a little boy. I used to play there all the time. But at the back, if you go under the lilacs, it was always incredibly dark, and whenever I went *there* I was always frightened. I knew something had happened, you see. When I was a child, that is. Something was wrong. And I didn't know what it was. She would never tell me, and after a while I would never, never ask. But *you* knew, of course. That was always understood. And I expect you know now. Why it happened. Why she did it."

David, for a guilty instant, looked away. Because they had never told Tim about what had happened to him, about what had happened to them. Years ago he'd known that this had been a mistake and wanted to tell, but always Diana had refused. Now, a little edgily, he tried to hold his ground. "I'm not sure I understand what you're saying."

"No? Well, it's clear enough to me. She killed herself for the same reason you were divorced. It's as simple as that."

"That can't be true, Tim. Your mother and I were divorced years ago. She killed herself yesterday—"

"Actually, the day before. I didn't call right away. I couldn't . . . I couldn't have . . . *said* it, I suppose. Out loud."

David closed his eyes. For one second he couldn't bear to look at anything. And then, realizing they were shut, he opened them again. Yet his voice was calm. "All right, Tim. But what's the connection? Why do you think—"

"What else could it be?"

"I don't know. Money. A love affair. Her health. You."

"No. I've thought of all that sort of thing. It doesn't make any sense. When I arrived, everything was just the same, she was completely . . . I don't know. She was just herself. She was glad to see me. She was . . ." He shrugged.

David waited a moment and then said, "I'm not quite sure of the chronology. You've been here for a few days?"

"Yes. I got here last Friday. I was going to take a week to study. I still have three exams to sit." He looked up at his father. "But you don't deny . . . ?"

"What?"

"That something happened, when you were divorced."

"Of course something happened."

"I don't mean that. Something happened . . . something . . ."

"All right. Yes. Something did happen. We should have told you, and I wanted to tell you, years ago. But Diana didn't—I'm not sure why, but she didn't. It concerns me, more than her, and if you really want to know, I'll tell you now, but it can't be the reason, not after so long. Because it was all over twenty-five years ago. And you have to tell me, Tim, what happened, here, the day before yesterday, out loud."

Tim looked down, and David could sense his shock. Of course: he would have assumed that the secret hidden in the darkness beneath the lilacs was unknowable, unspeakable. Its concession, so easily, was almost frightening. And perhaps, after all, he wasn't so sure he wanted to hear it, for his voice came quick and low. "There's not much to tell. I've been over that day a thousand times. We had breakfast together and then we went for a walk. We walked into the village, down to the water, then came back and around. Nothing happened. Absolutely nothing. She saw a bird that especially interested her, some kind of wren. We passed a few people she knew and we said hello, but they were only people from the village. It was all perfectly normal and she was completely calm. When we got back, I began studying, up in my room, and I didn't see her again until lunch. We ate that together up in her room; she made it, then knocked at my door. I didn't think about it, but I suppose she'd been there all morning."

"Painting?"

"No. I asked her about her painting, but she said she was giving it a rest for a while. She had her camera out, a couple of cameras actually—she said she was cleaning them. I don't think she'd been using them. Anyway, it was all perfectly normal, and we had the sort of conversation we'd had a hundred times before. She didn't seem different—I couldn't see anything different. I still can't."

"All right. So you ate lunch . . ."

"Yes. Then I took the things down—she told me not to, but I did the washing up—and then I went upstairs and began studying again. I didn't see her after that until four o'clock. I'm not sure where she was, but I think in her room, or at least the house. Anyway, at four she knocked at my door, with some letters in her hand. She wanted me to drive over to Cardigan to post them. She said the post was a full day faster if you posted things from there, and she had some bills that were a bit late."

"Is that true, about the post?"

He shrugged. "I suppose it is, if she said so. Why should I have doubted her?"

"No reason. But you didn't think that she was just trying to get you out of the house?"

"Well, of course I do now, but then, no, I didn't think anything of it."

"All right. So you went off in the car?"

"Yes. But just as I was leaving, she said she was going to have dinner with someone, and I should get something to eat in Cardigan or be prepared to fend for myself. So when I got there, I mailed the letters, looked around a bit, then had a sandwich in a pub. I didn't get back till seven, or a little after. She wasn't here. But of course I didn't expect her to be here. I just went back to work. I didn't look up again until nine, and then the police came at ten." Tim leaned back in his chair. It was obvious that he'd now come to the crucial point, and yet he almost seemed to relax for the first time; as if he was relieved; confident, now, that he was going to get through it and be all right. "You know the footpath that runs over to Tresaith, along the top of the cliffs?"

"I'm not sure."

"It starts on the far side of the village, and runs along the shore. It's probably a hundred feet from the top of the cliffs to the water."

"Yes, I remember now. There's a waterfall?"

"That's right. A small one. Two of them. Well, someone found her clothes there, some man from Tresaith who takes his constitutional along there every night. He saw a bundle of clothing off the path, at the end of a point. They were all neatly folded, everything. The police said that it was quite common for someone to do that. She'd even taken her glasses and folded them on top. There was just a little pile of her clothes and her glasses. The man phoned the police. They came and found a note in her bag, so they knew what had happened. They told me, and I had to go to say that the clothes were really hers, although there was never any doubt, and the next morning they organized a search. There are a few Royal Marines at the base, and they used rafts and a frogman. They found her the next morning, caught in the rocks."

"My God, Tim."

"Yes. It was awful."

"And what about the note?"

"The police have it. They said they'll give it back but I told them I didn't want it, they should burn it. What it said was: 'I am doing this of my own free will. This can't happen again.' She'd signed it. She signed it 'Diana Harper.' " Then Tim looked at him quite simply, without hostility now, and added, "That's partly why I was so sure the reason . . . 'This can't happen again.' . . . You know what that means, don't you? You know what she meant?"

David took a breath. "Yes. I suppose. But I can't see why it would mean anything now."

"It goes back, though. I was right. To when you were divorced?"

"Yes. But that was so long ago, Tim—"

"Does it have something to do with an American named Tannis?"

"Yes. It might. Why?"

"Who is he?"

"An American naval officer. Or he was. He was the director of security at an American base, a research establishment, like the one here. It was called the Naval Ordnance Test Station and it was in a place called China Lake, in California. But how did you hear about him?"

"He came here."

"When?"

"Tuesday afternoon."

"And what happened?"

"Well, I'm not really sure. He talked with Mother."

"Was she upset?"

"No, I don't think—"

But then Tim hesitated, and David thought he was going to ask a question and he said, "No, wait a minute, Tim. Just tell me."

"Yes. I'm only thinking. Because she did get upset. You see, I wasn't here when he arrived. I don't think she was expecting him—he just showed up. When I came in, they were talking, in the lounge. She'd given him coffee. She didn't seem upset then, but when she introduced us . . . I don't know. We shook hands, and she was smiling—the way you do—and for a second she looked very strange; a funny look came over her face. I don't know what it was. She wasn't frightened or anything; it was something else. I thought she might be sick."

"But that was when you came—he was already there?"

"Yes. But it was a funny moment."

"Then what happened?"

"Nothing, really. She recovered herself. There was just that one reaction. Then she laughed and said that Captain Tannis was interested in two Germans and had I seen them. She made it sound like a joke."

"What Germans?"

"They were called Buhler and Vogel. The American, Tannis, asked if I'd ever heard of them."

"And had you?"

"No. Of course not. Who are they?"

"I don't have the faintest idea. Do you think your mother did?"

"No. I'm sure she didn't."

"Well . . ." And then, as he saw Tim about to protest, he added, "I'm telling you the truth. I don't know anything about these Germans."

"But the rest—"

"Yes. But hold on. I have to know more about Tannis. Did you see his car . . . was it an official car?"

"No."

"Was he in uniform?"

"No. I would say he was too old. If he was in the navy, he must have been retired—"

"But was there anything at all official about him? Papers, perhaps, something he might have been showing your mother. A briefcase."

"No. Look, I don't really remember that much about him. He was American. You could tell that; he just *looked* American. I remember he was wearing sunglasses—the kind pilots wear—and he kept them on all the time. Even in here."

"All right. But if he wasn't official, if it wasn't like that, how did your mother explain what he was doing?"

"She didn't, really. She just said she'd known him once, in America, and that he knew you. She said she didn't know what it was all about, but how extraordinary it was, to see him after so long. She made light of it, in a way, but I could tell she didn't want to talk about it, she didn't want me to ask questions."

Because, David thought, she already knew. *It was happening all over again.* And she'd already made up her mind. Yes, the next day she'd been calm and composed because she'd already decided. He felt sick. It was true. It had been Tannis up on the cliff. Tannis knew something. He'd come—

"Father, what's going on? What is this all about?"

"I'm not sure. I've never—" But then David hesitated; and Tim in a sense paused as well, neither of them knowing what to say or quite what they were hearing: for David could barely remember a time when Tim had called him Father. With extraordinary grammatical dexterity, he usually avoided referring to him at all, either by name or in any other way, and certainly not as Father. Now the word was suspended between them, acknowledged for a single instant by their mutual silence—a tribute to the dead—and then ignored. We're in Wales, David thought, we can be more English than the English, and then he said, "We never told you because there never seemed much point. But it wasn't that we meant to hold it from you. If you'd really wanted to know—"

"Except you made sure I didn't ask. You made sure it was something I *couldn't* ask."

"I'm sorry, Tim. We tried . . . Or I suppose I should be honest. All right, we did keep it from you. We didn't want you to ask about it. If we'd told you, it would have been harder to forget ourselves. None of this was easy. And we couldn't think of everything—I can see now that we didn't think of you enough—but we had to save ourselves. You'll have to forgive us, both of us."

"But what did happen?"

David shrugged. "Well, why do you think we came here to live, to Aberporth?"

"Because you were working at the base."

"I always assumed you knew that, but did you know what I did? Did your mother ever tell you?"

"Not really. You were some kind of scientist. But it wasn't something we talked about. It was always just assumed, something you didn't have to talk about."

"All right. But that wasn't the mystery. I was a scientist, though I was very young. That's something else you have to remember. In fact, I was something of a boy genius. Cambridge, physics, all the right professors. And I was something of a cliché too: the grammar school boy made good. I didn't understand it then but—well, never mind. In any event, my special field was infrared radiation. You know what that is?"

"Heat. I see. Heat-seeking missiles."

"That's right. A lot of development and testing of the first British missiles went on right here. Firestreak, the first one was called, and that was followed by Red Top. But the first heat-seeking missile—and far and away the most important—was an American missile called Sidewinder."

"I think I've heard of it."

"Every Western air force uses it. The Americans, of course, the RAF, the Germans. All the NATO countries. The Israelis. Everyone. It's the most important small missile in the world. It was the first missile to ever shoot down an enemy plane in combat; they make it in many different models—"

"And you worked on this?"

"No. Or not really. They started developing it right after the war, and it was operational—the first models—in the late fifties. The man who really did it, almost single-handedly, was a man named McLean, one of those American native geniuses; some people actually claimed he made the first one in his garage. He was the technical director at China Lake."

"Where this Tannis man comes from?"

"Yes. But I met him here. He was a security officer, you see. He was escorting a group of Americans who came over here on an exchange program. And just a few months later I went over there on the same sort of arrangement."

"When was this?"

"Just before you were born. In fact, if it hadn't happened—we'd looked into this, all about dual citizenship—you might have been born there."

"So Mother was with you?"

"Oh, yes. She loved it there. She was much happier there than I was. But that's not the point, you see. The point is this: the Americans had learned that the Russians had Sidewinder. They were manufacturing it— exact copies. Not an independent development, but copies. Somehow they'd stolen it. And you have to understand how important that was. The jet aircraft had revolutionized air warfare in many ways, and for all kinds of reasons, but one of the simplest was that it was very hard to shoot a jet down. A jet could literally fly faster than a machine-gun bullet or the shell from a conventional air cannon. So Sidewinder had given the Americans an enormous advantage, and now it was gone. They were furious. They set up a huge security investigation, trying to find out what had happened."

"And what did this investigation discover?"

"That there was a traitor who'd given the plans to the Russians. And the traitor, you see, was me."

Tim looked at him. "What do you mean?"

"Exactly what I said. As far as the Americans were concerned I was a spy. The U.S. Navy hated me especially: I was the first Russian spy to really breach the security of an American naval institution."

"I don't believe it."

David smiled. "Good. But the Americans *did* believe it. They convinced themselves that I was a traitor. You wanted to know what happened, Tim, and I'm telling you. They said I was a spy, probably one of the more important ones since the Second World War. Just behind Philby, I suppose."

"But you weren't."

"No, I wasn't. In fact, they didn't even have enough evidence to arrest me, or charge me, or put me on trial. But it didn't make any difference. You have to understand what this meant. I was a scientist, working in military laboratories. Everything I did, everything I wrote, read, scribbled on a blackboard, was classified. Your mother's shopping lists were Top Secret. But once the Americans issued their report, I lost all my security clearances, first in the United States, but then all my British ones. Our people stuck up for me, just for appearances, but they were convinced too. Besides, they had no choice. Even at that point,

British and American defense research was all linked together, and the Americans wouldn't have funded or cooperated on any program that I was involved with. Even the university labs all had military connections. I was finished as a scientist. I was finished . . . who *I* was—that was all over. Everything I'd striven for was lost. I'd made so many people proud, you see. So many different people were counting on me . . . and it was all lost. I couldn't work, I couldn't even teach. So I began to drink. I lost your mother. I lost you. I lost—well, I lost everything."

"It's incredible."

"Only because it happened to me. Someone you know. But I'm sure I wasn't the only one."

"No. I still can't believe it."

"Maybe that's the difference between me and other people now. I can believe anything. I can believe that some children are born deaf and dumb; I can believe that innocent people go to jail, that people waiting for the bus are knocked down by drunk drivers, that people are tortured and murdered, that people—"

David stopped. And he could see Tim complete the thought in his mind: that people kill themselves. His face was stricken, as if the thought had driven through him like an ax through wood. And David could see inside, could see that the inside and the outside were the same after all. My God, he was young—his fear, his anger, his love were equally innocent, like the white wood of a tree.

Tim got up then. He turned away, went over to one of the windows that looked out to the garden, and he said, "You don't know how awful this is. You see, I hated you. I hated you for all those years."

"No, you didn't."

"I *wanted* to."

"Except she wouldn't let you."

"Maybe I even hated her a little because of that. But even if I didn't hate you—"

"Tim, up to a point, it wouldn't have made any difference. You should have known earlier. But even if you had, I couldn't have been a father like other fathers. They killed that. China Lake killed that. I had to accept it. I had to do the best I could. It wasn't my fault, or yours, or your mother's—"

"But why couldn't you have . . . I don't know . . ."

"Tim, listen. There's no point pretending. Yes, if I could have done things differently, it might have been better for you and for your mother. But I was fighting for my life. I was trying to survive. You don't necessarily have choices. If there'd been any other way, I would have taken it. Diana understood that. That's why—"

Tim turned around then. "Yes, that's why she forgave you, why she always took your side. And that's why—isn't it?—why she did it? That's what she meant, it was starting all over again?"

"Yes."

"And that's what you think too?"

"I don't know . . . Yes."

"Why?"

"Because she did. And because of Tannis."

"You think he was threatening her?"

"No. The opposite, if anything. I think he was warning her. You see, he was on my side. He always claimed that I didn't do it—"

"But this investigation they had . . . ?"

"That was all run from Washington. That was all above him. He was the local man, lower down the totem pole. Of course, I don't really know what happened—I was more or less a prisoner—but an RAF security officer hinted that Tannis was the reason they never charged me. They didn't want to without his support."

"So what do you think it means, that he came here?"

"I just don't know."

"Will you try to talk to him?"

"I'd have to find him. And maybe he won't talk to me. Maybe talking to me is already too dangerous for him. . . . I don't know."

Tim turned back toward the window. He was silent for a moment and then he said, very quietly, "This is all true. You swear it?"

"Yes. I swear it."

"I have to tell you something, then. When this happened . . . when I learned about it . . . At first, I wasn't going to call you. I was just going to do it all myself. The inquest, and the funeral, everything. I knew she might not have wanted that, but I didn't care. So I wasn't going to tell you. But then I knew I had to. Because when I went to Cardigan, when she sent me to mail those letters, when I mailed them, I think—I'm sure, in fact—one of them was addressed to you . . . here. You understand? She sent it to you, but with this house as the address."

"What did it say?"

"I don't know. I just saw your name on the envelope. I only realized what it was as I pushed it through the letterbox."

"But where is it now?"

Tim turned around. "Well, it hasn't arrived yet. It should come today. We don't get the post until just before noon."

So Diana had written a second note. That's what it came down to. Only then did David understand, and he sat still for a moment, absorbing the implications. She'd wanted to tell him something. Which could only mean that her suicide involved him, that it really was *happening all over again*.

Tim had turned away, back toward the window. David got up and could see, over Tim's shoulder, the long garden running back from the house into a hollow, with the dark lilacs at the back and the alders and the one big oak; and then, closer to the house, the honeysuckle and mock orange and the borders with the patch of freshly dug earth where Diana and Tim had taken up the iris, and he knew that Tim had been looking at that, and thinking of his mother. But as David stepped toward him (or was that really possible? could they, at this late date, put their arms around each other?) Tim turned to face him. And then, on Tim's face, David could see the peculiar, helpless look of understanding. Tim now knew; but he really knew nothing, and he understood this. There was no way he could understand or explain or be part of what had happened to his father, he could no longer even hate, and he understood this. There was nothing he could do. It was done, it was finished, it was past. Seeing this fresh pain on his son's face, the pain that he felt himself as such a familiar ache, David did reach out and touch him on the arm, for one instant. Then Tim looked away and said, "I don't know what to say or think."

"You don't have to say anything."

"Yes." He looked back and tried to smile, a kind of apology. "I suppose I was angry, that she wrote to you and not to me."

"Well . . ."

"What do you think it means?"

"I'm not sure."

Tim glanced back, toward the garden. "You know, I always wondered why we stayed here, in Aberporth. It seemed like such a strange place for her. Why didn't she move away? And I always thought that the reason was connected to you, to your divorce. But it's the opposite, isn't it? When you think of it, knowing what really happened, you wonder even more."

Yes, thought David, you did. But then this had been his question too, why Diana had stayed in Aberporth, and now that someone else had asked it, the answer, so obvious, filled his mind. Had the betrayal been so very close? But surely it couldn't be.

And then, in any case, Tim was moving. "Look," he said, "if you don't mind . . . I have to think . . . I think I'll drive around. There's no point, really—"

"Listen, Tim—"

But he was out the door, and a moment later David heard Diana's car start up. He wondered: Was it possible that Tim had guessed the answer to his question?

Why had Diana stayed on in Aberporth?

Why, after all that had happened, had she never moved away?

From this base and its secrets. From the scientists who lived their secret lives here. From the peculiar scene of his private catastrophe.

David knew he was innocent; he hadn't given Sidewinder to the Russians. But someone had.

CHAPTER 10

Dear David . . . I've been sitting here for ten minutes, wondering whether to call you "dear," whether you were ever dear to me or I was ever dear to you. But you're dear to me now, though I suppose it doesn't really matter, and it probably didn't even make much difference then. I don't mean it unkindly, but we used each other, didn't we, in our different ways? The other night, I was having a drink in the Hotel Penrallt—I don't think you'd remember it, it was probably still a private house then, but it's where everyone visiting the base stays and drinks—and I overheard two biddies in the lounge whispering together, and one said, "She was in love with love," and the other said, "No, my dear, she was in love with marriage," and I thought of us. Or me. Actually, I wasn't even in love with love or marriage, but I knew it was all right to be, that nobody could object. Dear daddy most especially—oh dear daddy dear. *Arthur, Diana wants to marry.* Yes, well, what could he do about it? I thought I could escape him that way, though it was impossible, *much* too late. What I felt for you was all mixed up with that, and I suppose it was the same for you, though I was never quite sure what you were trying to do—only, I think, that you didn't have a choice. Poor David. But I've no regrets, not even now when I know—Yes, you must believe that. I don't blame you for anything. I never had the right to blame you, and I never have. In all the years afterward, whenever we saw each other, at our little lunches (that's how I used to think of them, and I'd always look forward to them, talking about Tim or whatever it was) I'd always think, what an attractive man, and if he was interested, I certainly would have been. So we met at the wrong time, really. We ought to have met much later on and had a very nice affair—which, I think, is what I'm good for. Or was. My speed *exactly*. Hotels, motels, weekends, afternoons. My apologies. I'll start again . . .

There. You see? One of my little girl moods, my *daddy* moods. How sweet I can be if I try! Divertimento: That's what spoils my painting, the little girl in me trying to get out, but not quite getting out, a goody-goody two-shoes Victorian *young lady* all crinolines and *accomplishment* or a naughty girl, a kind of hippie child I think, psychedelic, *spaced* (I don't know why, no, actually I do, my mind has been going over everything from that time, and I've been thinking of all those words people used, which I never had the nerve to) who's all frizzy hair and long paisley dresses and pale fey looks with her mascara smudged. (I never use it.) Carnaby Street. My god I'm old. This won't be so bad after all. What do I have to look forward to? Everything, all over again. I was ten years old, and that's all it was, the same thing over and over, in and out, out and in. But my painting, that's what I was thinking about—I probably should have been an illustrator. That's what little girls are good for. Pets and petting. My speed again: your better-quality advertising with a children's picture book at the bottom of my drawer, waiting to get finished. Or I should have stayed with photographs. But you're so naked, aren't you, and you can cheat with painting, with metaphors; *like* this, not this *is*, you see. I am definitely getting to the point. . . . Tannis. Weston. Dead man in the desert. You. Charis. You and me. I took out my old camera, the one you gave me—do you remember? it was a very good one, a Leica—and I looked at the

pictures I'd taken over there. China Lake. I always have a hard
time saying it, thinking it. In the desert, anyway. I'll burn
them. Certain things *should* be taken with you to the grave.
Secrets. All those secret pictures in your mind that happened,
maybe didn't. Click click. I must think in pictures. Tannis. He
came to see me—there . . . That's what all this is leading up to.
He didn't call or I would have told you. He came here, then he
took me out for dinner (the Penrallt again) and at the end he
said he was going to see you, but I don't know. Don't trust
him, you mustn't trust him. I trusted him because he was
frightened, I could tell even though he didn't admit it. He's
retired now, but he still lives near there, he has a house, he
says, where you can see the sunsets. Over Hollywood. In Technicolor. He made that sort of joke, easy jokes, as if he wasn't
sure of me. What I would say. How I'd react to him. Would
I—But he didn't know, all the way back to daddy, that I'd
never let myself be caught, I couldn't face it. (Not what you'd
say, but what I'd have to say, and not be able to pretend.) But
what he said was (and I'm sure he was not pretending): One
night someone phoned him, he didn't know who, and wanted
to see him, but they didn't really say what for, and when he
said he wouldn't, they said your name. David Harper. David,
he remembered who you were. They said it had something to
do with you. He wasn't exactly sure that it did, possibly they
were only showing him, in a general way, that they had to be
taken seriously. (I keep saying they, but it was only one.) So he
finally went. There was a kind of trail of messages, but it ended
in the desert, near the base, and he found the man all right but
he was dead . . . You see—the camera you gave me, photographs, it all comes around again, I'm being quite logical,
though I suppose you don't know the photograph I'm thinking
of, not sharing my particular obsessions, in fact I didn't know
it either until years later when I saw it in a book. Click. He
took it (Weston, that is, you won't even know who I'm talking
about, sweet sweet Edward, all we little girls loved him, one
after another let me tell you) with pretty Charis on a trip, the
trip when he married her—she was the same age as his sons. I
understood. I understood her perfectly, what she'd want, how

much she'd want it. They had a black Ford sedan (in those days all the cars were black like the photographs he took) and as they drove through the desert they saw a cardboard sign on the verge that said there was a sick man at some creek (Caruso?? Creek) whom someone had left and then gone for help. So they turned off and found him, dead as a doornail (do you remember how they actually talked liked that, howdy slowpoke *well now I don't know*) lying with a bandanna tied up in a bundle that was full of milk coupons (apparently, you could save them up and they would give you a silver spoon) and Weston took a photograph, *made a negative,* as Charis always says, *click,* how I envy her! lying there very peacefully, frozen, but quite relaxed—natural—but then death is natural, isn't it, nothing at all to be afraid of. Click. He was from Tennessee, no he wasn't, he was from East Germany, click click, I'm getting the hang of this, now the picture is the dead man Tannis found, no doubt taken with a flash, whose name was Buhler. Tannis said he had no idea who he was, which I believe, and I'm sure I've never heard of him. He was an old man, in fact 65, which turned out to be important, because the East Germans keep their people in until they're 65 like sheep and then they let them out. (Or the West Germans pay them, something like that.) So in a sense there was nothing wrong with this man, it was all quite legal and there was no doubt that he wasn't an agent. So, officially, nothing is certain. Click. Flash. Secrets. Secret secrets. But: he did know your name, or the man who killed him knew your name. (Someone had killed him right there in the desert, Tannis heard it. It's so hard to keep this up, I'm like an actress who's forgotten her lines and has to make them all up as she goes along, but—Never mind. Never you mind, they'd say. *Never you mind, dear.* I want to tell you this. You have to know about it and I'm afraid he won't.) It's possible they don't believe what Tannis said ("they," those special navy police) but eventually they will. He investigated on his own—all men especially daddy have their little private eye—he said he got ahead of them. He thinks he knows who killed him—killed Buhler—a man named Vogel. I'm trying to go faster. Click click click. Tannis doesn't know him—he doesn't remember—he says he's run away—but I do. Yes. Click. Click. *Don't you remember the place where I rented the horse?* Diablo. You were there, you know, once, remember when you did come riding and I raced ahead, he had that little place on the other side of that nasty town (Indian Wells?) in the desert. And he had a little girl. I don't know if you saw her, but I did, I'd talk to her when I fetched the horse, her mother was dead, a pretty little girl—her daddy loved her—but really loved her. Click. Click. It's no use crying out for mummy when it's really daddy that you want. But her daddy wasn't there, one day, when I came, he wasn't there—in the morning—already so bright—like sunlight when you're peeking through—so I took Diablo out—but when I brought him back he still wasn't there, and pretty pretty was alone. Click. Marianne. Click click. Was her name. I can just see her, big dark eyes and dark hair, like a Mexican, although I'm sure she wasn't really. She'd been alone all night, she said. (But I hadn't seen her in the morning, I think she was hiding.) I was afraid to leave her, because I knew she was frightened, she said she was frightened of snakes under the house—I did drawings for her, trying to calm her—I drew her picture—she told me stories and we made picture books—and finally another man came, filthy, I mean with his hands and face all dirty—exhausted—it was the Boers who trekked but he had an accent like that—maybe he was German too—who said Vogel had gone somewhere suddenly—there was a story but I forget it—and he was to take the little girl to him, in Los Angeles or Mexico, I can't remember. Click. A tall man like a rake. Stooping down to sweep you up. Upsy-daisy Dina. Diana. I'm not sure—I don't remember exactly—if I believed him. But the girl Marianne did know him and she went with him, but though I kept waiting he never did come back (Vogel) so I just left the money and went away. $$$. But that's who Vogel was. Is. *Tannis didn't know this.* But I don't know if I believe him. He should have known it, although it was so long ago, perhaps he just doesn't remember. Why should he remember me or you? Why should Mrs. Hanson remember daddy playing with me on the swing, swinging me higher and higher until I knew my knickers showed? But he knew that I took the horse out, because I told them all that. Because that was the note, wasn't it, the one that trapped you? When you got caught. Don't get caught. Whatever you do, don't get caught. Get home free. *If you want to know where your wife goes riding and what she really does try* . . . but I don't even remember the name of the road they told you to go to. Because I never went there. But I did go riding. Oh David, I had to tell you this, but I can't tell you any more, if I did you'd know why, you'd understand, you'd—look after Tim. You have to. I saved him for you. I was always afraid of being caught, of anybody finding out—I just couldn't bear the thought. Let's pretend, David. I don't know. I can't stay here. But where can I go? Go far away. Dear David, go as far away as me

David had read the letter in the lounge, sitting in one of the smooth blue chairs by the pristine fireplace, surrounded by the immaculate blue rug and the off-white walls, the soft air lightly scented with the iris.

When he was finished he looked around him, wondering what the letter was trying to say.

He wasn't sure. It had been hard to imagine Diana living in this room, and so it had been hard to believe in her death as well; now, paradoxically, the very life in her letter convinced him she was dead. *Here* was the Diana he remembered. But the room . . . the room, he thought, was just as wrong. "You see? One of my little girl moods, my *daddy* moods. How sweet I can be if I try! Divertimento: That's what spoils my painting." For the woman who'd written the letter, David thought, this room had been a stage set. But what part had she been playing? How had she presented herself? As a widow . . . divorcée . . . artist . . . mystery lady . . . She could have played out any of a dozen roles. But which, and why?

He leaned back in the chair, shuffling her pages together again, fifteen sheets of blue airmail paper, covered, for the most part, with her easy script but finally degenerating into a Biro'd scrawl. It was definitely her writing; it was definitely her voice: only she could have supplied these details. He could now admit that in the back of his mind he'd wondered if her death had been more sinister than suicide, but he had no doubts now. She'd killed herself, and he could feel the finality of it spreading nauseously through his stomach, turning the liveliness of her voice—"That's what little girls are good for. Pets and petting"—into something grotesque, so that he folded the letter so he couldn't read another word. But if her death, in his mind, was now much more an *act*, he still had no idea what its cause and purpose might have been. As an explanation, he thought, the letter was worse than useless; it only deepened the mystery. She'd been desperate and guilty and confused—"Secrets. All those secret pictures in your mind that happened, maybe didn't. Click click"—but what had she been desperate, guilty, and confused about? Or was this question, he thought, only another way of asking the question that had eluded him yesterday: Why had she stayed here? Why had she stayed in Aberporth all these years?

He got up and walked over to the window, parting the curtains, his eyes moving like a camera across the empty drive, the lawn, the lane dappled with the golden sun filtering though the overhanging oaks. Such peace. Tranquillity. But lurking beneath the surface . . . glimpsed between the curtains . . . hiding behind the arras . . . was the *spy*. How many times had he watched this film? So often that he'd finally enjoyed the humor of it. *They'll catch me in a moment.* Yes, all those black-and-white films with B-actors whose names you didn't quite recognize, who searched for Red spies on ordinary suburban streets, or the next-door apartment, or the seat beside you on the train. Or right here in Aberporth. Why not? Someone, after all, had given Sidewinder to the Russians, and he knew it wasn't him. Diana?

It was, he thought, the obvious answer to his question—why had she stayed in Aberporth?—and presumably the reason it had been so hard to ask. She'd been the spy; she'd stayed here to go on spying. But could it be true? It struck him now that he had never before considered the question, even in the most general way. Who had done it? He'd always supposed—or had he supposed anything at all?—that the actual spy had been some professional, by definition anonymous, his actual identity unknowable and, finally, unimportant. But it could have been Diana. It was, he thought, just possible. One fundamental aspect of the whole case had been the fact, undeniably true, that the Russian version of Sidewinder, dubbed Atoll by the NATO secretariat, had been an *exact* copy of the Americans' missile; it could have been produced only from detailed plans. And he'd once had the plans—by mistake, though of course *his* mistake, and hence one of the elements in the case against him. He'd wanted to see some details of the seeker head but had filled out a form incorrectly and been issued the full plans, indeed the actual construction drawings, of the missile. That had actually happened in China Lake itself, when Diana had been with him. Yes. And though she had no scientific training—she'd studied art history but hadn't graduated—she had a phenomenal memory, and of course she also had her camera: "I took out my old camera, the one you gave me—do you remember? it was a very good one, a Leica—and I looked at the pictures I'd taken over there. China Lake. I always have a hard time saying it, thinking it." Well. Yes. But did he really believe this? Diana, or anyone, could have been a spy. Was not that the assumption that had been applied to him? But it was ridiculous. He suddenly felt a surge of guilt. He was doing to her exactly what had been done to him. Diana hadn't done it, and he knew it, simply because of who she was. *I am not a spy.* How many times had he screamed it in their faces? Besides, if she had been the spy—and framed him? then lived all those years with the guilt?—why hadn't she come out and said so? It made no sense. If she'd killed herself out of guilt, or fear that she might be discovered now, she would have confessed, or written nothing at all. So what did her letter mean? What had happened? But she hadn't known, he thought, again feeling a sinking, falling sickness in his stomach. She hadn't known, and that was the point. Something was happening, and she didn't know. Tannis. Germans. Memories of horses and little girls . . . That's why she'd done it—

It's happening again.

It's all happening again and I can't stand it.

Now David didn't move. He stood by the window, by the table with the irises, and he didn't move. He stood in the silence. And then he had that feeling, on the back of his neck, of someone watching him. But it was only himself. Watching himself. What was he going to do? What could he do? He wanted to run. He had run before and he thought he'd got away. But now. He wanted to run again. But he didn't move. What had happened. What had happened twenty-five years ago? What had happened now? He didn't know. But then he felt something turn inside himself, like the mirror of a microscope tilting light toward the slide—he was a scientist, after all—and when he did move, he moved toward the mystery. But with fear and trembling. He went up the stairs, each step sinking soundlessly on the carpeted tread, his hand sliding along the smooth waxed banister, and he kept wanting to call out, as if to warn away the monsters . . . "she said she was frightened of snakes under the house" . . . But he had no real idea as to what these might be; he had no idea what he was going to find, or what he was looking for. He held his breath; it took all his will to go ahead, and yet, if he hadn't, he knew his will was lost. "I suppose it was the same for you, though I was never quite sure what you were trying to do—only, I think, that you didn't have a choice. Poor David." The hall was dim. The second door led to the room that had been their bedroom. He couldn't remember it, but he had, after all, fornicated with the woman who had slept here, the suicide. He turned the knob and stepped ahead.

Inside the room—it was dark—he leaned back against the door and let out his breath. Then he took in another, and he could smell her. He almost gagged: the scent of her skin and hair, still lingering in the air, had touched a memory more than twenty years old. Diana. Lying beside him. Diana, as he bent down to kiss her. She had been alive, here, only hours before, and her life wouldn't quite let go.

Grisly. Macabre. Grotesque. Her death was all of that, all the more so because it was rooted in the absurdity that had destroyed both their lives. And there was nothing he could do about it, nothing at all. So what was he doing here? The question left him panicky, because he didn't know the answer, because, even if he had, it would have made no difference: he would have been here anyway. He had no choice. He felt cornered. He tried to calm himself, looking around, getting his bearings. He didn't remember the room at all, but then the renovations Tim had mentioned must have completely changed it, changed its proportions, certainly. A wall had been taken down, opening this room into the next beyond, so now the bedroom stretched all the way along one side of the house, right to the back, where a single window overlooked the garden. For a bedroom it was altogether too long and narrow, like a hall. But then, he thought, it really hadn't been a bedroom; as Tim had said, she'd led her life here, and he could feel that. It came to him as a kind of relief, actually; she was dead, but at least here she had been alive. He was aware as well that she'd become a rather different person from the woman he'd known, although it was a difference, he thought, that he could appreciate precisely because he could see the history, find his way back to his Diana. That day in Cambridge flashed in his mind, with the bright sun and the single rain cloud. She'd gone on from there, but she'd never entirely left that self behind. And then he thought of the letter again, her criticism of her style—"Divertimento: That's what spoils my painting"—and he could see traces of what she meant, hints of the exotic that were not quite brave enough, styles that were "revivals," something French and frilly, like Fragonard, around her bed; something Eastern but also Victorian— dress-up Moorish, like the Arabs of Gérôme—that clung to a sitting area with wicker and rugs and silk cushions; and then, farther on—at the very end of the room, where her easel and paints were set up, beside a couch with a rug tossed over it—there was even a suggestion of the Pre-Raphaelite, bourgeois dreamers of the decadent: Diana, in fact, having taught him all these painters' names years ago, marching him through the Louvre on their honeymoon. All these associations made the room definitely *hers*, although the details were actually hard to see; the curtains were drawn, it was very dark; shapes floated before his eyes. He wondered if that had been the last thing she'd done here, going around to all the windows and darkening them. But then, he thought, she never had been one for gestures, another reason her suicide was so hard to understand. But she had always liked the dark, needed it to sleep. So that morning, more likely, she'd simply never bothered opening the curtains. And indeed the principal light in the room, as he grew used to it, was a small lamp on the little desk near her bed. Another sign of her life, persisting. Unless Tim had turned it on. But that wasn't likely, David thought; he doubted that Tim had been in here since it happened. He crossed the room, his first movement into it, and went over to the desk. He was right; the pad of airmail paper was still lying on top of it, her last words pressed into it. "Dear David, go as far away as me"

He put the pad down and then turned to the bed. She'd made it. But she would do that, he thought; she was neat, organized. At least on the surface of her life, she usually knew what she was doing. So she'd woken, bathed—the bathroom was next door—then come back here, dressed. But not necessarily. In certain moods she could enjoy prolonging sleep, her dishabille. *In Scotland, you know, they always sleep* in—*and I know just what they mean.* David could hear her voice saying this. And then, before the thought was actually in his mind, he could feel a weak, trembly feeling come down his arms, and he was reaching out, lifting the pillow, revealing Diana's nightdress, which wafted another draft of her scent up to his face. Instantly he pressed the pillow back. But then his fingers lingered on its lacy cover, and he remembered "daddy playing with me on the swing, swinging me higher and higher until I knew my knickers showed."

Only now, only as he turned away from the bed, did David realize what he was doing, retracing her steps, thinking along with her through the last moments of her life. It was as if he were taking a death mask, tracing out the mystery. What had happened to her? In the end, what did she mean? Then he felt a mingling of woe and anger: he knew, after all, where her steps had led, and there was nothing he could do. But he couldn't stop himself, he moved on, into the shadows, farther along in the room. Here there was a kind of sitting area: a kilim rug, creaky wicker furniture, a low table with an engraved brass top—her arabesque. A mahogany butler's tray lay across the table, holding the remains of her morning tea. The pot was empty, she'd drunk it all—though its fragrance also lingered; Irish breakfast, a little heartier than he would have guessed—and the milk jug was empty too; but he couldn't find the cup. He looked around for it. It was, he thought, as though he were joining the dots in a children's puzzle; at the end a face would be revealed. What if he couldn't find the cup? What if he lost the trail? Yet he had an instinctive confidence that he wouldn't, that in fact he was being led somewhere. And there it was, still farther along, in the part of the room she'd used as a studio. Here there was a couch, covered in some sort of faded brocade, fringed with tassels, with another kilim thrown across it, and an old rough table covered with her painting things: bottles of brushes, piles of rags, tubes of paint. The cup was on a low table in front of the couch, actually an old piano stool, and he imagined her sitting there, setting the cup down, and leaning forward to look at the fragile watercolor easel that would have held what she was working on: some liberated Edwardian lady with a room of her own. But the easel was empty. Had she sat here staring at that emptiness? But that would have been another gesture, again not like her. She'd come here for a purpose. The next dot . . . He found it on the floor, beside the table. A photo album.

It was an old album, heavy black pages in a binder, the pictures held in with little stick-down corners. He recognized it immediately; these were the photographs she'd taken on their American trip. New York. Snapshots: views from Battery Park, then looking back across the water. She'd insisted on the Staten Island Ferry: *I want to do all the tourist things.* He'd been embarrassed, stiff, feigning a greater sophistication, though, he remembered, he'd been secretly scared out of his wits by the city. There were photos of shops, a surprising number, and then quite a few taken at the Bronx Zoo. Diana had loved all zoos. Greenwich Village, where she had wanted to go and he hadn't, for the sophistication, of course, had really been hers; so they'd gone to a coffeehouse and drunk espresso and listened to folk songs. . . . *CC Rider, see what you done done* . . . The words came back to him as he looked at a picture of himself, twenty-five years ago, on the corner of MacDougal Street. He was wearing a tweed jacket; the soles of his shoes must have been an inch thick. Thank God, he thought, that his eyes were good, or he would have had those National Health glasses that made everyone look like moles. What had Diana seen in him? The question flitted through his mind as he turned over the pages. They'd taken the train west. There were stops along the way, shots out the window: one, which he must have taken, of Diana, mugging, in an observation car, the Rockies and pine trees behind her. Los Angeles . . . Looking at these photographs—Santa Monica, the beaches, palm trees—he thought of an old friend from Cambridge, a physicist named Kevin Elton, who'd taught him how to drive, the one useful social skill he did possess, which had given him an initial advantage over Diana. There were shots from a trip they'd taken up the seacoast, along the Coast Highway, he remembered, which he'd known from Raymond Chandler, perhaps his only connection with that whole part of America; images of the sea breaking on the rocks, swirling into an inlet, incredible trees with fantastic roots . . . cypress roots. From Carmel, he remembered. And there was a very good photograph of two sea otters floating companion-ably on their backs in the water. And he recalled that Carmel was the home of Edward Weston (and was it not interesting, he thought, that Diana would assume he didn't know the name, though he was now a photographer of sorts himself?). With this thought in his mind he con-centrated on the photographs, for clearly, as they went along, they grew much better, more serious; photographs, in fact, as opposed to snapshots. She'd always painted, although, as far as he could remember, she'd had no interest in photography, and he'd bought her the camera only as a way of recording their trip. But she'd liked it, just as a thing, with its knobs and levers, an intricate little machine that she could master. But she'd obvi-ously become more deeply interested; he could tell from the composi-tions, the way she began to play with depth of field. There was a shot of himself that had been taken with a longer lens, which she must have bought out there. And as he stared down at this strangely familiar face, he admitted to himself how peculiar, *unequal*, their marriage had been. He'd always been aware of the social distance between them and a difference in their temperament, both of which had somehow been bridged by their mutual desire to move from where they were to somewhere else, but what he could see here was how much more sophisticated she had been than he—the eye that had taken these pictures had been so much more know-ing than his own—and that it would have taken him years to catch up to her. "So we met at the wrong time, really. We ought to have met much later on and had a very nice affair—which, I think, is what I'm good for. Or was. My speed *exactly*. Hotels, motels, weekends, afternoons. My apologies. I'll start again . . ." Yes. He'd been so innocent. Or had that been his attraction? "I'll start again." He remembered his fantasy that

Diana hadn't killed herself at all but had merely disappeared, wanting to start again. But had she been trying, even then, to start again? Or—the possibility returned—he would have been such a perfect mark or cover, or whatever word they used, if she *had* been the spy. Going back to the album, he flipped ahead, searching now for the center of all this, what Diana must have been looking for herself, her photographs from China Lake. But as soon as he got to that section, he knew something was wrong. There were simply not enough of them. A few pages, eight pages—that was all.

Half a roll: general views of the desert. Mountains, buttes, canyons, vistas. The rest: snaps around the base itself. Serried ranks of bungalows. The main building with the American flag. No shots of the labs, because that was forbidden. Everything was dated by the cars, bizarre crosses between speedboats and spaceships. One of him in a jeep, with a marine driver; the identical shot with Diana, the marine, one foot out the door, smiling broadly, his eyes lost in shadow.

A second roll was all close-ups of the desert floor, cracked and crazed, and monumental rocks—"art" shots that didn't quite work. A third was back in the desert, the walls of canyons covered with odd designs—close-ups of these; abstractions, stick men and deer or mountain goats, which he remembered had been put there by Indians; he'd never seen them himself, but an excursion had been organized for the visiting wives. A fourth roll contained a few people, the scientists he'd worked with, Jerry Something, Walter O'Hara, Don Whatshisname, and their accompanying wives. Some of these had been taken at a party, now-forgotten faces grinning at the camera and raising drinks. But that was all; the next page was more desert, but he recognized these pictures as part of a trip across Death Valley.

No Tannis.

Almost none of himself.

Only two photographs of Diana.

Not a single photograph that could have any connection to what had happened.

And yet she'd looked through this album within hours of killing herself.

This was a syllogism, David thought, that had only one conclusion: Diana had removed several pages from the album; and almost immediately, as he looked about, he noticed a package of paper matches on the table. She'd never smoked. There was a wastepaper basket in the corner. When he looked into it he saw it was a quarter full of fine, flaky ashes, ashes that had then been broken and stirred around to make certain that no one could ever determine what they'd been.

He leaned back on the couch.

He looked down the long, narrow room, as dark as a cave, looked past the empty easel, the brass table, her kilim rugs, the lacy bed; and then he closed his eyes and images of her flickered across his mind. It was all paradox. She was dead; but she was more alive to him than she had ever been. In this room he had learned more about her than he'd known as her husband, but this only proved how much a stranger she still was.

He was suddenly exhausted. He tried to think. He'd been joining the dots; the momentum, one to another, had carried him on, but now he could feel himself slow, sink down. What had happened to her? Tannis. He tried to think of what Tim had told him. Tannis had arrived without warning. Apparently she had given him coffee, amicably, easily; but then something had changed. At least, that had been Tim's impression; something had changed in his mother. But David couldn't see what this might have been. Tim, in a way, had literally been the issue of China Lake; he was a constant reminder of the whole affair. But under those circumstances, with Tannis there beside her, Diana could hardly have found that a shock. No. It was something else. His mind tried to find it. Germans. Vogel. The horses. He did remember about the horses: *Lord, David, you do look just like a cowboy. I can't believe it.* And in fact, he'd enjoyed it, riding well quite naturally, though he never had before. But Tannis had forgotten this, or pretended to, or was that significant? And he thought then of that terrible day when he'd found the note and he'd taken that jeep and gone off in the desert, the one note leading to the next, *burn this note or there won't be another, you're being observed,* following them like a paper chase, until he was walking along that dry stream bed—*dry gulch*—and he looked behind him, and there they were, marching up toward him. My God, the sheriff actually had a star on his chest....

But what did this mean? What did it all mean now? He felt dizzy. Literally: his head was spinning. If he tried to stand, he thought, he'd fall. Down into the morass again. It was all happening again. That was the point. That was what Diana had understood. There was no way out. If she'd known what was happening, she would have said so. Of course. If she had been the spy, why wouldn't she have confessed it in her letter?

She still didn't understand what was happening, and to try to find out what she knew could only lead to her ignorance. And her despair. And now, indeed, that was what he felt; he felt it wash over him in a wave: oh, it was hopeless.

Yet it was now that David got to his feet. He seemed determined. His face was set; and with this firmness, he actually looked much younger, rather like the face in the photographs—the innocent in New York, the awkward young man with the marine in the jeep. But he wasn't conscious of this, only that he had to go through with it, though it was unclear, for a moment, exactly what this meant—until, as he found himself in the hall walking toward the door, he realized that he had to complete the task he'd started; he had to follow her steps right to the end. He had to finish what he'd begun. She'd made up her mind. She'd burned the photographs. She'd written the letter, "Dear David . . ." Then she'd sent Tim away and for the last time she'd opened the front door of this house, closed it behind her, and walked into the road. He was a little earlier than she had been; he was aware of that. The shade under the trees would have been a little different, the breeze a little stronger, the evening breeze off the sea. But he couldn't help that. And she would have come this way. Quite directly. Up the hill, till she could see the bay, sparkling under the sun, beyond the headland and the base.

David walked on. The sun did sparkle on the water. High up clouds blew across the fair sky. Meeting no one he walked along the empty road till he reached the houses of the village, the shops, the little inlet with its half-moon of beach and its iron rail. He could hear the water there, lapping up, washing up; and bobbing on the waves was a bright orange inflatable, bearing a man and a boy, puffed up in their yellow life jackets, working their way in toward the sand. He paused to watch them a moment, distracted, in that moment, absolutely: he had no idea where he was or what he was doing. Then he went on. The way rose again. He passed a shed owned by an undertaker: a macabre irony he barely noticed. Then, stepping over a stile, he was on the footpath to Tresaith, the breeze and brightness off the sea ruffling his hair, dazzling his eyes. He could smell the water, the wind. He was thinking now of Diana walking here, hugging her arms around herself against the chill. She would have kept her head up; he sensed that in these last moments, she would have felt a particular curiosity about herself. She was going to do it, but would she really? To his left the path was marked by deep hedges, the cliff edge lying beyond; on his right, opening out, were open fields with caravans, uninhabited now, and a few grazing cattle. One of the caravans was bright green; "Wendy's," it said. The path dipped down into a gully, the hedges so high that the sea was lost. Then the ground leveled. There were no hedges. You could walk, easily, out to the edge of the cliff, which curved in here, making an inlet, and on the far side, coming into view as he neared the edge, was a waterfall, a long, thin plume of water slipping down, down to the sea, whose waves washed in heavily below, surging against the rocks, thudding into the hollows and caves cut into the cliff. Now he was right at the edge. He was looking out. There was no need to look down at all. He had no fear of heights, but he couldn't remember— had there ever been an occasion when he might have discovered it?— whether Diana had possessed such a fear or not. What had happened to her? He could feel her now. She had not been angry: whatever it was, whatever had happened to her, she'd accepted it, right at the end. But he knew that he didn't. Anger filled him. Hate filled him. He gritted his teeth; he wanted to scream into the teeth of the wind. He hated himself. What a coward he'd been, not to fight them the first time, to hit back. But how could he? He'd agreed, he'd agreed. That was the irony; of course he'd agreed. You don't have to tell me about the Russians. And then, quite insanely, his heart filled with hate for the British, their self-consciousness, hypocrisy, their absurd sense of superiority, which was maintained only by the ugly viciousness with which they'd put others down. And how it had all trapped him. What chance had he had? He was so polite, such a cheerful victim. Thank you, sir, could I have another? She must have felt this too, trapped. But by what? Well, he didn't know, really. But it didn't make any difference. Not the slightest. There was no way out; as soon as you found one, they took it away. He thought of Anne. What a fool he'd been, and like all fools he was the worst kind of danger; yes, it was happening all over again, not just to him. Of course, he would have to do it to somebody else.

Loser.

Yes.

He looked out.

He knew it was going to happen.

He wasn't sure, though, whether he was going to jump or fall; that wasn't quite clear. Perhaps it was neither. You flew. Up, for an instant, toward the sun. Then the wind rushed past and you tumbled, as a roaring filled your ears; and you were going down, down into an icy darkness filled with twinkling stars.

CHAPTER 11

For David that fall into the sea, the separate moments of it, would stay with him for all his life; and he would never really know what had happened. Had he jumped? fallen? There was a moment of surprise, as he dropped, almost as though he hadn't expected it. But his free fall, his *downward motion in a gravitational field unimpeded by a retarding medium*, was itself so long—two hundred feet, perhaps; more than six seconds—that he had time to prepare himself. And he entered the water . . . but he was never quite sure how he entered the water, feet first, on his back, his rump: only, his entrance was so clean, so precise, that he later thought of it in terms of the laws of refraction, *the change of direction that a ray undergoes when it enters another transparent medium*. For the sea was transparent. Falling, he and the water were utterly lucid. But all he could feel was movement; he had no sensation, for example, of being wet. And he had no sense of fear. His speeding, rushing motion wrapped him around, kept him safe. He'd been transformed, was more energy than mass. Yet he was completely aware of the element he was in, the vast, oceanic darkness, shimmering away, and he had an absolutely clear memory (and, later, would have no difficulty remembering that he had remembered this) of his father, swinging him up by the arms, up and down, up and down, *Up you go, up you go*—and it seemed to him that he almost laughed out loud, as he had as a child, twenty feet under the water.

But then everything stopped.

For an instant he was suspended, motionless: the downward acceleration of his fall was matched perfectly by the upward thrust of buoyancy; Newton and Archimedes in equilibrium. His heart floated in his breast. His center was absolutely still. He felt at peace, and all around him was brightness, a vortex of light, his own turbulence exorcised and reflected back upon him.

But this lasted, altogether, only an instant, and then everything went the other way. From energy to mass; outside him, back in. And that was all pain. He thought his chest was crushed: his lungs burned. *There was no air, no life*. Panic screamed through him as he was thrown up, shot up, with a roaring in his ears, a scraping across his eyes, a great blow upon his neck, and was finally hurled into the bright, blinding firmament again.

But it was not until he went down and came up a second time that he realized what a perilous position he was in.

David lay on his back, in the trough between two waves. The sky seemed amazingly high above him, far away, and dazzlingly blue, and the brown, rocky edge of the cliff towered over him, looming, a single boulder, like Gibraltar. At the hard line where the cliff cut across the sky three herring gulls twisted up a vortex, a whirlpool matched by the turbulence of the sea around him. He had dropped into a cusp of the cliff, which formed both; high up the wind beat into it; here it shaped the sea into a surge, which lifted, with deceptive gentleness, then threw itself into huge, cresting waves against the rock. He was not that far from "shore"—that is to say, the cliff face—but he realized instantly that once into that surf he was dead. And he was very close; with each surge he was pressed in closer. And he knew, too, that there was another danger, which he could feel tugging down against his legs; for the sea would have carved out grottoes and caves beneath the surf, so if he was not smashed to death on the surface he would be sucked down below. Yet David had the advantage of being a strong swimmer, and something of the peculiar calm he'd experienced underneath the water was still with him, so he didn't panic. In fact, he took time to pry off his shoe—one had already disappeared—then waited for a trough, drew in a breath, and dived. For David had already understood that this was his only chance, to get below the violence of the surface into some calmer zone. He dug down, blowing water, straining his arms—three smooth breaststrokes—and then found a cool, swift current that actually sucked him out, a backwash off the cliff. It gained him ten yards. Then he was on the surface again, blowing; and he was almost finished off, for he was smashed down by a breaking wave, and took in water. Now, coughing and choking, he did panic a little, but not so much that he couldn't get some air in and then get *down* once more, bobbing up again in the next calm. He lay back a second. Then he saw salvation. Away to his right, as the curve of the cliff arched out to sea, two huge rocks caught the surge in a series of enormous breakers; but behind them, between them and the cliff itself, was a smoother lee. He took another breath, got under just in time, and swam for it. He made it on the second leg. Gasping, he bobbed in the backwash of the surf. Only then did he become conscious of the sound—the roaring of the surf, the screaming gulls, the soft gurgle of the gentler water close to him.

For a minute he stayed where he was.

But for no more than a minute. Because David knew that if he stayed too long he would die another way. The water was very cold; already, he could feel a sort of feverish warmth in his center as his body drew in upon itself. In five more minutes he would be helpless from hypothermia, and in a quarter of an hour he'd be dead. He had to get out. He reached out, clawing, at the rock, but even as he did so, he turned back, toward the cliff. It was only twenty feet away and it was actually over his head, for the sea had undercut it here. And what he saw, as he looked up, was a fissure, a split right down the face of the cliff and, higher up, a deep cleft where the two great chunks of stone, which now made this little island, had fallen from. If he could get up there . . .

He lay on his back. The water bore him up, lifting him up and down, and he realized that every fifth or sixth wave carried him up higher than the others, and that these higher waves sent a plume of spray, like a geyser, into the fissure. Once he understood this, he didn't hesitate. His foot found the rock underneath him, and he pushed off, stroking hard, reaching the crack just as he sensed, behind him, chasing him, one of the larger surges. It caught him. It bore him up with a rush—his shoulders scraped on rock—the fissure was that narrow—and then his hands, reaching up, grabbed onto something, a crack. And then the water fell away beneath him and he was dangling by his fingernails. But he'd done it. The next wave surge spewed up around him, but he was wedged in the crack now, like a pebble. Another crested. He let it. But as it fell, he wiggled up. This was only a matter of inches, but four waves later he was out of it. The water reached up but couldn't touch him. He laughed. It was crazy, wild. But he'd done it. He worked up higher. Well, you know how to climb, don't you? Yes, he did. Up there, he could see a line where the rock changed. The tideline. Above, the stone was lighter. He'd get there, he promised himself, and then he'd rest. It was easy, like shrugging your shoulders; a kind of stretching, when you pushed off with your feet, as if you wanted to work stiffness out of the small of your back. And then he found a niche and could lean back, cradled. There was sun too. He felt it on his cheek. And then there was something more, something discovered . . . a piece of heavy, sodden paper. Tossed there. Thrown there. Pressed into the fissure by the wind or the waves, then matted down.

He turned it over.

And made a magical discovery.

But it was science too. Because turbulence is also governed by strict laws—*unsteady systems*—and the sea below was nothing if not wild. Conceivably, everything that survived that maelstrom was thrown up here, as he had been himself. So what he now held in his hand was a page from Diana's photo album. She'd not burned everything; she'd meant it literally: "Certain things *should* be taken with you to the grave." Even as he held it, one edge of the sodden page disintegrated in his hand. In fact, one of the pictures had come away completely—one secret was absolutely safe—but three others revealed . . . what? He was too tired to guess.

A short, dark man, holding the bridle of a horse, on which a little girl was sitting.

A shack, windswept, forlorn, with the Mojave Desert stretching out beyond.

And a woman whom David didn't know, her lips puckered for a kiss.

Exhausted, David exercised a peculiar, clumsy care, extracting each photograph from its corner and sliding it carefully into the button pocket of his shirt. If this was a prize, he'd earned it. And earned a rest. Ten minutes, he thought. No more. He could now actually feel the sun. He checked his Rolex. And then go on. Leaning back, he was looking up toward the sky, where he watched a little tern, *Sterna albifrons*, and a black-backed gull, *Larus marinus*, wheel and dive at the dizzying point where the cliff, the sky, and the sea all ran together.

From the time he began moving again it took David another forty minutes to reach the top of the cliff.

The climb, really, was less difficult than it looked, although probably only someone with David's climbing experience and his head for heights could have made it. Once he'd reached the cavity where the fissure ended, where the rock had broken free and fallen into the sea, the only way up was along a steep, narrow ledge, which also must have been formed when the rock gave way; unsupported, the whole cliff face had split, the split then eroding into this path, which was perhaps six to eight inches wide, so that he made most of the ascent on his toes, his heels hanging in the air. The last five yards were the worst. The top of the cliff had crumbled away, there was a lot of loose rock, and by that point he was truly exhausted. But finally he pulled himself over the edge, rolled over, rolled over again, and then lay back, staring up at the high, blue sky that was rushing here from Ireland.

For five minutes he lay there, gasping, and then pulled himself up on his elbow. He was looking along the path, toward Tresaith, and as he looked up he could see that a man was coming along it: an older man in a flat tweed cap. A walker, carrying a stick. David watched him a moment. Then, without thinking, he crouched down and scrambled into the cover of some gorse. He wasn't sure why he did this; he only knew that he didn't want to be seen. Hunched, panting, trying to control the rush of his breath, he hid there until the man went by. Only when the way was clear did he rise and move cautiously toward the path. He hesitated. It seemed unlikely that he could get back to his bed and breakfast without being noticed and, for reasons he did not even consider, he knew that he didn't want to be noticed. Yet he could not stay here, not, say, until nightfall, when he could move without being seen: he was too tired, cold, wet. He needed shelter. And so his eyes moved automatically toward the holiday caravans he'd noticed earlier on the far side of the path. They were all in a line, facing the water, and looked rather forlorn, down-at-heel, a blight on the landscape except for a certain eccentric, jaunty air: one was painted dark green with lemon yellow windowpanes, another was dressed out like a circus wagon, while a third sported a collection of weather vanes—traditional weathercocks, but also Spanish galleons, a witch-on-a-broomstick, Cupid shooting his bow—that squeaked about in the wind. They all seemed uninhabited, even abandoned. But David was cautious as he moved toward the green-and-yellow caravan, staying among the bushes as long as possible and then walking smartly, stubble stabbing the soles of his feet, as he came into the open. The cows eyed him a moment from the opposite side of the field, then went back to their grazing. But there was no one to see him. At the back of the caravan was a rickety stoop, with a door painted yellow to match the windows. It was padlocked. He poked along the foundation, trying to find a stone large enough to smash it, but discovered something better, a heavy spike. With a sharp twist he pried back the hasp and, having broken a serious law for the first time in his life, stepped inside.

Through his fatigue he sensed a mild surprise at himself; he waited a moment, almost as if expecting to be challenged. But the caravan was empty; as his eyes adjusted to the gloomy light, he saw he was in a kitchen, tidied up before departure, and it seemed clear that no one had been here for months. A pair of rubber boots stood in the sink, and the refrigerator door was open, its light bulb lying on one of the shelves inside. The elements of the stove had been removed as well and lay on the counter, while dinner plates had been turned over the openings in the stovetop. Quietly, setting each door back with delicate care, he went through cupboards: melamine plates, cups, saucers, all in kindergarten green or yellow and all finely scratched and worn. Four of each. There were odds and ends of cutlery in a drawer and under the sink he found a plastic pail. But that was it. Pushing through a bead curtain he stepped into the room beyond. It was equally barren, a sort of lounge. The windows had been covered in cardboard; light leaked around the edges. It was dark and dank. Holding his breath a moment, the bead curtains swaying behind him, he felt the strangeness of being there alone, illicitly. He tried to imagine who might stay here. An old man, an old couple? Grotesques? A television, with rabbit ears, sat on a bureau. Opposite this was a couch and an upholstered rocker, both shrouded in heavy plastic, the plastic taped down to the floor. They were so careful of their miserable possessions. A regular door led, presumably, to a toilet; another bead curtain took him into a bedroom. It was also damp, moldy, and since the walls were painted yellow and the floor was covered in green lino, the total effect was almost amphibian. An old couple, conceived, by a cartoonist, as frogs. A folding cot, but without its mattress, had been pushed into one corner, a braided rug hung on the wall by a nail, and a chest of drawers sat beneath another taped-over window. The chest of drawers was empty, but in a cupboard he discovered a rubber rain cape and two blankets encased in double plastic bags. Returning with these to the kitchen he stripped off his clothes and dried himself with one of the blankets and wrapped himself up in the other. To his surprise he discovered that the mains power was on. He put the elements back in the stove and switched on the oven. He warmed himself, then heated water to wash. Slowly he began to feel human again. Didn't Toad, he wondered, have a caravan? And slowly, too, he began to take stock of what had happened.

Because something had happened.

For a moment he wasn't sure what it was and he almost felt leery of thinking about it, of pinning it down too closely, but as he rocked back in the chair he closed his eyes and remembered how he'd looked up, way above him, through the dark green sea, the light of the sky shifting, shimmering, utterly quiet and remote. He remembered how incredibly far away it had seemed. Yet he hadn't felt frightened at all; he'd been perfectly calm. And this came back to him now, the peaceful, quiet solitude of that moment, and then he knew, in the simplest sense, what had happened: he had changed. He had changed, and the first consequence of this change (a consequence, not a decision, for no decision had been necessary) was already apparent: he was going to act.

He wasn't going to hide, or run for help, or pretend it hadn't happened. *It's happening all over again*, Diana had said, and killed herself. But he wasn't going to let it happen, not this time. They've made a mistake, they've given me a second chance. He thought: on the cliff, he'd dared them. That was what it had come down to. And he saw now that he'd had to do that. It was exactly what he'd had to do. He'd given death a chance, but death hadn't taken it. Now he had his life back, and no one was going to take it away from him, not without a fight. Quite deliberately he brought Anne's face into his mind. *Yes.* He wasn't going to lose her. And easily now he admitted the truth about Diana, that he'd never really had her. He'd been too young, a boy, too innocent; which was why it had worked, he thought, why they'd been able to frame him. He was utterly innocent. He'd done nothing at all. It had been a pure, perfect fabrication; he'd been a kind of tabula rasa on which they'd been able to write and draw exactly what they wished. But not this time. They'd have to kill him . . . and he knew that this was true, that he really meant it. Which was something to consider a moment, and he did. They would have to kill him. But then the tension was broken as a rustling sound on the counter made him look up. It was a mouse tiptoeing toward the sink. David watched as it sat up and wrinkled its nose, then scurried forward; then paused again. He smiled. What a perfect symbol it was. He was a man not a mouse. Or a man not a boy. But as he thought this, something about the image—the self-deprecation?—seemed not quite right; in fact, it was exactly the sort of comment he once might have made about himself. But now? He wasn't sure. But it didn't sound right. He was different, and now, however obscurely, he sensed this difference even though as yet he did not entirely identify with it. It was as if he hadn't caught up to himself; those two characters in his mind, who created the endless dialogue of his consciousness, weren't quite in sync. I keep missing the cue, he thought. I don't know how to prompt you—me, that is.

But this thought, in its turn, filled him with impatience. The mouse disappeared behind the countertop. (The place must be infested with them, he couldn't stop himself from thinking; hence the plastic on the furniture. They'd even nested in the stove.) Because he knew he couldn't delay, he had no time to think out this new self, he could only act it out, *him* out. And yet that was the problem: if, *now*, he was going to act, what was he going to do? He had no resources. No authority. No allies. He was on his own. Yes, all the implications of what he was embarking on rushed in upon him. But he was embarked; and his new self, even if he hadn't caught up with it, had preparations under way. Naked—his clothes were still drying over the back of a chair—he took stock. His wallet yielded £428, his Barclaycard, American Express. His checkbook was in the glove compartment of his car, and he could get more money if he needed it. What about his house? Business? This was presumably going to take time. But Mrs. Simpson (his secretary two and a half days a week) could deal with that, at least for a while. Anne. Tim. He'd already linked them in his mind and had decided as well that they might be in danger, even if he wasn't sure why or how. So he would send Tim to Scotland and then get them all away. Derek must be almost finished school, so that would be all right.

All these questions seemed to have answers ready even before he asked them; and it was the same with the larger issue, his strategy. Despite everything, it seemed to him, he had certain advantages. He still had Diana's letter—soggy, smudged, but more or less intact. Even if its details were obscure, it represented a simple fact. Diana had killed herself *because* of what was happening, because of her relationship to it, which meant, he thought, that this relationship must have been much more crucial than he'd ever imagined. The events at China Lake had involved her as well as him; her, separate from himself. And even if he didn't understand what this meant, he suspected that he was the only person who understood that she was important at all, so he had a leg up. Next there were her photographs, her secrets, but he had them now, and he wrapped himself in his blanket again and spread them out across the table. They were wrinkled from the water and the smooth coating of the images had blurred, but they were clear enough. The first showed an attractive woman, a blond wing of hair combed across her forehead. Her eyes were happy; her lips were puckered, making a face or perhaps offering to kiss the person with the camera. He couldn't be sure, but he thought she might have been the wife of a scientist at China Lake. Certainly the bright sunshine, falling into the garden of a bungalow (a redwood fence, a curve of flagstone steps, a string of Chinese lanterns) made him think of the desert; and the bright, forced expression on the woman's face (a laughing voice, tinkling like the ice cube in a drink, *our turn next*, and then a confidential retreat, arm in arm, toward the powder room) brought back the wives of the scientists, imitations of Doris Day and Debbie Reynolds (or were such allusions just another aspect of his innocence?), and he almost remembered—it was on the tip of his tongue—one man in particular, an engineer, a specialist in servomechanism: there'd been a party, Diana and the wife had become friends, spent time together shopping, afternoon trips to Los Angeles or Bakersfield. But her name, and any certainty that it belonged to this face, was gone.

The second photograph, as he turned to it, was actually more obscure. A tumbledown shack, the desert behind. Yet it had a particular quality—it was a photograph rather than a snapshot; that is, an attempt to create an image—and he remembered Diana's letter: "Weston took a photograph, *made a negative*, as Charis always says, *click*." That was it, he thought; this was a composition, framed, deliberate. But it was hard to know what the image meant. The shack, actually two stories high, was covered with peeling black tar paper, ghostly advertising messages still legible upon it—SOFT RINKS EDS OTEL—but the window frames were bleached white like bones and you could look straight through and out the other side to a desert dune. In front, toppled over, was a staircase, long enough, he guessed, to reach the second floor, and a crude table with two chairs pulled up to it, as if for dinner, so that the whole effect was a little surreal. In fact, as a photograph it worked well enough. But why save it? How could this be a secret worth taking to the grave?

He had no idea how to answer these questions, and picked up the final photograph, which in contrast to the others seemed easier to understand. A short, dark-haired man was holding the bridle of a horse, on which a little girl was sitting, leaning forward happily, smiling at the sun. It had to be Vogel, and Marianne, his daughter. And Diablo, the horse Diana had rented from him. Vogel, who'd killed the other German, the one called Buhler. Or at least Tannis thought so. Yet Diana, according to her letter, wasn't sure whether she trusted Tannis about him. "That's who Vogel was. Is. *Tannis didn't know this.* But I don't know if I believe him."

He set the photographs in a row; their secrets, for the most part, were still secret. But everything, he thought, intersected at one point. The fact of Diana's death, the letter, the photographs, what had happened on the Clints of Dromore; they all came to focus on Tannis. And David's new self, it seemed, had already prepared this ground. Finding Tannis was the key; that was already a settled question. And again, despite everything, he saw that he had one great advantage: no one, including Tannis himself, would know he was looking, or expect it. He remembered his fantasy about Diana disappearing into the sea so she could reappear with a new identity. But wasn't this what he had done? Right now, sitting in this caravan, no one knew where he was. Coming over the cliff, seeing that man walking along the path, he had hidden, and his instinct had been right. His own live existence was the greatest secret he possessed. No one else knew he was in the game. He had no resources or authority, except surprise and a completely free hand. He could do anything he wanted. And at least for the time being, he decided, that had to be his first principle: the preservation of his anonymity.

It was a principle he put into practice right away.

He had some luck. By this time it was early afternoon, and his clothes were a little drier; but it would be hours, overnight, before they'd look presentable. And he considered that, spending the night in the caravan, but he didn't want to delay that long. On the other hand, if he went through town dressed as he was he'd be as conspicuous as a scarecrow. But then it began to rain, a sudden drumming on the roof of the caravan and a steady drip that fell determinedly from the ceiling to the top of the refrigerator and then to a growing puddle on the floor; a pond within the pond. But after half an hour, as the rain came down even more heavily, he knew it would provide him with a perfect cover. He got into his shirt and trousers, but put on the rubber boots, which Mr. Toad had left standing in the sink, and then, over his sweater, the rubber rain cape he'd noticed in the bedroom. He felt damp and miserable but looked, he thought, no more damp or miserable than an unlucky bird-watcher or hiker who'd been caught out when the rain began.

He stepped out of the caravan. Despite the darkening sky he blinked against the light. But there was nothing to see, and no one to see him, except the cows in the field beyond who swung their dripping muzzles briefly toward him. Along the cliff path he didn't see a soul, and then he was in the village, blurred by the rain blowing in like mist from the bay and the gray horizon. Two boys in yellow slickers ran past him, heads down, bodies somehow twisting backward against the wind. They barely spared him a glance. A blue van chugged around a corner just behind him and disappeared. And that was all. Anonymous, unnoticed, he came up to the house. His car was as he'd left it. Diana's wasn't in the drive, so Tim wasn't back. Inside his first priority was a bath, and then, wrapped in a towel, he phoned Anne in Kirkcudbright. She was right there, and he had the feeling she'd been waiting.

"Hello."

"It's good to hear your voice," she said.

"Yes. Me too. How are you?"

"Good." Then she laughed. "I hate this. You sound so near, but you're not."

"But it's better than nothing."

"Absolutely." He could feel her smiling. "I can't believe it anyway. I'm too old for this. I keep thinking I really should have some doubts . . ."

"With a capital D, you mean. Like the vicar in a Trollope novel?"

She laughed. "Exactly."

He said, "Look . . . a lot has happened."

"I knew that, somehow. That it would."

"Well, it's all true. Diana really did kill herself."

"Oh, David. That's so awful. How? . . . No, don't say."

"It's all right. I'm not upset, or not like that. She drowned herself. She threw herself into the sea."

"My God."

"Yes. But it's more complicated. There's something I have to tell you. I would have, eventually, but you have to know now. Or maybe I don't have to tell you. I told Axel. Did he ever tell you about what happened to me? In America . . . at a place called China Lake?"

She hesitated; and David wondered, for an instant, if she was struggling with her loyalty to Axel's memory. For, of course, he'd been sworn to secrecy. But then she said, "He did tell me something, or hinted—he always said you had a secret. But I don't remember the details. It was political, wasn't it?"

"No." But then David stopped himself. "Actually, that's wrong, it *was* political, only it didn't seem that way. But in fact it was. Now it's come back as something else again. I'm not sure what." And then he told her everything, the whole story, straight out. His career at Cambridge. His time at Aberporth. Then China Lake, and everything that had happened afterward, and now: Tannis, Diana's letter, the Clints of Dromore. All he left out was his own peculiar baptism, because he didn't want to frighten her. When he was finished, Anne was silent so long that he prompted her: "Still there?"

"Yes. I just don't know what to say. I never knew, I never understood. It's awful. I can't believe something like that ever happened. They destroyed your life for something you didn't do at all."

"Well, I wasn't the only one. I was just thinking that. But they didn't destroy my life, or they only destroyed it as long as I let them. And my life isn't destroyed now, and I'm not going to let them destroy it again."

"But what can you do?"

"I'm not sure, but I want to find Tannis."

"But isn't he looking for you?"

"Except something must have happened. He came here and saw Diana and was open enough: he said he wanted to find me, warn me. But then, when he did find me, up on that cliff, he didn't say anything, or even reveal himself. He saved me but then wouldn't talk to me, and I don't understand why."

"Maybe that's *because* of Diana."

"Well, I don't know about that, but I'd like to find him. And maybe he's still in Scotland."

"I could check that, if you'd like. He'd be in Dumfries, probably, or Gatehouse of Fleet. I could simply phone around to all the pubs and hotels."

"All right."

"And what do I do if he's still there? He might be—"

"I don't want you to do anything. Just hang up the phone. I don't want him knowing—anybody knowing, if they don't know already—about the connection between us. You and me. You have to be careful. If Tannis was telling Diana the truth, then this all began, began again, with one of these Germans murdering the other . . . Vogel and Buhler. So one person's already been killed. And then there's something I've never really thought about. I was framed. So that means that someone got away with it . . . in the beginning. They could be very frightened right now."

"I don't like it, David."

"Then don't—"

"That's not what I mean, and you know it. I'm not in danger, but you are."

"Yes, and there's nothing I can do about it. That's just the way things are. What I want you to do—listen now, I don't want to get fierce—is check out Tannis and then leave. Take Derek and go somewhere safe. If you were to get out of Kirkcudbright, where could you go?"

"Edinburgh. I've friends there. London."

"Farther."

"Well, we could go to Derek's grandmother, Axel's mother. She's in Copenhagen."

"Perfect. That's what you do, then. Check on Tannis. Then phone my office, not here. I gave you the number—"

"Yes."

"And you'll either get Mrs. Simpson or an answering machine. Just leave a message. It's one of the kind you can get to play back."

"All right. But what will you be doing? I still don't like this. It's frightening. And I feel like the girl in a Western movie, wringing her hands while the hero slugs it out with the villain."

"Hopefully there won't be any of that."

"But there could be."

"I don't know. But it doesn't make any difference. I have to do this. This can't hang over me for the rest of my life—over *us*."

"David . . . it frightens me." He heard her breath come out of her. "I love you so much."

"I love you too. Don't worry. Everything will work out. I have an advantage, remember: no one expects me to do anything. They think it will be like the last time, that I'll take it lying down. They won't be looking for me because they'll assume I'm running the other way."

They talked a little longer, he took down the address in Copenhagen, and then he said good-bye. Then he sat by the phone, needing time to leave her, to get used to it, and then he picked up the phone again.

Tannis. Where was he? How to find him?

Maybe he was in Scotland; but just as likely, he thought, he might be here. Tannis had almost certainly stayed in Aberporth; he'd taken Diana to the Hotel Penrallt. Conceivably he was still there now or had left the beginnings of a trail. He gave Tim half an hour more and then got on the phone. He'd intended following the same strategy as Anne, but he called the Penrallt first and was first-time lucky. Though in fact he called them twice. The first time the receptionist told him, with a definite brusqueness, that they didn't have a Tannis there; a brusqueness so definite that, when he drew blanks at half a dozen other places, he phoned back and asked for Tannis quite directly: "Could I speak with Jack Tannis, please?"

"Sir, there's no one by that name here, as I think I told you earlier, and as I told the other gentleman yesterday."

David hesitated. "I don't understand . . . another gentleman?"

"We don't give out information about our guests. Good afternoon."

The line went dead. For a second, again, David hesitated; it took him just that long to see the ambiguity. But then he did. Tannis was not a guest; if he was, since David had asked directly, they certainly would have put him through. And no doubt the refusal to give out information about their guests was a general rule. But the receptionist could also have meant something else: that the "other gentleman," who'd also been asking about Tannis, had now become a guest himself.

That, in any case, was the possibility that clearly had to be investigated. But David waited, with the phone in his hand. Was he really going to do this? Could he even take this first, small step? He was a different person now, and if in the next moment he went forward he would in the moment after that be still more different. He smiled at himself. How absurd this was: he felt like an outlaw, ready to run up the revolutionary banner. Yet he still delayed. Tim. Where was he? And he went upstairs, to his room, as if that would give the answer. If it did, perhaps it told him that he was gone for good, because all he could feel was loneliness. Old schoolbooks leaned against one another on the dusty shelves, the alarm clock on the night table was silent and had lost one hand. He guessed that Tim had put up the posters on the wall—*Harold and Maude*, and one of Fassbinder's films—but that was probably years ago. He'd been studying; a notebook and a statistics text were open on his desk. But beside these was the *Lonely Planet Guide to India*, which seemed to suggest how separate his true desires and his life might be. The life in this little room seemed transient, little connected to the house. Had he really spent that much time here? Where was his heart? And David wondered, as he looked around it, whether over all these years he had misunderstood the relationship between son and mother, whether there'd been difficulties he'd never queried. Suspicions? It was, at the least, very curious that Tim had had the same question in his mind: Why had Diana stayed in Aberporth? He would have seen her life here. Had he sensed some mystery at the bottom of it? But then, David thought, he wasn't even sure what he felt about this himself. Yet he could wait no longer. He had to find the answer, despite Tim; and he wasn't so sure, in the end, that it wasn't better that he was gone. He was out of harm's way, beyond the focus of danger that David had now become. Still, it was a link, fought for so hard and so long, that he refused to break, and so he borrowed a shirt from his son, a sweater, a dry pair of trousers. And then it was after five; he was either going to take this step or he wasn't, and yes, he was. He put on his raincoat—it was almost dry—and went out to his car and headed for the Hotel Penrallt and the "other gentleman" who knew Jack Tannis.

CHAPTER 12

As usual, the name described the place.

Pen means top; *allt* is a wooded hill or cliff. And that's what it was. High up above the sea and close to the base—he must have passed this way a hundred times—David turned into a long, hedged drive that curved across a stretch of lay-land and then sloped down toward lawns and a grove of oaks. The hotel was just beyond. Like so many other houses in the area, it was vaguely Tudor in style—gables galore, chimneys, a lot of half-timbering—but was otherwise hard to place; probably Victorian, but conceivably built as late as the twenties, for it was entirely imitative, even if it couldn't make up its mind on the model it was copying: hunting lodge, farmhouse, great estate. But the view made up for any shortcomings, carrying the eye down the wooded ridges and ravines and the smooth, green fields of the farms that led to the village.

In the car park, with its new asphalt fresh and glistening after the rain, David paused a moment and took a breath. How was he going to do this? But he knew the real problem was in himself: How could he believe he was going to do this? He remembered the first hours after his arrest and how he'd stubbornly refused to accept that anyone could think he was a spy. It was all a mistake, and in a moment they'd realize it. It wasn't him. Thus: he wasn't him. He felt something like that now, although perhaps in reverse: a sense of his own unreality—could it really be him, acting like this?—transforming the world beyond the windscreen, the loop of the drive around the hotel, the neat lawns and the long view, a black-and-white image in the dead light of the low, gray clouds, and he remembered, as they'd locked him into a room at China Lake on the first night, how the sound of the key turning in the lock had brought back memories of Burt Lancaster or Mickey Rooney, someone raging through the bars of some prison film; this was a movie, it had to be. He'd kept thinking that. But it wasn't. He wasn't in the audience, watching; he was on the screen, acting. And yet that wasn't quite right, either. It was worse. Because it really was happening; he wasn't playing a role, from which he could escape: he was himself. That was when he'd felt the real horror, and now he felt some echo of it, except, again, it was reversed, because he was responsible. For turning this car park into . . . for insisting . . . No. He wasn't exactly sure what he was doing, except he was doing it; he wasn't going to let them get away with it. He thought, getting out, looking at the cars now: *Kim's Game*. Philby must have been named after him—that had never occurred to him before—and before he knew it—Was he not a scientist? Were these not his powers of observation?—he had all the licenses in his memory. But then he looked at the cars more closely. There were five altogether. Two were just cars, a Toyota and a dented Polo. Two others had MoD stickers on their windows, which presumably meant they were from the base. Reasonable: the hotel was close enough to be a local, and certainly, if you were visiting, the nearest lodging. But then he looked into a blue Ford Escort, hired from Godfrey Davis, and right in front of him, on the back seat, was the Routemaster for Western & Central Scotland. It was a shock to see it there—so real. Almost as if he'd conjured it up, an illusion. But it wasn't an illusion, and unless it was coincidence it had to mean . . . Well, what could it mean? Tannis had certainly been in Scotland, but he wasn't registered at the hotel, at least not under his own name. And why would he use a false name? Which left only one alternative. The man who'd cut his rope. Which was, more or less, what he'd been looking for. But he hesitated. It had never occurred to him that success would come so quickly. And he wasn't quite sure, now that the moment had arrived, what he should do.

But he was determined he wasn't going to let the moment slip. He turned immediately, heading into the hotel. He had no precise plan, but when he went inside he discovered that reception, a counter built into the angle at the bottom of a landing, was deserted. Through a doorway and around a corner he could hear the sounds of a bar and faintly, down a corridor, a Hoover whined and rumbled; but there was no one in sight. He looked up the stairway; there was a door at the landing, but it was wedged open and he could see a gloomy square of wall. He hesitated. Still no one appeared. He looked up and down. There were decent moldings around the doors; you could almost smell the paneling somewhere. But the place had the forlorn air of the private house turned to commercial purposes, and it was intensified by the dim, respectable, self-regarding light. Which made it all the easier to reach down behind the counter and find the register. The current page was marked by a rubber band. His hand was trembling, but all he had to do was flip it open. His eyes scanned down . . . no Tannis, and this one page held all the registrations for the past week. No one had signed in today, and only a single guest had registered yesterday: a Dr. Keller, from Los Angeles. Room 22.

Keller.

He closed the register, twisted it back into place, and leaned against the counter.

He wasn't quite sure: Tannis, of course, could be calling himself Keller. But he couldn't see any reason for it. Keller. He said the name over in his mind. It was, a little ambiguously, foreign. German. But somehow not very German. And it certainly wasn't Vogel or Buhler. But Los Angeles was right: that's where Vogel had killed Buhler, or Buhler had killed Vogel, whichever it was. And Tannis and California were inseparable in his mind.

But just then a young woman, passing along the hall at the top of the stairway, stuck her head around the corner. "Hello. Good afternoon. I'm sorry. I didn't see you." She gave David a bright smile, bustled down, and went in behind the counter. "I hope you haven't been waiting long? We should have a bell. We *had* a bell—"

"That's all right, really. I just arrived."

"I wasn't expecting anyone. I didn't think we had anyone in today. Do you have a reservation?"

It seemed easiest not to contradict the assumption she'd clearly made, so David only nodded. "I hope so. There should be one. Mr. Harper. A gentleman named Tannis made it for me."

She had turned on a desk lamp and now rummaged through a box and then felt underneath the counter. Tannis's name had apparently made no impression, and after a moment she muttered, "Well, I don't know what could have happened. We don't seem to have anything . . ."

"He would have telephoned at the end of last week, I think."

"Well, not to worry. We have plenty of rooms." She looked up brightly. "Only, we're not all open yet. Of course we're open all year, really for the base, but only with a few of the rooms. It would take me about half an hour to get one ready for you. If that's all right."

"Yes. Yes, of course."

"Lovely, then. The bar's through there. The restaurant's open. . . ."

He was signing, offering his credit card. "I was wondering. Mr. Tannis was supposed to have someone else with him, an American. I think his name was Keller."

"Oh, well, he's here."

"Ah. That's a relief. So Jack will be along."

"You're all friends, then?"

"Well, colleagues. Or at least I know Mr. Tannis. I've never met Dr. Keller."

"He's in the bar, I think. An older gentleman, with a tan. Jacket, not a suit." She was coming around the counter. "Will you be dining in? Because you won't have a key, and I should tell Wilma, so you can sign."

"Yes, I think . . . that sounds . . ."

But she was already bustling off ahead of him, through the doorway leading to the bar. David hesitated; his deception had left him a little breathless. But he'd brought it off, he thought, though he wasn't sure to what end. Following the receptionist, he went into the bar. It was small, square, newish, or at least recently tarted up. Too much bright varnish for his taste, but that made it easy to pick out Keller. As described, he was a tall, tanned man who was sitting by himself, with a whiskey and a carafe of water set out in front of him. He looked up as David came in, gave him a good, long look, and then glanced away. But he'd looked too long, and now there was an uncanny moment, for David was certain that this man had tried to kill him. It was extraordinary. He had tried to kill him. And now he was just sitting there. Later David would understand that the bizarre quality of the encounter had been a blessing, for he himself gave no sign that he knew who Keller was. There was simply nothing in his own vocabulary of gesture and emotion that matched the moment. So Keller didn't know he knew. And almost at once normalcy reasserted itself, and David felt the incredible recede, at least to the degree that he began to think. But there was no doubt. If this wasn't the man who'd tried to kill him on that cliff, then it had to be Tannis, and it simply wasn't. In his tweed jacket and open-necked shirt Keller looked as young and fit as he could possibly look, but he was still an old man. Older than Tannis must be. And, David thought, he wasn't heavy enough, and the face was all wrong. Tannis was a big man, he remembered, and had the face of a big man: solid, fleshy, massed. Keller, though quite tall, was thin and had a small, hard, bony head that was oddly hollowed: an indentation below his mouth squeezed out his chin, his cheeks were sunken, his eyes deep set; and when he turned his head to ask for another drink, David could see a deep depression at the base of his skull: as if a giant hand had reached down into his crib and squeezed his soft baby's head in strong, hard fingers. It created an odd impression, David realized; the man's head was virtually deformed, but as if along some consistent principle so that it didn't make you *look* away, as ugliness usually did; on the contrary, David had to stop himself from staring at the man and knew he would have been very conscious of him even under different circumstances. But he wasn't Tannis; that was the point. And he wasn't Vogel, either, for his mind, exhausting itself, considered that possibility too. He took out Diana's photograph of Vogel, leaned it against the stem of his sherry glass, and they didn't match at all. The man holding Diablo's bridle was short and dark, stocky; no matter how he had aged, David didn't see how he could have turned into Keller. Although, if these details excluded Keller, there were connections too. For Keller had the deep, dark tan that David would always associate with the desert. Keller, Vogel, Tannis: however they were joined and separated, they all came from the same world. But what was his place in it?

It wasn't until after dinner that David began to find the answer.

By then he was settled in a room. It was long and narrow, a larger room that had been divided, but it was comfortable enough, and it had French windows, opening onto a little balcony, which gave him a view down to the drive, and Keller's car. He watched it till eight o'clock, then returned to the bar. Keller was still sitting there, with a menu in his hand; David asked for one as well, and they were taken into the dining room at the same time. There was even a moment when David thought they'd be seated together for, with the exception of an elderly couple, they were the only diners. But they ended up on opposite sides of the large, darkly paneled hall. It was gloomily lit: rows of empty tables only making the room darker, like an empty church or, David thought, one of those great seminaries you sometimes read about that now housed only three or four students, or, to be absolutely exact, like one of the better schools he'd taught in, before his drinking had gone really bad—an impression that was reinforced by the single matronly server and his own decision to order the fish. Which was actually rather good. And then he realized that Keller had ordered it too, so that their movements, as they dealt with the bones, almost mimicked each other—which meant he almost missed the fact that Keller ate like a European not an American; that is, he didn't transfer his fork, although what significance this had he couldn't guess. Dizzyingly, as the scene played on, he couldn't guess the significance of anything at all. Knives clicked against plates, a chair squeaked back. There was something almost macabre about it: this man had tried to kill him, but life went on. Perhaps he was mad. Or Keller was mad. Yes, Keller would get up in a moment and try to stab him with his butter knife.

But this moment passed. It was curious. But David realized there wasn't anything he could do; he had to watch Keller, and he didn't want him to suspect that he knew who he was. So he couldn't just get up and walk out. And neither did Keller, although his motives would have to be different, for he really had no reason to believe that David knew who he was. He might be fearful that David knew, but he wouldn't definitely think so. If anything, as he caught the occasional glance that Keller directed his way, he began to form the opposite impression: Keller didn't seem fearful at all. When Keller had first seen him in the bar, he must have thought he was seeing a ghost, but now he seemed quite easy, even complacent, as if everything had somehow worked out for the best. And as he slid some Caerphilly onto a cracker, David thought he could at least imagine a reason why. Diana, after all, had died under strange circumstances. If he'd fallen to his death in Scotland, a second violent death so soon after the other, it would have created a coincidence too great to ignore. Lights would have flashed; he wasn't sure where, or what they would have meant. But Keller, he was guessing, was relieved that they hadn't. From which you could conclude (a) that Keller hadn't killed Diana; and (b) that he hadn't even known, in Scotland, that Diana was dead. Or was he letting his thoughts run away with him? Because you still had to ask the question: What was Keller doing in Aberporth? There was an outside chance that he'd actually followed him here, looking for a second chance to kill him. But David doubted that: he'd discovered Keller, it wasn't the other way around; and Keller, in the bar, had thought he was dead. So the only other connection was Diana. And if Keller hadn't killed her, what was the connection between them? In the end this was the question he carried with him into the lounge.

The lounge, where their coffee was served, was as dark as the dining room, and dominated by a huge fireplace, in which a fire was laid but not lit—in fact, so perfectly laid, almost ceremonious in its composition, that David doubted it ever was. Soft chairs and sofas, surprisingly modern, were deployed around it. The elderly couple moved off by themselves; it would have been awkward to join them. But equally, David realized, not having foreseen this possibility at all, it would have been difficult for him and Keller not to sit together and exchange a few words. In fact, it was Keller who took the lead, leaning forward after the waitress had deposited their tray and saying, "A pleasant meal."

"Yes."

"Better than I remember, at least."

"Really? I've never stayed here before."

"Oh, neither have I, not at this hotel. I don't think it existed when I used to come here. But in those days, there wasn't anywhere decent to stay in Aberporth at all."

"I never had that problem. I used to live here."

"So then you must have worked at the base? Perhaps we even met. I had many friends there. . . . My name is Keller. Thomas Keller." He smiled. "Though for some reason people always call me Rudy."

The man was leaning forward; there was no way for David to avoid offering his name—and his tongue almost stumbled on a false name before he realized how fatal that would have been, for it would have told Keller that David knew who he was and what he'd done. But he caught himself in time, took a sip of coffee, and smiled himself. "David Harper. I don't think—"

"No doubt I was before your time. And of course I never worked here. I was always one of your American visitors. That was when I was still with Hughes."

"Do you still live in California?"

"No, no. I am retired for many years. I live in Mexico. A beautiful place, a colony called San Miguel d'Allende. It's full of artists—even I paint. But you're right, I love the heat and the sun. I loved it in California. But on a pension, the Mexican sun is just a little cheaper."

"I see. But it sounds a pleasant life."

"Yes. Definitely. And I can travel. I never thought it at the time, but my work gave me friends all over the world."

"Including Wales."

"Exactly. But it's the first time I've been back for a long time. And you lose track, of course."

"Yes."

"And you, Mr. Harper? What brings you back?"

"My wife. Or at least my former wife. She stayed on here after our marriage ended, but she's recently passed away."

"I'm sorry."

"Well, it's been difficult."

"You say recently . . ."

"Yes. In fact, only in the past week."

"I am very sorry, then. I feel . . . I have been indiscreet."

"No, of course not. But you're more fortunate than me. I find I have really no friends here at all. I hadn't realized how long ago it all was. You say . . . in the old days, you worked for Hughes?"

"Yes. Radio. Telemetry."

"Really. My own work—you understand, I haven't had anything to do with it for years—was physics. Infrared."

"So you would have sent aloft experiments whose progress my equipment would have beamed back to earth."

"No doubt."

"Now, though, you say you've left that work?"

"Yes. I make documentary films. Nature films."

"Fascinating. As I mentioned, I've learned to paint. I could ask you, do you prefer artistry to science?"

"Well, I'm hardly an artist."

"Perhaps you're being modest. Or not quite frank. In a documentary film—isn't it true?—any creativity must be carefully hidden."

"I think I know what you mean. Yes."

"But that's always true, of course. The best art is the simplest. Or think of nature. At San Miguel I often paint the flowers, the birds. If you were to consider them creations, artistic works—God as the greatest artist . . ."

"Yes."

"Well, then, their artistry, their real beauty, so often passes unnoticed. We are always talking about the beauties of nature, but we really don't mean it. It becomes the cheap print in a broken frame on the wall. We always overlook it. Who stops to think how beautiful an orange is?"

"We can't. There's too much beauty in nature. We'd be overwhelmed. Which I expect is the reason we destroy nature so readily."

"We're not up to it?"

"In a way."

"So, in a sense, man isn't worthy of nature. It's an interesting view. Man can't appreciate God's artistry. It is too demanding of him. Which is why we turn to science: it demands so much less. We can be so much smaller. What do you think?"

"I'm not sure. Perhaps I'll reserve judgment, Doctor."

"Yes . . . Well, you can tonight, Mr. Harper, but not forever. Don't you think, eventually, you have to choose . . . art or science?"

"I suppose you could say that I originally favored the latter but am moving closer to the former."

"Me too. Or possibly we are both growing old. Anyway, listen, it has been a pleasure meeting you—"

"You're off, then?"

"I think so. I should make an early start tomorrow."

"But perhaps we'll meet at breakfast."

"No, no. I mean truly early. I must."

"Well, then, good night. It has been a pleasure."

"Good-bye." But just at that instant Keller hesitated, turning back. "I was just wondering . . . perhaps you knew a friend of mine, a man named Stern? I used to work with him as well. Perhaps you . . . ?"

David shook his head. "I think I do remember the name. But I'm not sure."

Keller smiled. "For some reason I just thought of him. He also retired to Mexico, you see, but we lost touch." And then, with a smile and a wave of his hand—he did not quite offer it—he departed.

David stayed where he was.

He took a deep breath and felt his heart race. He didn't dare move a muscle. Because right there, right at the end, he'd almost given everything away. He'd been so smart about his own name, about the cunning of his own honesty, that he'd almost been trapped at the last. But as he watched Stern go out to reception, where he did seem to be settling his bill, he could at least hope that he'd gotten away with it. Because "Keller" was Stern; as soon as David had heard the name, he'd remembered, known. Not much. But enough. *Stern* had been the telemetry man, the expert on instrumentation, the man who'd beamed the results of their experiments back to earth. He was not Keller's friend but Keller himself. Stern. Yes, it was Stern, all right. Despite its strangeness, David still could not remember his face—too many years had passed—but he'd recognized the name at once, although somehow Stern had missed that flash of recognition. He'd been too sure. He'd blinked at the wrong moment, revealed himself rather than revealing. And there would have been a lot to see. Because for David it was a recognition that indeed went behind the immediate moment. The very directness of the lie, face to face, was telling. After that, he could not refuse to believe; there was no way around it. The worst was true. Stern, or Keller—whatever name he wanted to call himself—had attempted to kill him on that cliff. Now he was playing him for a fool. But he was not going to play the fool, not this time; and so that night, in his room, wedged in a corner of the window so he looked down toward the car park, he watched and waited, sitting perfectly still in the darkness, waiting, as he'd so often waited, for a fox or a badger to come into range of the camera, keeping himself awake with a hundred tricks he'd learned, a sixth sense alert to any movement. Until, at 3:02 a.m., Stern finally showed himself.

The night had turned cool by then, that cool that keeps you wakeful. The clouds had gone; there were stars and a moon. It was a lovely early-summer night. Two tall trees framed his view: down the gullies and valleys to the village, where a few lights sparkled, quite separate, distinct, all by themselves in the dark. Stern's car was still there; David raised himself to look but then let himself fall back. For before he actually saw Stern, he heard the scuff of his steps; and then, all at once, he was there, the back of the car already opened in the dark. It was definitely he. His posture and a quick glimpse, in silhouette, of his strange squeezed head made it certain.

David held his breath.

Thump. Stern had closed the back.

For a second David lost sight of him. But then he was around the side, the driver's side, getting in, the inside light went on, and David was already rising, gathering up the blankets . . . but then he froze. For Stern hadn't gotten into the car at all; he was just leaning inside, fetching something, and now he backed out. He closed the door and locked it. Walked away. Walked out of sight.

But David could hear his steps, and they weren't going back to the hotel; they were heading down the drive. David moved. He hadn't expected this at all: he'd expected Stern to leave early in the morning, at six or seven, say, but not this. What could Stern be doing? The hotel was quiet. There was no one at the desk. David eased open the hotel door and stepped out, listening. Nothing. But Stern could have gone only one way: to the main drive, leading back to the road. David came up to it, squatted down, an old trick, making a horizon, and for an instant caught Stern's movement above it.

He followed.

It was easy enough. Stern could still be going only one way, and after a few minutes David had closed up the ground between them, getting close enough to see him. They reached the end of the drive. Turned left. Away from the village. Along the crest of the hill, the *allt*. And then David knew, with Stern below him, that he would be visible above the horizon, and he stepped quickly across to the verge, into the rustling shadows of the hedges. He was all right there. At the bottom of the hill Stern turned off. Left. Inland. Again, it was the only way to go. They passed into a very dark lane, with big trees on either side. At the end, another turn. All the houses were dark. Two more turns. Two more again. Stern seemed to know where he was going, but David was lost, though he was guessing they were close to the airstrip. But why would Stern be going there? It was very dark. Here, in among the trees, you couldn't see the stars, and the wind bowed down branches and darkness around him. Stern kept walking. He walked fast and never looked back once. And he wasn't going to the airstrip at all. Suddenly they were beside an open field, a wide pasture silver with the dew, humped with sleeping sheep. Stern, without a pause, went right over the fence. And David had to follow, moving right into the open, because on the far side there was a dark line of trees, and if he wasn't close to Stern when he reached it, he'd never find him. So all he could do was walk directly in Stern's tracks, a perfect spoor in the dew, stepping into his footprints as if playing a game—but a casual glance back might miss him—and then, as Stern's body pivoted over the creaking wire on the other side, drop to his knees. Stern disappeared. Quickly, running forward, David went over himself. And suddenly knew where he was. To his right the ground dropped away sharply into a gully, a path curving down to a stream that sparkled in the dark light; beyond, up the side of a hill, was a little house, all dark. But to his left, the path ran straight and level, between two long files of trees whose thick roots intersected across the way and whose branches made an arch above it. A tunnel. Stern had gone that way. And the road at the end was not a hundred yards from Diana's house.

It was the only destination Stern could possibly have in mind, and David immediately felt frightened. He was thinking of Tim, naturally. Had he come back? But he was able to beat Stern to the house, pushing through trees and then cutting across a neighbor's long garden, which brought him to the back of Diana's garden, to the very lilacs where Tim had hidden as a child. And from there he could see the drive. And Diana's car wasn't there, so presumably Tim hadn't returned. Staying where he was—he was perfectly hidden—he watched the house. It was a dark bulk of shadow against the deeper black of the trees on the opposite side of the road, but a little light glinted on the windows of the kitchen. There, about five minutes later, he saw a flicker of movement. Stern was at the back door, never thinking that the front was open, though in fact it was, for David had left it on the latch for Tim. But it didn't delay him much anyway: in about ninety seconds, David judged, he had got inside. It was then three thirty-five. For the next hour, until quarter of five in the morning, David waited and watched, hidden deep in the lilacs *it was always incredibly dark, and whenever I went there I was always frightened. I knew something had happened, you see. When I was a child, that is. Something was wrong. And I didn't know what it was. She would never tell me, and after a while I would never, never ask. But you knew, of course. That was always understood. And I expect you know now. Why it happened. Why she did it.* And maybe now he did, for he didn't have to ask himself what Stern was doing, for he was certain he knew: Stern was searching. Stern had come to Aberporth because of Diana, and now he was looking for . . . letters, a diary, the photographs that David had already found. If so, he was too late altogether, but which had he particularly wanted? The picture of the woman, with that sweep of blond hair over her eyes; or the tumbledown shack in the desert, the ghost-town hotel; or the picture of Vogel and Marianne and the horse Diablo . . . or some photograph altogether different that had vanished under the waves? But then, David thought, it was possible that he wasn't searching for any specific photograph at all but only wanted to make sure that there was nothing in the house to incriminate him. Incriminate him—in what? And why would Diana possess such evidence? But the only answer he could find to such questions was the obvious one. What was the only possible connection between Stern and Diana? *Why had she never left Aberporth?* And the answer still seemed unavoidable when Stern emerged. By then there was a kind of light in the sky, wet, silvery, turning the world into the negative of a black-and-white photo. In the shadows Stern was a ghost; David watched as he vanished in the mist that hung over the road. David hesitated then. He knew he could lose Stern now, but something drew him to the house. He ran stiffly up to it, through the back door that Stern had jimmied so skillfully it was hard to tell he had been there at all. Inside, he supposed he was looking for some proof that what he suspected couldn't be true. But of course, he told himself, that was like trying to prove a negative. But whatever Stern had found, David knew what *he* had found. How could he now avoid the truth of what Diana had done? All around him he felt the house, cold, dead, abandoned; and in the end all it could provide was a kind of cold comfort. He was about to leave when he saw it: an envelope, on the hall table. The scrawl across it was almost illegible, but it must have said "Father." And when he opened it, there was a note from Tim, who must have returned, found he wasn't there, and left again. "I should go back. I have to deal with my exams. We didn't talk about this, but the policeman to see in Cardigan is Wilson, if you want. There will be an inquest, I think, but not for a couple of weeks." David put this in his pocket and took it as a sign that the way was clear. Tim . . . Diana . . . all that had happened: it was all there, out in front of him. Running back to the hotel was like falling again into the sea. And effectively he was someone else and could live it all again. Nothing could stop him. Stern's car was long gone, but where could he go? Unless he was heading into the depths of Wild Wales, he could only be heading for Cardiff and London. Twenty minutes later, on the A478, he found Stern's little Escort speeding, quite literally, into the dawn's early light.

CHAPTER 13

David picked up Stern's car around five thirty in the morning. He lost him, north of Bristol, sometime after eight. And then he found him again, in London, at one o'clock that afternoon.

This sequence of events had been dictated by luck: bad luck first and then some good.

To begin, following Stern had been easy enough; there were virtually no other cars on the road. But traffic thickened at Abergavenny, and on the M4, going over the Severn Bridge, it became very heavy. David was a good, fast driver, but so was Stern. It became increasingly difficult to keep up with him. Then for a stretch of five or six miles David was boxed in by two big lorries, and by the time he got free, Stern had vanished. It was no use; David drove on as fast as he could, and Stern simply wasn't there. But he didn't give up; he kept driving. Because the M4 goes to London, and that, surely, was Stern's most likely destination. But where in London? David had only one clue, and at Reading he used it. He turned off, went into town, and bought a fancy briefcase with a fancy lock and even waited twenty minutes to have TS monogrammed on it in gold. Then he went to the local agency for Godfrey Davis and concocted a story that, he thought, was just confusing enough to be plausible. He'd met Stern in Wales. They'd dined together. Somehow, when they parted, each had gone off with the other's briefcase. He'd only discovered this now. Could they tell him where Stern was? No, they couldn't, but they let him call their main office in London, and after ten minutes of bureaucratic shuffling he ended up with a man named Fortsmann.

"You say this person's name was Thomas Stern, Mr. Harper?"

"That's right. He said he was from Los Angeles. We were comparing notes at dinner, you see. I have a car from Baker's. He mentioned that he'd hired one from you."

"Yes, we do have him on our files."

"Do you have any idea where he is? Could you give me his address?"

"Well, I'd rather not—you'll understand that we prefer not to give out personal information about our customers. What I suggest is that you leave his briefcase where you are, and we'll see that he gets it."

"But that doesn't do me much good, does it? I'm assuming he has mine—he must have. And it's got some quite valuable papers in it."

"Well . . . I suppose he'll turn it in as soon as he discovers what's happened. I really don't see that there's anything more—"

"But that could be days. Weeks."

David could hear the sounds of tapping at a computer terminal. "According to our records, Mr. Harper, he took the car at Heathrow and is due to return it there, tomorrow. Of course he could extend that. But most likely—as you say, he's from Los Angeles—he'll be flying back to America. If he doesn't turn in your briefcase then, what you might do. . ."

Heathrow.

As a discovery it wasn't exactly earthshaking. As he thought about it David realized that at some point Stern almost *had* to go to Heathrow. And he was certain that he was going there now, not tomorrow: this certainty being part intuition but also part deduction. The more he thought about it, the more it seemed that there'd been something purposeful, *final*, about Stern's actions. His search of the house, his early start, his hard drive into the dawn: Stern was winding things up. In any case, whatever the basis of his feeling, David acted on it. He got back in his car and drove. Now he had his good luck. Perhaps it was Stern's turn to be held up by traffic; possibly he'd taken time for lunch. But one way or another David managed to get ahead of him, for he arrived at the airport about twenty minutes later. And then his good luck got even better, for he blundered, or so he thought, ending up in a terminal for European flights—for Los Angeles, he should have been in Terminal 4.

But it was just then that he saw Stern. There was no doubt about it; his tall frame, surmounted by that peculiar head, was unmistakable. And he wasn't going to Los Angeles. He loaded at the departure displays, bought a ticket, and checked himself in to a British Airways flight, Frankfurt-Berlin. David waited a decent interval and then bought a ticket for himself. Forty minutes later he was in the air.

The trip itself was uneventful. David had no difficulty avoiding Stern in the lounge; and although the flight boarded by rows and he and Stern were both in the first group, Stern had taken a seat farther back in the plane and David was already settled and slumped down behind his chair back before Stern sat down. And as far as David knew, Stern didn't move from his place the whole time. In fact, David had only one real worry. It was possible that Stern was leaving the plane at Frankfurt, and if everyone had been allowed to get out there, he would have had to follow him into the terminal. But the problem never materialized; ongoing passengers were told to stay in their seats, and after a quarter hour the plane was in the air again, beginning the series of sudden swoops and banking turns that always seemed to characterize flights in the Western Corridor. David looked out the window; when you flew to Berlin you occasionally had that rare experience, a glimpse of another plane in flight, and once he'd seen a MiG, far off. But that afternoon there was nothing except huge, fluffy clouds; everything was routine. Or at least it was routine for him. He'd been to Germany many times, and Berlin three or four times, but he wondered about Stern. When they landed at Tegel, he seemed unsure about where to go, and David, though he tried to stay behind him, ended up in the taxi ahead. That was only a slight perturbation, however—after all, this was the headquarters for the spy who came in from the cold—and a quiet word to his driver took care of it. Discreetly they slipped back in traffic and followed Stern to an ordinary, modern, high-rise hotel on the Hardenbergstrasse called the Excelsior. As Stern registered, David wasn't twenty feet behind him.

This whole sequence of events—on the one hand, so ordinary, so commonplace (he'd endured a tedious plane flight, no movie, the usual indifferent wine), but on the other, so bizarre (he really had said, *"Folgen Sie dieses Taxi!"*)—created, strangely enough, exactly the mood he needed. It provided a kind of respite, a relief. There'd been nothing to do; he'd been suspended in time and place. And so he found himself drifting away, looking down at the proceedings from some unspecified but distant vantage point that allowed him to see himself as part of an action that couldn't quite be real. There'd been a mistake. Of course Stern was just an old man. He'd imagined everything. He'd wake up soon; it was all a dream. Yes . . . Stern was leading him to Tannis, or Buhler or Vogel—or *somewhere*—but he was also leading him back into his own strange past, and in the plane, after they'd left Frankfurt, after he knew they were flying to Berlin, he began thinking of all those novels and films from the sixties about espionage, so many of which had been comedies, like *Our Man Flint* or *Modesty Blaise*, films he'd watched from an utterly bizarre perspective, listening to the laughter all around him while he recalled the smell of tobacco on the breath of one of his interrogators in RAF security, a man named Bill Tell, his crazy name entitling him, surely, to take his place among the characters on the screen. That whole time had been like that, and on the plane it had come rushing back to him, Carnaby Street, James Bond, the Beatles, Philby, movies like *Blow Up*, yes, Jane Birkin, that little gap between her teeth: he'd drifted through those years in an alcoholic haze, booze having been his way of going mad or staying sane, he was never quite sure which. But no matter how mad that mad, mad, mad world had been, it hadn't been mad enough. There was still no connection between what had happened to him and the world other people believed in, no matter how bizarre it was; ultimately, he'd had to forget the former so he could step into the latter and believe along with everybody else. And he'd never quite managed it. But that gave him an advantage now: ordinary realities were just as hilarious as "Follow that cab," and he could take Stern at face value even while he acted *as if* it wasn't true. As if. Even though. Strangely enough. Those were the phrases he knew best: qualifications, reservations, conditions, refusals of commitment, letting you step back, at least in your mind, even though he knew, all along, that it didn't make any difference, you had no choice, you were part of it whether you liked it or not. But the trick was, don't let it be a burden. That was the trick that had got him off drink, and it was the trick that he used now as he followed Stern. He was deadly serious but he managed not to show it, even to himself, acknowledging what was happening only behind his back: he went into the hotel's bar, Rum Corner as they called it, and ordered a double brandy, one of his favorite drinks, took a swallow and then turned his back to the glass. Somewhere, though, connections were being made. Hooks gave birth to other hooks, a Velcro strip between past and present. Berlin now. The 1960s. Stern. Sidewinder. The front of his mind was working out how to keep track of Stern, a real difficulty, because the hotel had virtually no lobby at all—there was certainly no place to sit and hide behind a newspaper—but the back of his mind was remembering that dream he'd had in Aberporth, the basic science of the infrared, with all its links to this country. Was there some connection? *Germans*. Buhler: according to Tannis, this was the German who'd been killed by Vogel, owner of Diablo, father of Marianne. But Stern simply couldn't be the man in that photograph. On the other hand, he might be Buhler. The only evidence that Buhler was dead came from Diana quoting Tannis, and conceivably Tannis, perhaps wanting to frighten Diana, had invented his murder. Well, he just didn't know. But one fact was now clear. *What had happened to him at China Lake had ended up here, in this strange, special town.* And so he was not particularly surprised the next morning, a Sunday, a soft, sunny, windy day with the church bells sounding across the diminished traffic, that Stern, on foot, wearing a windbreaker and cloth cap, not only led him down across Berlin but also into the past.

Of course, in every way, Berlin was anachronistic, and on a Sunday that feeling was only magnified. The city had paused ever so slightly and seemed out of step with itself. And in any case, every day of the week there was the paradox of an old European capital that was at the same time the purest example of a fifties city outside of Texas or California, a city whose wide boulevards demanded American cars and whose steel-and-glass "modern" architecture was as out of date as fins. Here, America was still king, and in the cafés people fought against the wind to read their *International Herald Tribune*s. Here, it was still and always yesterday. There was no need for nostalgia; this remained a city of variety acts and Johnnie Walker Red, of wisecracks, hot deals, and dames. David caught the mood: on a Sunday morning, what was more natural than following someone along the Ku'damm? David, waiting outside the hotel for Stern to appear, had felt a normal part of the crowd. Surveillance. Subversion. Subterfuge. The city seemed designed for it, with its huge sidewalks and handy advertising kiosks. Stern, in any event, seemed completely unconcerned about anyone following him—he hadn't looked back once, David thought, since they'd left Aberporth—though he wondered about the people in the cafés: Did they guess what was going on? As they looked up from papers and cigarettes, a palm cupped above their ashtrays against the swirling breeze, eyeing him for an instant before they returned to the whipped cream whirlpooling atop their coffee. But whatever they saw on this sidewalk, dwarfs, angels, llamas, spies, they'd seen it all before. As for Stern, David remained uncertain: Did he know the city well, or had he never been here? He walked briskly, purposefully, and never referred to a map; but David had the sense that he was following a carefully worked-out route and probably taking the longest, but simplest, way around. Ku'damm to Potsdamerstrasse, then along to the canal: main streets and obvious landmarks. He stayed on the right bank, curling back, and then crossed over to Potsdamerplatz on the first of the bridges. But only as they reached Anhalter Strasse and David sensed, then saw, the Wall did he realize they were heading for Checkpoint Charlie. Which shouldn't have surprised him. If Berlin was an anachronism, the Checkpoint was the perfect doorway to his past, for the past of the city was already being swallowed up by its own myths, and here was one of the greatest: but less real, right in front of him, than it was in old newspaper files. There was a museum, tour buses, souvenir kiosks. Even a tower that the timid could climb to get a view of communism. Checkpoint Charlie was an exhibit in Madame Tussaud's or a film set. As he went through it was hard not to believe that the border guard, staring him so squarely in the face (checking his passport photograph in obedience to some bizarre and ruthless training), was one of those actors you've seen a thousand times but whose name you never can remember, just as the older officer, stretching his uniform a trifle, was probably Curt Jurgens, and the British spy, two ahead of Stern, was undoubtedly Dirk Bogarde. After paying for his visa and changing the obligatory twenty-five marks, David stepped across a line that divided the Technicolor world from an old, scratchy black-and-white print, an ancient production by some long-defunct company whose name, logo, and antecedents were no longer comprehensible—RKO International, say, or Vitaphone. Even the weather reinforced the unreality; the bright sun and the wind, the fluffy clouds driving across the perfect blue sky, reduced the gray, darkened buildings to stage flats or illustrations in some obscure historical text, as if even nature had left this world behind. Stern, in his own way, did the same; he paid no attention to anything around him and just kept on walking, David falling into step behind, losing himself easily in the trickle of people heading for the Unter den Linden and the big museums. But Stern didn't go that way; still on foot, ignoring the taxis at Leipzigerstrasse, he turned right and away from the crowds. At which point David began to revise his earlier notions: Stern seemed to know exactly where he was heading. Over the Spree, onto the island. David guessed that Marx-Engels Platz was somewhere to his left, and then he glimpsed the city hall along the angle of the street, a sagging banner flogging in the wind. Over the Spree again. Under the S-Bahn. Left. Right. Soon David was entirely lost. Looking back, far in the distance, he could see the shape of a plane sinking down against the lovely blue sky toward Tempelhof, on the far side of the Wall, a world away. And this was a different world, which now closed around him like a bad dream. Big stores looked like car parks, apartments like factories, factories like prisons. Even the sounds belonged to a different time. Chain clattered over the tailboard of a lorry. A child's boots hurried up a metal stair. Water rushed darkly below a grate. David was trying to keep track of landmarks—what if he had to return alone?—but it was useless. Possibly they'd passed a railway station; there'd been that sense of open space behind a line of buildings. He'd noted a post office, a small park. And then they were into a built-up area of blank, faceless apartments and corroding concrete, and Stern disappeared. This happened so quickly that for a second David kept on walking, the momentum of his steps carrying him on, as if he was mesmerized by their rhythm. But then he realized that Stern simply wasn't in front of him, although, just as quickly, he also realized what had happened. There was a stairway, like the entrance to a subway, that led down to a basement entrance in the building at the corner. In fact, there was clearly a sort of well that ran along the side of the building, guarded, at the level of the sidewalk, by a low, iron railing. Then David realized that the building was actually a church: he hadn't seen this immediately because the street was so narrow—you couldn't get back from it—and its main entrance was on the opposite side; but leaning backward he could see there was a squat steeple and windows that were vaguely ecclesiastical. For a second, taking all this in, David didn't move. And just as he began wondering what Stern was doing, and started to decide that he must be meeting someone, Stern reappeared, coming back up the stairs with a bicycle under his arm. He was holding it carefully, lifting it up so the wheels kept clear of the steps, and he set it down gently in the road. Then, with a quick look up and down, he pushed off from the curb, wobbled a little, and wheeled away. Now he really did disappear: turning left at the corner, he passed right out of sight.

For David—though he scarcely realized this, so quickly had it happened—this was almost the end; he now came very close to losing touch with Stern altogether. Unlike the M4, this little street had no obvious destination, and he had no clue, no Godfrey Davis agency, that could help him. He also delayed; he misunderstood what had happened: for some reason he assumed that Stern had placed the bicycle there in advance or had arranged to have it left for him. And he kept trying to think why. Everything he thought, really, was too complicated, and only when he approached the building and looked down the stairway did he grasp the simple truth. Stern had stolen the bicycle; that was all there was to it. The building was definitely a church—this close he could make out the murmur of the sermon inside—and the stairs led down to a side door. Set below grade, in the well that ran down the side of the building, was a bicycle rack. This held perhaps twenty or thirty machines, most of which were locked, but many of which weren't. Stern had just taken one. And now there was nothing for David to do but steal one as well . . . yet again he delayed. It was hard to bring himself to do it; was there not something especially awful about stealing a bicycle? By the time he'd manhandled one up the stairs, Stern was long gone. In panic, realizing now what was happening, David rode quickly up to the corner, but the cross street, which Stern had turned into, was empty. He rode down it to the next intersection; nothing. He went along to the next, and when, as he looked up and down, he still couldn't see anyone, he was tempted to turn, just to do something. He swore to himself. He was sure now that he'd lost him. After sticking with him all the way from Aberporth. But finally he continued straight on. And that was the lucky choice, for when he looked to his right at the next corner he could see Stern, two blocks away, waiting for a light to change. David turned up the street; the light went green; he pedaled harder . . . and for the next five hours he never let Stern out of his sight again.

By any standards it was a strange journey.

David had a long time to think about it—twenty-five or thirty grueling miles—but he never finally decided why Stern had done it the way he did. A car would have been so much easier, and the DDR has perfectly good buses and trains. Moreover, stealing a bicycle had meant taking a chance—not a great one, perhaps, but a risk nonetheless. On the other hand, it was so anonymous. A car meant forms, a train meant handing in a ticket; but even in East Germany, officialdom considered a bicycle unworthy of attention. It looked so innocent. The sun was out. There was enough wind to fly your kite. And look, there was an old man, bicycling along. No one would guess the extremity of his journey, for they'd see only the tiniest slice of it and assume he'd be turning up the next lane, down the next crossroad. Soon, indeed, they were in the country, and David, without a map, was thoroughly lost. But that, he decided, was the brilliance of it. No one knew where Stern was, nor, later, would they be able to trace where he'd gone. After he returned to the West, the only record of his trip east would be in his passport, which he could destroy in a minute. Although this notion, and all David's other speculations, was only assumption; he really didn't know what Stern was up to at all.

In fact, he didn't know anything, as the miles rolled by, except the constant ache of his thighs and the grim determination of his breathing. Stern, David saw as he drew close enough on a couple of occasions, had equipped himself with a decent machine, not exactly a racer but fitted with some kind of Sturmey-Archer gearing; whereas David's bicycle was heavy and slow, coasting down only the steepest hills, which it had almost killed him to get up. The worst of it, he thought, was not knowing how far he had to go. There was no sense of progress, or any expectation of relief; he just kept on, and on, and on. Stern stopped only once, and even that was a torture. By then, they were well into the country (though David knew only that they were heading south and that they'd crossed under an autobahn) and were on a secondary road, paved but very narrow, which for a time paralleled a major highway; he caught glimpses of it in the distance. At a crossroad, which would have continued on to this larger road, an enterprising East German had set up a charcoal grille and was selling sausages to people coming off the highway. Of course, Stern stopped—and David, sitting in a ditch about two hundred yards away, watched as he enjoyed a leisurely lunch. Whereas all he could manage, when they went on, was a bottle of East German pop, a revolting combination of root beer and Coke. That was at about one thirty.

David had no way of knowing, but he'd only another hour to go, although the end, when it came, gave him little warning. They'd been riding through flat, open farmland that was narrowing into a shallow valley, the soft, green fields on the hills dipping down to meet at the road, as if the road were a stream. Ahead he could see that it meandered through a gentle curve, and a few houses and big trees were pressed against it on either side. It was a pretty spot, but there was really nothing to distinguish this hamlet—for it was not even a *Dorf*—from so many others they'd passed. But Stern slowed right down. In fact, he slowed down so much that David had to stop his bike altogether. And when Stern pedaled on, David stayed where he was, sensing now that they'd arrived: all the miles from Aberporth led here; out there in those hills, with the sun still bright in the sky, the day had awaited this moment.

David's instincts served him well. Stern rode on a few hundred yards and then turned into a patch of waste ground and scrub, disappearing into some trees, only to return a few moments later on foot. But David was already off the road, his bike pushed under a clump of cedars, whose hard shadows hid him. Those shadows were probably crucial. For Stern now looked back. Up to this point, he'd only glanced over his shoulder a couple of times, but David had been so far behind that there'd never been much danger of Stern's spotting him. On a bike, David had reasoned, Stern wasn't going to get away from him, and so he'd cautiously stayed well behind him, only closing up the ground when they'd approached settlements or turnings. But now Stern stared straight toward him, shading his eyes against the sun. David didn't move a muscle; and even after Stern had turned and begun walking toward the village, he stayed just where he was. Only as Stern finally passed out of sight, as the road curved, did he run forward, and even then he was careful to keep three large pine trees, growing just where the road began to bend, between himself and Stern's retreating figure. Panting, he came up to them. Peering around them he could see beyond that there was no more cover at all.

In any case, Stern was nowhere in sight. He'd disappeared completely, which meant that he must have gone into one of the houses.

Catching his breath, David knelt down behind the largest of the pines and studied this little hidden hamlet. Now that Stern had gone, there was no sign of life, with the exception, he saw, of two brown hens pecking along the side of the road about a hundred yards away. But no people. No smoke from the chimneys, but of course there wouldn't be at this time of year. Everyone was probably inside resting after lunch, or conceivably—how many people would live here? twenty-five?—the whole place could be off visiting in the nearest town. He counted the houses. There were only eight altogether. The largest was farthest away, leaning out over the road where it curved back again; it was partially hidden by a pine as big as the one he was hiding behind. Nearer to him and on the same side of the road four small cottages stood in a row, separated from one another by muddy tracks and low wooden sheds; the chickens perhaps found a home in these. Directly opposite were three other houses that were joined together by a cement wall; it was about eight feet high and formed the front of each of the houses, their roofs sticking up over it. David presumed there were gardens behind. All the buildings were constructed the same way—of brick, but bricks so off-square that the mortar had fallen out. Accordingly, they'd been plastered over with cement, the cement then falling away in great blotches. Again, the place was almost bizarrely out of joint with any possible present, yet because it was so isolated, the effect nearly worked. After following a man on a bicycle, he'd naturally ended up in a peasant village, circa 1935, a bizarre combination of *Cabaret* and *The Sound of Music*; any moment a huge Duesenberg would come roaring and hooting over the hill. Yes, such an image worked; but what role did Stern play in it? It was impossible to guess, and for the time being, David realized, there was nothing he could do to find an answer. For he couldn't get any closer. Stern could reappear at any time, and he'd be caught in the open. Moreover, Stern would be returning this way; he'd have to, if he intended retrieving his bicycle. The pines David was lying in gave him good cover, though they were only a few yards from the road, but they were the only cover around. So he had no choice except to stay where he was; and for the next thirty-two minutes, that's just what he did.

Very little happened. The hens nodded energetically up and down the verge; a man in a white shirt with the sleeves rolled up appeared briefly at the door of the big house and then went back inside; and overhead the blue sky and the bright sun and the white clouds—the beautiful Sunday afternoon that made this whole country seem incongruous—turned on toward the evening. And then Stern was stepping out the door of the farthest of the three cottages joined by the wall.

He wasn't there, and then he was; and two seconds later, as he stepped down the road, he could have been coming from anywhere.

It was that quick.

And yet there was nothing surreptitious about him. Here he didn't even look a stranger, an old man in a cloth cap, a Sunday visitor, somebody's uncle or grandfather. He seemed to favor his right side a little, not quite a limp, and possibly artifice; but one way or another it made him look all the more innocent. Only as he came level with the pines did David see that he had something under the windbreaker. It was wide and flat and had been shoved into the top of his pants, possibly a file of papers or photographs. It might even have been a book—David couldn't quite tell. Then he was past him, and David was looking at his back again. He continued down the road, perhaps stretching out his stride a little, and finally disappeared up the track where he'd hidden his bicycle.

David, however, stayed where he was. By this time he'd already decided there wasn't much point in following Stern back to Berlin, which was where he had to be going. And the fact that he was apparently taking something away with him only reinforced his decision. Stern had looked for something in Aberporth but had found it here; and, David thought, if he wanted to find out what it was, he had to go to that house.

He gave Stern five minutes for second thoughts and then stepped into the open.

At this point David felt easier than he had all day. He was tired and aching, but he was free of the stolen bike and Stern, and only now was he able to admit how much that had troubled him: to be on the wrong side of the law in a totalitarian state whose secret police looked as absurd as Boris Karloff but who, unfortunately, were also real. He guessed that he was in technical violation of his visa, but that couldn't be the end of the world, and as long as he got back by midnight no one would know anyway. So he didn't think he was in much danger. Especially, he told himself, because Stern, whatever he was up to, was clearly operating in terms of a private agenda: he didn't have allies on this side of the Wall any more than he did himself. So fairly confidently he went right up the road. There was no sense trying to hide, although as the road turned into the village high street he realized there were more people about than he'd thought. On the far side, behind one of the detached cottages, he saw two children playing with an archery set, the girl in her Sunday best shrieking as her arrow hit a paper bull's-eye on a stake. And behind the wall, as he came up to it, he heard a sudden rise of voices and a burst of laughter, so perhaps there was some kind of holiday. But no one took any notice of him. And there was no one actually in the street. The wall, as he walked along it, was about eight feet high, dirty concrete, flaking away. But someone had neatly swept along the base—he could see the marks of a broom in the dirt—and the cottages, despite their sagging brick, were well cared for. All the windows and doors sported fresh blue paint, and each of the doors that led through the wall had been painted as well, a glossy brown. At the third cottage, the one Stern had visited, this door was standing partly open. It didn't actually provide access to a drive—it wasn't wide enough, and you had to step over a little threshold—but David could see a small white car parked against the side of the cottage, so presumably a lane led behind all the cottages, back to the road. And presumably, too, the person Stern had seen was still in. David stepped along to the front. For just an instant he hesitated. What was he going to say? How would he explain himself? But he wasn't sure it made much difference. Probably the most important fact he could discover was the name of the person who lived here.

He knocked.

There was no answer.

After three more tries, there was still no answer.

David glanced around. He couldn't see anyone in the street; but standing where he was, he thought, he must look conspicuous, even suspicious. And now he was uneasy. In a place like this, people answer when you knock at the door. Something had to be wrong. Unless . . . Stern had a key and had let himself in. Or the place was empty and he'd broken in. But that didn't seem very likely. Something had happened, and everything inside him was saying *run*. But he couldn't. Not after coming so far. Quickly, just to get out of sight, he stepped to the side and through the doorway in the wall. Now he was in a cool, dark side yard and was hidden not only from the street but also from the next cottage, for there was a wooden fence. He listened, and the voices and laughter, from farther along, seemed quite normal. He was all right, then. He looked about him; the yard was bare earth, hard-packed for the car, which was a Skoda, drawn up tight to the house. Squeezing around it he looked through a window, but this revealed an interior as dark and gloomy as an old painting. But another window, to the back, revealed the kitchen, empty; a wooden table and four wooden chairs; wheatstone canisters for flour, sugar, and coffee neatly arranged along a counter. The window he was looking through was directly above the sink, and he could see a mug with a spoon in it. But he couldn't see or hear the person who'd been drinking from it, and he kept moving along the wall to the wooden addition, which was a kind of attached shed; it was right at the back. Beyond, there was a track, which was how they must take out the car; and, on the other side, the neat, leafy rows of a carefully tended vegetable garden. But here he was out in the open again: the fence ended before reaching the track. So he moved quickly. Two wooden steps led up to a door, which had a hasp for a padlock, but there wasn't one, only a latch, which lifted easily and he was in.

It seemed very dark. He waited a moment, letting his eyes adjust.

Then he could see that he was in a combination storeroom and pantry. In the far corner was a stack of old car tires; wooden shelves ran along all the walls, stocked with glass jars, the vivid red of pickled beets, tawny onions, cucumber pickles, peaches. For some reason a metal hook, with a length of black iron chain, hung from the ceiling. A big tin contraption he thought might be a smoker was pushed up under a painted table; and against the back wall of the cottage stood a huge cement sink with one steel tap. David stood quite still, taking all this in. The place smelled of dust and damp and peeling paint. Then he wanted to call out, but he didn't, though he suddenly realized he was so tense he was trembling. He took a breath. He went up to the door leading to the house proper. It had a glass knob that turned easily. He went through. And went right across to the opposite doorway and did call out then, *"Entschuldigung ... Entschuldigung!"* But there wasn't an answer, and he was sure now there wasn't going to be. In front of him was a short hall leading to the front door, outlined by the light outside. He went slowly toward it, his steps quite soundless on the carpet runner, which for some reason caught his attention: he thought of a Victorian boardinghouse, it was so ugly, dark, ornate. There were no lights on, no light except the outline of the door, but now he could see in the dimness. He came up to an archway, on his left hand, opening into the room he'd looked in earlier from the yard, but even before he really saw it, his eyes had moved the other way, across the hall. He supposed it was the "best parlor." It had that sort of forlorn, determined decency—neat and clean but threadbare, old-fashioned, like a radio with tubes; though in fact a television, with a big round bluish tube, stood in one corner on spindly metal legs. It was a room for Sunday best. Tea for two, with china from a pretty wooden tray, with inlaid dancers all in lederhosen. There was a doily for the African violet to sit on and plumped cushions on the cumbersome high-backed couch. A picture on the wall was indecipherable; a clock ticked heavily. A light was on: a floor lamp, with a brown, tasseled shade, casting a yellow circle across the lower half of the woman's body, her plump, brown-cotton-stockinged legs, and her gray skirt tugged up a little—she would have slipped down from the couch. She leaned back against it. On her upper part she wore a white blouse, a buttoned sweater over; a broken string of pearls spilled down her neck, dribbled down her bosom.

For a moment David didn't move.

He knew she was dead, and there really was no surprise in that—not from the moment his knock had come emptily back to him—except, perhaps, that she was a woman, not a man. But even though he'd been sure, it was still a shock. He was frightened. He wasn't frightened *of* anything; he just felt fear, like the silence, all around him. He had to close his eyes for a second to find himself, but then he did and went forward into the room. Yes, she was dead. He thought she might have been strangled, for that was the look on her face, a twisted, strangled look. Leaning down a little to see, to be absolutely sure, he smelled face powder, which made him think of his aunt, her little house in Burslem, the little room at the back, no bigger than a cupboard, where he'd slept, falling asleep listening to the adult voices murmuring together deeper in the house. His aunt. That smell. The almost-silence. Her front room . . . Her bag, she'd never been without it, her face turning anxious the moment she missed it under her hand. Perhaps this woman had been the same, for her own purse lay beside her, its contents spilled across the floor. He searched quickly through this jumble. And discovered—there were any number of documents, papers, cards—that her name was Buhler, Elsa Margrit Buhler, that this place was called Niederberg, and next week she would have turned sixty-three years old.

CHAPTER 14

David turned out the light. Stepping away from Elsa Buhler's body, he instinctively covered her in darkness. It was the least he could do; it was the best he could do. And then he went into the hall. He wanted to go farther, but he didn't dare. You could see into the kitchen, and the opposite room, which he'd looked into from the yard. Only here, with the keyhole outline of the door in front of him, was he quite safe.

He stood there, leaning against the archway, as his heart raced in a second wave of shock. But on the other side of the horror was the realization of what he'd found. *Buhler*. It was a terrible way to find out, but here at last was proof. He hadn't gone on a wild-goose chase. Buhler was one of the names Tannis had mentioned, that Tim had overheard, and Diana had put into her letter. So it was all real. Buhler, Vogel, Stern—they were all connected.

He stepped back farther, so he couldn't see into the room. After a time he felt the horror recede. It was still there, but on the other side of . . . across a line, in any case. He realized that: he was divided from it, and divided, too, from some previous definition of himself. No, he was not quite as horrified as . . . he would have been? might have been? should have been? As the shock passed off, in fact, he felt a trickle of curiosity. He stepped toward the doorway again and looked down at poor Elsa Buhler. And he could feel all sorts of responses to the sight of her (head thrown back against the couch, her legs splayed out under the little table, like a fat Japanese matron about to eat dinner), but they, too, were on the other side of that line, perfectly reasonable responses, which he could even recognize as his own but which now seemed impossible, absurd. He remembered something then, the memory summoned in part by the darkness of the room but also by the light, which he could see from the corner of his left eye, that showed through the crack around the front door, as if it were the end of an endless corridor or tunnel: a memory of the brief time (indeed, only a few hours) when they had actually held him in the jail of a military barracks, questioned him in a real interrogation room, with a heavy door, a grilled window, bright lights, and a white tile floor like a urinal or a morgue. He'd finally rebelled. *I must speak to a lawyer. I won't answer another question until I speak to a lawyer. I have a right. It's my right.* Later, he'd cringed at the innocence of this. A lawyer! Of course, if he'd insisted, they would have given him one; no doubt they had several on retainer. And if he'd asked for his own lawyer, they would have taken care of him too.

Yet that had been his response; and he could feel the same response forming now, despite everything. Put your trust in some legitimate authority. Oh, yes. Just tell the truth. Be reasonable. And he could feel all this now, on the other side of that line: phone the police, here, right away and explain. Or go back to Berlin and tell the authorities there. They could follow Stern. They would—Yes, that response was right there, ready and waiting; all he had to do was take it. What made him curious, however, was the fact that he wouldn't, that he wouldn't even seriously consider it. And this had nothing to do with being in the DDR. It was the line—and now he was on *this* side. He was different now; that leap into the sea had changed him forever, and now the change was at work. Looking down at Elsa Buhler's body, he even knew what the change was. She had nothing to do with him, absolutely nothing. It was as if he were reading a newspaper story about a total stranger, murder photos splashed across the *Sun* . . . and suddenly discovered his own name in the middle of it. Which was exactly what he had thought at China Lake. *This has nothing to do with me; just let me explain.* Except it had everything to do with him, and he couldn't explain a thing; that's what he'd learned, what he knew now. No one would help him except himself. But what help did he need?

He stepped back again into the hall; but he was quite calm now.

Stern, Vogel, and Buhler were connected—Tannis must have known
this—and the connection lay in what Stern had taken away with him. But
what could that have been? Obviously he wasn't going to find it; at the
same time, was it not possible that there might be some other way of
spotting the connection? He had, he thought, a few clues as to what Stern
had been after. For one thing, *whatever he'd found here, he'd also looked for
in Aberporth.* Two: Mrs. Buhler had given Stern coffee, so presumably she
didn't know him as an enemy and probably didn't know him at all. And
there was something else. Stern had been in the house for barely half an
hour; in that time she'd greeted him, made their coffee and served it, then
he'd killed her and . . . It was a sequence that didn't leave much time for
a search. So whatever Stern had been looking for, it couldn't have been
well hidden; it probably hadn't been hidden at all. It was something
sitting right out in the open, whose importance Mrs. Buhler simply hadn't
understood. But, a final deduction, once her attention had been drawn to
it, she might have understood, which was why Stern had killed her. And
then taken it away, so that now it could be revealed only by its absence.
All of which meant, David thought, that he should be *looking* more than
searching, keeping his eyes open rather than turning the place upside
down. He didn't know what he was looking for, but he had to make sure
that he recognized it when he saw it. Something simple, something that
would *connect.*

So now, quietly, scarcely touching anything, he began moving
through the house, trying to let the place sink into him. There was a skill
to that, and he did have it, he told himself. Lying up in the bush, with his
camera tucked behind his ear, he'd try to go very still, disappear into the
world around him, stop consciously looking for anything, stop consciousness altogether, allowing the patterns outside him to sink into him so that
any slight disturbance of them would alert him. He did that now. What
had been moved, touched, displaced? The sign could be something very
small, a note stuck into the frame of a mirror . . . a calendar . . . a name
in a telephone book . . . or something cruder, larger: the arrangement of
the furniture, the pictures on the walls. And indeed there was a phone,
with a phone book beside it. But it had no listing for Vogel, Stern, or
Tannis, and the only calendar he found was blank. The furniture was as
fixed as the features of an old lady's face, and as for pictures—they were
more interesting; he found himself pausing in front of them. There were
two in the hall, posters, reproductions, in mahogany frames. A leopard,

with a green-eyed panther stalking behind, vaguely art nouveau in style, probably from the twenties, when children under twelve paid twenty pfennig to get into the Munich Zoo. The other made him think of Klimt or Rossetti: chivalrous figures flowing mystically together, bright as butterflies. And in the dining room, the dark room across from the front room, was a reproduction of a landscape in the Staatliches Museum, Berlin, *Hauptstadt der DDR*, by a painter called Menzel, whom he didn't know. It was rather dark, formal: gardens, with some sort of great house beyond, a palace. Upstairs, in the hall, were several others like it; and now these images gave the first hint of a pattern, for the panther and bright knights were so different from the others. Elsa and Buhler. They had both lived here, but those two pictures, David thought, were the only tracks or sign that Buhler had left; they were an expression of him, whereas the rest of the house, the dark tables and cramped chairs—a kind of ersatz Victorian—was all Elsa. Unless he had it backward. But he was sure that he didn't; somehow, Buhler's departure was proof. And then, still just *looking*, he was rewarded more concretely. He'd assumed that Elsa Buhler and the Buhler who'd died in the desert, Vogel's Buhler, were man and wife; but even before he proved it to himself, he was fairly sure they weren't. Separate bedrooms along the upstairs hall and, more generally, domesticity without intimacy, housekeeping and companionship but nothing sexual; on the contrary, a tidy, well-kept barrenness. You could feel all that in the very air of the rooms. And then, in her bedroom, he found a collection of photographs on a table under the window; framed and arranged in staggered ranks, they provided a family history. Three of the photos were obviously quite old: Papa and Mama, stiff separate portraits, heads propped up by starched collars and stern rectitude, and then one of them together with Mama holding a swaddled infant. And then his eye moved to a less formal shot of Elsa in pigtails, carrying a straw basket over her arm, with a boy on either side, each holding her by a hand, one rather younger than the other, one in short pants and the other in trousers, though both were buttoned almost to the chin in tweed jackets. These had to be her brothers. Two of them. There was no indication of their names, but as David followed them through the years he realized that by the time the modern pictures had been taken (beside the cable car for the Weisser Hirsch, in front of the Thomas Church, wearing walking shorts outside a workshop at Seiffen) one of them had disappeared; in fact, the last image in which the two brothers were together clearly dated from before the war—the cut of their jackets, the heavy boots, some quality in the light itself, made that clear. So one of them, the older of the two, hadn't made it to 1945. That wasn't anything to be surprised about. But it was something he'd found out, and it gave him confidence. And questions, which also helped define a pattern. Why hadn't Buhler married? What was his relation to his sister? And why did he live in a house that was so much hers rather than his own?

Buhler's room was the place to find the answers. Separated by the bathroom from his sister's, it was at the back of the house and because of the line of the roof it had a low, slanting ceiling; so it was like an attic room, comfortable but also like a cell, a refuge, a place to lie up in. The furnishings were simple, almost institutional—his plain wood bed could have been a bunk cut down—and the emotional quality (gray light falling on a gray wood floor) was precisely the loneliness that haunts communal life, the life of barracks and dorms. Abandoned? Yes, but not *fled from*. . . . David had the feeling that Elsa Buhler hadn't touched a thing in here, nor would she; it was still waiting, this room, it had always been *waiting*, a waiting room for?? He didn't know the answer, but that was the pattern he felt: someone waiting, biding his time. In the interim Buhler had read—there were a lot of books on shelves—and collected stamps; their albums lined a wall above a little table, just a plywood plank laid over trestles. His name was Walter Joseph Buhler, or just Walter Buhler; it was written neatly across every book's flyleaf. David flipped through them randomly. A few novels and some poetry by standard German authors, Heine, Mann, Feuchtwanger, Fontane; a few foreigners, Jack London, *For Whom the Bell Tolls*, Jules Romains; but mostly reference books, texts on a variety of subjects: geography, geology, birds, bridges, butterflies— all rather carefully arranged, as if he'd taken courses about these subjects, learned what was in these books, and then rarely looked at them again. But what had such study been preparation for? Or had it, precisely, been an end in itself, his way of waiting?

With that in his mind, David looked through his stamp collection, and it seemed to represent much the same sort of thing. He remembered how he'd collected stamps himself as a boy, but that had been rather different, for his albums had been like books, with little pictures of the stamps: you'd match one and then stick it in. Buhler, by that standard, was a real collector, almost professional; his albums were ordinary three-ring binders, but had special plastic leaves, the stamps being slipped carefully into pockets. Many were from South America or Central America, also Africa, although as he went through them David began to realize that Buhler didn't collect by country or period. It was a question of theme: for all the stamps were of birds or butterflies, anything that *flew*. Which confirmed, in David's mind, his earlier feeling about the posters. It was a colorful, rather beautiful, collection; stamps from Costa Rica and Zanzibar, Venezuela, Peru, Mozambique, some triangular or very large, most very bright: emeralds, monarchs, peacocks—among the butterflies—and all the bright, exciting birds, parakeets, macaws, cockatoos, lories, hummingbirds, condors, eagles. They were so light, so bright, so frivolous, so much in contradiction to Buhler's world that it seemed fitting, in the end, that they revealed it: for it was the emerald butterfly, slipping off the page and fluttering to the floor, that gave away his secret. Bending down to pick it up, David realized that one of the floorboards, just at the edge of the bed, had been cut. This had been neatly done, on an angle, so the cut was nearly invisible. But he stuck his knife in, prized it back, and it came right out. Underneath it, in the space between the floor and the ceiling of the room below, was a metal box, screwed into place.

Buhler's hidey-hole.

But it was empty.

The metal sides of the box, yellowishly lacquered, glinted back at him with a golden, mocking light. Stern had beaten him to it. Whatever had been here—letters, photographs, a diary—had been taken. Of course, there was a certain obvious logic to this; the best he could do was discover such negative signs of what Stern had been after. But it was a letdown nonetheless, and with a sigh he sat back on his heels. Which only served, as it happened, to frustrate him all the more: for as he rocked back, David's eyes came level with the small painted table by Buhler's bed, and he could clearly see, imprinted by the years into the very surface of the wood, the marks of two small frames. Getting up, he ran his fingers over them. Photographs, he supposed. Two photographs in frames, like the ones in Elsa's room. But these pictures had been different, not images of family history but something else, something crucial to Buhler, for he'd kept them by him all the night; and something crucial to Stern, for he'd stolen them away. But what could they have shown? Some atrocity. Stern himself, in some compromising situation. It was impossible to say, but it was clear again what Stern was doing. Covering up. Covering his tracks. Just as he'd been doing in Aberporth. On the Clints of Dromore? Severing his connections with and to . . . but what?

Well, he didn't know, that was the simple truth of it, and David swore and sat down on the edge of Buhler's bed. And for a moment now his resolution did weaken; he was suddenly very aware of Elsa Buhler, dead in the room on the floor below, of the sunshine falling through the cracks around the black front door, creating an arc of light her eyes would never see. But this moment passed and in fact he suddenly felt a grim satisfaction. For he'd discovered something, after all, confirmed the thrust of Stern's intention. And his own method had been confirmed as well; whatever he was going to find, whatever Buhler had to offer him, this was the way to look for it, and once more he followed his instincts and actually got up and left the room, letting himself be drawn along, searching through the bathroom and a cupboard (soap, shampoo, a tin pail, a shelf with neatly folded rags), though fifteen minutes later, when he finally found it, found all he was going to find, he was in Buhler's room again. He'd been reaching a decision: he'd have one last look in here, then try downstairs again, and if he still had no luck he'd take Buhler's car back to Berlin—he could still get there before Stern—and confront him. But as soon as he stepped through the doorway, he glanced down and saw the little wicker basket on Buhler's table. It was the sort of basket you'd keep fruit in, but it was full of stamps, envelopes, and torn pieces of envelopes; people must have saved them for him. He poked through them, not actually looking at all. But don't look, and you'll find what you're looking for; he'd been right about that, because, as he picked up a piece of envelope, he saw that it had two big, bright American stamps on it. They were twenty-cent stamps, both the same; they commemorated the California state flower, the poppy, and the bird, the California valley quail, which would have been Buhler's interest. And the postmark was clear: Lone Pine, CA, and only a few weeks ago. But the "envelope" was even more interesting. In fact, it wasn't an envelope but a corner torn from an aerogram, a folding letter of blue airmail flimsy. Moreover, the aerogram was German, a *Luftpostleichtbrief,* which meant that Buhler must have purchased it in West Germany and carried it with him to California, where he'd bought the sort of stamp that interested him and which Elsa Buhler—out of habit? as some sort of private gesture?—had saved. But this explanation came into David's mind only incidentally; what attracted him immediately were the few lines of writing that had survived, on the reverse.

There was not much: only the tag ends of half a dozen separate lines. Remembering how an aerogram folded, he guessed they were from the middle of the letter, but because of German grammar—verbs tend to pile up at the end of clauses and sentences—even that wasn't certain. Had Buhler written from top to bottom or side to side? In any case, only a few cramped words were left

the truth about our brother and Vogel. The Red Cross,
friends, other refugees, the organization UNRRA
all the letters in the box under
Nordhausen and Dora remember. It always seems so small. I
like the last time. But that was my choice.
filled in. However, I could still see them.

What this meant, as he read it over, was scarcely clear, and yet it was clear enough. Letters, refugees, "the truth about our brother." UNRRA—the initials were in English, but it took David a moment to remember precisely what they meant: United Nations Relief and Rehabilitation Administration. After the war, they'd fed refugees, settled displaced persons. Buhler had apparently written them, and others, looking for a brother, or Vogel, or both? And he'd kept the record of that correspondence in the box beneath his bed. Which Elsa had known, which Stern had found. Had he got that out of her before he'd killed her? Those letters and what they revealed had been a secret, possibly so secret that Buhler hadn't even told his sister about them until he was out of the country. In any case, the connections they revealed had been a secret to kill for. And there was one other connection, which David would have found eventually, but which in fact he'd already noticed, or at least half noticed, for they'd been given no particular prominence on Buhler's shelves: a couple of little pamphlets, one of which was called "Chronik der antifaschistischen Mahn- und Gedenkstätte Mittelbau Dora." It was modestly printed, not very memorable, a bare recital of facts illustrated with rather bad black-and-white photographs. But its pages told David what he needed to know. Dora was a prison camp, on the outskirts of a railway junction called Nordhausen. In many ways, as the pamphlet showed, it had been little different, even in its horrors, from any other camp. For there were photos of the crematorium on a little hill, and there were photos of *die Häftlinge*, the prisoners, by the barracks behind the barbed wire fences, and there were photos, taken after the war, of schoolchildren, trade union delegations, so on and so forth laying wreaths and flowers in front of monuments to the thousands of dead. There were even poems:

> *Viele haben das Lager D gekannt,*
> *D wie Dora, so habens die Faschisten genannt*, etc. etc.

Yes, all of this was entirely familiar, but what grabbed David's attention were other photographs and images, pictures of a huge underground factory where the prisoners had slaved and of the terrible weapons that they'd assembled. For it was in Dora that the Germans had built the V-2, the Vengeance Weapon II, the first ballistic missile in the world, building them at *Konzentrationslager Mittelbau Dora* in the Harz Mountains just as the U.S. Navy was searching the deserts of California and then settling in at China Lake.

CHAPTER 15

It took David about three hours to drive to Nordhausen.

The trip was uneventful; there was really no reason it should have been anything else. The car was a risk. But only briefly. Once he was out of the village, where someone might have recognized it as Buhler's, it would have been bad luck if anyone had stopped him. He scrupulously kept to the speed limits; as soon as possible, he left the main highway for smaller roads; and there was lots of traffic to lose himself in—strangely, "the Sunday drive," that great American custom of the fifties, was still observed here in the East. As he drove along David was actually unaware of his greatest potential danger, which was running out of petrol. He had only a few East German marks and of course none of the coupons, exchangeable for *Benzin*, that tourists with cars were compelled to buy as they entered the DDR, so he would have been forced to use deutsche marks to tank up, and though they would have been accepted, they were still illegal and would have marked him out. Even so, this would have made little difference. No one was looking for him. The problem never arose in any case, for the car's tank was full and ran low only later that night as he came back to East Berlin.

But that was the end of the trip, when he was full of the exhilaration and anxiety of the last dash for the Wall. In the beginning, as he angled south and west through the afternoon sun, what he felt was curiosity and a particular determination. He knew, absolutely, that he would see this through to the end, but where would that take him? He really had so little to go on. All he knew was:

He had nothing to do with Elsa Buhler.

But he had everything to do with Elsa Buhler; he must, for he was one of only two people on earth who knew she was dead.

He had nothing to do with Dora, a concentration camp in East Germany.

But no, he had everything in the world to do with Dora the *Konzentrationslager*, or why would he be driving there now?

And he had nothing to do with what had happened at China Lake, five thousand miles away in the desert.

Except that, too, was quite wrong. He had everything to do with China Lake, for wasn't that where he had started?

But David was always careful about such speculations, though they were true enough. It was the story of his life, he thought. His life had never been his own; it had all been decided by other people, it was something that had happened to him. But that didn't make him so special. Looking through the windscreen he could see a "Communist" world and "Communists" driving along in their cars, "communism" being a shorthand expression for describing what had happened to *them*. Of course it was crazy. He had been suspected of "working for the Communists," but if the East German police picked him up now, they'd accuse him of working for the CIA . . . which would make a perfect ending, he thought, like one of those television plays where the protagonist ends up where he began and the music either goes solemn or seems to come from outer space. He smiled—well, you could take comfort from that. Life, whatever it was, couldn't be like a television play. He was smiling. Yet only an hour before he'd discovered Elsa Buhler. But that was part of it too. It was part of what had happened at Aberporth, he thought, *what he'd done himself*, finally, after all these years, taking his life into his own hands. He could admit that to himself now. The world outside was utterly removed from him, but that had nothing much to do with its political complexion or his immediate situation; really, he'd often felt just as far removed driving through the Cotswolds or France, and this world, after all, had never done him any harm. Whatever he might fear now about the East German police he'd only ever suffered at the hands of the FBI and RAF Security. Yes. If he didn't feel at home here, how ought he to feel in California? But the truth was, his distance from the world had existed long before China Lake. All that had changed now was his acceptance of the fact, and he could admit it now because he had something beyond this world to live for. And that was how he thought of Anne, that was how she came to him then. He could just feel her, inside him. Or more exactly, he could feel himself become the person he'd become with her. Two moments merged in his mind. The first was the moment, under the sea, when he'd stopped falling, when the water had held him up and for an instant he'd been weightless, hanging, floating, suspended by his own momentum: and he'd let himself go, let the last of his breath stream out of him, bubbling bright—and then had been flung up to the light. And joined to this was the instant, making love to her the first time, when she'd called out to him and he'd also hung up, high above himself, and then let himself go, let himself fall down into her. He didn't understand what had happened in either case, not really, but it didn't bother him. It had happened. And the consequences were irreversible; there was no way he could lose it now. He mustn't lose it. Those two moments, which were really the same, had saved him. Anne had saved him. She had literally saved his life. It was a vast, improbable coincidence, but that was what it came to. As he drove on he could feel the tension ease out of him, down his arms as they stretched out to the steering wheel and out of his shoulders so his head could ease back and his eyes open more easily to the world. He was all right, he thought. He was going to get through this. But if it hadn't been for Anne, if he hadn't crossed the room that night and kissed her, if she hadn't called out to him, he would be dead. He would have killed himself, as Diana had done, for she'd been right, in the end. It was all happening again, but worse, with dead bodies this time: and he could see now in his mind's eye the white bulge of the back of Elsa Buhler's thigh where she'd slipped down on the floor pressing the back of a coffee spoon under her. He could see that, and he could bear it; but the man he'd been before Anne—no, he wasn't sure about him at all, wasn't sure if he wouldn't have opened his mouth to the Irish Sea and drowned.

But of course the day wasn't over yet; David knew there'd be more to bear. But he'd get through it, that was also settled, and so he kept on driving, one eye on the rearview mirror, though he saw nothing except this strange world that had nothing to do with him but of which, none-theless, he was a part. Dessau, around Halle, west to Eisleben: finally he could see the Harz Mountains, soft under the haze, and then at Nordhausen he began to check for signs. But what kind of sign do you use to mark a concentration camp? What kind of "attraction" had it become? In fact, when he came to it, he thought of a forestry commission—the sort of sign, posted at a viewpoint, alerting you to the animals you might see. It was quite large, with a formalized "eternal flame" and green lettering. *Mahn- und Gedenkstätte Mittelbau Dora*, this read, "Memorial to Mittelbau Dora." But of course there'd have to be a commission to administer such a place, with a board and bureaucrats. The opening hours were posted underneath: from September to April, till four thirty in the afternoon; from May to August, to half past three. *Montags geschlossen*. By his watch it was almost six, so he assumed he was too late, but he turned along the road anyway, a large hill beginning to fill the landscape on his right hand, and saw that there were still a number of cars in the car park.

He pulled over. At first glance there was very little to see: a big hill covered with small trees and loose rock, an impression of a quarry or wasteland that was being reclaimed. But there was a path, and he followed it along till he reached a directory and a map set up on a sort of lectern. "You Are Here." It indicated roads, a railway line. The hill on his right was called Kohnstein. And other areas were filled in and neatly labeled. *Appellplatz*. "Roll Call Square." *Wachtturm*. "Guard Tower." *Hier wurden 7 Italiener erschossen*. "At this point 7 Italians were shot to death." *Mehrzweck-Gebäude*. "Multipurpose Building." *Museum ehem. Krematorium*. "Museum Formerly Crematorium." Each of these "sights" was depicted, on the map, with a little formalized drawing, but David couldn't see them immediately. Ahead there was a line of trees and a rise in the ground, but he realized that two of the points indicated were almost directly across from him. *A-Stollen*. "A-Tunnel." *B-Stollen*. "B-Tunnel." These were drawn out, on the diagram, with rail lines leading into formalized depictions of tunnel entrances, rather like a road sign on a mountain highway as you come up to a pass, though all he could see in the hill itself were two scarred areas in the rock; but the rails were still there, sunk into the crumbling remains of a cement roadbed. And as he walked on farther still he came to a huge block of concrete, which at one point someone must have attempted to blow up: it was blackened and cracked and canted to one side, but the concrete blocks were so massive that their original purpose was still recognizable. A strong point. A pillbox. In fact, drawing closer he realized that this must have been the camp entrance; it wasn't hard to imagine the guard barrier and the soldiers with their machine pistols and trucks idling as papers were checked. Finally, stepping by this, he came up to the gates of the memorial: *K-Z Mittelbau Dora*. He stepped beyond it.

But again there was very little to see.

Ahead of him was a large open area, about the size of a football ground. It was very flat, and part of it was paved, with the same old cement that the tunnel rail lines had been sunk into. Judging by the map he supposed that this must have been the *Appellplatz*; and at the far side, high on a scaffold, he recognized the guard tower, absurd, like something from a movie set, terrifying because it was real. And up on the hill, which still filled the scene on his right, was a brick building with a big chimney that could only be the museum *ehemals Krematorium*. A long flight of steps wound up to it through the trees, and he looked that way for a moment, because there was a small knot of people around it, really like the figures you might see grouped around a grave during a funeral; but then his gaze shifted to the only other structure in the whole place visible aboveground. It was in the middle of the open area and consisted of a wall, built of blocks of rock, perhaps ten feet high and fifty feet long: a memorial, like an enormous headstone. It faced the hill, as if the whole of this open space was a burial ground, as if the earth beneath his feet was filled with buried bones. And stepping closer he suspected that there was no "as if" about it: he was literally walking across an enormous grave. Closer to, he stopped. He stared ahead. Now that he could see it properly, the memorial was a compelling sight. Figures were carved into the rock in bas relief. Ghastly, skeletal figures, cramped, bent, crouched. Buried. Curled into the postures of the dying. Many had shovels and picks in their hands. Corpses who'd dug their own graves. Diggers. Tunnelers. Burrowers. Burrowing even here in the rock that memorialized them. Miners buried in a slide or . . . what came into his mind was a photograph he'd seen in an archaeological text, a skeleton taken from a cave in Shandinar, an example of *Homo erectus* (or was his mind playing a trick to supply this irony before these bent specters?) who'd been buried beneath the communal hearth a million years ago. The significance of this find, if he remembered correctly, was the trace of pollen found with the body, evidence that a flower had been put into the grave—had anyone put flowers on these graves?—a thought that caused him to turn his head, up to the *Krematorium* on the hill, for he could see flowers there, heaps of them, and he realized that some kind of service or observance must be proceeding. And then all these thoughts passed out of his mind, and he simply felt the sun and the breeze. What more could you feel? Every feeling was choked off by shame, mocked by its own inadequacy. How dare you feel. How dare you be alive to feel. What good do your feelings do? But then that passed out of him. Unexpectedly he discovered that he felt quite unafraid. He was protected here. This was a true sanctuary. Moreover, he felt a sense of recognition, of an expectation fulfilled. He wasn't in the least surprised to be here; everything he was going to find out, he knew already. That's what it amounted to. There were so many connections. And all the particular connections now filled his mind. Rockets and war and science—those connections that, in the beginning, had been the crucial connections in his own life. The simple connection to Germany. He thought of Wernher Von Braun, the original rocket scientist. If they'd built the V-2 here, then Von Braun, whether or not it had ever come out, must have stood right on this spot. And hadn't somebody said, at China Lake, that the cine-theodolites on the base had been taken from Peenemünde or some other German base? Yes: Our Germans Are Better Than Your Germans. It had still been a little joke, even in his time, and could not Stern have been one of those Germans? It was at least a possibility. And Buhler had come here, and Tannis was drawn in as well, for Tannis, he remembered, spoke very good German, and surely he'd learned it while serving here. But it was more than these specifics, this sense of connection. This was where it had started. This was where the first principles of everything had been laid down.

What were those principles?

How were they embodied?

David turned and looked toward the crematorium, the museum; if the answers to these questions existed, they must be there. And he would have to find them quickly. There was still a soft, hazy light in the sky, but it was after six, and Berlin was at least four hours away. But there was also a sense that he must not go too quickly. This place, of all places, demanded discretion, and at the top of the hill the group he'd seen before was still gathered together conducting their ceremony. A trick of the wind brought the sound of voices down to him and drew him across the open ground to the hill. At the bottom he realized how high the hill was. Stone steps curved up it, wide steps, as if to ensure a leisurely pace: you had to go up slowly, through the long grass and the trees, and when he reached the top David could see that a second monument occupied the crest of the hill, a small square, paved with the same gray stone as the memorial, with a sculpture at its center, whose gaunt figures also echoed those below, and an eternal flame, the palest flicker in the sun. Flowers and wreaths had been heaped around the sculpture, and off to one side stood a double line of uniformed schoolchildren who were listening to an older man addressing them. Twenty or thirty other people looked on. David hesitated. One of the men in the crowd turned his head and saw him. David looked into his face; for just an instant, there was a question posed there, but then the man smiled and turned away, and that was almost like a permission. You get on with your business; we'll leave you alone. Quietly, around the back of the crowd, David made his way to the museum. The door was open, actually slightly ajar, and he slipped inside.

The museum was small, like a village school or a changing room at the beach. There was no one in it, but the lights were on. The ceiling was low; after a moment David realized he was stooping, but that really wasn't necessary, and he pulled himself up and began looking around. There wasn't a lot to see; in this whole place, he thought, there wasn't a lot to see: empty spaces, absences, maps of buildings that were no longer there. Almost nothing was left at all. So the exhibits, even the crematorium itself—a trolley mounted on rails that ran into an old cast-iron furnace— weren't very spectacular. Most were grouped along the walls of the building, and he walked slowly past them. One glass case displayed a *Gummi*, which David had learned as the German for rubber but which apparently was also a truncheon used to beat the *Stücke*, or "scraps," as the SS called the prisoners; another spread out a tattered prison costume, the candy-stripe uniform of a silent-movie crook, with a striped beret called a *Mütze*; and still another displayed a bucket, in which prisoners were killed by drowning them in their own urine and feces—though the bucket was just an old rusted bucket. And other "exhibits" were actually models: of the tunnels, of the V-2 under production, of V-2s being transported out of the camp on railway cars. And many others were photographs: of the camp barracks; of the missiles; of Wernher Von Braun, of Von Braun receiving a medal from President Eisenhower; and quite a number of someone called Albert Kuntz, a Communist deputy in the Reichstag who'd been murdered here; of an SS guard called Sander who'd been tried for numerous murders and sentenced to eight years by the West German courts. All of this was low key, and David found no buttons to press or cassettes to listen to or slide shows to view; but it worked just the same. As he moved quietly among these modest displays, he learned all he had to know about Dora.

What a history it was.

He knew a little of it already, for Dora's history belonged to the history of modern rocketry, and Aberporth and China Lake were both part of that. But in Germany rockets went back a good deal farther, in fact to 1927 when a group of young science enthusiasts had formed the Society for Rocket Propulsion, or *VfR* (*Verein für Raumschiffahrt*), and began building a series of small rocket motors at Breslau. They were amateurs, but the best in the world. By 1930 they'd fired a rocket with a thrust of 7kg, and only two years later the success of their *Repulsor* engine had attracted the attention of the German military. The group almost split over this; one side believed that their research should be purely scientific and peaceful, while the other was not so squeamish. Perhaps, in the end, it was money that decided the issue, for in 1932, Germany was in the grip of depression and the *VfR*'s membership, and financial resources were quickly dwindling. So it was the "war party" that carried the day—war, after all, was only the continuation of science by other means—and of course Wernher Von Braun was their leader. In the autumn of 1932 he began working for the Army Ordnance Office under the sponsorship of a young officer named Walter Dornberger, and for the next thirteen years these two men dominated German rocket research. Von Braun was an aristocrat, the son of a financier who'd served in Hindenburg's cabinet, while Dornberger had more modest origins: his father was a pharmacist, and he was a career artillery officer. But both men were engineers, and their talents meshed perfectly. Von Braun was one of those rare scientists who understands politics, especially military politics; and Dornberger was one of those rare soldiers who understands science. Though they wouldn't have used the phrase, the interface between science and the military was their meat and drink; and very quickly they established Germany as the most important power in rocketry, even if few people knew about it. In 1934 a first effort, the A-4, reached an altitude of 6,500 feet over the island of Borkum in the North Sea; in 1936 they started construction of a major test facility at Peenemünde, a small fishing village on the Baltic coast; and by 1941, when the failure of the Luftwaffe in the Battle of Britain finally convinced Hitler to give their projects top priority, they were ready to proceed with the very large rocket that became known as the V-2. Almost 50 feet long, and weighing about 15 tons at takeoff, it could reach altitudes of more than 110 miles and speeds of 3,500 miles an hour. By October of 1942 it had been test-fired successfully, and by the end of the year the missile had been ordered into production. Initially, this was to be carried on at two locations, Peenemünde itself and the Zeppelin works at Friedrichshafen, on Lake Constance. The Germans were aiming for production of 600 missiles a month by September of 1944, a hopelessly ambitious target, but long before then the Allies intervened. This, too, was a story David knew, as indeed most English boys of his generation did. It was the story of the daring daylight reconnaissance missions flown over the Baltic in little wooden Mosquito fighter planes; of the mysterious objects in the photos they took, some kind of bomb but unlike bombs anyone had ever seen; and of the final deduction made by a genuine heroine, Constance Babington-Smith (played in the movie by . . . but David couldn't remember), that these were indeed rockets. In any case, though the tale was rather less dramatic than this—the British had known something was going on at Peenemünde for several years—the end result could not have been more spectacular. On August 17, 1943, 595 RAF bombers dropped 1,800 tons of high explosives and incendiaries onto the base, seriously damaging it and certainly putting an end to the idea of using it as a production center. An alternative had to be found, and it was. Two weeks later the first prisoners arrived at the hill in the Harz Mountains that would ultimately be known as Dora: twelve hundred French, Russian, and Polish inmates transferred from Buchenwald.

The German plan was simple. Von Braun's secret was out, and any attempt to manufacture his weapon in conventional facilities would only attract more raids; so they'd build a factory underground, literally inside a mountain. The Kohnstein hill was selected for two reasons. First, it was on the outskirts of Nordhausen, and Nordhausen was a major rail junction; completed rockets could be shipped easily to launching sites within range of Britain, especially London. Second, the Germans had already surveyed Kohnstein and knew that it represented, in rudimentary form, what they wanted. For Kohnstein had originally been the site of an ammonia mine, developed in 1917 with prison camp labor from World War I. It had been abandoned in 1934, but on the advice of I. G. Farben—and how fitting that was, for Farben supplied the poison gas to Auschwitz—its tunnels and shafts had been converted into an underground storage depot for oil, gasoline, and other chemicals. Now all the Germans had to do was expand the tunnels and . . . But of course the Germans didn't do it, the *Stücke* did—and the "all" was Hell.

The first prisoners, all from Buchenwald, were transported in trucks and then ordered out of the trucks into the old shafts running into the side of the hill. SS guards drove them, and with picks, shovels, and dynamite they hacked and blasted at the rock, digging hundreds of feet of tunnels and caverns. They slept in the holes they dug. They had no beds except the shelves they hollowed in the stone, and they had no water except for the drops they lapped from the bare rock walls. They died by the hundreds, but there were hundreds more where they came from, and when they died by the thousands that, too, was no problem. They were infinitely replaceable. They were worked to death, and when they could work no longer they were beaten to death, and those who were not quite dead would be transported back to Buchenwald where they were gassed and cremated, for in this first phase of its history, Dora did not have its own crematorium. The *Stücke* labored all through the autumn of 1943 and the winter of 1944. Those who did not die in the first few weeks—and most did die—those who managed somehow to survive often spent days at a time without seeing the sun or drawing a breath of fresh air. But they built Von Braun's factory. It was enormous. The two main tunnels, which were about five hundred feet apart, were ultimately two miles long, forty feet wide, and thirty feet high: and they were connected by forty-seven cross tunnels, *Hallen*, thirty feet wide and twenty feet high. This added up to more than one million square feet of usable space. And over it all was the roof of Kohnstein mountain, two hundred feet thick.

With the factory complete, work could begin on the missiles themselves. This second phase of Dora's history was inaugurated with two grand visits. The first was from Albert Speer, head of German armaments production, who made a tour of inspection in early December 1943. He was appalled at what he saw. Speer would not have used expressions such as "the leading edge of technology," or called the V-2 "a ground-based IRBM," though that's what it was. But he knew that Dora's exhausted skeletons were incapable of building anything requiring precision. He immediately called Peenemünde, and Von Braun arrived at the camp on January 25, 1944. Accompanied by his retinue and an SS guard—"*Mützen ab!*" they ordered the prisoners, "Caps off!"—he marched through the tunnels and agreed with Speer. The quality of both the camp and its inmates was not up to his rocket. So both changed. By the end of March the *Stücke* were out of the tunnels and living in barracks—cold, drafty, and lice-infested but dry, and the air was free of the choking stone dust in the tunnels. And new drafts of workers arrived. French. Czechs. Italians. Russians. Poles. "Actually," Von Braun's personal secretary said, "we got to work quite well with the foreigners—it was a veritable melting pot. But they often fought amongst themselves. Remember, many had become prisoners for criminal or homosexual reasons as well as for political and religious beliefs. We needed the laborers, so we tried not to mistreat them. It was a top secret operation, so once you were in, you stayed." As long as one maintained a proper sense of irony, there was a good deal of truth in this; of the sixty thousand people who passed through the camp, many did stay, for perhaps half of them died. As for the political complexion of these men, whatever their sexual habits might have been, most were certainly opposed to the Nazis. Some, especially among the Germans, were Communists and many were captured Resistance fighters; this was especially true of the French, who formed a much larger proportion of Dora's population than they did in other camps. And Dora was certainly a melting pot, a hellish caldron of *Kapos* and *Commandos* and *Sonder-Truc*, the SS term for a "special event": a whipping or a hanging, with the victims strung up in the *Holzhof*, a wooden enclosure beside the infirmary, or in the tunnels themselves. Still, despite the horrors, the missiles rolled out. Precisely designed by Von Braun to fit under mainline rail tunnels, they were shipped to their launching sites and fired, about three thousand altogether. The most famous target was London, which was hit 517 times; but more than 1,200 struck Antwerp, and lesser numbers reached Paris, Liège, Lille, Maastricht, and Hasselt. But of course it wasn't enough. Even wonder weapons couldn't stop the Allied advance. And so, in the last days of the war, the final period of Dora's history began, in some ways the most dreadful. The camp's population swelled, as other prisoners were evacuated before the Russians in the east, including thousands from Auschwitz, who found Dora worse than what they'd left behind. And the camp guards and administration, fearing that they might be called to account for their crimes, began eliminating witnesses; there were mass hangings and quiet executions, the bodies piled up. Hundreds of bodies. So many that the ovens couldn't handle them and they were burned with oil-soaked cordwood in the *Appellplatz*. . . . But finally it ended. On April 11, 1945, about a week after Von Braun and his colleagues had fled the camp, tanks of the Third Armored Division, First American Army, rolled in.

That was Dora.

That was it.

There was little else to say. With the museum's booklet in his hand—"KZ Dora: Produktionstätte des Todes"—David went around the cases four times, compared models to maps, stared at photographs, but finally he knew it was useless; there was nothing more. There couldn't be any doubt that every rocket ever built, every spaceship that man would ever fly, had its origins in this place, but there was less here than an archaeologist would turn up from a minor Roman site. *Stücke.* "Scraps." Well, it fitted. And altogether, he supposed, it was enough. What you could see, he thought, what you could feel, was a certain consistency. The minds that had built the rockets had also built the camp; the one was implied in the other. It was all of a piece. It hadn't just been necessary to build the rockets, it had been necessary to do it in just this way.

But how did he fit in?

It was an appalling question . . . to think that he did. It was almost too much to bear, but in the peculiar sense that this was an honor, or a title, that he didn't deserve. He felt so small. What had happened to him—it was all in a different dimension . . . and yet it had happened. And Elsa Buhler was dead, and Vogel and Stern—if Stern wasn't Vogel under a different name—had some dreadful, legitimate connection to these events. Tannis might too. At least tangentially. David now wished he knew more about Tannis, but he'd been an intelligence officer, he knew that much, and there was the whole history of how Von Braun and his men had reached America and how a few had come to China Lake. An intelligence officer might know all that. Did Tannis know about Buhler? It was a question, David decided, that probably had one of three answers. Buhler must have been a prisoner here. Or a guard. Or, in fact, one of the scientists.

Then, as he was trying to focus his mind on these questions, the door of the museum opened. An older man stepped in from the brightness outside. He was rather in a hurry and for a moment didn't realize David was there; when he saw him, he looked startled. "Oh, I'm sorry. Are you with the delegation?" he asked in German, although David's reply, for some reason, came out in English:

"No, I'm not. I just came in. I hope it's all right."

The man switched into English. "Yes, yes, of course, but we are now officially—please, just a moment. My colleague speaks very good English."

"That's all right—" David had said in German, but the man was already out the door. And a moment later, when it opened again, a much younger person came forward. He had curly red hair and a thick red beard. He looked both eager and yet a little nervous.

"Yes? You are English?"

"But I speak German," said David in German.

"No, please, I like to speak English. It is only that we are now closed. We are only still here because of the ceremony."

"I'm sorry. I didn't know."

"It is quite all right." He smiled. "Look. Look."

"That's very kind of you, but I think I've seen everything."

The first man was holding the door open, and David had the feeling that they wanted him to go, probably to leave themselves. But they didn't want to offend. Smiling, he stepped past them, blinking in the glare—his tour of Dora hadn't taken very long after all, and it was still light.

At the entrance the younger man smiled. "You are English? From England?"

"Yes."

The young man nodded, apparently pleased. And it was then that David asked, "I was wondering . . . you don't have any records of the prisoners, do you? I mean of individuals . . . names?"

The young man looked doubtful. "Names?"

"That's right. I wanted to know about one prisoner in particular. One man who was here."

The red-haired young man began to shake his head, but then he stopped himself. "Please, a moment," and then he turned, and ran toward the eternal flame and the statue, calling out as he went. David followed slowly after. The ceremony was clearly over. The schoolchildren, in their uniforms, were winding down the stairs, and the adults, in twos and threes, were preparing to go. But the young man broke up one of these groups and brought a man over to David. He was short and looked very fit, his face slightly pockmarked and brown with windburn. David guessed he was in his early sixties. He wore a good gray suit with a navy sweater under; a white collar showed, and his tie was tightly knotted. His expression was curious, inquiring. Some quality he had—his vigor—made David think of Joseph Conrad. In fact, when the young man from the museum made introductions, he turned out to be a Czech rather than a Pole. His name was Jan Zalenda. He spoke good English.

"Rickert says you wanted to know something about a name?"

"Yes. I wanted to know about Walter Buhler."

Immediately, the man shook his head. "He isn't here."

"But he was a prisoner in Dora?"

"Certainly. But he isn't here today. He would be normally. But he isn't even in the DDR."

"I don't understand."

"Well, that's their policy, Mr. Harper. At retirement, under certain conditions, you can leave. I saw him six months ago in Prague, and he told me he would go. But normally he would be here. He is a member of our group."

Rickert, the red-haired man, was looking on, and smiled.

David hesitated. "But Walter Joseph Buhler definitely was a prisoner here?"

"Yes. Walter and also his brother. His father was in Buchenwald. He never came out. They were trade-union men, railroad men. They took his father right away, while he and his brother were later. His brother was a skilled man: the Nazis were mad, you understand, but not entirely. And Walter was very young."

"I see. But the brother—?"

"Johannes. They hung him."

"Hung him?"

"Yes. In the B-Tunnel. You want to know this . . . ?"

"It's hard to explain."

Jan Zalenda shrugged, though he didn't seem very perturbed about this lack of explanation. On the contrary, he seemed to relax. "Well, they hung him. I saw him. Don't have worries about that. They always did it the same way. They took a wooden peg, the end of a handle or a broomstick, and they wedged it in your mouth, so you wouldn't swallow your tongue or bite it off. And they strung you up. You strangled. There were always a few hanging there, to frighten us."

"And . . . they just hung him? There was no reason?"

"They thought he was in the Resistance."

"Was he?"

The Czech shook his head. "No. He always wanted to be, I think, to do something; he knew I was. But he couldn't, because of Walter. It would have been too easy for the SS to put the screws on, you understand? They would threaten to kill Walter . . ."

"Yes. I see."

Thoughtfully, the Czech nodded. David realized he was dizzy; he wondered if he would be sick. But then the Czech went on. "In addition to this, he was named by Vogel."

Vogel. So there it was, a connection. But David kept his voice level and asked, "Who was Vogel?"

"Do you understand about the camps, Mr. Harper? There was a Resistance, many Resistances. Each nation had its Resistance. The French—they were very important. As were we Czechs. There was a Russian Resistance, the Poles . . . Every nation had its group. But there was also a certain amount of coordination. The center of that was in the hospital. It was down there, over there. Not that it was really a hospital, but that's where the 'Muslims' went—that's what we called the patients, those who were too exhausted for work; they were praying to Allah for deliverance. In any case, the doctor had a radio, which some of us could listen to and spread the news. So it was very important, and the SS and the Gestapo were always trying to penetrate it with informers and agents provocateurs. Somehow, they caught Vogel and tortured him."

"So he worked in the hospital?"

"That's right. As a kind of orderly, and he was in charge of certain records. That made him important, for it meant he had a certain freedom . . . of movement? That's what you say?"

"Yes."

He nodded. Then shrugged. "But they caught him. I don't know how. They beat him with their *Gummis*. Then, one morning at roll call we all stood down there, with our caps off, in our 'Hurons,' and Vogel was marched up and down the rows by the SS and he picked out the 'Resistance leaders.' "

"But I don't understand. He picked out Buhler's brother, and you just said he wasn't part of the Resistance."

"Oh, yes. That was true. Vogel picked nine men at random, every one of whom the SS hung, and not a single one belonged to the Resistance. The SS didn't know it, but the Resistance was still intact."

For a moment David was silent. He was aghast. And as he stood there in silence, the Czech reached out and touched his elbow, steering him toward the stairs. He, too, wanted to be on his way. They started down the hill, toward the old *Appellplatz*, which was now falling under the shadow of the hill.

Finally David asked, "What did they do to Vogel after this?"

"Well, you know, that was always a mystery, because they didn't hang him. I don't know. At the end, who knows what games the SS thought they were playing. Perhaps they thought to use him further. But of course it was a catastrophe, at least for Vogel's name. In the camp most people didn't belong to the Resistance, so they didn't know what Vogel had done; they assumed he must have been an informer. Only people like me, who couldn't speak, knew the truth. So . . . after the Americans came . . . it was so confused. We survivors were broken into groups, according to our nations. All I knew for certain about Vogel was that he had met a woman, one of the people who came here from Auschwitz, and that they were together. She was a Jew. But she was also an American. That was how Walter tried to find them. She had been born in Chicago. She only lived there as a baby, only for a few weeks, but technically she was an American and so they could go to that country. Walter wrote to all the agencies, you see, to the United Nations and the Red Cross; after the war, there were many such organizations. He had hundreds of letters. Once he showed them all to me."

Hundreds of letters, David thought, that he'd hidden below the floorboards beside his bed. He said, "What did Buhler mean to do . . . by trying to find them?"

"Oh, well. He swore he would kill Vogel, that he was going to follow him to the ends of the earth. What could he think, with the body of his brother hanging above him in the tunnel? But later, I don't know. Because Walter knew the truth. I saw to that myself, I assure you. I don't know . . ." He hesitated. They had reached the last step. For a moment, Zalenda stopped there and looked out, toward the memorial stone. "Truthfully, it's hard to know what Walter really thought about it. He must have understood. What could Vogel have done? Men were going to die. Everyone was innocent. Vogel did what everyone did, what he had to do in order to survive. He thought he was going to die himself, I'm sure of that. So he was probably thinking of how to get through his own last second as he bit on the stick, and at least he would have known, you see, that he hadn't betrayed his friends. So he made that choice. Yes. I think Walter must have understood that: Vogel was trying to survive, like everyone else. You might even say he helped Walter to survive, through hating him." Zalenda smiled, a quick flash in his hard brown face. He said, "You don't want to tell me why you have come here?"

"As I said—"

"No, no. That is all right. But it's important, that I tell you this?"

"Yes. For me, this is very important."

"Good. Well, then, I can tell you something else," he said, turning as he spoke, beginning to walk along the base of the hill. "I can tell you why *I* come here. I now only come on this day—it is the day most of us Czechs were well enough to leave; they began sending us back—and I suppose I come in order to remember. You can either forget, you see, or remember . . . although I would be afraid, if I didn't remember, that I might forget. In any case, there is another reason. I'm ashamed of what I did to survive. Do you know what that is? Are you a Christian?"

"No. Well, I don't know."

"In any case, I don't want to offend you. But the way I survived was by faith."

"You were a Christian?"

"No, not exactly. But I came to have faith in God. Or faith, in any case. Before I came, I didn't believe, but here I learned all about it. You see . . . You have to understand. Here, you only wanted to live one more day, or even one more hour, and when you did survive, you were thankful. And who could you thank? Others died, and you didn't. How could you explain it? There was no way. So you found faith. Soon your faith truly did seem the reason for your survival, the reason you didn't give up while the others dropped dead all around you. God! Yes, and the stronger your faith became, the more it seemed a reason all in itself, justifying and forgiving everything you did to sustain it. Even betrayals, betrayals even of yourself." The Czech had been walking as he'd talked, so fast that David had been working to keep up; but now he stopped and looked along the hill toward the scars in the rocks that marked the tunnel entrances. He shook his head and gestured with his hand toward them. "No, forget God. I always think that here. You know that line in Dostoevsky, 'Without God, everything is possible'? It is so silly, and no one ever says so. I can never understand. We've always had God and *exactly* everything has been possible. That was the trouble with Von Braun. He always said that when he was aiming his rockets at London, he had his eyes on the stars, and people always laughed. But I believed him. Yes. Exactly. Because he had his eyes on heaven, he never saw London, or this place. That was the trouble, in general. The men here believed in God but knew chemical formulae as well. They were scientific believers."

David said nothing: here, it seemed, the only response you could have was silence. But then, as the smile faded on the Czech's face, he realized that this man rather wanted to be rid of him, that he'd been tagging along beside him, not letting him get away—to an appointment, to meet friends, to get on with his life—for all these events, and the ideas arising from them, which for David were so extraordinary, were commonplace to him. So he said, "Look, could I ask one more thing?"

Zalenda frowned, then shrugged. "Yes, surely. But I have my car, and tonight I am in Erfurt. It is getting late, you see."

"I'm sorry. But . . . do you think . . . I only want to ask you this: Would it be possible for Walter Buhler, even today, to kill Vogel, to want to?"

Now for the first time the Czech seemed alarmed. "No . . . I don't know. I don't understand. Why do you want to know?"

"Well, could you just look at this photograph? The man holding the reins of the horse. Could that be Vogel?"

"Vogel?"

"Yes."

"But you didn't know about Vogel. You asked about Buhler—"

"I understand, but could you just look at the photograph. Could you just tell me . . . It *is* important."

The Czech hesitated a moment longer, then took the photograph and looked down at it, held it at an angle to catch the light, and David wondered if he didn't see, just for an instant, some flash of recognition, and then wondered, too, if the man's suspicions might not hold back the truth. But finally he shook his head. "I'm not sure. Perhaps. I can't say." The Czech looked up. "It is an old photograph?"

"More than twenty years old."

"That is the desert?"

"Yes, the Mojave Desert."

"Well, I couldn't say. I'm sorry. The last time I saw him, he was a skeleton, his face was the color . . ." He shrugged.

"I understand. Thank you."

"And you still don't want to tell me why you wish to know all this?"

"It is hard to explain, believe me. But no one will be hurt. This won't hurt anyone."

The Czech nodded and seemed about to speak. But then, with a quick smile, he turned and simply began walking away. David let him go, watching him stride firmly toward the entrance of the camp, his back quite straight: not once turning to the side, not once looking back. Then he was gone, and after David was sure he was gone—quickly now—he started to his own car. He had a long drive ahead of him. But this trip had been worth every mile. His mind was full of a thousand thoughts. Whatever he might think of the Czech's metaphysics, he had made the great connection, found the premise on which everything else was based. As he drove through the night he was sure of it. Vogel had killed Buhler's brother, and Buhler had set off in revenge, all these years later. But Vogel was still the survivor and had survived once again. He'd killed Buhler and, traveling as Stern, was now covering his tracks, erasing the last traces that connected him to this place. That had to be true . . . or much of it had to be true. And as he drove along he wondered if this was a quarrel that he had any rights in. Could he judge Vogel? Could he even contemplate what this man had gone through, or the choices he'd faced? It was none of his business. Yet it was. That was the trouble. But even after all this time, and this terrible trip, he still didn't see how. So as he went his thoughts settled back to where they'd been as he'd set out, and as he reached Berlin and saw the brilliant lights of the Checkpoint ahead, he made sure he was thinking of Anne. That, he knew, was the only way he would survive. And at 11:32, in company with a dozen Turks and three students from Illinois, he regained the West.

CHAPTER 16

Copenhagen was lovely in the June sun, with the water sparkling in the harbor and canals and the sky blue above the spires of the churches. It is a city where you look up, and there is always something to see: a spire; a watchtower; a verdigris cupola; the red roofs of the tall, narrow houses in the old town. David didn't know the city well, but he had always liked it. Walking along you might catch a glimpse of the sea at the end of a street, and the sun warmed the stone to earth tones, joining the town to the land around it, that low, undulating, Danish landscape that meets the sky in a line of pearl. Stroget, the city's main shopping area, was bustling. Bare legs. Bicycles. Tourists flapping maps and laboring, unnecessarily, with pronunciation guides. In the café a young girl and her boyfriend took the next table, the girl hooking her feet behind the legs of her chair and shoving her dress down between her thighs: So there! she seemed to say to her boyfriend, as she leaned forward, chin in hand. Everyone seemed happy, and David was determined not to be left out. He was amused at himself. But that wasn't going to stop him. Did that make him more amusing? Watching Anne, enjoying Anne, he sipped at his Carlsberg. It was now Tuesday afternoon; he had arrived the previous day. He'd discovered Anne and Derek were enjoying a pleasant Danish holiday; nothing untoward had followed them from Scotland. Frue Brahe, Anne's mother-in-law, turned out to be a delight. She lived in a fine, airy apartment in a wonderful old building with stone stairs and a beautiful bronze banister. David had never met her, but Axel had evidently told her about him, so her scrutiny was of the gentlest sort. He'd sensed a tiny pause, a beat of melancholy; he supposed that Anne, with another man, was one more confirmation of the loss of her son. But that was only a moment, for she was also full of good humor, with a vast store of the Danish equivalent to Polish jokes, stories about people from someplace called Mol. To her great delight, for she doted on her grandson, Derek could never resist breaking in with the punch line, or an explanation. "You must understand, David, our Molboers are very simple folk. . . ." Two Molboers are sitting in an inn and their lantern dies. They have two matches between them, but one drops his. The other crawls about on the floor, searching for it, until his own match burns out. And so they are left utterly in the dark. "Don't you get it? They're so stupid. . . ."

David smiled, remembering, as Anne sipped her campari-soda. She loved campari. He was, she had told him, now seeing her city self. They'd been shopping; she'd worn no makeup, just a clear gloss on her mouth, and her gold-red hair was loose on the shoulders of her linen suit, a contrast that made her stunning. Beside her David had felt positively scruffy and had bought some clothes himself, even wearing his new blazer out of the shop. Now he looked good. And he felt good. And after a good night's sleep and a few hours of simple Danish sanity he was beginning to understand what he had to do. He watched Anne set her glass down. She'd told him about Tannis in Scotland, tracking him down—he'd spent two nights at a hotel in Dumfries but had left by the time she phoned— and David had told her the whole story about Stern, Vogel, Buhler, working back and forth over the ground, working out what it all meant. Now between them on the table was Diana's photograph of the man, the horse, and the little girl, and Anne said, "I want to get this right about the photograph. You're saying that Stern is *not* Vogel?"

"No, no. They're the same person and his name is undoubtedly Vogel. But Vogel isn't this man, the man in the picture."

"But Diana thought he was. What else could the picture mean? There's even a horse in the picture, and she'd hired her horse from him when you were in China Lake together."

"Yes, that all fits. The trouble is, the man I met in Aberporth was definitely taller than this man. There's really no resemblance—it's just all wrong. Then you work on from there, you see. You come to Buhler. We know that Vogel sent Buhler's brother to his death at Dora. We also know that Buhler turned up at China Lake and was murdered. It's obvious. Buhler was trying to avenge his brother, but Vogel won out. Since then, he's attempted to erase any connection between himself and Buhler in Europe. That's why he killed Buhler's sister. But of course the man who killed Buhler's sister was Stern. So Stern and Vogel have to be the same person—"

"And not the man in this photograph."

"Right. God knows who *he* is. He probably has nothing to do with it. When you look at the other pictures I found, they don't seem to be connected, either."

"But you are, David. I mean, you have to be, because you saw Stern—or Vogel, rather—go into Diana's house in Aberporth."

"Yes, but I'm just wondering if that doesn't lead to another obvious conclusion. I think Vogel was the spy. Vogel was the man who gave Sidewinder to the Russians. And somehow he framed me for it." He leaned forward. "It's not such a leap, if you think about it. Sidewinder was my original connection to China Lake, the only reason I'm involved at all. There were three big elements in the case against me. The first was the material I handled; I mean, I certainly could have done it. Probably Vogel didn't know that. But he would have known I was a scientist; it would have been natural for Diana to tell him . . ."

"And she might have let something else slip, that you were actually—"

"No, I doubt that. Diana was always careful to obey the rules. But he could have found out easily enough that I was a scientist working on the base, and that's all he really needed to know. Point two. That trip I made to Czechoslovakia as a student, to visit my godfather. Maybe I've always looked at that the wrong way. I was always so concerned to convince them that the Russians didn't recruit me that maybe I've missed the important point. The Russians might well have known I was there. They could have told Vogel about it, if he was working for them. They would have known exactly how the Americans would react."

"And the third point was the letter. . . ."

"Yes. Well, I actually destroyed the letter, which turned out to be fairly stupid, although I suppose they would have just said that I'd written it myself."

"But it claimed that Diana was having an affair. Do you think she could have been?"

"I don't know. I guess so. Though we'd just been married. But she was so far ahead of me; I was so innocent. I suppose it's the only word. But I'm not sure it makes any difference. I keep trying to see things from Vogel's point of view. She hired a horse from him. She was usually alone. Perhaps it just put the idea into his mind; all he needed was a way of getting me wandering around the desert. So he made up that letter. Then he arranged for the Russians to meet me. You see that's what it looked like. . . ."

"Yes."

"But the real point is Tannis. One way or another, I know why I'm involved. We know about Buhler and Vogel. But if the whole business, what's happened now, was just a private quarrel between them, going back to the camp, why would Tannis even know about it?"

"Well, he must have been the man on the Clints of Dromore that day."

"Yes. And he was definitely in Aberporth. I was thinking . . . you see, I asked Tim if Tannis seemed to be there officially, when he was at the house, and he thought he wasn't. And I can just see that. You can imagine. Buhler, an East German, is murdered at China Lake, right on the base, for all we know. They'd have to do something about it. They couldn't ignore it."

"Yes."

"And say there was also some connection to what happened to me. Maybe something they found on his body. I'm not sure what it could be, but something. They might feel they had to start some kind of investigation, but they'd be reluctant—"

"So they'd have a chat with Tannis on the QT?"

"Exactly. They'd ask him to look around on his own, find out if there was any fire under the smoke. But if Vogel learned about it, he'd be frightened. From his point of view, everything might start coming unraveled."

"So Tannis is the key."

"Yes. In the end." David hesitated. Tannis was the key, and he knew what that meant: he'd understood last night that he would have to go back to China Lake. That's where Tannis was. And Vogel, too, most likely. Buhler had been murdered there. That's where everything had started. But he was reluctant. Afraid? Vogel, who was really Stern, had tried to kill him on the cliff that afternoon? Probably. But that made sense only—

"David?"

"Yes?"

"You don't want to go back there, do you?"

"I'm not sure. In a way I do. But I'm not sure I should. Maybe I don't have the right. Say Vogel is the spy. Think of what happened to him in Dora. Do I really have the right—"

"Yes. Think of what happened to you. You have any right you want to claim."

David shrugged. "I suppose. But then there's Tim. I phoned again. No one seems to have any idea where he is." Anne began to say something, but he shook his head. "No, I don't really think he's killed himself. But he was so upset. It wasn't just Diana, but what I told him about me. I think I always misread something there. Something was going on that I didn't understand. I can't think what he's doing."

"So what do we do?"

"Maybe we should go back to London. Forget everything else. Let bygones be bygones."

"But will other people do the same? Stern, or Vogel, or whatever his name is. He certainly isn't."

"I know. That's the trouble."

Anne finished her drink. "David, you know it's up to you. We can go back to England, or we can go to California, whatever you want. Just remember, though, I'm coming too."

That point, at least, had been settled earlier. Anne had insisted: Derek would be safe in Copenhagen and she wouldn't let David go on alone. He hadn't argued with her. He hadn't wanted to. But his exact aim now was something of a question. He had no tracks to follow, no one like Stern to give the lead. Of course they would go to California; since he'd climbed out of the Irish Sea, there'd been no doubt that he'd go *on*. But what would they do when they got there? He would find Tannis, but what would he say to him? He felt now a kind of suspicion of himself. Did he have the courage? Yet he was not sure of the test his courage might fail. Was he afraid that he would run away? Or possibly, he considered, in seeking out Tannis he was trying to make peace, effect some sort of reconciliation. Tannis would have a line into the FBI; given the events of the past weeks they'd surely have to revise their old conclusions. So would he be satisfied with that? Was that a victory? On the other hand, his true intention might lie in quite an opposite direction. Perhaps, after all, he simply wanted revenge. Yes, despite his fine words about Vogel and Dora, did he want to settle the score? Anne had given her permission, if that's what he'd been asking. And there was another possibility, the simple desire to know . . . though it was hardly simple. This was his history. He'd been made by all this, that's what it came down to, and he would either understand it now or he never would. Deep inside, he must still be a scientist. Was he really going to live out his life in ignorance of how that life had been defined? But even as he posed these questions, he drew back from them; in fact, it still seemed crucial not to insist on answers. He'd recognize the answer when it appeared, and that would define the question well enough. Meanwhile, he did have one certainty, and that, in fact, was Anne.

They flew to Los Angeles by way of London; he needed to get some money anyway, and it gave him another chance to get in touch with Tim, although he didn't, not in Aberporth, at his college, and no messages anywhere. And that was a worry. But as the miles drifted by thirty-five thousand feet below him there was no doubt in David's mind that he wanted Anne beside him. They kept saying to each other that Tannis was the key, but David knew she was, at least for him. Again, as he'd understood in Germany, she was literally his salvation, the only reason he was looking down at these clouds at all. More than anything else, he couldn't get over the coincidence. Formally, he knew, the story of what had happened to him began with Vogel and Buhler, long before China Lake. But he couldn't help but believe that the true beginning was also in Anne's cottage, when he'd come across the room to kiss her. And that almost hadn't happened. There his courage had faced a little test, and his nerve had almost failed. And what if it had? Everything that had happened later—the Clints of Dromore, Diana's death—would have divided him from Anne and any hope for himself; he would have been lost, he knew it. That moment had changed the course of everything, even though he hadn't known at the time that there was a course to be changed. She had changed him, or he had changed himself, and he could still feel the changes running through him. He felt a touch self-conscious in the simple sense, but also more profoundly.

At Kennedy—they only changed planes; they flew straight on—he stripped and washed and changed his shirt; and when he looked at his face in the mirror, he immediately glanced away. Yes, that was him; but it was a face a little different from what he'd expected. He would have sworn, too, that his voice had changed. He seemed to breathe more easily.

Not that he mentioned any of this. He wasn't quite sure what it meant, and in a way he didn't care: Anne's presence, right there beside him, was far more important. He felt impatient. He thought of all the conversations they hadn't had. So many gaps remained to be filled in. He almost regretted the urgency of his feelings for her; he longed for a normal moment, an ordinary day. As it was, he enjoyed the moments offered: her hair brushing his face as she slept against his shoulder, the way she took his arm as they walked along.

Finally, as they came into Los Angeles, sliding high above swimming pools and bungalows and superhighways, he felt himself withdraw a little. Since China Lake he'd managed to avoid L.A., and no wonder, he thought, as the memories came back; for they all seemed vaguely humiliating, memories of uncertainty, strangeness, impotence. Or was that making too much of it? Hadn't he just been very young, much too young?

"We're so simple," he said to Anne. "We try to pretend we're complicated, but it's all a ludicrous front. We spend all our time trying to avoid the embarrassment of the most utterly banal revelations. Or is it even banal to say so?"

She laughed. "Of course, that may be what being English is all about."

"I was all at sea. These people were so obviously savages but they didn't seem to know it."

"But Diana liked it?"

"She wanted to stay, I think. When she got pregnant—that was only a week or so before everything fell apart—she checked on what it would mean if she had Tim here. I remember one time . . . we had a car, someone had lent it to us. I was petrified. I could barely drive anyway, and of course this was all on the wrong side of the road. But we drove here, and on the way we stopped for petrol. It was night, and there was another car, a convertible full of people. We were out in the desert, and I remember looking into this car, with all these shadowy, laughing people and the light gleaming on the hair and the shoulders of the girls, and I can just hear Diana saying, 'Oh I wish we could go with them!' "

"You were horrified?"

"No, no. I probably wanted to go; I just didn't know how. I shouldn't make myself sound like a total prig, and even if I was, I didn't want to be. The problem was, I knew that if I tried to fit in, I'd only make a fool of myself."

As they walked on the beach at Santa Monica, with the day's last warmth still lingering in the sand, his tone was easy, and he could talk like this. But he wondered how he would be seeing things if he hadn't changed; if he'd passed an uneventful time here, adding one more line to his c.v.; if he'd gone on at Aberporth, or Ferranti-Packard, or BAe . . . if he'd lived the life of that man he'd seen in Aberporth, walking his dog. What was his name? *I'll always have a fondness for California, you know—Timmy started there, after all.* He'd remember meetings and seminars and colloquies, and his successes, one experiment in particular—*On their range, you could really run a proper* test—that indeed had increased the "look" of Sidewinder some crucial number of degrees. He'd have contacts (*Bob and I go back a good long way*) and memories of Diana: Diana beside a pool, on that horse, sipping California wine. After all, those things had happened too. You could remember it that way. But now he said, "I was awkward, arrogant, lonely, frightened, pompous, priggish, young, brilliant, of course—"

"You're still brilliant."

"Thank you." He kissed her.

"Not here."

"No one will notice. We are surrounded by Americans. I told you, they're savages. Well-fed, well-groomed—"

"All the same . . . Besides, we have to think about tomorrow."

Tomorrow was Tannis.

They spent the morning finding him, which wasn't so much difficult as tedious. He was listed in the phone book, but all they got was a recorded message, in a bad imitation of Mae West's voice, asking callers to leave a message. The listed address was a numbered road. Trying to narrow it down, they called the post office in Ridgecrest, but they weren't much help. Nor was the gas company. Finally, using some Yankee ingenuity and appealing to the entrepreneurial spirit, David phoned a real estate agent in Mojave, telling him a cock-and-bull story—perhaps made convincing by David's accent—about moving to California and having an old friend out in the desert and they were thinking, wouldn't it be nice to have a property out that way? This worked, but at a price, for there was no way to avoid driving out there and taking a tour. They saw four houses, were given brochures on new developments, even checked out condominiums, a whole tract of them, built at the edge of the highway in the middle of nowhere, looking across miles of rock and sand. But eventually their patience was rewarded. Around four o'clock the agent said, "I think your friend must be right along here," and sure enough, after a few more miles, they saw his mailbox, J Tannis, at the end of a long asphalt strip that ran into a canyon and then curved around, ascending to the cliff top. They could see his house, a bungalow, hunched down among the rocks.

Two hours later, in their own car, they were back.

At that time of the day, the sky was still high and blue, but shadows were also darkening the canyons and creeping out from under rocks. Rather in the same way, David could feel his caution stirring. But the only approach to the house put them right out in the open: they drove straight up the drive, visible from the house, indeed visible from ten miles away.

"What are we going to do if he isn't there?"

David shook his head. "I don't know. Leave a message. I wouldn't mind getting into his house. Seeing what—" But he broke off, his eyes glancing around, though there was really nothing to see at all.

Anne felt nervous. When they stopped and got out of the car, she could feel the hot, dry wind against her face, but she couldn't hear it, and nothing moved—not a branch, a leaf. This unsettled her. Do you like the desert? The question formed in her mind, but now ordinary thoughts were beginning to seem inane. Instead, she said, "That must be his car."

There was a carport where the asphalt ended, redwood posts roofed with lattice, an old Chevrolet zigzagged with shadow. David nodded. "Yes, but he probably has another one. Or a truck." In fact, a patch of dirt, to the left of the car, was dark with oil. He hesitated a moment, waiting to see if anyone emerged, but then went up to the door. In his own mind he was certain that Tannis wasn't here, but he rang anyway. Or, rather, chimed: three separate notes, a musicality that seemed out of keeping with his memories of the man. No one came; and after a moment he motioned Anne to follow and headed around the side of the house. Like many desert dwellings it was little more than a pretentious shack, with split-log corner posts and beams, rough clapboard siding, and a cedar-shake roof. But it was larger than it looked; their steps scuffed along a path, four bricks wide, that ran all the way around, to keep the runoff from eroding the foundation, he supposed, and at the back, surrounded by a brick wall, was a tiled patio. This had a pleasant, formal air. The wall was spectacular, in fact, for beavertail cactus was growing all along the top of it; there were hundreds of plants, and they were all in flower, huge mounds of rose and lavender. A wrought-iron gate led through the wall, and in the middle of the patio was an ornamental iron grille, some kind of drain, with a mesquite planted in its center. A white plastic table and a couple of chairs had been pulled into the scrawny shade of the tree, and everything was coated with a fine film of sand.

Anne said, "You have the feeling no one's been here for weeks."

David nodded. He felt it too. Tannis wasn't here, but his absence was more emphatic than that; he'd *gone*. He thought about leaving a message but what would be the point? And finally he said, "I want to get inside."

A large glass patio door led into the back of the house, but it was curtained, with a white, gauzy curtain liner and a dark blue curtain, drawn tight. They couldn't see in. But a wheelbarrow had been tipped up against the wall, and there was a shovel and a spade beside it. The spade looked heavier. Anne realized she was frightened, as David smashed in the glass; this was against the law. But she didn't say a word. She thought, You came to help him, not to stop him; and as he put the spade back—rather punctiliously, as if to make amends—she pushed through the curtain and was first inside.

Quietly David stood beside her.

He didn't move, and he was glad that she didn't speak: he realized he was trying to fix this image in his mind, like someone awakening who wants to catch a dream. He'd come back to China Lake; for the first time he now really felt this. Yet he wasn't sure why. Why hadn't he felt like this in Los Angeles? All morning he'd been trying to decide if they should drive up and see the base; there, he thought, he would discover if he still had anything left to feel. But he felt it now, quite clearly, in this ordinary living room, with a brick fireplace at the far end, and the usual California-style furniture, a low-slung sofa, leather chairs. There were no explicit reminders of the past, he couldn't see a photograph, nothing was emblematic, everything was neutral. Indeed, the most obvious feature of the room, the huge expanse of beige shag carpet that covered the floor, wall to wall, was anachronistic in every way: out of date, but not even invented at the time when he'd been here. Yet something now brought it all back. Perhaps it simply came from being in a desert room again, that smell of closed-up heat, the quiet that lay inside a deeper stillness, although, as he strained his ears, he thought he heard the sound of dripping water, like the slow drip-drip of the evaporators they'd used for air-conditioning in the offices and labs, and very far off, in fact, he did hear that other familiar sound, the rumble of a distant plane.

Finally, Anne called out, "Mr. Tannis?"

David smiled and felt himself relax. "It's all right," he said. "There's no one here."

And there wasn't. Tannis was gone, all right, or, more precisely, probably hadn't returned from Aberporth, the Clints of Dromore. Yet it wasn't so easy to determine exactly what had happened—the terms of his leaving, so to speak. They went through the house and found clothes in his bedroom closet and two Samsonite suitcases on the upper shelf, so perhaps he hadn't gone very far. On the other hand, there were no socks or underwear in his bureau. And though the milk in his fridge was off, the tap in the kitchen sink was dripping, as if he'd just stepped out and would be back in a moment. Even the one big discovery they did make didn't give them an answer to their question. This came in his office. It had obviously been tidied away—pencils in jars, a notepad lined up with the corner of the desk—but again, whether the man who'd worked here had left forever or would return tomorrow wasn't obvious. But they both immediately noticed the flashing light on the answering machine.

"And look," said Anne, picking up the wastebasket. "He must have just bought it. Here's the carton it came in."

"Yes. He can't be that far away; otherwise, why bother?"

"So play the tape back."

He bent the neck of the old brass gooseneck lamp that occupied one corner of the desk and shone it onto the machine, winding the tape right back to the beginning. The phone would ring. The caller would hang up. A stockbroker, calling all the way from Denver, left his name and number. Electronic peddlers: selling magazines, light bulbs for the handicapped. "Just to remind you, Captain, the next VFW meeting is on Tuesday, usual time."

"What's the VFW?"

David shook his head. "No idea. Veterans . . . ?"

But then they hit it. Unfortunately, there was no indication of when the call had come; no one here, it seemed, was in the habit of giving the date and time when they left their message. But there weren't that many messages altogether, so this one couldn't have been that long ago.

"Jack? Bill Matheson. Look, uh . . . I don't want to be too unsecure about this but uh . . . the other people think they've found the subject B, you know, the unfortunate foreign national you discovered out there, might have been trying to get to. Someone called Vogel? It didn't ring a bell with me, but, ah, evidently . . . evidently there's a farm or a house near Indian Wells that he owns, or at least he used to; evidently no one lives there and the county's taking it back for—Christ." It broke off there, but the next call was from the same man. "Me again, Jack, the tape ran out, I think. But I want to get it straight. Have you heard of this Vogel? And there's someone with the same name up the Trona road. They sent someone out there, and there's a woman living in a trailer with a kid. She says her father isn't there. He's supposed to be in Mexico. Okay? Could you give me a call on this? Thanks." He hung up. The tape ran on. The stockbroker, one more time. A hangup. Another. And then another half-dozen calls before their own, that morning.

David turned off the machine and Anne said, "So that proves it, David. There *is* an investigation."

He smiled. "You're just beginning to believe this, aren't you?"

Her face was serious. "It's real now, in a different way."

He touched her hand, then opened the drawer of the desk and found Tannis's phone book. He looked up Matheson. "He's in the navy, a commander. He works at China Lake."

"You're not going to phone him?"

In fact, for an instant, that's what he thought of doing. But he shook his head. "No. I suspect I'm the last person they'd want to see at this point."

"Yes, bureaucracies don't like to admit mistakes, do they?"

"Exactly."

"So what do we do?"

"I still want to speak to Tannis. The question is, will he come back here?"

"You know, he doesn't have to. Didn't you hear a couple of beeps, those tones? Look at the box, David. This is one like mine. He has a beeper; he can get his messages from any phone."

"Well, that could be all right. He phones, starts to play back his tape, and I pick up the receiver and talk to him. All we have to do is wait for him to call."

It was the simple solution and probably it would have worked, but it was never tested.

By this time it was almost seven o'clock; they hadn't eaten since the morning, and so even though it felt rather strange to be making themselves at home, Anne heated a can of soup and they ate it in the living room, sitting in the middle of the floor, with the lights off, for a light would show for miles. Anne was quiet. She was afraid, of the dark house, of the desert, of what was happening. Most frightening of all, she realized they had nowhere to go for help. Now that he'd decided differently, she understood how much she'd been hoping that David would go to the police, that some "reasonable" solution would present itself. With a few additional facts and some rational arguments, "normality" would be restored. But now she knew that was impossible: some quality in Matheson's voice, his casualness, had convinced her of this utterly. He was getting his job done. He had no interest in solutions, would have no interest in David; his only concern was in preserving "normality" itself, a normalcy that assumed people like David couldn't exist. So the police, authority, "other people"—they were no help at all.

What she also saw was how important this must have been for David. He *pretended* to believe in other people, he could play the part quite perfectly, but really he didn't believe at all. He couldn't. It was too dangerous. But he believed in her. How had that happened? Why had he chosen her? She acknowledged these questions but didn't really press them, because she knew, as she thought along, that she was understanding how deeply she believed in *him. You're just beginning to believe this, aren't you?* His voice had been light—or had he meant it? no, he hadn't—but there was truth in what he'd said; each day was like an additional confirmation of him in her mind. And then she understood what she'd been working up to. I love him more than Axel, she thought. Up to now, she couldn't have borne making the comparison, but now she did: I love him more. And then she thought of Derek. Oh, I love him so much too.

But she didn't say any of this, nor did David guess what she was thinking. His thoughts and fears were more immediate. He was still thinking about Tannis and the answering machine. They'd drawn only the obvious conclusion: Tannis still wanted a certain connection to this place, at least to its phone number. But you could go further, he thought. Tannis had bought the machine, and recently, because he wanted to record messages, but he was also *expecting* one. And who could that be from? Matheson . . . the FBI . . . David didn't think so; Tannis could call them anytime he wanted. No, the more he thought about it, the more he felt sure that Tannis was expecting a call from Vogel; that was the message he didn't want to miss. But there was an alarming side to that. He'd felt, from the moment he'd come in here, that Tannis had abandoned this place, and now he was certain that Vogel had frightened him off. And David could see why. It was so isolated and so out in the open. That's why he'd insisted they keep the lights off. Even when he picked up their soup bowls and carried them out to the kitchen, he didn't turn the lights on. He washed up in the dark—"If we're going to move in, we might as well be good houseguests"—and all the time he kept an eye out the window, for the kitchen was the one room that had a good view back to the highway, and in fact you could see for miles, so that he'd been following the lights of a car for several minutes when he realized it was slowing down. It was slowing down, just as it came up to the drive—

"Anne. Come here. Quickly."

His fears jumped up in him as the car turned, but in fact it wasn't turning as he'd thought; the car—*except it wasn't a car, it was a truck*—made a U-turn on the highway, then drew up on the shoulder. As Anne came in, as a figure moved through the beam of the headlights, he suddenly realized what was happening.

"What is it?"

"His mail. Christ, I never thought of that. Look, we have to get outside—"

"Is it Tannis?"

In fact, as he'd seen the shadow passing in the headlights, he hadn't thought so—the figure looked too slim and young; in fact, he'd thought of Tim, there'd been something that youthful in the movement—but it couldn't be, and he said, "I don't know. Maybe. But it could be Vogel. Anne, I want you to—" He wanted to get them out of the house; he didn't want to be trapped in here. Vogel, after all, could kill. He'd killed Buhler, he'd killed the woman in Germany. But even as he spoke, he realized that the truck, rather than coming up toward the house, was retracing its route back along the highway.

"It's all right," said Anne.

David's feelings swung suddenly around, 180 degrees. "No, it's not. If that's Tannis—whoever it is—we're going to follow him. Look, go out and start the car."

Because he didn't have his shoes on; they were in the living room. But the comedy of it was a relief; it calmed him. Finally, with his shoelaces still untied, he ran out of the house and got into the passenger seat, and

Anne headed down the long, steep drive around the canyon. This was probably a mile. But it wasn't hard to pick up the truck; as they came down the hill, they could see its taillights drifting down the highway. And though they lost it as they came lower, that was for only a moment, until Anne put her foot down and caught them up again. She was a good driver. There were few cars on the road—a single set of lights, far, far behind— and it was not quite full dark, so she didn't have to deal with that un- nerving desert blackness, the black of the road merging with the desert night, the feeling, as you wind through a curve, that you're heading off, into nowhere. Besides, the truck wasn't going particularly fast; there was certainly no sense that it was trying to get away. So, hanging back, keep- ing their lights out of the truck's mirror, they headed north and east, along Route 14, the day dying out behind them, their shadow racing far ahead, and then the truck turned and David could see, strung across the darkening night, the lights of Ridgecrest, though all he thought was *China Lake*, and when Anne looked at him, he shook his head. "No, I don't remember this at all. It was so much smaller. Look at that." To the right a long, low slope of land was lit up, bright as the Milky Way . . . and now, too, there were many more cars, desert cars, pickup trucks, Western dreams: polished tailpipes, racks of lights on the tops of cabs, big mag wheels and tuneful horns.

Anne said, "I think I should get closer."

From the corner of her eye she saw a street sign—CHINA LAKE BLVD., it read—and she thought, Now I've arrived officially. She felt less nervous if she talked a little. "Where exactly is the base? Is that where he's going?"

"It's all over there; straight ahead, and over to the right."

But the truck didn't get quite that far. She was one car behind it as it turned—they all made the light—and then the car ahead turned off, into a motel.

"Don't get too close now."

"I don't think he can see us from here."

"No, but he might slow down and then it would look unnatural if you didn't pass him. Actually, you don't have to worry about him seeing us. You're driving, we're a couple. That's not what he'd be looking for."

She nodded. "Where are we?"

For all at once the lights were gone. The highway and all the land around was black, all black except for the two red lights ahead.

David had a map on his lap. "We are now on Highway 178, heading west. The next town is called Trona, and then it goes along for twenty miles and divides; there's a junction. If you go left, you cut across the top of the base and end out at the highway—Route 14, the one we were on before. The other way, to the right, you head toward Death Valley and Las Vegas."

They were silent then.

Anne kept them close, but not too close; she'd fall back, then ease up a little, closing the gap as they whipped through Trona, then stretching it as they headed down the smooth, black road again. She was frightened. She could feel it in her shoulders, and when she let her eyes look right, down toward the Panamint, she'd jerk her gaze away: she couldn't bring her mind to bear upon the emptiness.

Then, quite suddenly, the truck's lights disappeared.

"David—"

"No. Don't slow down. That's it . . . just a little." He peered out the window. "Over there, you see, he's turned."

She looked, but in fact she didn't see; that way there was a huge bulk of mountain against the sky. "Is there a road? I haven't seen a sign."

"I don't know. But just keep going. If he sees our lights . . ." His voice trailed off. But Anne understood what he meant. Quickly they reached the point where the truck had left the highway, and then, as they went by, David turned and looked back, trying to fix the spot in his mind. "I don't think there is a road. He just turned right onto the desert."

"What do I do?"

"The trouble is, you can see lights so far out here—"

"Yes."

"So go on for a few miles, say three. Push the button. Then turn off your lights. If he's watching, he'll think we've gone over a rise. Then double back. But you'll have to keep your lights off."

"God."

But she did it. With David turned around in his seat, trying to see the truck—but it was gone—they went along, made their turn, Anne flinching as her front tire bit into sand, and came back along their route, all in darkness. She kept her speed to twenty, then realized that she must be invisible from behind and glanced in the rearview mirror—

"No. Keep your eyes on the road. I'll watch for anything back there."

She wound down the window then, stuck her head out, drove one-handed, so she didn't have to peer through the reflections in the windshield. She narrowed her eyes against the grit, felt the desert wind flowing through her hair, felt the excitement of a curve, and then jerked back in and said, "That's a road."

"No, no, we haven't come far enough."

"But it *is* a road. Look, just there."

She slowed. Stopped. And she was right. There was a road, or at least a roughly graded track, running back into the desert.

David shook his head. "This isn't it. We've at least another two miles to go." But then he hesitated. "Still. Do you think we could get up it?" He peered out into the darkness; against the lighter sandy sea the shadows of the creosote and shad scale, brittlebush and sage, were thrown out like an enormous net.

"Yes, I could get up it. It isn't very wide, but it looks quite solid."

"Put your lights on."

"No, I'll be all right. I'll just drive slowly."

She didn't go more than five miles an hour, dropping the transmission into first and keeping it there. And she stuck her head out the window again, to see, though the line of graded ground caught the light more cleanly than the desert and wasn't that hard to follow. At length they tilted up a slope. At the top were two big boulders, sharp as teeth. Then they were looking down into a long, shallow bowl, where lights were gleaming.

Anne braked instinctively.

They thought it together, but it was Anne who said, "David, on the answering machine—they said someone had been sent to the Trona road. That's the trailer. We've found Vogel."

David squinted. It wasn't exactly a trailer, but it was enough like one. "It works out, doesn't it. Tannis must be watching this place. That's why the truck turned off where it did. He's up in those hills somewhere, watching us now."

For five minutes they watched too: staring silently from the car at the little chain of lights . . . like a single railway car, forgotten for eternity on this surreal siding. A shadow moved. David was sure it was a woman. But he wasn't absolutely sure. And if Vogel was down there? His fears returned. But if Vogel was actually in the trailer—David worked it out—Tannis would not be watching, he'd go down and get him. Tannis was watching *for* him; which meant Vogel wasn't there. He put his hand on the door handle.

"David—"

"Don't argue. Turn the car around, so it faces the highway. Then I'm going down there. I don't think Vogel's inside, but if anything happens, drive like mad. Go back to Trona and get the police."

He opened the door and got out, giving her no chance to argue; then he waited till she'd backed around. She wound down the window. "If it's all right," she said, "wave from the doorway and I'll come too."

"Okay."

"Be careful."

He walked quickly down the slope, his feet slipping in the sand; but if Tannis, or anyone else, was watching he didn't feel observed. Above all, he saw no movement from the house. He came up to the dark shadow of a car. It was a Peugeot, which surprised him, and then he could hear music, pop sounds from a radio. He waited a second, but no one emerged; surely no one was standing guard. So he went ahead. A couple of cement steps led up to a flimsy door. He knocked. After a moment, the radio went off and he knocked again. Then a woman called out and he answered, "Miss Vogel? My name is David Harper."

There was a pause; then the door opened. He had to step down to the ground and so found himself looking up at a slim young woman in silhouette—a square of yellow light shone from behind her, bright enough to dazzle. Then his eyes adjusted and he thought, If Stern was Vogel, then he was an old man with excellent taste in young women. She was smoking a cigarette. Her lean, tanned face was lit with a reddish glow; she was very beautiful. "I don't think I know you," she said.

"Is your father here?"

"Why do you want to know?"

"Or is he in Mexico? San Miguel d'Allende?" David watched this register on her face, and he added, "I know your father, Miss Vogel. We met in Wales. Could I come in?"

With a nod she stepped back but leaned forward to hold open the door. He came inside, into the light, brushing against her, and smelled her perfume, something soft and rosy. She was very attractive, which shaped a little of what came after. "I have a friend, Miss Vogel, up at my car. A lady. Would it be all right . . . ?"

She looked uncertain; she had great brown eyes, and David expected them to fill with fear. But the fear stopped in a tensioning of her jaw; and she nodded, a quick bob of her small dark head.

He turned and waved to Anne, then watched her get out of the car.

Then the sound of the slamming door came, cushioned, through the air. He wondered how far it would carry, but decided that Tannis would not be so close.

"Would you like something? A drink . . ."

David looked around him. It was a strange little room, for there was really no furniture, only Indian blankets tossed down in a bright quilt of carpet; and there were more rugs hanging from the walls, and even two that hung, like flags or baffles, from the ceiling. It was like a tent. In one corner a blanket had been rolled into a cushion, and she must have been sitting there, for beside it was the radio he'd heard, a bottle of liquor, and a small cloth bag woven with bright beads.

"I don't think I want anything," he said.

"No. A cigarette? I have some grass."

He said, "I found you by accident, Miss Vogel. I was following a man called Tannis." He watched her face. "Have you heard that name?"

"Maybe." She shrugged. "Why?"

"I think you have."

"Someone wanted a farm, a place they said my father owned, on the other side of Ridgecrest. That could have been him."

"He's watching for your father, Miss Vogel. Do you know why that might be?"

They heard Anne coming to the door, and the girl glanced that way. Then, rather neatly, she sat down, crossing her legs as she did so, on the same spot where she'd been before.

David hesitated, then sat down beside her. "Why is he watching, Miss Vogel?"

"Marianne. That's my name. He's not interested in my father, Mr. . . . David?"

"Have you ever heard of a place called Dora?"

She shook her head.

"A man called Buhler?"

She shook her head again, but David wasn't sure; it could have been a lie.

"Don't you have a child, Marianne?"

Her eyes glanced down as she answered. "Anna. She's with her father."

Anne. Anna. Marianne. "And that's all right?"

"I told you. Whoever this person is, he's not interested—"

"So why is he watching?"

"He wants gold."

"Gold?"

"That right. It's almost exactly this color. . . ." And she picked up the bottle of tequila and, with surprising daintiness, took a sip.

Anne was standing in the doorway now. Marianne Vogel looked up at her and smiled, an acknowledgment, Yes, you're beautiful too. Then, opening up her little bag, she said, "I'm doing some peyote. Would you care to join me?" And she reached down into the bag and pulled up a fistful of dark, leathery buttons. She held these out, in offering.

"No, thanks," he said.

"You should. Really."

David hesitated. And then, to Anne's astonishment, he took one, put it in his mouth, and chewed.

CHAPTER 17

Why had David taken the peyote?

What was he doing with this strange woman?

David could see questions in Anne's eyes, and he wasn't necessarily certain of the answers. I seized the moment, he might have told her. It seemed the only thing to do. I felt I had no choice.

And that was true enough, but it wasn't only a question of intuition. On the one hand, it was rather more concrete, for he'd simply been responding to Marianne's obvious fear by trying to calm her, come over to her side. Look, he was saying, I'm with you, there's nothing to be afraid of. At the same time, it was also more subtle and complicated. At the root of Marianne's fear was a mystery—she was so terribly frightened—but (and this was the point) she already knew the solution to it. She already knew the answer, but the trick was to get her to admit it to herself. David saw that at once; it was part of picking up on her being just a little crazy. It had to mean something: this crazy, beautiful woman, alone in the desert with Tannis watching her. Yes, the mystery of her fear seemed congruent with the larger mystery—Vogel, "Stern," Buhler, Tannis, Sidewinder, AIM-9B—the solution to one gave the answer to the other. The answer to his own mystery, David thought, lay in hers.

And the peyote itself was a part of this. Peyote was a mystery. Peyote was a part of the mystery of the desert. And peyote connected his own time in the desert to the present; it could take him back, back to the time he'd lost, a time, for everyone else, that had been saturated with sex and drugs and politics but that he'd missed. Hadn't Aldous Huxley, the first evangelist of lysergic acid, visited this place? Expand your mind. Well, that couldn't hurt. In any event, the peyote seemed to connect with everything else; here was his *second chance* in yet another form. So all that was part of why he took the drug. But most important of all David was still a scientist. By taking the peyote he was performing an experiment. On himself. On the whole situation. He was trying something out, trying something on. Will this work? He didn't know. But what he realized only as he put the button into his mouth and chewed (the first marvelous unpredictable consequence of his act) was that it made Anne crucial. Everything now shifted toward her. In a way, cunningly, David had withdrawn, turned himself from subject to object, offered himself up for a kind of examination, the scientist merging with his experiment. He'd allied himself with Marianne—they became the couple—and so Marianne was disarmed; that was one side of it. But the other was how Anne now became his secret witness. She was his eyes and ears but would also be able to discover things he couldn't hear or see. From this point almost everything would be worked out through her. He realized this only at the very last moment, and he tried to get it across to her, for he could see, as she came into the trailer, as she saw what was happening, how astonished she was. And then how abandoned she felt. She was odd man out, thrown back upon herself. So he looked at her and tried to make his eyes tell her that this was all right. I'm still here, he tried to say. Just play along. Do your best. Be yourself. . . . But of course that wasn't so easy, especially in the beginning. When he couldn't actually tell her anything. She watched him put the peyote in his mouth and couldn't believe it. What was he doing? David . . . Oddly, she suddenly felt ridiculous. Yes. *She* felt like a fool. Which was silly, since *he'd* done it. She wasn't sure what was going on. She didn't understand a thing. But that, in a sense, was perfect. For the time being, that's exactly what David wanted. She didn't understand; all she could do was take it in. Himself. The frightened girl. The trailer. The solution to the mystery, whatever it might be.

*   *   *

Anne looked around the trailer. She was shocked. That's why she felt ridiculous; one wasn't supposed to be shocked today. Not by drugs, at least. Drugs were passé. A *bore*. Well . . .

The trailer was strange, set up like the inside of a Red Indian's tent—actually, the woman, Marianne, looked a little like an Indian. Or a Mexican. Yes, the room was like that. Lamps tipped the light over the floor, which was covered with colorful woven rugs, but everything else was dark and shadowy. . . .

"Sit down," Marianne said. "Look, if you don't do dope, that's okay. I've got plenty of tequila. Really. It's okay."

The peyote, Anne had to admit, frightened her a little. And she would never have expected David to do it. It wasn't like him. Except it had to be like him, since he'd done it. He'd done it so easily. Then she understood why: being able to do it like that was connected to what had happened to him in the years after China Lake; watching him, that became more real to her than before. For David a little peyote wouldn't mean so much. He'd been desperate, he knew all about desperation, that's what he'd seen in this woman now. Looking, she could see it too. Yes, that was the first point. Marianne was desperate.

"Anne. My name is Anne. Thank you. Just a little, just enough to cover the bottom of the glass. All right . . . I like lime . . . but I don't think any salt . . ."

The rugs were so beautiful and strange: that's what Anne noticed first.

They had a soft, warm, musky smell. They felt slightly greasy between her fingers, or smooth as linen. The patterns were diamonds, like stars or snakes. They wiggled around borders, hung in chains, turned inside out. The colors were dark rose, indigo, sepia. They were the colors of sand, the hot white sand on the surface beneath the sun, then darker deeper down, when you dug with your fingers. And they were the colors of blood: pale and almost milky in the flesh, but welling up crimson in a wound. They all had names, and Marianne said them aloud, touching each in turn: *moki*, Ganado, Klagetoh, White Clay, Two Gray Hills, Burnt Water, *yei*.

Marianne certainly knew a lot about Indians.

"No, the rugs are Navajo. The Indians around here never learned to weave. They were Paiutes toward the Sierras, on the other side of Route 14, and Shoshone over here. They were like cavemen. They lived on roots and pine nuts and jackrabbits (they clubbed them; they didn't even have bows and arrows). They might have been five feet tall. That was a real big Paiute. Most of them would never have seen a white man till the 1860s, when the Nevada Comstock opened up. Sacagawea was the most famous Shoshone. The Crow captured her as a child and sold her as a slave to the Mandan, who took her east. Then Lewis and Clark met her and she led them to the Pacific, and she actually did find her way back to her people. I'm sure they made a movie about it. Wovoka was the most famous Paiute. His real name was Jack Wilson and most of the time he wore a suit vest and a big hat. He invented the Ghost Dance religion. The whites would stop moving west and the Indians would inherit the earth, provided, of course, they did his dance. It took about a week. They were like Indian Shakers. Really. The Shakers were at their height then, this is about 1870, and Wilson knew them. When the Indians danced, they went into a crazy trance and thought they were invulnerable; hence the Ghost Shirts, hence Wounded Knee. They charged the soldiers, thinking the bullets wouldn't hurt them. Peyote wasn't actually a part of that, although it was all connected. Peyote was magic. Peyote made you invulnerable too, protected you from witchcraft. The Tarahumara thought that, and the Apache, the Lipan, the Mescalero. The modern peyote cults started not far from here, and that's what they were all about. They really knew how to push dope. Joaquin Brown was a Paiute, around Fallon. Joe Green was a Paiute. Chief Grey Horse—Ben Lancaster, that is—was, I think, a Washo, or half, from Gardnerville, Nevada. He worked in the bars in Reno, and he was the most important. He spread it. He taught a lot of the others to make the moon, tie their drums. He lived with Mary D. Creek. I know where he got his, and that's where this comes from; he cut it and dried it near Sanderson just like I do. It's almost extinct; you have to know where to look. He's extinct too, of course. He died in 1937. Wyatt Earp died in 1929 in Hollywood; I think that's one of the most important dates.

But there really never were any Indians. The Navajo, all the wool in these blankets, they got that from the Spanish, like the horse, guns, iron. Indians, what they had, the wisdom and beauty they'd accumulated from the beginning of time, you could put it into a small bag. Of course, if they'd been left alone long enough they, too, would have come up with the transistor. But they weren't, were they? And as soon as they met the whites they were finished. As soon as they met the whites, they turned into myths; by *as soon as* I mean, say, within thirty-six months. So if one of the things you *did* have was a drug, and you'd been turned into a myth, you'd probably want to take it."

"You studied anthropology?"

"Only for a year. But out here, one thing you've sure got lots of is time to read."

Marianne was frightened. So she chattered on. That's what David had seen, how frightened she was. There was a moment, as Marianne looked away, that Anne was able to look into the darkness of her large, dark eyes, an absolute, absorbing darkness, which was both terribly frightening and terribly afraid: Anne had been able to look there for only an instant, and then she'd looked away herself.

David said, "How many should you take?"

"Have you taken it before?"

"No."

"Just one. Or two or three. I'll take half a dozen at least." All the time she was talking to David, but Anne knew she was also watching her. Then she said to her, "Are you sure you don't want one?"

"I don't know. I'll wait, if that's all right."

David said, "Where does it come from?"

"I told you. Sanderson, Texas. The Indians used to find it around Laredo, up and down the Rio Grande. But it's all gone now. You have to go to Mexico."

Did David want her, as it were, to stay sober? Was he counting on that? Well, she had never taken drugs, only a little grass. Of course. But it had never been important. Face it, basically you are a good girl. A Good Girl.

A mother. You are well brought up. Also English. You were not a virgin when you married because you'd determined that to be a virgin would be more embarrassing than otherwise. But embarrassment was certainly the key.

There were two lamps on the floor, spilling their light across the bright rugs. Marianne had said the red in the rugs was cochineal. It came from a bug, which they crushed into dye. You can see them; they look like bits of wax on the cactus. They suck juice out of the cactus. The sun, the cactus, the juice, the bug, the dye, the rug—

"Do you think they hallucinate when they feed on peyote?"

"They prefer the prickly pear," David said. "*Opuntia polyacantha.*"

A tongue of light reached beyond the rugs and through a doorway to the kitchen, gleaming on cheap metal cabinets faced to look like wood. I couldn't bear living in a place like this, Anne thought, and then she looked back to David. He was still there. As it were. All there. *Opuntia polyacantha* indeed. What was he doing, expecting? Only recently, only retrospectively, had Anne understood how much David relied on his instincts. He pretended to believe in what other people did and was very convincing, like a terrifically good actor; but he trusted only what he could see, touch, smell, divine.

Tannis had killed a rattlesnake under her house, Marianne said. Which was one reason she was happy to have her daughter with her father. Vogel. Who wasn't Stern: she had to remember that. Or was it the other way around? And maybe, anyway, Marianne wasn't as happy about it as she said. No. The drink, the drug; that's why she was doing this, that's why she was so frightened. Her daughter, Anna. Across the room, in a corner, Anne could see a picture of the little girl, a photograph in a silver frame that would have done well for Marilyn Monroe. But probably Anna had picked it out herself.

It was clear to Anne that Marianne had been taking the drug long before they'd arrived. And had been drinking the tequila. She was tough. That also was part of it, something between the two women. I got your man to take the drug with me, and you won't. So . . . So what?

"I'd like some water," said David after the second button.

Marianne looked suddenly alert. "Let's go outside. It's a lovely night, and I know a beautiful spot." She got up. "Everybody take a blanket. *Everybody take a blanket, I'll get the water, and we'll go outside.*" Only a mother, Anne thought, could catch that rhythm; and you were a good girl, so you did as you were told. But it was indeed a beautiful night. It was full dark now, and the black velvet sky was scattered with diamond stars. She had never seen the stars so bright. So white. Far beyond the trailer was the dark mass of mountains and the other way, toward the highway, was the pale reflection of the Panamint, like a lake in the sky. Anne was wearing sandals. The sand sifted through them, rather cool. The air was cool but soft. David touched her hand.

How are you?

All right.

I don't—

Don't worry. She understands everything. She knows it all.

Marianne caught up to them. She led the way, and they came to a small hollow down among some big rocks. They stretched out all the blankets in the sand. It was wonderful, as soon as you got down on them. You were quite surrounded, and hidden, by the rocks, but high up it was so open, all the way to the stars. The water was in a metal bucket. She'd brought a mug, and David ladled some up and swallowed, then immediately moved away behind one of the big rocks; she could hear him being sick. He kept being sick.

"Are you all right?" she called.

"Don't worry," said Marianne. "Almost everybody is, especially when they take a drink."

"David—"

"It can be lonely," Marianne said, "if you're the only one not doing some."

No.

But then: what you should do, she thought, is what they least expect.

The peyote button looked like a piece of dried fruit.

Dried apple.

Or apricot.

Or a dried fig.

Anne put it in her mouth and bit it. It tasted salty and bitter and harsh, like the inside skin of a walnut. And it turned all stringy, as she chewed, like a tough, gristly piece of meat; in fact, it wouldn't quite be chewed. Should she swallow it? At once, her mouth was full of spit, flowing with it. And turned numb: not like the dentist, but all on the surface, tingling, though her tongue could feel beneath the numbness the incredible softness of her mouth.

In the end, she did swallow it. Since, apparently, she'd only sick it up.

Slowly, lustrously, the night sky revolved behind the stars. Anne followed it, turning around and around. She grew dizzy, turning, but then was turning all within herself, quite calmly. The stars streamed past. They took on colors, like ribbons, or neon, or crayons. Time-lapse photographs of Piccadilly. Times Square. Really, she thought, isn't this rather . . . but she couldn't find the word.

The weaving in the blanket was incredibly close and fine. Warp and weft. Diamond twill and tapestry. She followed a single thread, over and under and back. She thought she'd lost it, but then she found it again. She looked up, and the red diamond in the pattern lifted with her eyes, took wing—red ash drifting above a fire—and flew away; quickly, zipping along, bright as a parrot.

Off by herself, behind a rock, Anne was sick. She was going to get down on her hands and knees, but in the end she just bent over at the waist. She was going to be sick. She knew that. Nothing could stop it. Gently, she felt her asshole tighten. She had no time to take a breath. Her belly twitched and then it came up, her throat and neck were open and gaping like a fish, and she threw up, her ass and belly were twitching to get all of it up. My God. It was like breathing, backward. My God. She was sick again. Oh, *fuck*. She'd got some on her shoe, and of course she was wearing sandals.

David. Divad. "David, did you know you were a palindrome? Or almost."

"What does that mean?" asked Marianne.

"Well, it's the same, forward or backward. Upward or downward."

*　　　*　　　*

Blue milk spilling from the Milky Way . . . The whole experience, Anne thought, was rather at that level: banal, like a line from a popular song. Lucy, or whoever it had been, in the sky with diamonds. The effects were actually less intense than those in a dream, though in a way the most important aspect of it was that you weren't dreaming. It was like a dream but you knew you weren't. Except she wasn't sure what this had to do with Marianne. But the stars, the constellations, truly were incredible.

They lay on their backs on the blankets, looking up at the stars. David understood the zodiac, and this was California, after all; science and astrology were not so far removed. "But it doesn't work anymore, the earth has moved. The stars aren't in their houses. At the equinox the sun is supposed to be in Aries—that's where the ancients saw it—but I think it's moved all the way to Pisces now." How very calm his voice was. Anne, staring up at the stars, let her eyes fall shut. Inside, high up, a friendly yellow Leo bounded along. Anne watched him. He was supposed to stop and yawn and roar, but he didn't. She opened her eyes and he just kept going, absolutely enormous bounding along the top of the mountains, leaping quite clearly from peak to peak. She could hear David saying, *He was aiming for the stars and he never thought of London at all.*

She drank some more water and went behind the rocks. But this time she didn't feel sick. She waited, expecting to be sick, lifting her eyes up and looking out toward the Panamint, waiting; but she was quite calm. After a time, though, she leaned forward. She wasn't exactly sure she wanted to try this, but she was curious to see whether or not she could. She relaxed her throat and opened her mouth, loosened her jaw somehow. Then she worked at the muscles of her belly. Nothing happened; but then she laid her hand flat down there and pressed, and the resistance gave the muscles something to work against. They fluttered. She had to close her eyes and concentrate, but relax at the same time. She made them flutter again, like a belly dancer, she thought, but way inside. And it started. She was suddenly terrified. But she refused to be afraid. One, two, three. The water spewed out in a perfect crystal stream; she watched it float. The individual drops were bright as diamonds and absolutely weightless, float-ing up into the sky like balloons.

Houdini could do that. He'd swallow a key and then bring it up and get out of the box or whatever. He could be sick at will.

Where was Marianne?

Colors, Anne thought. It was all about light and colors. An Eagle pencil box. Primary colors. Like the seats in a McDonald's. Flower children, flower power . . . there was a decidedly childish side to this. But was there anything wrong with that?

She was now very tired. I want to slow down. But the colors didn't stop. She closed her eyes and they were still there, like a separate element. Swimming through them: like schools of bright fish, coral heads, trembling weeds. But she moved so smoothly. It was like swimming, nude. Very pleasant. Just glide. That was it, you just went with it, the currents, the breezes, rolling over in the sun when you get too warm. Lie on the rug and you can sleep. Close your eyes and you can sleep.

And then, it seemed, she did sleep.

But Anne didn't quite recall the end of it.

Later, she would have hazy memories of leaning against David as they walked through the sand. And there was some strange business about "taking the long way round." But she didn't recall going back to the trailer, and only when she awoke some hours later did the peculiar difficulties of falling asleep come back to her. This was on account of the colors, which were evidently the principal effect of the drug. As soon as she closed her eyes and tried to relax, they started. Apparently you couldn't control this; she had some power over the shapes the colors assumed but not over the colors themselves; they simply wouldn't go away. It became rather annoying. *All right, I've had enough*. It was like listening to someone tell you a story you'd heard a dozen times before: she could feel that particular, set expression forming on her face. And when she awoke, this was the first test she made, closing her eyes and trying to find the colors, and then looking around and seeing if they were "out there." Although, as soon as she realized she was doing this, she thought, Well at least you can draw the distinction. In the end it seemed that they were, but only slightly; to get them, she had to work at it.

Relieved at this, she drew herself up, leaning on her elbow.

She was in the main room of the trailer and realized now that she was lying on a very narrow mattress, with some of the Navajo blankets over her. David was beside her, covered too, and he was still asleep. She tried but couldn't remember at all how she'd got here. She listened. But she couldn't hear Marianne, nor indeed anything else, except for the soft whir of a fan that she couldn't locate. But then that faded into the easy, quiet sounds of herself. After a moment she realized that she wanted to pee. And rather than blunder about looking for the toilet, she pulled one of the blankets around her, for she was naked, and went out the front door.

It was very cool, and the sky was overcast. She found this a relief; the sky now seemed to draw down around the vast landscape, almost protectively, rather than retreating into the harshness of space. But some stars were still out; and it didn't seem light enough for dawn. She wondered where her watch was. But then she stepped down and began walking away from the house. Finally, about a hundred yards on, she squatted down. She settled herself, held herself for a second. The air was beautifully cool, and she took a breath, then let it out, peeing at the same time. Up on her toes, back on her haunches . . . she stretched back, shaking out her hair, feeling it lovely and smooth on her back. She was feeling rather good, actually. She looked down. If it's bright blue, don't panic. It wasn't. She had nothing to dry herself with, so she waited a moment, dripping. My God, she thought, this is crazy. You're a hippie. Navajo blankets! All you need now are some beads! It all seemed very amusing. Then, draping the blanket over her shoulder, letting her skin enjoy the cool air, she walked back to the trailer. The bucket, with the mug, was sitting by the steps. She wondered if she might be sick again, decided she wouldn't be, and had a drink, and then splashed some over her thighs. Finally she went inside. The trailer was quiet. David hadn't moved, and she went back to sleep.

She slept now for a good hour or so. And the next time she awoke, David was sitting up beside her, and rather to her surprise he was smoking one of Marianne's cigarettes.

"Are you all right?" Anne whispered.

"A little zingy. But okay." He spoke in a normal voice. "She's in the bedroom, absolutely flat. She won't move for hours."

"You're sure?" Anne found she was still whispering.

"God knows how much of that stuff she had." He leaned down and kissed her cheek. "Are you angry? You didn't have to take it, you know."

She thought for a second, then smiled. "No, I'm not angry. I don't know whether I enjoyed it . . . Well, I suppose I did. I kept seeing colors."

"Yes. So did I."

"But what were you trying to do?"

"I'm not sure. I wanted to surprise her. See what she'd do. How she'd react . . . To you, partly. And how you'd react, what you'd see."

"I thought it was something like that. But I'm not sure I saw anything very much, except that she's terrified."

"It's her daughter. Vogel has the child. That's his way of keeping her under control. I'm certain of it."

"Which means?" Anne asked.

David hesitated, thinking; and if he answered her question she didn't recall his reply; for almost immediately, it seemed, she was waking again. So she must have fallen back to sleep. Yes, because now she was waking up again. And there was a sensation of time having passed, rather as though she'd fallen asleep on a train, so her sleep, her dreams, the moving of her body, had also been measured out in miles. It was much lighter: lying on the floor she could look up through the slats of a venetian blind on one of the windows and see the sun. And the air was warming. Now David was sitting at the end of the mattress, and he gave her a quiet smile. His face was damp; drops of water glittered on his unshaved cheeks. He was naked, and his skin glowed red, as if he'd just toweled himself. Lying there, Anne realized that she wanted him, though with the usual delayed reaction; there was always an instant of dulled sensation and her mind clouded, as if her senses were striving *not* to feel; and then she did feel it, and her heart pumped more strongly. Always she felt desire first in her lips and her breasts.

She pushed the blanket away.

To show herself to him.

But she still wasn't certain. She heard herself whispering, "Is she still asleep?"

David nodded. "Dead to the world."

He rose up to his knees. Anne could see that he was already thick and lifting, and she closed her eyes. Could she turn his cock into a snake? Or perhaps a flower, a tulip, a nice Dutch tulip still in bud, a fat red bud right at the end so heavy it bends down the stalk? But it didn't quite work; if the peyote was having any effect, it was only to lend a certain polished quality to the world. He was glowing. She reached out her arms. Leaning forward he began to kiss her, rather lazily. Opening her mouth to his lips she felt an easy cool breath slide down her throat, and then she bit at his lips, as if to say, Now now, not so lazy as that. She was sighing. She was suddenly more aroused than she might have expected. Turning her face she felt his fingers trace back through her hair, then the back of his hand eased her throat back, sliding down along her jaw and then turning over to cup her shoulder, drawing her to him. Her shoulders felt so round and smooth in the palms of his hands. Holding her shoulders, he kissed down to the base of her throat, his tongue smooth, cool, calm. Then it was all about his hands. His hands were burning, and she couldn't keep up with them—she was still gasping at their weight on her breasts as they began stroking her thighs. Her belly trembled beneath them. His fingers teased at her nipples till her breasts ached, and then his mouth took the ache away. He had big, hard, horny hands, a gardener's hands. They knew just what to do. They spread her open and then his thumbs, pressing together, found all her secrets. Her hips were moving, she couldn't stop moving, but his tongue was tireless, imperturbable, wicked, for he merely leaned forward a little and licked her ass, guessing just what she wanted, to be cooled there: and he kept on and on, on and on; then she began to come. Or she could feel it start. She tensed herself in a particular way that she had, the way she always did. Yet, to her momentary consternation, it didn't work. She strained, but something didn't catch. Something slipped, or bent, missed. It felt good, though, warm, soft, flowing. She sighed. The sigh went all the way down, and she cried out. Something was happening. His tongue didn't stop, and now she felt his hands again. He was so strong. He could climb cliffs. He could pull himself up on ropes. Now his strong hands reached down behind her knees and pressed her legs back, and his fingers, on the inside of her thighs, spread her legs wide. His hands felt huge and powerful. They bent her back farther and wider. Farther and wider. Wider . . . A confusion filled her mind. She felt sick. Oh, no. Stop. She didn't say this, but she thought it quite clearly. Yet David kept easing her back and down. She didn't like it. No, she didn't like it. Gently, he kissed her. But it hurt, to be bent back so far. Or it wasn't exactly pain. She was suffering . . . an imposition. Yes, she was angry. He was forcing her. She wanted to cry out. And as she began to cry out, she choked, or at least there was a constriction in her throat, and for an instant she thought she couldn't breathe. She was gagging. She felt close to panic. She was straining back against David with her legs, but she couldn't cry out, though she wanted to, she didn't actually tell him to stop. Did he know what he was doing to her? Perhaps he didn't. But in fact he now did exactly the right thing. For he pressed himself forward all the more, bending her back even more deeply—she was spread so wide that she felt she would split, that some terrible mess would come pouring out of her—and then, with his face pressed against her cheek, he reached back and down with his hands and stroked her backside very gently. And the touch of his hands was magical. She just couldn't resist the lovely touch of his hands. That touch went right through her, into her bowels, and now everything eased and softened inside her, from her asshole to her belly to her breast. And then the anger passed right out of her, and the pain; as if the pain was in truth the anger locked up in her, down there, right in her hips. And realizing this, startled, really, she took a breath, her throat opened some crucial millimeter, she could breathe—well, she realized, she'd actually been holding her breath all along—and without the least effort, all on her own, she drew her legs back still farther and she could feel herself swollen and open for him, as open as the lips of her mouth. She breathed him in. It was so good. She loved him. She felt a crazy happiness, which she didn't quite understand; it felt so good, but why so crazy? She was sighing as his cock moved in her. Slowly, he began to fuck her, and it was like a game, for he seemed to be fucking her in time with her breathing, in and out with it. Her head went back then, for she could no longer sense the light around the window, beyond David's shoulder. She was in a cool, calm shade. And with astonishing clarity, so clearly that she might have wondered whether the drug could still be working in her mind, she saw the image of her father's hands. It was extraordinary. They were big, strong, rough, brown hands; stubby and strong. She was looking at the thumbs, the big base with the shorter, crooked finger above; she was looking at his clenched hands, but from the palm side, as it were. And somewhere in her mind she knew exactly what this image was. She was on the swing in the garden and her father was holding the ropes, pushing her: this fucking was just like being on that swing. He pushed her faster and faster, and her legs worked, pumping her faster, and then she leaned right back, her whole body lifting her higher. Till she was frightened, right in her middle, in the pit of her stomach, almost screaming with terror. But of course she wasn't really frightened. She opened her eyes. And her hands weren't on the ropes of the swing but David's shoulders, reaching far down his back, and she pressed up to him and came, as easy as a kiss on the cheek.

*　　　*　　　*

That's what made it happen. The drug, the sex. The waking and the sleeping, the sleeping and the waking. But she still had no idea. That, the idea, didn't come until later, until . . .

She had woken again. But David had still been sleeping, there'd been no sound from Marianne, and so she'd wrapped herself in her blanket and once more gone outside on her own. She'd been still half asleep. It had been so hot; but there was a water tap at one end of the trailer and she'd washed, and then she'd washed out her blouse and her panties—they were too soiled to put on; and at last, looking for a spot to set them out to dry, she'd noticed the two big rocks jutting over the depression in which the trailer lay. So she'd walked up there.

She'd looked around. She wasn't thinking very much. There was nothing to see but rock and creosote, creosote and rock, hot and empty. She knew that no one could see her. She weighed her clothes down against the wind with a couple of stones, she stretched out on the slope of one of the rocks. Opening the blanket she showed herself to the sun. Well, why not, if there was no one to see her? Her eyes closed, her mind moved on its own. He fucked your brains out. Now they can fry. She smiled. She could feel her body soaking up the heat from the rock below her, the sun above. Salvador Dali, Georgia O'Keeffe. White skulls. Clocks melting in the heat. Chocolate time. Those colors.

She wasn't thinking very much. But after a time she began wondering if she might be pregnant, knowing she didn't want to be, no, definitely not, she'd done that, and she began counting back from her last period, how many days had it been? . . . but in the end that had proved too much of an effort, so she gave it up. Only something came to her then, apparently quite out of the blue, just as her mind was drifting away, actually at the moment when she closed her eyes, exchanged the blue of the sky for a dark pulse of blackness, which then changed, behind her eyelids, to a shifting flag of yellow. And it was rather strange. There was a kind of absence in her mind, as if she'd forgotten something. But attached to this a peculiar alertness, as if she had to be on the lookout for whatever it was . . . she'd forgotten; or so she supposed. But what came into her mind instead was the thought: Sex had nothing to do with getting pregnant in any case. She thought this, but then she didn't quite understand what she meant. She had to think about it again, and what she meant was, the point of sex, the reason for a man and woman coming together in that particular way, was not the pregnancy but the orgasm. Physically, biologically even, that was the reason for it; sex was about coming, not babies. They were actually a secondary consideration, especially if considered in light of the method. Reproduction could take place in so many ways—cell division, rutting, whatever—but the way we did it, you came, and that was the main point. Anne saw all this quite clearly, but was at once rather startled. It wasn't the sort of thing she normally thought about at all. Moreover, she wasn't certain whether the thought was original or utterly banal, although as she considered it she guessed that most people would put it the other way around. The point of sex was pregnancy. Coming was a reward, a prize. A bribe. An inducement to fuck like rabbits in order to reproduce like them. But that wasn't true, not even biologically. The point of *our* way of reproducing was coming, feeling like this, having this warm, easy feeling all through your body: a kind of refreshment, as if you were waking up after an especially deep sleep. In fact, her own eyes were still closed, and she frowned a little. Did she really agree with this? It rather smacked of blood, the mystical, something D. H. Lawrence might think of; and she'd never liked Lawrence, she was suspicious of any sort of thinking that put the body, biology, at its center. On the other hand, it was true. She knew it. Something had happened to her, with David. She was different now. And that difference was the point of everything. Sex, however it had begun, had evolved into this, not so much a way of making babies but remaking ourselves. Yes? Wasn't this the real advantage we had over the animals? And then, whether as a validation of this whole line of thought she would never be sure, a memory flooded into her mind. How young she'd been, as young as the world is old; but she could see it all so clearly. It was very simple. She was being held by her father. She was in his arms. His hands held her. She could see her father's face, the slope of his cheek. She could smell her father—now, in California, she could smell her father. Then her mother had bent down, her eyes smiling, and kissed her on the cheek *and she'd known her father was holding her, rather than her mother.*

Yes, that seemed to be the point of it; and it was so startling—it was the earliest memory of herself that she'd ever had—that she was shocked into consciousness. And this consciousness, as she sat bolt upright, was so acute that she barely had an instant to enjoy her memory, for at once she understood why she'd had it. None of this was accidental. None of these thoughts and feelings was irrelevant. Just the opposite. From David's hand to her father's hands, hand over hand, she'd been led to this point, as if ascending a cliff. David had sent her climbing ahead, on a route he couldn't have taken. And now she was here, at the top, at the edge. Which was this question: If Marianne had enjoyed the memory she'd just had, whose hands would *she* have seen? Father and daughter were separate links, but how did they join? Vogel was Marianne's father, but who was Anna's? Or, putting it the other way around, who was Marianne's *husband*, the father of her child?

A great urgency now overcame her. She scrambled down from the rock, got her clothes back together, stepped into her rather damp panties. She began walking, then running, down the sandy slope to the trailer. Inside, the darkness overwhelmed her, the sun had been so bright; and then she realized that she had to go into the sun again, for she wanted the photographs David had found in Aberporth and they were still in their suitcase, in the trunk of the car. So there was a little confusion. But David slept through it all. She thought of waking him, but this seemed her business to complete. He was the scientist, he'd begun the experiment, but it had worked by leading *her* toward this conclusion. Quietly, then, she took the photograph of Anna that she'd seen the night before and prized it out of its shiny Hollywood frame. It was a portrait; according to the stamp on the back, it had been taken in Sears. Formal, artificial, the light and the pose a little too cute—but all that she needed. She carried it into the bedroom where Marianne Vogel was still fast asleep on her bunk. One glance was enough: there was no doubt at all, not that she'd really had any doubts. Anna was Marianne's daughter. The mother's face was tense, taut, tight, as if her cheeks and her forehead were trying to restrain the fear in her large, dark eyes; but her daughter had just the same beauty. Next, back in the living room, squatting on one of the Indian rugs, Anne set her two pictures side by side. Again, the resemblance was indisputable. Indeed, the little girl sitting on the horse might have been Anna, though of course it wasn't, for it had been taken more than twenty years earlier: it had to be Marianne, only a little older than her child today. And a second point, Anne thought, was equally obvious: you couldn't look at the photograph without believing that the short, dark man holding the reins of the horse was the little girl's father. You could see, she felt, that Marianne had been proud to make her father proud by sitting on her horse so confidently.

Now what did this mean? Anne's heart was pounding already, for her intuition had seized the answer instantly. Yet she forced herself to work it through. She moved her fingers back and forth across the pictures, like a child tracing letters as she learned to read. There had always been a Vogel in this part of the desert. David's wife had rented a horse from him; there'd been mention of a second property, not far away from here, that he'd once owned. Marianne was the daughter of this man. But who was the father of *her* child? And Anne knew that this was the question that lay behind Marianne's fear, the horror both she and David had seen, the oldest horror of all. Wasn't it obvious? Vogel, whom Marianne thought was her father, had fathered her child. Her father and her lover were the same man, so her daughter was also her sister. But here was the extraordinary point. *It wasn't so.* It couldn't be. David had been absolutely certain. The man he'd met in Aberporth, who'd called himself Stern, was *not* the man in the picture with Marianne as a child, the man who was so obviously her father. Vogel was Stern, or Stern was Vogel, but it made no difference. In some crucial fashion, Anne realized, they'd got it wrong way around.

When Anne had worked this out and was quite confident that she was right, she found that she wasn't sure what to do. She almost shook David awake; she wanted to tell him everything. Yet she didn't. She felt a kind of delicacy, which restrained her. Partly this was because of the peculiar nature of her discovery; but it was connected, as well, to the logic that had led her to it. She did not want to violate that. It was all so very private, and even private to her. So finally she simply picked up the photographs and went into the bedroom. Marianne was still asleep, her mind presumably streaming with the colorful dreams of the drug. Yes, that was also a reason to wait. The only chair was small and very low; Anna's chair. She sat herself down in it, placed the two photos on her lap, and tried to think how she'd tell Marianne the amazing truth.

David was outside when the screaming began, and the way it worked out he didn't have that much to do with it. Which was all right: even though he didn't know it, his experiment was already a success; all he had to do was note the results.

By then it was after ten. Waking up, he'd felt rested, relaxed, and he'd assumed that Anne was outside. So he'd gone to look for her; and then, as he'd done the first time he'd got up, he filled the bucket from last night with fresh water and ducked himself. He searched behind the trailer for Anne and was just coming back to the door when it started. Screams of terror. Screams of desperation. Screams of the most frightened child in the world.

He froze, but then ran forward, though he knew at once this wasn't Anne's voice. But then he discovered that he'd managed to lock the door behind him, and by the time he jerked it open and got inside and into the bedroom, it was almost over. Anne was on the bed, holding Marianne, whose screams had choked down to sobs. She was gasping, like someone who's been running for miles and can't catch his breath. David thought it was all because of the peyote at first, a bad trip, the worst of all possible trips, but Anne tried to explain, holding the woman, cradling her, talking through and over her sobbing.

"I worked it out, David. Vogel is the father of her little girl and she thinks Vogel's *her* father too. You see? But he isn't. He can't be. She's the little girl on the horse, in the picture. Look at the picture of *her* little girl and you can tell—"

"He's my father," Marianne kept gasping this out. "He's my father, my father . . ."

She kept on and on, and Anne tried to soothe her. "That's right, he *is* your father, that's right. . . . So you see? The other man isn't, don't you see? Anna's father . . . He *isn't*."

"But he took me. He took me away. He was the one who did it. And you were there, I'm sure, because your voice . . ."

Anne shook her head at David. "I don't understand it. She keeps on about my voice. That's what frightened her, as soon as I tried talking to her. . . . Somehow, waking up and hearing my voice set her off."

But David saw it then. If, to this point, he had been operating by indirection, he now contributed one crucial, particular insight. He was kneeling by the bed, and he reached out and eased Marianne around so she could see him.

"Try to remember. It's not Anne's voice, you see, it's her accent. Listen. She has an English accent. There was a woman with an English accent when the man took you away, but that was a different person—my wife, I think. Her name was Diana. She hired horses from your father. Rented horses. Do you remember?"

"But my father didn't take me."

"That's right."

"He didn't come back. I was just a little girl—"

And now David could see it all quite clearly and he nodded and said,

"That's right, your father didn't come back one day, and the other man took you. And my wife saw him, the woman with the English accent. But he told her some kind of story and took you away, and then he pretended to be your father, didn't he? And then he married you when you were older and you had your little girl?"

"Yes. Anna. He's got Anna."

"Yes, he's got Anna. But you see, he wasn't your father after all. He was never your father. He was a different person. Your real father never came back. Do you understand? Do you know where your father is? Your real father?"

"No . . . No. I just know he never came that day—"

"But you know where Vogel is, don't you, with your daughter?"

She nodded, and David rocked back on his heels. She knew where Vogel was, but in truth the man wasn't Vogel. Vogel, her real father, had disappeared years ago, had *never come back*. Someone else had taken his identity, even his child. And Diana had been a witness to it, its very first moment. Diana had returned her horse, just as she'd explained in her letter, but Vogel had not been there. His daughter was upset, frightened, and so she'd waited: "I did drawings for her, trying to calm her—I drew her picture—she told me stories and we made picture books—and finally another man came, filthy, I mean with his hands and face all dirty— exhausted." And this other person had taken the child and had then pretended, for all these years, to be the girl's father, sealing her in the secret with him through some awful seduction. Who was he? David, now, was almost sure of the answer: Stern—surely it had to be—who hadn't worked for Hughes Aircraft but right here at China Lake. Stern had become Vogel, *as Buhler had discovered*. Because Buhler had known the real Vogel in Dora; he'd discovered the switch. That's where it all must have started. Buhler had come looking for Vogel but found Stern instead, and Stern had panicked and called Tannis. . . . Why? *Because . . .*

"David?" Anne was holding the woman now, rocking her into tearful silence. "What are we going to do?"

David leaned down and kissed her, and then he turned to Marianne. "Take it easy," he whispered, "just rest awhile. Then you'll take us to Anna. All right?"

"She's with him."

"That's right," he answered. "I know she is. We'll all go together and find him. You just show us where."

PART III

The Cassegrain Telescope

Development of this wholly Israeli AAM, derived by Rafael Armament Development Authority from early Sidewinders, was started in 1961, and by 1965 Shafrir had in many respects overtaken the US missile. Many details are still classified but it is clear that all models have a Cassegrain optical system behind a large hemispherical nose, pneumatic control fins, and fixed wings indexed in line and containing recessed rollerons similar to those of Sidewinder.

—BILL GUNSTON,
Modern Airborne Missiles

CHAPTER 18

Tannis, on his knees, leaned forward and scooped the cool, clear spring-water over his face, licking a little from his lips. The water was so pure it was virtually tasteless. But it felt wonderful on his skin. Even here, in the shade of the high rocks, it was already very warm.

Dripping off his face, droplets rippled the surface of the pool; but in a moment it was smooth again. Looking down through his own reflection, Tannis could see right to the bottom, which was formed by a huge gray rock as smoothly curved as a lens but cracked in the middle; it was here that the spring welled up. There was a little current, a trembling that caught the light, but the surface was perfectly still and everything was absolutely clear. And just then, as he looked down, the image of another face appeared, Harper's son—he was also bending down to drink—and as soon as he saw it, Tannis knew. *To see yourself as others see you.* For a moment his breath was suspended between horror and amazement, and then, released, it disturbed the smooth surface of the pool and briefly hid the truth. But there was no doubt. The water grew still, the boy's glistening image mingled with his own, and was his face as it had looked forty or fifty years ago. His eyes. His mouth. Even his expression. Only without his life yet written on it.

Tannis couldn't believe it, but he had to. Careful not to give anything away, he looked to the side, at the boy's profile. He looked at him for a long, long moment, and there was no doubt at all; once you'd seen it, you couldn't miss it. Son, you've got my eyes. A queer feeling passed through him. He felt unsteady, and his own eyes refused to come to focus; then, after an instant, he finally settled on another horror. Son of a bitch, he thought, that's why Diana killed herself. That's how it must have happened. When the boy had come into the room, she'd seen them side by side; and she'd seen what he'd just seen. And known. Everything. And couldn't take it.

As he eased back on his heels, an image came into his mind. A woman, rolling away from him, on one of those English beaches that were all smooth round stones. Yes, that was the first time: three wet pebbles had pressed into the soft flesh of her hips and he'd brushed them off, watched her skin turn pink. Except, he thought, that couldn't have been the time, the boy couldn't have come from that. He worked it out. That first time he'd been guard-dogging a scientific delegation from NOTS, and then later that summer—or was it the next summer?—Harper and his wife had come over here. So it must have happened here; yes, maybe even right by this very spring—well, not likely. But this was just the sort of spot where she'd come out to meet him, riding on that horse, or he'd take her to one of the motels. He hesitated. He tried to conjure up some image of her, some sensuous detail, her breasts, her skin, her scent; but only those three wet pebbles and then that other memory, his first memory, in fact the clearer memory: her voice, the hat bouncing on her back, *Heavens! I must look just like Dale Evans!* Everything else was now long gone. Except, it seemed, her son.

Discreetly, as the boy cupped water to his mouth, Tannis leaned back farther, withdrawing his reflection from the pool. And his voice, entirely normal, gave nothing away. "You're sure it was your father?" he asked.

"Yes."

"And he was naked?"

Tim, gasping at the cold shock of the water, wiped his mouth and nodded. "Absolutely. Not a stitch."

"I assume you didn't wave, or run down and say hello?"

"It didn't quite seem the moment."

Tannis liked him. Tim. Except for the name. But he stood up for himself. Which was a touch surprising, given the way he looked. The tenderfoot. Still wet behind the ears. Blue jeans neat as suit pants. "And what about this woman?"

"I'm not really sure about her. That rock, you know, is behind the house—you can't see the front, it blocks your view. I only saw my father because he came round the back. He seemed to be looking for something. So the woman might have been inside and walked away and I just missed her."

"But when you saw her, she was coming down that slope, where the ground dips down there?"

"Right."

"I don't suppose *she* was naked?"

"Almost, actually. She's quite good looking. She has the most beautiful hair."

"Blond, with a lot of copper in it?"

"Yes." Tim looked up. "Do you know who she is?"

"I saw him with a good-looking woman, with long blond hair like that, up in Scotland."

With a flick of his wrist, Tim sent a spattering of water across the pool. "That could be right. He has a friend there. I've never met her, but her name is Anne Brahe. That's where he was when it happened. That's where I called him."

Tannis grunted. "Brahe? What the hell kind of name is that?"

"It's Danish. Her husband was Danish. He made films. I remember, when I was younger, that he had a film on the BBC. My father worked on it."

Tannis stepped back, well away from the pool, and Tim looked back at him. "What do you think's happening, then?"

"Who knows . . . but if they're running around naked, you'd have to say they're getting pretty friendly."

"My father must know something."

"You think you saw Vogel in Aberporth. Maybe your father did too. He could have followed him. It doesn't make any difference. He's here."

Tim settled back on his haunches. "So I should go back to the rock?"

Tannis shook his head. "Don't bother. Eat something. They'll stay put. Only an idiot would go out on the desert this time of day."

Tannis had set up his Coleman stove under a deep overhanging ledge. It was a perfect camp. In the desert good water is everything, but he had never seen this spring on a map. The high cliff behind them, and the deep ledges, hid them and gave them shade at the same time. Beyond the pool, which was only three or four feet wide, the rocky ground rose up steeply, then pitched down again into a narrow, blind arroyo where they kept the mule. It was the sort of place you could never find; you either knew about it or you didn't.

Tim began making coffee. He liked to do things, and now Tannis let him. He needed time to think. After what he'd seen in the pool, the boy was doubly a complication. His presence was bad enough. In Wales it had been natural to leave his number: *If you see any of these people, I want you to call me at once.* But of course he'd never expected the call to come; and when it had—from Los Angeles, no less—Tannis had been astonished. But it had worked out well. The boy had proved useful. He could pick up his mail. It was a lot easier watching with two; and with Tim to run errands, he could stay out of sight himself. Even as companionship, Tannis thought, the boy was all right. They liked each other—and given what he'd just found out, you had to say that was natural enough. But then that was definitely another order of complication, what he'd seen in the pool. He watched the boy priming the stove. Did he suspect anything at all? Eyeing him, Tannis decided that he didn't. But maybe he didn't have to, maybe he'd just sensed a connection, picked up on something without knowing what it was. That would be in keeping with what he seemed to be about. In some obscure fashion, Tannis realized, Tim wanted to re-write his own history. Hearing about his father had freed him from some burden—Tannis couldn't exactly guess what it was—and now he was seeing his whole life in a new light, was trying to be someone quite different, something different from your Oxbridge boy. That, in any event, seemed the best explanation of why he had come and was the root, Tannis guessed, of his own appeal: warmonger, spook, Yank, Wild West gunslinger; he was now a curiosity, attractive. There are more things in heaven and earth, Horatio, than are dreamt of in the *New Statesman* or whatever the fuck they read now. In a way, the kid actually reminded him of Harper, all those years back, for he'd always had the feeling that Harper was trying to put distance between himself and something in his past, where he came from. And Tim was just a nice kid in the same way his father had been. Innocent. Scared. Had he had a woman? Presumably. But you wondered. Tannis took a cup of coffee from him and a sandwich; somewhere he'd found some fancy Italian sausage, which wasn't bad at all.

Tim said, "I wish I'd brought my camera." He was looking along the hills, the ragged black line the upper ridge made against the sky.

"You take pictures?"

"Yes. I'm actually quite good."

Tannis remembered that the woman, his mother, had brought a fancy camera. "This has all been done," he said. "The desert, all the hills around here."

"Ansel Adams."

Tannis shook his head. "He was more in the mountains. That's how I think of him."

"He did shoot the desert, though; but I suppose you're right. Edward Weston would be a better example."

"Sure. He was all through here."

"You know about Edward Weston?"

"I know about the desert."

Tim smiled. "Anyway, just because he took photographs here doesn't mean I can't."

"It wouldn't be the same. If you take a photograph of something, it changes. Because of his pictures, everything you see here is different."

Tim smiled. "You remind me of one of those natives . . . you know, in Borneo or somewhere. Take my picture and you steal my soul."

"Interesting."

"You think the desert has a soul?"

Tannis shrugged. "That's hopeless."

"Well, think of painting. How many thousands of pictures have been painted of the hills around Rome, or Dutch dikes or English cow pastures?"

"You're proving my point. That's all changed; no one can see those hills anymore—all you get are abstractions, spatters. Or just think of a bowl of flowers. You can't paint that anymore; people just laugh. Flowers aren't as beautiful as they used to be."

Tim smiled. "I can't decide whether this is *cracker-barrel* or *home-spun* philosophy, but I think it's very American and I want to say I appreciate it—as part of the tour, I mean."

The boy was like that: you could push him, but not too far. He could stand on his own two feet.

Still, no matter how agreeable this was, there was no disguising the fact that his discovery in the pool had left Tannis in a state of shock. The boy was his son. He was connected . . . connected to . . . but he couldn't have said to what. Though this was part of what disturbed him. In any case, it was a recognition that had brought the opposite of enlightenment.

Who am I? The question was now precisely answered, yet seemed all the more mysterious. And his own face, his own past, so perfectly expressed in the water's surface (was this not the youthful image of himself he saw in the mirror of his mind?), opened up a host of possibilities only to shut them off at once, almost in mockery. *What might have been.* Everything might have been, everything might have been different. But now he was . . . who he was . . . and what was that? Not that it mattered, Tannis thought. *It was over with and done.* That, too, was clear enough, and this disturbed him most of all. The moment he'd seen the boy's face shimmering beside his own, the moment he'd understood what it meant, he'd also understood that something was over. And he felt a surge of anger. He'd been tricked. The woman had tricked him. She'd suckered him, she'd— But how unreasonable that was. The trick, after all, had been played on her; and it was so horrible, once she'd discovered it, that she'd killed herself. And she'd just got herself pregnant, which was what they were there to do. . . . What did it mean? Why did it mean anything. . . . But it bothered him, that he could remember so little of what had happened; just those three pebbles, three pink spots on the whiteness of her hip. And even so, that hadn't been the time. No, it must have been the time . . . but he couldn't remember the time. He couldn't remember any of the times; not with that woman, or any other woman now that he thought of it—and he felt a touch of panic. But then he told himself, You were never supposed to remember that. It was a feeling. You felt it, then you didn't; and you only felt it when you felt it. But he didn't feel it now. He felt nothing now. Would he ever feel again? He wouldn't, he wouldn't . . . he dreaded that it was true. He wanted to run then, to flee—he could, he could. Or could he? The jungles of Brazil, a sandy beach on Tahiti, a room above a bar looking down on a stone square in Nicosia—he could get to any of those, he could go anywhere he wanted. But there was no point, he knew; he couldn't live there. Could he live apart from here, away from the desert? Whether the desert had a soul or he had a soul, he didn't know; but he knew he would die away from here. He could no more live in the jungle than a cushion cactus; this sand was ten thousand years distant from the sea; Greeks don't drink tequila.

Yes, it was all done now. All that was left was to make his move. He watched a black-throated sparrow nervously flitting about in the creosote, felt a breeze stir cool on his still damp face. Came back to himself. Saw nary a single cloud in the hot, chalk sky. Yes, this was the height of the desert day, but he knew that he had to make his move; that was the decision his mind was making. He'd been playing out the string, and this was the end of the string. What he'd seen in the pool, that forced the pace. Because there was no going back. That's what Tim meant. He'd lost an illusion he hadn't even known he had, a freedom that wasn't free at all. Still. Still. Forget all that. Regardless. He hadn't liked it this morning when he'd phoned his number. Something seemed wrong with the tape; it hadn't wound back right. You could almost think someone had been up there, wound it back. In any case, there'd been no message from Stern, if it really was Stern. Although, more and more, he was sure it had to be. But he didn't like it. And the FBI were close. He'd had a running start, but not so far, and there'd been that man, with cop written all over him—even his mind would run at fifty-five miles per hour—who'd visited the Vogel girl at the trailer; they'd watched a couple of days before. Now Harper was here. And even if nothing else had happened, he thought, that would have forced the issue. But he didn't blame himself. Harper was hardly something you could have predicted. Harper was going to roll over and play dead; that was the probability. If he'd thought otherwise, if he'd thought Harper would do whatever the hell it was he was now doing, maybe he wouldn't have saved him on that cliff. Although there hadn't been much choice. If Harper had died up there, given what had already happened to his wife, all hell would have broken loose; even the navy couldn't have pretended nothing was going on. Anyway, there was no going back, and it could be a lot worse. Tim, Harper, and the woman were all complications, but they were complications for everyone else as well as him. He could still pull it off, but he had to do it now. The question was, what should he do with the kid, though why was that a question? He sipped his coffee, lit a Lucky, turned over the old brass Zippo in his palm. Say it came to that. Why should Tim be different from his German just because he'd shot his jism up that woman, which he couldn't remember anyhow. But he was, he was. The pool had changed— Tannis watched him. It was like damnation. He was damned if he did, damned if he didn't. But at least the kid was entirely oblivious.

When they'd finished, Tim began cleaning up. In that self-mocking way he had, he said, "I feel like I'm the dude in a Western. I ought to be wearing fancy boots and a funny hat."

"Yeah? Well, you are a dude. Listen, are you sure you want to go through with this?"

"What do you mean?"

"I mean, don't be a hero. In this script you don't even get the girl at the end. You've been a good boy. A good son. No fooling. What you told me *was* important."

"You don't really think I'm going back to England?"

"No, but what about L.A.? A nice hotel. Or one of the motels in Ridgecrest."

" 'Mo-tels.' I like that."

"Except there's no joke. It's going to get rough now. I don't want to insult you, or your intelligence. You understand what I'm saying? It took guts to come here, to *think* of coming here. I appreciate that. And it hasn't done you any harm; a dose of the real world never does. Quit school. You can do something useful now, like running a restaurant or selling video-tapes."

Tim laughed. "I'm not sure what you're getting at."

"What I'm saying is, you won't save your father by killing yourself."

"I'm not sure that's why I came here . . . to save my father."

"It'll take the rest of your life to figure out why you came here. In the end, let me warn you, the answer will be selfish as hell."

"Everything's different now."

"Okay. And for you, that's fine. But I don't have time for it. For me, in its own way, this is serious business."

"What do you mean?"

"This is it. I'm making my move."

Tim hesitated now. He had his own questions, after all. Why had he come? What did he want to do? Since Aberporth, since David had told him the truth, the condition that had governed his life had been critically revised. He'd always known that he hadn't known . . . the truth, some secret, something. That had been implicit, almost openly conceded between his mother and himself. As a little boy he'd always expected some revelation; he'd discover that his father hadn't perished in a shipwreck, after all, but had been sent to Australia as a convict where he'd died rich, leaving an immense trust. . . . That was the trouble, however; his fantasies had invariably been supplied with happy endings, whereas this seemed much more complicated. He couldn't blame his father, not as he'd done in the past. But he couldn't exonerate him completely. Had there really been no choice except abandoning them? As well, the truth only posed more questions, especially about his mother, just because she'd known the truth from the beginning. Why, for example, hadn't she told him the truth herself? Still, he thought, he was now clear in his mind about one point, something he'd understood only as he'd stared down at the trailer this morning. His father and that woman. They were together; it was obvious. Shocking? But also distancing. That was what he'd understood, in fact. His father with a woman who wasn't his mother. It had made David seem more like an individual, with his own continuing life. His father had *moved on*. All that had happened to him was being put into the past, a past, Tim realized, that still consumed himself. But this actually cleared up a little mystery about his own behavior: the reason he'd come to Tannis rather than to his father. Of course, there were practical considerations. David had disappeared, whereas he'd had a telephone number, with a California area code, for Tannis. But now he realized that he'd recognized in the American a connection to the past that was more like his own, similar questions that were still not answered. He looked at him now. "You don't really think I'm going back to some motel?"

"I just want to be sure you know what you're doing."

"I thought what we were doing was waiting for Vogel to go to his daughter . . . or for her to go to him."

Tannis nodded. "But your father changes that. Something's happened down there. He knows something more than I do. I don't know what the hell he knows, but he knows something."

"Maybe we should ask him."

"No, no. This is a Western, just like you said. So let him play his hand. He won't know it, but we're his ace in the hole."

" 'We,' though. You said 'we.' "

"You're sure?"

"Yes."

Tannis didn't know if this was the answer he'd been angling for, but if he didn't take the kid, what the hell would he do with him? "All right," he said, "let's get going."

"Now? You only just said that it would take an idiot to go into the desert at this time of day."

"Yeah, well, I'm a mad dog and you're an Englishman. Let's get some of that noonday sun."

In fact, it was shortly after noon that they left.

The kid, Tannis thought, really was all right. No dumb questions and he worked fast too, packing a little food, clearing up their sign, taking the truck up as far as it could go. Finally, all by himself, he filled the water jugs, empty plastic milk jugs, and helped string them on Prince, the mule. The mule, though, was a minor problem. Away from his stamping grounds he had proved proverbially stubborn. And the only way out of their hole up, its sole disadvantage, exposed them for a time: they had to circle down and away from the hills, even leaving themselves visible from the road. So Tannis didn't want to take too long, and he sent Tim up ahead to check that the coast was clear. "You said this was a Western. So go down there and flash a signal."

For a mirror Tim took the top of their jar of Taster's Choice, and about ten minutes later Tannis saw the flash and encouraged Prince to move. He did; perhaps he'd felt cooped up at the end of his arroyo, for he seemed almost willing as he staggered into action. Tannis, working up his nerve, banged him to a trot, which he fell into, although with a kind of jerky, irritated motion as if to say, Listen, don't push your luck. Quicker than Tannis could have hoped, they reached the hills again, drawing into the cover of an enormous boulder, where they waited for Tim to get up to them. His walk, not half a mile, had left him dripping sweat.

Tannis, perched on the mule, looked down at him. "You're going to really feel it in this heat. If you want to go back, just say so." He wondered, even as he spoke, why he kept offering the boy a second chance, especially since he knew he wouldn't take it.

Tim leaned over, panting. He raised his head. "Which way?" He pointed. "Up there?"

As a good navy man Tannis was reluctant to put much faith in the Army Corps of Engineers, but since his last trip he'd equipped himself with maps and put together a rough route. Now, with a wave of his arm, he pointed it out. Essentially it was three long ramps or defiles up the massive, rocky confusion of the mountainside, one defile higher than the other, each extending farther north—like scratches on the wall of a prison cell, counting off three days. In practice, of course, it wasn't as neat as that. Tim had no idea where they were going, and Tannis was content with "more or less"—his "ramps" weren't trails, merely lines of least resistance, barely perceptible patterns in the chaos of boulders and twisted stone. Then, at the end of each of these runs, they faced the problem of reaching the one above, and that meant two brutish scrambles, bulling straight up the hillface; the first ripped Tim's jeans to tatters, the second left an ugly gash above Prince's knee. The heat was awful. The sun burned. There was no shade. Tim would never have believed that he could sweat so much, drink so much. And the higher they went, the more blinding the light became, and the black rock soaked it up and scorched their hands—basalt rough as cinders, obsidian sharp as glass. Once started, though, there wasn't much else to do but keep on going; a look back gave even Prince courage. And eventually, as the last tracing on Tannis's map led them closer to the summit—they were about two hundred yards below it—he pulled them up. They'd reached a spot where three great boulders, like bombs that had refused to detonate, created a high shield of cover.

Tannis pointed ahead of them. "Look there."

The whole summit of the hill had cracked and shifted, and the exposed face, jutting out, made a smooth, gentle slope as easy as the walkway in a park. It apparently went right to the top.

Tim gulped air. "It looks too good to be true."

"You don't think I planned it?"

"No, I don't think you planned it."

Tannis thought a moment. Going over the final ridge, they'd be exposed, profiled against the sky. "But we can't wait till dark," he said aloud. "And the longer we wait, the more we have the sun in back of us. So we might as well go now."

Over they went; the final ascent was simplicity itself. As things worked out, they weren't even much in the open; just beyond the point where their path ended, a lump of rock—the nub of some enormous batholith intrusion—bulged up, blocking them from view on the far side, absorbing their profile on the near. They went along a hundred yards, reached a small hollow, and Tannis stopped.

"Let's take our break."

Tim flopped down.

"For Chrissake"—Tannis could be relentless—"let him drink."

He meant the mule. They'd brought a poncho, grommets at the corners, and Tim rigged it up between some rocks and poured four jugs into the center of it. Prince slopped it up. Finally they all lay down; even the mule lay down. Stretched out, Tim could feel his heart beating against the ground, reverberating against the stone, and the animal's heat ten yards away was like an open fire. Tannis watched him. And if, as they'd climbed, what he'd discovered in the pool had receded in his mind, now it all came back. For the resemblance was truly uncanny, as soon as you knew to look: their faces, their size, and even a quality in their movements. But Tim didn't suspect a thing. Why should he? And what difference did it make anyway, to either of them? His genes. His blood. One dipping of his wick in the universal ooze. So the boy didn't know who his father was; neither did he, come to that. He thought of Oedipus. He'd read the play in *The Complete Greek Drama*, edited by Whitney Oates and Eugene O'Neill, Jr., two volumes, boxed, fancy; he liked reading plays. Oedipus had killed his father at a crossroads, not knowing who he was. Well, Tim Harper wasn't going to kill him, God knows. But then the other side of that was Herod, slaughtering the innocents, killing every Jewish man-child to make sure he got the right one, the Bible tells me so. But why should he kill Tim? Why was he even thinking that? Well, why not? But he didn't even know the secret; he wasn't going to tell it. No, what got to him, he thought, was the woman; he wasn't sure why. You shot it up them anyway; it wasn't as if they stole it. But something had happened behind his back, that's what it amounted to. Mummy and Daddy. He remembered now, there'd been a lot of that. He'd been old enough to be her father and what was she doing fucking him with a new husband waiting? You had to wonder. No, but he'd given her a special thrill, doing it with Jack, he was her first Yank, he remembered that now, she'd liked that. *You're my Marlboro Man*, she'd said that, Christ, but then she'd tricked him. Making him play God the Father begetting his only begotten Son, himself all over again. That's right, he looked at Tim, that's you, *next*, that's the next you down the line. That's what it meant, that's what it all meant now. He was making his move and he could still pull it off *but what comes next* . . . But then, looking at Tim, he thought again, Christ, he's just a kid, and tried to laugh it off: all those fucks and this is what you get. But now it was working in his mind, what comes next, even if he pulled it off. And he knew it.

It was late afternoon. After a time Tannis got them going again, working along fairly easily just below the ridge, then gradually angling down the slope. His plan was to reach the point where he'd lain in wait before—that ledge, jutting out from the hillside; the ravine running down to the valley below; and he wanted to reach it before early dusk. He assumed that the woman, Marianne, would be leading them, and she wouldn't cross in daylight—and it would stay light, this time of year, till almost nine. On the other hand, she might not want to cross in total darkness. So he pushed them. Still, for a time, he let Tim ride the mule, an experience that didn't necessarily incline Tim to credit him with great compassion. But finally they reached the spot, and it had just turned seven, the oaks and pines only now spreading their shadows back through the deep, sere grass.

Tannis drew Prince up and Tim got down, all stiff legs and aching back. Then Tannis handed him the reins and pointed down the ravine. "They'll come along there. Drift him back a couple of hundred yards and give him some water. There's enough grass. But make sure he's well away. If he smells them, he could make a hell of a racket."

As Tim worked back along the trail, Tannis got some food together: wedges of Swiss cheese, more of the sausage, oranges. They ate quietly, and then Tannis made Tim drink a lot of water. "Drink till you have to piss," he said, "then piss. Then drink until you have to piss again."

Finally they lay back on the grass and Tim watched two jets fly high across the slowly darkening sky. They were F-15s, said Tannis, not even navy planes; no concern of theirs. "That's Loose Deuce they're flying, practicing combat air patrol."

"Loose Deuce?"

"The name of the formation. Two aircraft, line abreast. They'll have a mile of horizontal separation, about. One plane engages, the other covers. Or they'll go back and forth, trading places. And let me tell you: they'll both have Sidewinder on their wings."

Tannis had replaced Vogel's broken glasses with a fine pair of eight–by–thirty-two "Trinovid" binoculars, and Tim followed the planes until they disappeared. "It's incredible," he said, "to think that someone would actually do that."

"What?"

"Fly at a thousand miles an hour while people are trying to kill you . . . and you're trying to kill them."

"What's funny about that? What do you want to do when you grow up?"

Tim laughed. "I don't know. Not that."

"The hell. How do you know? Maybe you'd enjoy it."

And as Tim considered this, even considered it for a moment quite seriously (for his mind was as open now as it had ever been), Tannis watched him and thought of all the choices that still lay ahead of him, all the times he could still change his mind, start over. While he, on the other hand—what choices remained to him? Tim would see what he would never see, go places he would never go . . . and yet the only reason he thought this, Tannis knew, was the pool, and what difference did that make? And yet it did. And he said, as if to drown his own thoughts out, "You know I was a scientist, once upon a time?"

"Really?"

"Oh, yes. CalTech. Around here, look up and down and almost everything, except the rock, is mothered out of CalTech."

"But you never worked as a scientist, with my father, on the base?"

"No. That was before he came, at the beginning of the war. All my life, one way or another, I've been around here. I first came through here . . . I don't know how old I was, but I was just a kid. My father was a gambler. He'd won a truck in a poker game in Vegas and we drove it across Death Valley; we came right by here. He wanted to sell it in L.A."

Tim set the glasses; there was only vapor now. And moment by moment it was growing darker. "When do you think they'll come?" he said.

"Give them an hour. If not then, probably a lot later. After midnight."

"As I understand this, you're expecting this Vogel woman, and my father, to go to *him*?"

Tannis had stretched out, his hands behind his head. He was silent; but then, apparently making a decision, he rolled over, leaning on his elbow. "Right," he said. "Except it isn't Vogel."

"What do you mean? I told you I saw Vogel in Aberporth."

"It's the same man, but in Aberporth he was actually calling himself Keller and his name is really Stern. He's pretending to be Vogel. The real Vogel . . . I'm not sure who the hell he is. Or was, because I think I found his body. But he didn't live down in that trailer. There's a place on the other side of the base—the county's going to take it for back taxes, but the deed's in Vogel's name. Vogel's dead, though. Has been for years."

"Stern killed him?"

"Uh-huh."

"And you found his body?"

"That's just a guess. But if there's enough light, I'll show you, when we go across." He rolled over on his belly, so he was looking down toward the valley, pointing with a blade of grass. "There used to be Indians in all of these hills. I don't mean the Indians we know about; long before that. They didn't even have bows and arrows. They hunted with a kind of spear thrower called the *atlatl*—"

"I know what an *atlatl* is—"

"I keep forgetting. You go to school. Anyway, they hunted with magic. You can see all this down there. They cut drawings into the rocks, set up stone sculptures, in order to make the sheep—that's what they hunted, mountain sheep—come up into these little blind draws. The Indians would be hiding up there in stone blinds, like little forts, and jump out and slaughter them. They wiped them all out, in fact. That's what finished *them*. The Indians, I mean. But here's the point: when I was down there, I looked at one of the blinds. It was tumbled in. There were a lot of bones inside, charred bones. Stern killed Vogel. But he couldn't bury the body—the ground's all rock there. So he pushed the blind over it and burned it."

"My God."

"I told you, this could get rough. You know how to use a gun? No, of course you don't. All Brits worry about is how to use a knife and fork. Look." He'd brought his .30-30 Marlin, lever action, a good cheap gun, and he began showing the kid how to use it, the sort of thing he should have learned, age of twelve. Tim, tentatively, worked the action.

"It's made of steel, for Christ's sake. You're not going to break it."

"You still haven't said. Why did Stern kill Vogel?"

"The gold; that might be a fair guess. I showed you his cave. Even the way he's doing it, you're talking a lot of money. I'm not sure, of course—maybe I've got it backward. But I'd say Vogel, whoever the hell he was, found the mine, which must be the mother lode to end all mother lodes. Then he went to Stern. He probably needed money for equipment or something. Or Stern could have helped him get it off the base—that would have been a problem—"

"You know who Stern is, don't you?"

"If it is him, yes. He was a scientist. One of the Germans who came over after the war. There were quite a number besides Wernher. Most of them went to White Sands, then on to Alabama, but a few came here. He was an instrument man. He could measure the flicker of your eyelash, anything. He was very good, but he was also very, very easy to blackmail."

"Because he was a Nazi?"

"That tree down there. Sight on it . . . Easy. It's a peep sight, so peep. Relax . . . No, it didn't make any difference that he was a Nazi; they were all Nazis. Von Braun was in the SS. But the Nazis passed a law in 1933, called the Law for the Restoration of the Career Civil Service, that kicked non-Aryans out of all their state institutions, including research institutions, and Stern used it; that's where his troubles started. He was young, ambitious. He organized things to get rid of a few people ahead of him, one Jew in particular, one of his old professors. He shunted him into Auschwitz, along with his daughter. Who was really the problem. She'd been born in Chicago. Technically, that made her a U.S. citizen. It probably wasn't enough to hang him, but they wouldn't have let him work here. . . . Go ahead. One shot, the first shot, people never hear. They just think they heard *something*. So they start to listen."

Tim fired. To his surprise, bark flew off the tree.

"There you go. Just remember, you can hit someone with that thing a hundred yards away, but more important, as long as you're shooting they'll keep their heads down."

"How do you know all this about Stern?"

"Well, I was a security officer. I was in Germany right after the war. I conducted that investigation. I knew all about him, believe me."

"So *you* could have blackmailed him?"

"Sure. Maybe I did. If I'd known about the gold, I certainly would have. And it would have worked. If what I knew had ever become official, Stern was finished, no doubt about it, and somehow I think Vogel found out the same stuff I knew."

"How?"

"I've no idea. Maybe he was in a concentration camp with them, maybe he knew the daughter. Who knows. But he figured it out, tried to use it, and Stern killed him. Or that's my best guess."

"So Stern killed Vogel and then . . . he took his identity?"

"Right. Which was neat. He retired; he had to. I remember he moved to Mexico and I lost track of him, thought he died, in fact. But when he killed Vogel, he must have kept his papers. Smart. Anyway, you know how to use that rifle now. Just remember: Stern's a killer. So you just *might* have to shoot at him."

Tim said, "We have to tell my father this."

"No, we don't. I told you, we're the hole card, we're the cavalry coming over the hill. That's the one thing Stern will never expect."

Tannis sat down as he said this and took the empty package of Kraft cheese wedges and flattened it out. On the cardboard he scribbled, "Matheson, Believe everything he tells you." Then he signed it, "Cracker Jack." He handed it to Tim, who said, "Who is Matheson?"

"He's head of security at the base—my old job. Listen. If something happens, you give this to him and tell him everything I told you. Understand?"

Tim folded the cardboard and stuck it in his pocket. Awkwardly, with the rifle, he stood there. He wasn't sure what to do or say, and oddly, all that Tannis had told him only underlined his ignorance; it surrounded him now, like the slowly gathering dark. But he wasn't even sure what difference it made. Everything went back so far. It was all such ancient history. The facts were astonishing, but their persistence was extraordinary. China Lake and all that history—he suddenly had a sense of claustrophobia; there was no escape. But you can't turn back now.

And Tannis, in his own way, watching him, was thinking much the same. He sat down at the base of an oak, leaned back, felt the weight of the earth press down his spine. Smoking a Lucky, he almost laughed. He looked at the kid, who looked like him. Immortality; what a joke it was, to take this form. The cells in your balls had it better than you did; they took that leap, then kept on going. While you, no matter what you did, who you were, this was what it came to. He thought of the woman then. What a bitch she was. He wondered if this wasn't the way to pay her back, kill her only begotten son. Which he certainly could do. He could do anything he wanted, still. Yes, he could. Wasn't that why he'd told the kid so much, to get them both out on a limb? *You have no choice.* But then there was the other question, he thought, of what good it did you. If you didn't like the trouble your dick got you into, you could always cut it off. That's what it came to. No matter what happened, he could still pull it off, *but what comes next?* The hell. That's what he tried to tell himself. It makes no difference. So there was nothing to do but wait.

They didn't have to wait that long. The sun was gone. The sky turned that deep, rich, U.S. Navy blue; then the haze of dusk appeared, a golden powder in the air. Tim had slept for a time. Twice, as it grew darker, Tannis checked the mule, and finally looped a tether around a rock. Then it was after nine; from now on it would get dark very quickly, and Tannis knew that Marianne would either come or she wouldn't.

She did. There was nothing to hear, only that sound that is merely the dislocation of other sounds, the sound men make moving across the world. Silence. Then a hoof pushed a little run of rock, a horse blew, leather creaked; and Tannis could see them, winding down to the ravine. They moved in and out of sight; lost focus; were there again. All within themselves; not knowing they were watched. Tannis turned and saw

Tim's face, saw he was entranced: for the first time, watching men moving under him, unknowing. But only one man, of course. Marianne Vogel took the lead with the woman with the copper hair behind her, both on donkeys, while Harper, on a horse, brought up the rear. At length, as the cut dipped deeper, they sank into the gloom and disappeared.

As they did, Tannis felt Tim begin to move and grabbed his arm. "No," he hissed.

"But my father dropped something."

"Don't move. You might slip. The horse could get a sniff . . . What do you mean, he dropped something?"

"I saw him."

Tannis gripped him tighter; waited; then released him. "All right. Go get it."

Tannis watched him skidding down the side of the ravine. Even in the few moments since Tim had gone, it had grown perceptibly darker; it was hard to see him. When he appeared again, he seemed to jump up before his eyes. "Look." In his hand he had a lump of crumpled Reynolds wrap, bright and shiny, about the size of a golf ball. "What do you think it is?"

Tannis looked at it. Shook his head. "Who knows. Don't worry about it, though. Take the glasses. Get on the ledge and see if you can see them. I'll get the mule."

By the time Tannis had brought him up, Tim could see Marianne and the others at the edge of the valley floor. There, in the open, it was a little lighter. "They're waiting, I guess. I'm not sure, but it looks like they might be having a drink."

"Okay. We'll let them get out a ways, before we move. We have to make sure they don't double back."

Ten minutes passed. Then they had an anxious moment, for Harper and his party apparently disappeared; but the light was playing tricks, and they emerged again, already well into the valley. Tannis gave Prince a kick; he was reluctant, having assumed that his day's work was done. But in the ravine, his spirits rose—familiar scents, a familiar trail—and he moved on more happily. They came down to the edge of the valley and halted by the same big rock. And both of them saw it at the same time: another lump of foil, glittering in the sand.

Tim said, "Jack, he knows we're here. He's leaving us a trail."

"Uh-huh. I guess you'd have to say so." He smiled in the darkness. "Smart fella, your father."

"What should we do?"

"I don't know that we have to do anything. Just keep going. Maybe it'll make things easier. At least we don't have to worry about them spotting us."

"Why don't we just catch up to them?"

"Listen, he's thinking along with us, so you think along with him. He *wants* us to keep our distance. So just keep your shirt on and start walking."

They started off. They kept an easy pace. Tannis, up on Prince, could see them through the glasses, long shadows against the lightness of the ground. They weren't hurrying, either. Stars were coming out, but it was growing cloudy. He could feel a breeze. A cool, dark night. Which was fine. And no planes now. The mule trudged on. With each step he swung his head down, as if considering the possibility of lying down to sleep, or perhaps, as Tannis had thought the first time, he was following a scent. But he kept on going. They came up to the wash, where he'd picked up Vogel's tracks, or Stern's—who the hell was Vogel? who the hell was Buhler? he'd probably never know—and found three lumps of foil and then, on the other side, two more. Yes, Harper was laying them a trail. Now they were more than halfway there; the hard hills on the other side bulked up, a black horizon. He thought: We're going to get there. And quite suddenly Tannis felt lighthearted, quite easy, and he wanted to walk, wanted to feel the desert under his feet again, the hard stone, and the soft, steady warmth that even now came up from it. So he got down from Prince and tried to think, he tried to think of all the thoughts he'd never thought before. He could pull it off, but what came after? He remembered—why couldn't you remember everything at once? He walked on. Thank God; there was nothing else to do. And gradually it became harder to see them, up ahead; as they drew nearer the farther side, the forms ahead merged into the darkness of the hills beyond. Then, ever so slightly, he could feel the ground slope higher beneath his feet, as they hit the old streambed of rock and gravel laid down a million years ago—everything here was a million years ago—and almost imperceptibly, on either hand, the shadow of the canyon drew in around them. They were inside it now. He began working out the landscape in his mind, from the first time. Walked more slowly. The canyon ran on like this awhile, quite broad, with low, indistinct banks on either side. Then it narrowed, formed a pass; and on the far side of this the canyon was itself much narrower, its walls suddenly steep and higher. Here were the petroglyphs, the hunting blinds, Vogel's bones, if he'd guessed that right; and up on the cliffs, the dummy hunters. He remembered some water, a "sand tank" at least; and beyond that point lay a second turning, which he'd never reached. But Vogel's mine would have to be there.

Tannis stopped.

He wasn't sure, but they seemed to have stopped ahead.

He pulled back on Prince's reins, stuck his arm out, and caught Tim across the chest.

"Wait."

They waited.

Tannis wasn't sure what was going on. He could barely see them; the sun was all gone now, there were so few stars. He certainly couldn't tell Harper from the women. But then shapes seemed to drift apart; he blinked, wondering if his eyes were playing tricks.

Tim's eyes were better. "They're splitting up."

"Easy now. Which way . . . ? To the right . . ."

"Yes. I can see the donkeys. They're leading the horse. I can't see my father at all."

"Just hang on." He looked with the glasses, but they weren't much help. Still, he thought, what they were doing was obvious. Here it was still easy to get up the sides of the canyon; they'd go up there, then work along the ridge. He waited. And two minutes later, for an instant, he could see them profiled in a line against the sky: two donkeys and the horse coming up behind. That way, a few stars were out to light them.

Tannis put the glasses down. "Okay," he said, almost to himself.

"What do you mean?"

"Just that you're going up there with them. Take the mule. Don't ride him, lead him. Go straight up the slope here. Then go over the other side—not far, just go down far enough to get out of sight. You understand? Then work your way up toward them. Slowly, though, don't frighten them. They're going to meet up later, you see. The Vogel woman knows where she's going. They're going to wait for him."

"So what will you do?"

"Well, your father's on foot. It won't be hard to catch up to him. We'll go in together."

"I want to come with you."

"Uh-huh. Fine. You said that, and it does you proud, but don't play dumb. We don't need three guns down a mine to get one old man; we'll just shoot each other. But I want you up there with them. Say something happens. You never know. At least, this way, they'll have a rifle."

"Jack, I don't like this."

"You don't have to like it. In this film, given that it's only a mule and all, I'm probably no more than Rory Calhoun, but you're just Richard Egan."

Tim smiled. "I know this is a mistake, but I don't think I've heard of either Rory Calhoun *or* Richard Egan."

"Exactly." Tannis chuckled. "But you're real good looking, take my word for it. Just the man for the ladies. You get up there with them. They need you, they always do. That's something you want to learn early in life."

Tim didn't reply, but he smiled in the darkness. For Tannis had found exactly the tone to let him accept what was happening; knowing he was being manipulated, he still had to let it happen. He took the reins out of Tannis's hand. Only when he'd led the mule a few yards off did Tannis hear him whisper: "Good luck, then."

But he already had that, Tannis thought, aces and spades. And the kid had been part of it. On the whole. And what the hell, it was better like this, and he did want him to be safe. So he waited till Tim went over the ridge before he started forward. Of course, he had no intention of catching up to Harper. And if Harper waited for him . . . but he didn't; that was one bridge he didn't have to cross. Harper had a plan, though, that was soon clear, for when Tannis reached the point where the women had turned off, he found three more of Harper's aluminum golf balls arranged in a triangle, pointing straight ahead. He walked on even faster. He went through the gap. Beyond, it was very dark. The canyon walls climbed steeply higher; the sky constricted. He looked around, found the hunting blinds, dark pools of shadow as he hurried past them. Looking up he could barely see the petroglyphs like faint scratchings on the black glass of the night. Only the dummy hunters on the high ridge, catching what little light was left, were plain, looking down silently as he reached the sand tank—more aluminum—and then the second turning. This was very narrow. On either side the high rock cliffs rose straight up, and the entrance was almost blocked with boulders; the sheep would have died here by the hundreds, pierced and screaming panic. He picked his way through as quickly as he could. There was, he thought, no reason to delay or be especially careful. Stern couldn't suspect that anyone was coming;

he was probably asleep. But he hoped to catch a glimpse of Harper. Marianne Vogel would have told him exactly where the mine entrance was, and it might be difficult to find if he didn't actually see him go inside.

As it happened, he didn't see Harper at all. Once through the gap, it was very, very dark. He could scarcely see his hand in front of his face, let alone another figure; and, of course, the first time he hadn't come this far, so he couldn't be sure how the land would run. In fact, it scarcely ran at all: he could have been at the bottom of a well, the canyon walls were so high; and the bottom of this well was a stretch of boulder-strewn ground no more than twenty yards square. At the back—he began to get his bearings—this tumble of rock pitched up, forming a steep ramp that climbed to the very end wall of the canyon, like the turbulent, petrified course of a waterfall. But then it almost was that; over the centuries, boulders and rocks had dropped down from the cliff above and had piled up here, trapped by the narrowness of the opening to the outer canyon. In the darkness and this confusion of stone, the mine entrance might have been hard to discover; in point of fact, it was simple. Stern, or quite conceivably Vogel himself, in the beginning, had made a path through the boulders, levering them aside, a project that must have involved vast effort. But as soon as Tannis realized what he was looking at, the way was obvious, curving among the boulders of the ramp, until it finally disappeared into a dark hole in the cliff face. The mine had to be there.

For a moment, crouched behind a boulder, Tannis waited and watched.

He got out the Colt, cocked it, but kept it on safety. In fact, he didn't think there was anyone there. He looked up. He had to crane his neck right back to see out of this massive cul-de-sac, and only the faint light of two stars proved that the canyon walls did not go on forever. An odd, soft sound reached his ears. The air was absolutely still against his face, but high up it was moving, like breath over the top of a bottle. Apart from this, however, the silence was perfect, and he still sensed no danger. He decided there was no reason he should have. He must have been very close to Harper; Stern obviously hadn't shot him, and even if he'd tried to take him by hand, with a knife, Tannis would have heard the scuffle.

Still, as he stepped onto the path he kept his gun out and moved forward slowly. The path was about a yard wide, and the ground had obviously been worked over by animals, which made him think, Where did Stern keep his horse? A question his nose almost immediately answered. If the air had been moving at all, he would have smelled it before, but now he caught the odor of warmth and sweat, and then he realized that his eyes had deceived him. He'd assumed that the darkness in which the path ended marked the opening into the cliff face, a hole; but instead there was a very deep indentation in the rock, a gouge, almost deep enough to make a shallow cave. The top of this had been slightly extended by a kind of roof—brush, boards, with rocks scattered over them as camouflage—that was propped up by two timbers. A horse was sleeping under this canopy, comfortably bedded down in straw. Tannis, looking about, saw that the entrance to the mine wasn't in the back of the indentation but opened into its right-hand wall. Nothing had been done to hide it, but in fact you couldn't have found it unless you came right up to this point.

Tannis paused a second, worried about the horse. But it scarcely stirred. Satisfied, he then studied the entrance more closely, realizing it was actually the natural opening of a cave. It was a good six or eight feet wide, but less than his height; he would have to duck to get through. He hesitated; he was a dead man if anyone was waiting within, but he really had no choice, so he just kept as low as he could and went ahead.

At once, the darkness—the complete, total, utter darkness—enveloped him. It was a blackness so deep it might have been galactic, an absence of light so total it had a peculiar force of its own. He was paralyzed. For an instant he simply couldn't move. And then, with a silent curse at himself, he dropped to his knees. He waited. Surely his eyes would adjust. But they didn't. He was blind. He was a dying man. His eyes had closed, and all he had left were the sounds of his body, the touch of air on his cheek. One by one, those would go too. Fuck it. He had brought a small flashlight, but he didn't want to use it. It would simply give him away. So he began crawling forward on his hands and knees, reaching out carefully ahead of him. Had Harper used a light? Whatever this dark hole represented, he'd gotten through it quickly enough; had the woman told him a light was safe? Maybe she had, maybe she had, but he was damned if he'd put much faith in that, and so he just kept working forward, reaching out with his hand before sliding ahead, a prudence that was rewarded when his arm flapped about in a void. There was nothing ahead of him. He was on a ledge. His hand, pulling back toward him, encountered an edge of stone. He gripped it. Found it with his other hand. And arbitrarily moving to his right, he felt his way along until his knee hit something hard. He froze. But now his right hand discovered a length of wire rope. He traced it back; it was attached to the metal fitting his knee had encountered; and as he felt his way along and discovered the same attachment two feet farther over, he realized it was a ladder, leading down into the black emptiness before him.

He had to see more than this.

He knew that, but he didn't like it. Sonofabitch. Sonofabitch. Well we all aren't we. . . . He got out his old Zippo, worked the wheel; the wick caught with a yellow flame and a smell of gas so pungent it seemed to bring him back to the world. Its light showed him a little of where he was. On a ledge of stone. With the two heavy iron escutcheons bolted down into it and the lengths of metal rope attached by turnbuckles to them. Yet this was hardly enough. What was this place? What the hell was down there? And how far was it? So in the end he got out the flashlight, sending its beam back behind him, toward the entrance—he could just see it—and then cautiously up to the roof of the cave, this vestibule, and then along. Shapes emerged. A derrick of sorts. Pulleys. Lines. Running back, apparently, to an engine . . . They were the arrangements, in fact, you might have expected, thinking of the other smelter cave; somehow, the ore had to be hauled up here so it could be loaded onto the donkeys. He turned out the light. Leaned forward. The question was: Should he go down there?

Stretching out on his belly, he stuck his head over the edge. He couldn't see a thing. Each region of darkness was darker than the last. Yet he could sense a shift in atmosphere, a hint of coolness, moving air. But not a sound. He told himself: there's nobody there. And he had heard nothing at all. If Stern was lying in wait, then he must have dealt with Harper, and surely he would have heard that. . . . It made sense, but sense enough to stick his ass over the edge? Yes. He turned around, lay on his belly, inched his legs over, grabbed those two big chunks of metal tight in his hands, felt down with his feet. . . . He found the first rung. The second. The rope swayed a little and creaked. If someone put a light on him, he was dead as a doornail. His head was below the level of the floor above. He kept on, and on, but stopped counting after thirty rungs. It was at least fifty down. Then his feet hit the ground again and his hand felt forward into a darkness deeper than anything he'd known before.

He couldn't take a step. He pressed his hand to his nose and could not see his fingers. And when he worked the Zippo again, his pupils were so vastly expanded that the flame was dazzling and painful. But it was really no light at all. Sticking his arm out, he moved it around in a circle, and all he saw was the yellow, flickering flame moving about him, its little light mocking him, revealing nothing at all. Finally, again, he had to turn on his flashlight. He found the ladder in its beam. Worked across the ground he was standing on and about ten yards away picked out a set of metal rails, with a piece of wire rope running alongside. He worked this out. The rope would be attached to a winch at one end, and some kind of truck, which it would pull along the rails, at the other. This was how Stern moved the ore. Picking out the rope with the flashlight, he followed it on, till it ran through a small entranceway leading out of the cavern he was in. And at this point, just as he was fitting all these bits and pieces of industry together in his mind, he heard the first shot.

Instantly Tannis snapped off the light.

The sound echoed, reverberated. Died. But it had definitely been a gunshot. But a considerable distance away. He listened, and now two more shots followed in quick succession, the reports and their echoes piling up on each other in waves. A rifle. And a pistol. Or so he guessed. And far off. A deep silence followed in their wake. He could hear nothing. The silence, after the sudden roar of the shots, almost reverberated itself, bringing up in his ears the sound of his blood, his beating heart, the wash of air in his lungs. He waited a time. Then, when there was still no sound, he felt out with his arms and worked across to the entranceway that the flashlight had revealed. The shots, clearly, must have come from some deeper cavern to which this led. He found the edge of it with his fingers and traced it out. He would have to crouch. He ducked inside, stretching his hand before him, encountering a curved metal wall. Bent over, he shuffled forward, and only after he'd gone a couple of yards did he understand that the structure he was in, though rather like a culvert, was actually fabricated from the panels in the fuselage of an aircraft. They were not entire—he now passed a gap of bare stone—but of course it made sense: if you searched over this desert, you'd find plenty of panels from old target planes. Water trickled and dripped. His hand, reaching out, came away covered in grit. And then he saw a little light. It was not the end of the tunnel, but a curve; and a small gleam of light, which indeed must have come from the end of the tunnel, reached this far.

He edged up to it. Then, squatting, he watched that light to see if a shadow would form against it. Only when he was certain that no one was there did he go forward again. Now he could see the end of the tunnel itself, a truncated disk of dim, golden light, and he worked on more quickly; and finally stopped, and squatted, about three feet from the end. At this point he could see out but remained hidden himself.

There wasn't much to see, however; he was obviously looking into a cavern much bigger than the one he'd been in, and it was apparently lit in some fashion, for long tongues of light gleamed on damp rock. But only one detail revealed itself. Some ten feet beyond his opening was a low mound of broken stone. He waited again. He still couldn't hear anything. And then, coming forward in a low crouch, he scurried toward this mound.

Nothing happened in response to his movement, but he pressed himself right down into the stones. Keeping his head down, he got his breath; and only when he was very sure did he look around. The pile of stone gave him cover from directly ahead; and to his right the stones also spilled down, like a dike, protecting him on that side. Only on his left was he exposed, but as he twisted around on his back, training his gun over the gloom, he realized he was safe here as well, for he could see nothing but the back wall of the cavern, which rose up—his eyes followed it—in an astonishing vastness. It was immense. Even the other cave could not have prepared him for this. The cavern had the size, the scale, of an old railway station; he couldn't even sense, let alone see, to the top of it, not in this light. Yet it was the light, above all, that filled him with awe. It was a dark, rich, soft light. It was a light that had penetrated here from some far distance, like the light that illumines a deep woods or the depths of the sea. And it was a golden light, for this was indeed Vogel's mine, a strike, a claim beyond all claims, a dream of mother lodes, the Paiutes' golden hoard; in fact the old legend of the Panamint came directly into Tannis's mind, the secret cave guarded by a balanced rock—those dummy hunters?—for even though it was anthropologically impossible, this was nonetheless a legendary trove. Looking at it he could feel some echo of the pressures that had formed it pressing on his mind, the magma welling up, exploding and hissing, but finally pouring from the earth as pure as gold poured from a ladle. This cavern had been left behind, the gold growing through the stone in branches and leaves, covering it like the scales of great fish, studding it with crystals, octahedrons, and cubes, wrapping it with tendrils and wires, breaking off it in flakes as perfect as snow. And all through the gold, its lustrous setting, were chains and chains of crystals, soft, gleaming, silvery white; in some corner of his mind he knew this was arsenical pyrite, but that was thinking, and how could he think? For a moment he forgot everything. The gun in his hand. Vogel, Stern, Harper. Even himself. He felt his breath go, and then an awful, dreadful desire passed through him, like the desire of a dying man for life. What a hoard it was! He trembled. . . . But finally, as he got a grip on himself, the passing shock left behind true satisfaction. Well, here it was. Here was the reason for everything. No need to ask *why*. And he shouted at the top of his lungs, "Harper! Harper! Where the hell are you?"

His voice echoed in the vast hollow. Died. And then an answer came back, surprisingly calm.

"Tannis?"

"Yes."

"I was beginning to wonder."

"Where the hell are you?"

"Over here."

Harper's voice had come from his left, and in front of him; but now two shots exploded off to his right. He was looking the wrong way and missed the flashes, and in frustration let his own great gun off, straight up in the air. Sonofabitch. Well we all aren't we. Yessir. But his shots drew no fire—there was nothing to see in the gloom—and only when Harper's voice called, "Watch it," was he able to tell where Harper was.

Down the left wall of the cavern—he was beginning to pick out details now—was a scaffold of a makeshift, teetery sort. Presumably it had enabled Stern to reach some especially rich deposit (though how did he choose?), and beneath it was a lot of rubble, a number of piles, of the same kind that hid him. And it was from there that Harper's voice had come, although he couldn't quite see him. His eyes moved on. The light was magical, but there was not much of it—only a few lanterns, dangling from the scaffold, or hung on hooks bedded in the stone, lit the scene. But he realized now that there were many piles of rubble on the floor, and then he saw that the floor itself was pockmarked with diggings; wherever Stern put in his pick, he had gold. At the very far end of the cavern, lit by another lantern, was an area of darkness, a cavity or tunnel.

He called out, "Is he down there? At the end?" And before an answer came back, he'd leveled his pistol on the light. It was a very long shot, but he was a very good shot, *might as well get your eye in*, Wham! The light was gone. "There!"

"No!" Harper called. "There's a room there. He lives there. That's where the little girl is."

What little girl? "Where the hell is he, then?"

"Right across from me. There are two tunnels, about forty feet apart. They go straight into the rock. And then a cross tunnel joins them. Almost like an H."

"You're sure?"

"I've a map."

The woman would have given him a map. Smart thinking, son. That's why he'd come ahead so quickly, confidently. Local knowledge. Tannis peered ahead, trying to find the openings. They were up ahead, on the right-hand side of the cave: two dark cone-shaped holes, easy enough to see once you knew where to look. "I want to try to get him out."

Sure you do. But maybe it wasn't such a hot idea. Stern would talk. He would try to make a deal. Or he might, anyway. Tannis wondered how much Harper knew. If he'd come this far, he must know a lot. Amazing, actually. Well done, lad. The fucking Brits! On the other hand, what difference did it make? In the end, that is to say. Except there might be complications. Harper, after all, had a gun. Or presumably he had a gun. "Harper! You got a gun?"

"Yes. A rifle."

"So get him out, if you want."

"Tannis, say something to him. He knows you. He thought I was you, in fact. I think that's why he panicked."

"Well, he's not going to panic any less to hear me. . . . But all right . . . Stern! This is Tannis! Stern! There're the two of us. You don't have a chance! Come on out!" That sounded pretty good, he thought; then he waited a moment as the echo of his voice died away. Nothing happened. "Guess what. He's not coming out."

"Tannis, watch it. He says the entrance is booby-trapped. I think he's got some kind of transmitter."

"If you believe that, you'll believe anything—"

"Tannis—"

"Shut up and listen to me. Get your gun on the farther of those tunnels, the one on your left. Count to five, then start firing, nice and easy."

Silence. A hesitation. But what was Harper going to do? Probably he'd been working up his guts for twenty minutes, and he wasn't going to. Not that you blamed him. After all, he made films about squirrels. He fucked nice ladies. Certainly he'd never fucked a girl with his boots on, now that was convenience, fucking them as easy as taking a piss. So it was all working out. *What comes next?* This comes next. Count three, four, five. Until the cavern roared and boomed as Harper started shooting, keeping Stern out of the far tunnel, hopefully driving him deeper in. And even Tannis, up and running forward like an old jackrabbit, put in his two cents worth, *boom, boom, boom*, as he dodged into the open, crouched low, legs driving, then diving down and rolling behind a scattering of rocks. But rolling to his *left*. Away from the tunnels. That was the trick. And Stern, bless him, even helped out with a couple of shots as well, a pistol, but something big, not much smaller than his own huge blunderbuss—so that there was enough noise and dust and whanging metal to keep everybody's head down, but not Jack's. No sir, he was slithering away, squirming, twisting, his big belly scraped across the rocks, his throat half choked with dust. Moving very fast; big men often move much faster than you think, so that by the time the smoke cleared no one had any idea where the hell he was. Certainly, Harper had no idea that Tannis was now in behind him. Face it, son, you just weren't cut out for this sort of thing. But actually, no; just keep facing the way you are, dead ahead. He crawled a few more yards. That's it; just give me a minute to pin you down. But for the moment he couldn't quite manage this. He'd circled way off, to the left. On the far side of the cave he could now see the tunnels clearly—he was almost level with them—but he couldn't quite pick Harper out; it was too dark. Still, Tannis knew more or less where he was. The scaffold, like a derrick looming against the dusk, marked the spot, although the light from the dangling lanterns, rather than showing Harper up, hid him in a maze of shadow. He was probably there, right in front of him. If he'd only move or . . . With his mind Tannis passed into the darkness, trying to feel out Harper's, egg him on: Have a go! Have a go! Isn't that what you said to a Brit? Of course it was. And it worked. Well done, lad. For now Harper fired twice, two muzzle flashes that lit the scene, if only for an instant, as bright as day. There he was. Tannis could see his leg, his back, his crouched form down behind some rocks, all intent on the far side of the cave. And as the echo of Harper's shots came back, and back again, he crept up closer. But just before he got close enough, two more shots exploded near him, Stern's pistol. One of the lanterns was swinging wildly, *poof*, was out, and a second exploded in an orange ball of flame.

Tannis dropped right down.

Because he couldn't see a thing.

It was a lot darker—although one of the lights was still burning—but that was not the problem; it was the afterimage of the lantern's fireball, which was now as blinding as the sun. It drifted before his vision, so bright and real that he even waved his hand at it, but he could see nothing through it. A minute went by. The light swelled and pulsed, seemed about to pass, but then brightened once again. He heard a sound and cursed beneath his breath; had Harper moved? Then silence. Then something clattered, something thrown. Feeling with his hand, Tannis made sure he was behind a rock. His vision began to clear. But he wasn't sure what was going on. Another minute. And when he could see again, he could not see Harper; it was now much darker, and the shape his eye expected did not appear. But he had to be down there. He could not have gone far. Tannis gripped the big old Colt, he rose, he stepped ahead. He could see the scaffold, the single lantern. He didn't like this . . . and then he suffered a moment of confusion. Because there was Harper. But facing him, leaning back against a rock.

"Harper." Tannis hissed the name.

And then a voice came from behind him: "Jack, don't move. Don't move a muscle. Don't take a breath."

Tannis froze. He stared at Harper. And reflected in Harper's eyes, he could almost see the man behind him. "Stern?"

"Jack, you have a mind, but I know how it works. You would get him first. I knew that. You see, you walked straight into your own trap."

"Stern—"

"You used to call me Rudy. *Nos conocimos muchos años atrás, mi almirante. Yo soy un amigo. Un viejo amigo.* You remember."

"So it was you on the phone. You should have said."

"No, no. I was too afraid your line was tapped. Remember, it was you who taught me to be cautious. Buhler made so many threats. He was obsessed. I didn't know who he'd spoken to—I didn't know where you stood. Besides, an old spook like you . . . listening on your line could be routine."

Keep him talking. He doesn't want to kill you. He's afraid to kill. They all are, aren't they? If he was going to kill you, you'd be dead already. . . . "So why not meet in the restaurant?"

"Plans change. . . . Jack, the gun. It's in your right hand. Don't worry, I can see it. Throw it away from you, to the right. Don't even think of trying—I'm behind a rock—even if you got off a shot, you wouldn't hit me. So throw the gun away."

And Tannis gently threw the gun, but ahead of him, not so far from Harper.

"Jack, to the right, I said."

"So shoot me, Rudy. Pull the trigger, Rudy."

There was a moment. A silence. But Tannis felt nothing; he knew he was not going to die this way. And after a second Stern said, "Walk there, toward him. Then turn around and sit down. By the rocks."

He shrugged, then took a step, looking toward Harper, who hadn't made a move or said a word. But he seemed quite calm, removed. His rifle glinted in the dark, but too far away. Tannis turned around, sinking down—yes, that was a good move, making them sit down—but five or six feet from Harper, far enough. You can't shoot two men at once. He'd have to recover from the recoil, aim again. Was that what he had to make him do, shoot Harper first? But surely he wouldn't be such a fool. Unless he could get Harper to make a move, go for the gun . . . But Harper wouldn't. Harper wouldn't do anything. He'd wait. He was hopeless, Harper. It was a miracle he'd come this far. And he let Harper go, let him drift away, watched him only from the corner of his eye, as Stern now emerged from behind some rocks. Yes, Tannis wanted to catch *his* eye, and did, whispering, "Rudy," just to draw him close, close enough to reach out and hold his eye. "Rudy, it's amazing to see you after all these years."

And Stern felt it, felt his power; hesitated; smiled. "Jack—"

"About the restaurant."

"That's history. Isn't that what you say? Ancient history."

"Sure. It all is." He smiled with his eyes. Cooled him out a little. He almost had him now. That's it, ease off. There's nothing to fear at all, sweetie, it won't hurt really. . . . "I was wondering, though. How Buhler got out there, up that road."

"But that was simple. When I called you, I was in a pay phone near Darwin Springs, and he was right outside. I was going to bring him to meet you. That was the arrangement. But it had to be in secret, which he believed, you see, because of the base. He hadn't known about the base, not till he got here; he had no idea. So I built that up and then I dropped him on the way. The same place we used to meet, didn't you remember that? Because of the radar? Because there was no way they could listen through the radar? Anyway, I came into the town and left you the note. But I was thinking then. So I left a lot of time . . ."

"And drove back to that place of yours and got your horse—"

"So you understood about the horse. You were always so smart, Jack."

"You killed him, though."

"But that might have happened anyway. You know? And I must admit, you made me panic. You were there, all at once you were there. I never heard your car. Your truck. You see, I'd wanted a little time with you first, to explain, so you'd know what to say. Which would have been easy enough, you see; we could have talked right in front of him because he had no English—"

"But which would have been even easier, Rudy, if you'd just come into the Hideaway. No. Fess up. You'd worked it out. You were going to set me up." Which I'm saying almost lightly, Rudy, it's almost like a joke, but you can't even smile, you've lost that much already. That's it. Just look me in the eye. "You were going to frame me."

"If you like. Or you can just say that I was going to involve you whether you liked it or not. You see? You would have to protect yourself. And that meant protecting me as well." He hesitated. He was nervous now, but in a different way. He said, "That's what I need to know, Jack. How well you've done. What's going on, what's out there now for me."

"In Scotland you almost blew it."

"I realize. But I didn't know . . . about the woman . . . that the woman was no longer a threat. But you saved me. Or us?" Not *him*, not Harper, sitting right there beside them. They didn't even cast a glance his way; indeed Tannis didn't move his eyes an inch, he scarcely blinked. Quietly, he sucked up Stern's eyes and felt them weaken. I've got you now. I always had you. I knew your secrets and you were glad I knew, oh yes you were. He murmured: "And Vogel, Rudy?"

"That's all covered, I'm telling you."

"Buhler came looking for Vogel, but found you instead. That was the trouble, wasn't it?"

"Yes, yes. But that's all covered. Vogel knew what you knew, Jack. In the beginning. There was a woman who came from Auschwitz, a Jew, and in the end they put her in the camp where Vogel was. She told him—about it. You know?"

"Uh-huh."

"He only wanted money. I think he married her. He found me anyway—"

"Rudy, you should have told me."

"But I only had to give him money. But there was trouble, you see. Buhler had a brother in this camp, and there was some trouble between him and Vogel—I'm not sure how it worked—but Buhler tracked him down. He was almost crazy. I tell you, Jack, he was obsessed. He told me how he did it. He had letters, photographs, everything . . . but I've taken care of that. That's not a problem—"

"But Vogel found this place, he came to you for help. And you saw your chance. You killed him—"

"Well—"

"But there were loose ends, Rudy."

"I didn't know he had a child. But that's not a problem, I assure you—"

"But Rudy, there are still loose ends. His house. Why didn't you think of that? It's still in his name. They'll find it. They're slow, but eventually they'll get there."

"Maybe so, Jack, but that's just the sort of thing you know how to fix. Really, isn't it? You could do it, Jack. I think you could."

"If I wanted to."

"Jack—"

"This is over. Everything. It's all done now." Yes, what comes next, that was the question.

"No. I have a lot of money—more, from here, than you could dream of."

Money. If that's what he'd wanted . . . "You've had a good long run—"

"Jack, listen . . ." That was it, make him beg. He'd lost it all now. He could barely lift the pistol in his hand. He needs you and he knows it. Well, they always do, that type. Someone to share their secrets with. They don't have the strength. He could just walk across there now and take the gun. But what comes next? That was the question. And Stern went on. "We could do it. It would all work out. There'd be no problem except . . ." Yes, Stern was no problem; Stern was dead meat already. He could kill him and there'd be nothing left except . . . Harper. What else could Stern have meant? Except Harper. Though Harper had never been a problem; he could hardly be one now, except . . . It was just then that

Harper made his move. Tannis even saw it. Well, they both did; a shift of his weight, a movement that drew his leg up—he was sitting, half reclining—so that, if he'd wanted to pull up his socks, all he had to do was reach down his hand. And Stern's eyes even flickered; for the first time he unlocked his eyes from Tannis, but only to glance toward the rifle, glimmering in the dark five yards away. His pistol didn't move, though. It was still pointing toward Tannis. Who, for his part, only grasped in the instant it was happening, what was happening. But it was too late then. It had never occurred to him that David would have another gun, that he would know anything about guns. Though it might have. A man, after all, who's made films about snakes, about aggressive animals in wild parts of the world, might be expected to know one end of a gun from the other. He might even know how to carry a small gun comfortably, if he was sitting in a blind, or up a tree. In any case, Tannis only saw at the very last second what Harper had strapped to his leg: the cheap little Charter Arms revolver Marianne had given him. Tannis even moved himself, to stop him, but he was too far away, and even if he'd been much closer it would have made no difference. For Stern had moved his eyes; he lost him for that crucial instant as Harper got the gun up and Stern's finger squeezed the trigger. The shots fell one upon the other, Stern's and Harper's; they roared and roared; and Tannis screamed in agony, hearing his own scream from far away, as he felt his knee blow up beneath him and watched Stern double over at the belly. And then he was down and rolling. And Stern had ducked away in the gloom underneath the scaffold. Stretched out, trembling, shock, that is—just let it pass—he gasped out his breath and a moment later saw Stern heading for the tunnel. And he must have blacked out then, that's it, get it back, hold it, hold on, for now he could see Harper, crouched, careful, working in that direction. Son, this may not be wise. And then there was a shot, and another shot. Then one last dreadful scream—what a sound that was—but there you have it. Isn't it so true? This scream not words or laughter or the various other possibilities that really told the men from animals, screaming not from agony but from knowing you will die. Yes, that is what it comes to. This big brain full of equations, facts, melting points and atomic numbers, coefficients of expansion, spectra, wavelengths, problems, methods, definitions—really, it was the same as red blood and yellow gore pooling in your hands, no better, all attached, just the fucking same. Yes! Scream your guts out! It's all the fucking same. . . . Or was this Tannis, biting on his arm, trying to keep from screaming in an agony of his own? For he was sweating with it. His eyes were bugged with it. He lay there, listening, hearing this terrible silence, but still thinking, You can pull it off, it's not over yet. Oh, yes. That was plain. But then the ground shuddered, and there was a tremendous roar, a concussion so powerful it rolled Tannis right over on his back. Stern, it seemed, had not been bluffing. The place was booby-trapped. Tannis covered up his head as stones rained down around him, and then he was choking in a terrible dust. Through which, a moment later, Harper's face appeared, stricken, ghostly, but finally visible, close up, beside his own. And one thing more. His hands were empty. The horror of the tunnel had been too much for him. He had no gun.

CHAPTER 19

The dust was terrible.

Tannis watched it roll, belching back from the explosion, in a great wave across the cavern, and then rise up in a towering, roiling plume.

In a moment, lying on his back, looking straight up, he could barely see. His eyes were blind with grit; his mouth was choked with stone—one breath and he was gasping. He turned his head to the side, but here the dust actually grew thicker. It seemed to come from everywhere. All the lights had gone as well, so the dust was a kind of smoke, as if the cavern had been transformed into a boiler or a chimney.

Still, in the middle of it all, Tannis knew he'd done it, he was home free now; and the fact that Harper, in the end, had done it for him was only the perfect crowning touch. Poor Harper. He was the final step. And then it would be done, all done. The dust swirled around him. He closed his eyes against it. His fingers squeezed the gun—yes, even in his agony, he'd found it in the dark—and now he worked it out. It was the sort of thing you wanted to get right; he didn't want to look a fool. He'd shot out the light, way up at the end of the cavern. One. Then he'd fired in the air, just for the hell of it. That made two. Then he'd encouraged Harper on his way with three, four, five. Or had there been another? Call it six. Which made it perfect, anyway. Almost poetic, in fact; just one left, the only one he needed, that nice comfortable seventh round of your U.S. Govt Issue Pistol Automatic Cal.45.

All done . . .

That was the trouble. Of course he knew this. Hadn't he known it all along? It was this very finality, the perfect closing of the circle, that made you think: *And what comes next?*

But not now. Don't think it now, he thought, which meant he must be thinking.

Why not?

Why not now after all?

But the answer slipped away, taking the question with it for the moment. (Or do you forget anything at all? Isn't it all just waiting for another moment to reappear?)

But not now. Not this moment. Carefully, gingerly, he rolled over on his side. The pain in his leg wasn't so important, but it was there. Well, he could still feel it. If you can feel it, like they say, it isn't dead. And there was a light after all. Lying on his back, he'd been looking straight up into nothing anyway, so no wonder he couldn't see. But now there was a light, way over there. Harper had gone to get it, he remembered: one lantern dangling from the remains of the scaffold, way over on the other side. It shone obscurely in the murk. Yet you could see by it, and in fact in its light the dust wasn't black after all. Dancing crazily, madly, randomly, the motes were silver, soft, or a soft dove gray. He grinned. Well, it was probably the arsenic. He closed his eyes. His leg was agony. But not that bad. The worst of it was the taste in his mouth, and he began spitting, trying to get rid of it. Jesus Christ. You could hardly breathe. He watched Harper; he could just make him out, like a shadow. The lantern was high up the scaffold, and he was trying to get it down. Then he'd come back here. Tannis squeezed the gun. One round, that was all he needed. Then it was all over. *All over.* Yes, well, he knew that, but his mind slipped away again. He was remembering . . . the memory was very obscure, though he knew exactly what it was: the peculiar darkness, his discomfort, the gun—they all combined to bring it back. December 2, 1943. Or was it the third? Nobody knew for sure. Nobody'd stood around taking notes about themselves. But it was the night before the very first test at China Lake, and always when he remembered it he wondered why he'd pretended to be asleep. It was nothing, really. But he always wondered. He'd been lying there, he'd been awake all night, curled up in his sleeping bag, and he'd heard them call out his name, and he'd closed his eyes, pretending. Pretending to be asleep. It was so long ago. Yet he remembered it so well. He'd gone up with some others in the CalTech station wagons and a few trucks, joining the main team, Emory Ellis, Burnham Davis, Calvin Mathieu. Those were the leaders. He remembered them all. He'd liked Ellis. He was a sharp-faced man with glasses. A chemist. He was a specialist in bacteria, well, there you go. He came from the Midwest, Illinois, and he'd worked for food companies or something, but he knew how things worked; for example, he was an excellent desert driver. That's right. He knew how to get things done, practical things, which made him perfect for China Lake. In fact, he saved the day, because he had his pistol with him; that was the problem. When they got up there, with forty 3.5-inch rockets, they discovered there was no security, not even a shed with a padlock to put them in. There wasn't a single building on the base that was actually finished. In fact, nothing ever was finished, not for years; they were always building—the sand and the cement dust were as bad as this. And it was freezing cold that night. Freezing your nuts off in the fucking desert. They'd rolled out sleeping bags in a Quonset hut with no windows or doors—somebody shoved a panel from a packing case across the doorway to try to keep out the wind—and nobody could sleep. Tannis couldn't sleep. He was too cold. Excited. But the idea was, they'd take turns standing guard with Ellis's pistol—this one gun on a military base that was going to defeat the Japanese, no less—and here was the point: when it came his turn, when someone whispered, Hey Cracker Jack, he pretended to be asleep. That's what he remembered now, as he lay in the dust, how he'd been lying there, huddled in his sleeping bag (pulled up above his head, his hands jammed between his legs) trying to keep warm and pretending to be asleep. Why? Why had that been so important? He wasn't asleep, he hadn't slept a minute, he'd been lying there, hearing the others talking quietly, someone had a radio, he could still hear the hiss of it, a newscast, they were fighting in Italy then, on the Winter Line— Jesus, it can't be any colder there—but as soon as he heard his name he shut his eyes, pretended. Feigning sleep. Why was that so important? To pretend to be asleep. He knew he was awake, but they didn't—was that it?

"Tannis?"

It was Harper. Suddenly, he was right there, with the light. "Are you all right?"

The light swung in the gloom ahead of him. He could see Harper's face, and then he couldn't, as it swung back and forth. Did Harper understand at all? Did he have any idea what was happening? Going to happen?

Tannis heard his voice say, "There's got to be something . . . a piece of wood or something. I want to get up."

"Don't move. You need a doctor."

Yes, presumably, whatever happened next, that would be a part of it. "I'd feel better, standing. Get something."

He squeezed the gun. Yes, he'd found it in the dark, felt it heavy in his hand. Harper moved away; a second later, he was back with a short-handled spade. Perfect. He pulled himself up. Now his leg throbbed in a different way. Down to his knee was agony; below it, things were a little vague. Harper helped him. They felt through the gloom and found one of the rubble piles. Half standing, Tannis leaned back against it. He caught his breath. "I don't suppose that map shows another way out of here?"

"No."

Except there was one. There had to be. And in fact, standing, he could feel a very faint current of air against his cheek. He squinted, trying to pick out some pattern in the movement of the dust, but even with the lantern it was much too dark. All the same, it was there. He could find it. And maybe he was thinking of that as he got out his Luckies and his Zippo, and held the smoking cigarette in his hand.

Harper said, "I've got to do something about the little girl."

Tannis coughed and spat, thinking he wouldn't mind some water. "This is the Vogel woman's kid?"

"Anna."

"Where is she?"

"In that room at the back."

Tannis nodded. "Suit yourself. I'm okay here if you want to go. But she might be better off there until this settles down." Yes, and no doubt it would make for fewer complications.

Harper hesitated, considering. Tannis spat again and watched him. He watched Harper. Harper was a big man, almost as big as himself. Yeah, but you've got the gun, and he hadn't come back with his. Still, that surprised him, somehow, how big Harper was. Had he thrown it away, in disgust, in horror? Of course he'd been so young. A boy. The boy genius. He thought of Harper's wife. Well, we all make some mistakes. But he was different now. Yes, all in all, Tannis was glad he had the gun. Harper wasn't tough, but he was clearly tougher than he looked; it seemed he wouldn't take it lying down. And he had to be smart, your bona fide genius. But real smart anyway to get this far. Now he had all the answers too. Vogel. Buhler. Buhler had pulled the string and it all came unraveled. That's it. Playing out the string. We've all been playing out the string. You could see it there in Harper's face. Nature, Tooth and Claw, my son. No one likes to shoot an old dog dead. Was it horror in his face, or anger? But neither, really. That was the point. He just knew, that's all. He knew everything. Why not admit it?

"So now you know it all. Including me."

"But I knew anyway, I think. Stern stole Sidewinder, but not by himself."

"And you had it figured?"

"Pretty much."

"Interesting . . . I mean you had to do it some completely different way. You had to work it all out backward, beginning with yourself."

"But then that was the advantage I had, wasn't it? I knew I didn't do it. And Stern didn't know me, and I didn't know him. But somehow I was brought into it. All these years I've had that much to go on. It had to come out that the Russians had Sidewinder, and so there had to be a scapegoat— that was convenient for everybody—and I was nominated. But not by Stern. It took somebody else. For a time I thought it might have been my wife. Because whoever set it up knew everything about me, how I'd react. Where I was going to be. But of course it wasn't her, was it?"

Well, well, he really has figured it all out, thought Tannis, and she must have, too, at the end. One look, and she'd known, not just about the kid but everything. She'd betrayed him *that* way, and every other way as well. Still, forgive and forget, let bygones be bygones, and you don't want him to know everything, do you? You never know, it never hurts—keep something in reserve. Besides, there was the kid; best steer clear of all *that*. So he said, "Don't you remember how it happened? Your wife didn't have anything to do with it . . . except I said, in that note, that she was fucking a Mexican or whatever. Or did you think she was? Well, maybe she was so far as that goes, but it had nothing to do with me. Pure coincidence. I just needed to get you out there, into the desert. And then I organized the Russkies to cross your trail when of course it looked like you were going to them. But don't blame her for Chrissakes."

He watched Harper consider this, take it in, and nod. And then Harper said, "But there's one thing I still don't understand. You had some hold on Stern—"

"Sure. A son of a bitch who had bad luck. It happens. He shunted a Jewish girl into Auschwitz except she had aunts and uncles all across Chicago."

"All right. That's Stern. But did the Russians have a hold on you?"

"Don't be crazy. No one had a hold on me." Tannis chuckled. "You don't think I'm a Com-U-Nist?"

"No, I didn't think so. So why then . . . why did you do it?"

Tannis grinned. Well, here it was. Why not now? This now as opposed to the next now, or the one after, the one that just comes next—But he said, "You still don't know why?"

"How could I? Isn't that your greatest secret?"

"Maybe I have others."

"But that's the great one, that's the one that counts. If anybody found that out . . ."

What was Harper up to? Why didn't he make a run? Tannis could feel his finger tighten on the trigger. Tighten. Tighten. But he didn't pull it. . . . Not this now. Wait a moment longer. He leaned back instead, felt the pain wash over him—it's only in your mind, it's all in your mind—and then he said, "You really want to know?"

"Yes."

But what Tannis said was, "I keep thinking about something. I keep remembering the first time I ever came out here."

"When was that?"

"Before the base, before everything and everybody. There were no planes then, just hawks and vultures. I was a kid. My father was a gambler—I ever tell you that?"

"No, you never did."

"Well, he was. He looked for gold too—Christ, what he would have thought of this place—and he did look up this way some. But of course it's all the same, prospecting and gambling. Anyway—" He coughed. His mouth filled with an awful taste. But then he kept on talking, he could hear himself. *His voice said.* "He won this truck, in Vegas, in a poker game. It was ancient, well, I suppose not so ancient then, a Mack Bulldog—forty horsepower, solid rubber tires, radiator behind the engine, a kind of chain drive. The idea was to sell it in L.A. He took me with him. We went across Death Valley and you could get killed doing that in those days. But we made it. He had two beer barrels he filled with water. We slept out in the back. But then, over here, it died. I'm not sure about the road. Maybe it was paved. Or maybe they just oiled it down. But anyway, that old truck died and he couldn't get it going. . . ."

"And this wasn't far from here?"

Yes, Tannis could just see him, his father. Except he knew he wasn't. But that was okay. He was damned angry, because they were so close, almost there. We'll have to hoof it. Of course, Tannis knew you weren't supposed to do that; you were supposed to stay with your car. There were signs by the road. But they headed off. And got lucky right away. The truck was barely out of sight when they spotted a car, or a van: not actually on the highway, but a half mile off it, apparently just parked in the desert. Sitting there like that, it seemed an odd sight—Jack noticed his father's hand slide into the side pocket of his jacket, where he kept his gun—but they headed toward it, following the tracks it had pressed so neatly in the sand. As they drew nearer, the car looked odder still, an ordinary black sedan, but modified by the addition of wings or flaps, metal frames with canvas stretched across them, that had been folded out from the car's sides and rear, making three dark areas of shade. At the back, sheltered in this way, two men and one woman were working to mount a large square camera on a wooden tripod.

"That's right, they were photographers, out from L.A., I suppose. I never knew. No, that's not right actually—Glendale, that's what they said. And they introduced themselves—Christ, I wish I could remember who it was. The older fellow was forty, thick blond hair, and the boy—it was his son—might have been twenty. But I tell you it was the girl you noticed. She caught the eye." He could remember her like yesterday. A tall, tanned blonde, dressed in a fringed buckskin shirt and gray trousers and wearing heavy army boots. She was no older than the son, but her attachment was clearly to the father. And Tannis knew this, or at least knew something, even if he did not yet know what it was he knew. Perhaps she even sensed how she disturbed him; in any case, she was the only one of the three who took any notice of him at all, giving him a friendly smile as she extended her hand, a long, cool hand with a surprisingly rough palm. "You know, I think she was the first beautiful woman I ever saw. Or at least the first woman I ever saw as beautiful. You know what I mean."

"So what happened?"

"Well, what did happen. I don't know, nothing much. They loaded up the camera, drove back to our truck." This was like a dream. He was in the back seat, squeezed between his father and the boy, the woman just ahead of him, so that he could see the fine golden hairs that curled around her neck and smell the heat that rose up from it. Like a dream. It was like a dream. The girl, the strange black car, the patch of bouncing yellow sun against his face, the unlikely, strange devices piled up behind him; and when they reached the truck, events developed as in a dream. "Well, the older fellow was furious, of course, he was missing the light, but what could he do? He had to give us a hand. I remember the girl kissed him, that was to make it all right, cheer him up, and then his son and my father went off in their car to find a garage, leaving the three of us behind. Just the three of us, you see." At the last moment the woman took the camera and the tripod, to make room she said. And then the three of them were standing there in the desert wind, the dust, Jack, the golden girl, the man. The car disappeared. And precisely then Tannis became conscious of a sinking feeling, deep inside. He was not afraid, and it had nothing to do with his father leaving him. Maybe it was partly because the man and the woman were rich and he was poor, but something made him feel so small. He sulked. The poor girl. Lord, now she had two of them. For the older man, if not quite sulking, was at least disgruntled. She tried to cheer him up again. Look, she said, they were here, they might as well do something; they should take a picture. But the man shook his head; he had too little film, and did she know what each plate cost him? Twenty-seven cents, he said, twenty-seven cents. She called him a spoilsport then, and when he gave her a dirty look she stuck her tongue out, and then—Tannis could hardly believe his eyes—she began skipping up and down, up and down, beside the road, going around and around the man in circles, her feet kicking up the dust, her hands thrust deep inside the pockets of her trousers. But he just folded his arms across his chest and said, "My dear, you are so very charming," and then stepped around the broken-down truck—the sun was rising now—to find some shade.

It was at this point that she turned to Tannis. She smiled a kindly smile at him, and then she bent down toward him, and she was so very tall that her golden hair fell across his eyes and she flipped her head, to swing it back, and then leaned closer still, so he could smell her breath, spicy warm, and feel it brush his cheek.

But he didn't like that smile; he didn't like her to smile at him like that. Which perhaps she guessed, for now her face turned serious.

Did he know what a camera was? she asked.

He nodded, and he truly did: he'd read an article once about how you could make a camera from a shoe box.

And had he ever had his picture taken?

He never had.

Would he like to?

No.

Why not . . .

How much he wanted to say yes, to please her; but he couldn't. There was still the matter of her smile, that too-kindly smile. And perhaps he guessed what she had in mind. Tannis, age thirteen, wearing an old tweed jacket and baggy pants, like jodhpurs, with his flat tweed cap—she might have perched him on the hood of the truck, triumphant, or sat him on the back, his legs dangling over, his poor white boyish face peering anxiously at the lens. But he wouldn't have it. With those lovely clear gray eyes of hers she tried to catch his glance, but he looked away, and his face, his jaw, his heart, locked up: tight as a vise, a virgin's last resistance. Except, in the end, he blurted, "You want a picture, miss?"

"Yes. I want to take your picture."

He shook his head again. But then, "I can show you a pretty picture."

"Where?"

"Over there."

He pointed toward a canyon in the distance, the only damn thing there was to point to.

"What's over there?"

"You have to see."

"Tell me."

But he wouldn't. Of course. Since he had no idea that there was anything over there. Even in retrospect, Tannis was never sure what he'd been trying to do: escape; extricate himself; deflect her . . . but hold onto her for one last second longer.

And she saw him weaken. "Tell me," she said again.

But he was stubborn now, as only boys can be, and as he shook his head he could see something shift inside the woman: all at once she was bored with this little game, suddenly conscious of the heat, the tedium that lay ahead of them. All at once she stood up straight and turned away and stuck both hands in the back pockets of her trousers and stared down the empty road.

But she, too, couldn't quite let him go. She swung right around, pivoting on her foot.

"Over there?"

"I can show you."

"But you couldn't," he heard Harper say. "Could you? Had you ever been there before?"

"I told you: this was the first time I ever saw this part of the country. But the point was, she believed me. That was the first thing. I never understood, really—was she playing some trick on that man, trying to get his goat, or what. The hell. I just never knew. And it happened so fast. She turned around and got the camera and I picked up the tripod." God, he thought, it was so heavy on his shoulders, it cut down across them like a knife blade, but of course he couldn't let that show. So they struck out across the desert, the girl ahead. Tannis listened to his heart, beating like a bird's. He was heading into nowhere. He had no idea where he might be going. Ten paces and he was desperate. He thought, if he didn't find something for her to take a picture of he was going to die, right there; and then he realized that he wouldn't die, not for real—he was a shrewd little boy—but that he'd suffer something worse: a wound, a blow that would finally heal but would leave him twisted forever. So he was truly desperate, which was no doubt why he was able to carry that tripod the way he did. In ten minutes he was sweating, staggering; but ten minutes later, when he took a quick look back, he could barely see the truck. As for the girl, she trudged ahead, each step of those army boots leaving a neat chevron in the sand for him to follow, and looked back only once, her hand moving across her cheek to sweep her hair behind her shoulder, her lips arcing in a smile to urge him on. Finally they reached a wash, which spread in a broad, sandy estuary, merging with the desert. They were both exhausted, and as though on signal they slumped down against a couple of boulders, the girl leaning forward, head between her knees, her arms draped along her legs. Now, in secret, Tannis watched her. The way small strands of gold curled from the parting of her hair. The way her golden skin wrinkled around the tiny bones of her long, flexed wrists. The way sweat glistened in the corners of her eyes. Never, in this way, had he seen a woman's body—for a moment, like a raindrop quivering on a windowpane before it trickles down, he felt her—and then he loved her. And when she looked up and looked into his eyes, he didn't look away.

She smiled. "You okay?"

He nodded.

"Let's trade."

"I'm all right."

"I know. But your shoulder must be aching and my arm feels like it's falling off."

He was astonished: that the two of them, right there, hadn't vanished in a puff of smoke. Then, catching the movement of her eyes, he turned, and now could see the man, standing by the truck. They stood up at once, and as they hurried on he could feel that man's eyes burning in his back. Ahead of them the wash grew narrower, becoming a hard-packed strip of sand and boulders, with a deeply undercut bank that was edged with scraggly mesquite. For another quarter hour they labored on, until finally they reached a canyon. Which had nothing to distinguish it from a hundred others: a box canyon gouged from this knob of hills, its walls rising an impressive, but not spectacular, two hundred feet or so. Yet as soon as they were in it, Jack did feel something: a sense of space, folding around him, becoming his. And then he saw it, exactly what he wanted, and he stopped dead, his heart stopped dead, and he called out to the girl, "Wait"—a command uttered with such conviction that she obeyed at once. Yet what he had seen, once more, was nothing out of the ordinary. The back wall of the canyon, at the point where it began to form the angle of the box, had crumbled, spilling a great ramp of boulders to the canyon floor below, making a structure that geologists call a talus. The only thing peculiar about this one was the quality of the rock itself, for the boulders were a uniform dark gray in color, the color of the volcanic rock called andesite. Did Tannis know this? Had he seen it before? Had his father shown it to him? This was possible, though it made no difference. The plain fact was that Tannis headed for it instantly, scrambling out of the wash, dragging the huge camera perilously behind him. The girl followed, and from the top of the bank, through a gap in the mesquite, she could see the man, floundering across the desert. She hurried after Jack, and a moment later they were both standing among the first of the big dark stones. And he could hear his voice say, "How close do you have to be?"

"Here, you mean? Those rocks?"

"You'll see."

"What?"

"Just point it there, above the rocks. Get it ready."

As she wrestled with the camera and the tripod, Jack looked around him and began picking up small stones, until he had enough to fill his hand; doing this almost leisurely, so surely, as if he had all the time in the world, as if this was the only place in the world he wished to be, and then standing and waiting and watching the woman, almost smugly. For now he knew. He wouldn't lose. He wouldn't die. He'd live forever. And something of his conviction got through to her, for she worked quickly, without question, and when she was ready, she gave a nod, a little quiet sign. He looked toward the rocks, rocks so dark that they held the heat of the desert day, held it so the dew of the desert night condensed against them, trickling into little pools among their crevices—and then his arm swung out and the pebbles flew, like the pebble that killed Goliath, and when they landed, the rocks exploded in a great fluttering cloud of white, a thousand, ten thousand butterflies, pearly marblewings, who hung there, glistening, like a snowstorm in the desert. And though he didn't hear the shutter click, he heard the girl suck in her breath. "Jack . . ."

Her face was shining, more beautiful than anything he'd seen before.

"My God . . ."

They still hung there, fluttering.

"Jack . . ."

"I told you. I told you." He felt so weak and breathless; his whole body trembled.

"Yes . . . But will they settle down, go back? Could you do it all again? I should change the speed. My God, they're beautiful."

"Sure, sure. Just wait a minute."

He couldn't look at her; so he turned, looked back across the desert, watched the man come closer, till he could see his face. But he didn't care. He waited. He wanted him to see. Slowly he gathered up another bunch of stones, and when the man was almost there, he pulled his arm back— but just before he threw them, he looked toward the girl and whispered, "Do you love him?"

His voice was pitched so low, he spoke so much within himself, that she probably didn't hear him; it would be one more thing he'd never know. Yet for a single instant she pulled her eye away and looked at him and could have been about to speak, except he didn't give her time, to break his heart or steal it; his arm snapped back, the pebbles glittered in the air, and the miracle came forth again.

"That's why. Do you understand?"

"Take it easy now."

Why didn't he make his run? Didn't he understand what happened next? It was almost as if he figured he didn't have to, that this was the end of the line and it didn't matter. Now. This moment and the next. But this was now. Here it was. But finally, what came after? Oh, he could do it. He'd pulled it off. He had him dead to rights. But what came after? That was the problem; it would always be the problem; and worse, looking at Harper now in this awful gloom, he guessed that Harper knew.

"You understand?"

"Yes. I understand, about the butterflies—"

The butterflies. Had he told him that? "You wanted to know why I did it. Well, because I could. I can. I can do it all. Anything—"

"Just take it easy, though."

Yet now, even at the very end, his mind kept working. It tried to slip away. He thought of all he might remember. He thought of that time he'd had a dream of three Joshua trees signaling on a hill, a dream so vivid that when he awoke he was sure they must be real and spent days driving through the desert trying to find them. He thought of that, and then he didn't think of that; and he thought of other things. He tried to remember it all at once. Why couldn't you remember it all at once? He remembered. . . . Memory lane. Whistling Dixie down memory lane . . . He went off on some long reverie, and when he came back he wondered, "Why don't you try to take the gun, Harper?"

"What good would that do?"

"Have a go. Isn't that what you British say? Have a go, matey. Jump me. You'd have a chance. My word of honor: there's only one bullet in the gun. So say I missed."

Once he'd screwed a girl on what the British call a beach, pebbles, like a gravel pit, and when he'd rolled her over small stones stuck along her soft white thigh, and with a single motion of his hand he'd brushed them off. . . . That chalk blue desert sky, like faded denim stretched tight across a young girl's ass . . .

"It wouldn't do me any good."

"What do you mean?"

"You're indestructible. I couldn't kill you with a hundred guns."

Tannis grinned. Well, shit. So he did know after all. Had he been playing him along? Had he always known? He was a bona fide genius, so just maybe. Anyway, you had to give him credit. He'd figured it all out some other way, working backward from himself. "Those butterflies. You understand that? What that meant? The power of a woman, you turn that right around?"

"I understand."

"I had that power. You understand? I have the power. I decide."

"I understand."

"You fucker. You fucker, Harper."

And Tannis pointed his big old Colt right at David Harper's head. But then he thought, What the hell. This moment or the next. What comes after? Son of a bitch. Well we all are aren't we? So he turned the gun around and he was looking down the barrel, like the German in '45. *And I haven't told you the half of it. There's a hundred things you'll never know. Like—*

Tannis had to use his thumb, but he squeezed down on the trigger, nice and easy, just the way you're supposed to do, and never heard the roar that blew him miles and miles away.

So Tannis was dead, and in the dust and gloom of Stern's mine was transformed, almost instantly, into a ghost. It was hard to believe, so strong had his presence been, though David had been quite certain he was finished as soon as he'd laid eyes on him: Stern's bullet had caught him high in the chest, and even a hospital would have meant little. It had been extraordinary, in fact, that he'd managed to get up at all, leaning on that spade; for some reason David didn't understand, he'd dragged himself along, as though he'd been wounded in the leg—he seemed to be pretending that to himself. And then he'd talked, or at least rambled. What had he meant? What had he meant to say; had he meant to say so much? David now was far from certain, although the butterflies and the beautiful girl—he wasn't sure, but he could see it—it all made sense. And even if that wasn't entirely clear, the Colt had been definite enough. Covered in his own blood and gore, Tannis had still had the strength to squeeze the trigger; there'd been no doubt of that. Which of them would die? That was finally *his* decision, and was that not the meaning behind all the others? In any case, he'd managed it—and added a fine symbolic flourish; falling, he'd knocked over the lantern, so David was now entirely in the dark.

He was not afraid; as a child, he'd found no special comfort in the dark, but he'd not been afraid of it. Now rather than fear he felt a curious reluctance, some suppression of feeling at the back of his throat, in his nostrils, a reluctance to take too deep a breath; a kind of repulsion, or loathing. Tannis, dead, was lying a few feet away from him in this pitch-blackness; soon, he'd be able to smell his blood, his rot. And then there was Stern in the tunnel, lying in the pool of his own vile blood, which would be seeping along now, searching for its level in this horrible place, flooding it. Horror: he felt it. But not panic. He simply wanted to be away. This was the end, certainly the reduction of everything living; this whole ghastly place was. Here, one way or another, was what it all meant: the peculiar horror of the history that came so close to destroying him.

He had to get out. This one last step remained. But he knew that nothing could stop him now, that all he had to do was keep calm. He could see nothing; he could not see himself. But he was there, all of himself, he could count on that; yes, he could . . . see, as soon as he bent down and felt about, he found something. Metal. A lighter. An old Zippo lighter. Tannis, talking, had actually lit a cigarette with it. And now when David worked the wheel its flickering flame not only showed him the lantern but something else as well: the air was moving. Or it seemed to be. He moved toward it. And it took him just where he wanted to go, to the rear of the cavern, where the little girl was. The ground was treacherous, as pockmarked as the moon; but the lantern, fed from a bottle of gas, worked pretty well, and he was able to move quickly on, his shadow swaying out ahead of him, and he barely noticed the great golden walls of the cavern, the riches. He just wanted to see the way out, and he did, working across the back wall of the cave until he felt the opening Marianne Vogel had marked on her map, and he was through it, the lantern spreading a bright arc ahead of him. He thought, You're the light at the end of the tunnel. But no, he wasn't; that honor was definitely Anne's. But he could see here, finally he could really see: see that the tunnel was about six feet high—he only had to stoop a little—and was shored up with timbers and roofed along part of its length with metal panels. He hurried along it. And about twenty feet in he found another door, off to the left side. There was light around it. This was the room, Stern's living quarters, where the little girl must be. Yet he didn't stop, because now he could actually feel a breeze, smell fresh air. Ten yards farther on, he discovered why: one side of the tunnel had virtually caved in, and whether this revealed a second entrance, which Stern had never told Marianne about, or whether the explosion had actually opened it—well, that made no difference to him. He set down the lamp and shifted some of the larger stones, and then he shouldered his way through a gap and found himself at the bottom of a chimney, a crack in a single enormous piece of rock, a fantastic boulder. It must have been eighty, ninety, a hundred feet to the surface, but it was one rock all the way. And way up there he could see the sky, lit by a few faint stars.

He was in a fever now. It was so close; he could almost grasp what he'd been longing for, almost knew the name to call it. And so he hurried back to get Anna, the little girl, but she was frightened, and it took him a time to convince her to open the door. But finally she did. She had that look of terror, when a child feels there is no choice: she was too desperate even for tears. But he held her hand, he promised that her mother was close by, and he let her help: she held the lamp for him while he found some rope and a shovel and cleared the way. Finally he held her up.

"Do you know how to ride piggyback?" he asked.

"Yes, I do," she said.

"Good. I want you to ride piggyback on me, except I'm going to put a rope around us to hold us close together."

"Why?"

David pointed. "Because I'm going to climb up there."

"You can't."

"Oh yes I can."

And yes he could. It was a heroic feat. He was a climber, and a good climber, so he knew just how tough a climb it was. And if no one saw him do it, and the child, crying, clinging to his neck, was no good witness, well, that was all right too. But finally he knew they'd make it. He could breathe fresh air. He was coming up to the world again, and he could hear the breeze moving across the face of the desert. And then he could see the night itself, an edge of cloud beyond which the stars were shining. Finally the edge of the earth was beneath his hands, and he pulled himself up and over.

He was exhausted.

With the child's arms wrapped around his neck he crawled away and almost fainted and then, untying the rope that joined them, rolled over on his back.

David closed his eyes and didn't move.

When he opened them again, he was looking straight up, and he could see a couple of stars, which seemed to swing and swell with the beating of his heart, the pulse flowing through his retina. He watched them till their motion settled down, till his own breath was slow and easy through his body, like the breeze. Now he knew he'd done it. He'd made it. He felt a great relief, his breath flowed out of him in a long, easy sigh. It was all done, and he'd done it. Working backward from himself, as Tannis put it . . . He lay there. His mind was very still. He didn't think. Nonetheless, the meaning of all that had happened was now very clear to him. He'd changed himself, he was a different person; that's why he'd won through. Well, it was not so much. On the other hand, it seemed he'd given up a lot—at the time it had seemed a lot—and so he should give himself a little credit. The scientist. The Man of Knowledge. Master of Eternal Laws and Principles. Except such knowledge, by its own definition of itself, could only become power, which then could only seek for yet more power in an endless cycle: power over the world that only divided you from the world. He'd moved on . . . that's what it came down to. And in the months that followed all this, as he began to build a new life for himself, he'd sometimes wonder if the world hadn't moved on too. Did people still believe that science would come to the rescue of mankind? Did people still believe in that kind of truth? He wasn't sure—you could argue it both ways—but once upon a time the world had seen itself through the eyes of God and that had passed; so maybe things were starting to change again. He could even flatter himself: 1952, the H- bomb; 1955, Salk vaccine; 1958, Sidewinder becomes the first guided missile to destroy an enemy plane in combat. The historians would undoubtedly argue in their way, but couldn't you see the great scientific zenith somewhere in there? Before science became thalidomide and poison and air pollution? People had once believed and now they didn't. And he'd been part of it and survived, escaped!

But now, he thought, Come on! He was probably a little loco, here in this desert, which was certainly what the desert could do to you, when what he really needed was a little *locomotion*; and so he pulled himself up to his feet, which prompted Anna, who'd decided he was probably dead, to run over and hug his leg. She began to cry. She wanted to see her mummy. Was bold enough to say, "You promised."

Indeed he had; and so that was one last problem. He had no idea where they were; somehow, they'd emerged both behind the canyon and above it, certainly not where they were supposed to be. But then he remembered that he still had Tannis's old Zippo, and so he pulled the wick out and worked the wheel, and it flared up, so much so that he could only hold the hinge by two hot fingers as he circled it above his head. And a moment later he saw an answering light, just a glimmer, and from the corner of his eye—and, of course, in the last place he ever would have looked. Perhaps they'd been uncertain of his light as well, for it went out at once. But he'd seen it long enough; in front of them the desert lifted in a high, cleft mound, and behind them, at the edge of a bank of clouds, he could see a star. All he had to do was keep on that line.

But as soon as the light died, the little girl grew very frightened. It was so dark, they were lost, and she would never find her mother. Kneeling down, David tried to comfort her, saying he could find the way, but she wouldn't be consoled: they had to have a light, they couldn't see. They should have brought the lantern.

"Never mind," said David. "Listen. I've got something better than a lantern. It's a poem about a lantern. If you get it by heart—do you know how to get a poem by heart?—I promise we'll see everything." He looked down at her, and she seemed entirely dubious. But then she cocked her head expectantly, and before she had a chance to change her mind, he began.

> "The Lantern is to keep the Candle Light,
> When it is windy and a darksome Night.
> Ordained it also was, that men might see
> By Night, their Day, and so in safety be."

David watched her face, and after a moment she said, "Do it again," and he did, this time playing with the words, drawing them out, blowing them across to her, so that her eyes began to smile and then her lips began to smile, and finally at the end she made a little jiggle with herself. Then he said it one more time. And finally Anna tried, and then tried again, until she had it quite by heart. So David took her hand, and the little girl said the poem, and with its words and his bearing star to guide him, David took a step, and then another—carefully, for the ground was steep and rocky—until he found the path down from the canyon rim and away from China Lake.

A NOTE ON THE TYPE

This book was set in Janson, a recutting made direct from type cast from matrices long thought to have been made by the Dutchman Anton Janson, who was a practicing type founder in Leipzig during the years 1668–1687. However, it has been conclusively demonstrated that these types are actually the work of Nicholas Kis (1650–1702), a Hungarian, who most probably learned his trade from the master Dutch type founder Dirk Voskens. The type is an excellent example of the influential and sturdy Dutch types that prevailed in England up to the time William Caslon developed his own incomparable designs from them.

Composed by American–Stratford Graphic Services, Inc.
Brattleboro, Vermont

Printed and bound by R. R. Donnelley
Harrisonburg, Virginia

Designed by Cassandra J. Pappas